GENESYS X

22
100

FAIRWOOD PRESS
Bonney Lake, WA

GENESYS X

A Fairwood Press Book
November 2020

First Edition

Fairwood Press
21528 104th Street Court East
Bonney Lake, WA 98391
www.fairwoodpress.com

Cover and book design by Patrick Swenson

Hard Cover Edition ISBN: 978-1-933846-99-6
Trade Edition ISBN: 978-1-933846-97-2
First Fairwood Press Edition: November 2020
Printed in the United States of America

In memory of my parents Henry and Anna
and my friend and sensei, Shinsuke Yatomi

GENESYS X

BOOK ONE

The meaning of life is that it ends.
—Franz Kafka

CHAPTER ONE

2041 Los Angeles, California

ORDINARILY A STRIPPER'S FATAL OVERDOSE WOULDN'T HAVE landed in our laps. LAPD's Homicide-Special Division, a select downtown unit with citywide jurisdiction encompassing 468 square miles and 21 communities, handled only the city's most complex, brutal and high-profile murders. But that first Thursday in October my Handy pinged and the tired face of Lieutenant Rodriquez appeared, floating in the L-shaped space of the glove phone, between my thumb and forefinger.

"Sorry, detectives," Rodriguez said. "Looks like another hype offed herself." His sigh underlined what all us cops knew. Drug overdoses and gang-related homicides were at an all-time high in the city. "If NOHO didn't have every detective out on call already, I wouldn't make you guys do the drive. But you know the area, Piedmont."

I nodded. Before I got bumped up to Homicide Special downtown, I'd done a tour in North Hollywood.

So, two hours after the dead woman had been found in her tub, my partner Shin Miyaguchi and I were inching north off the 170 Freeway onto the Magnolia Boulevard exit in North Hollywood.

"No wonder the city's so screwed up," Shin said, shaking his shaved head as he watched a stoner prophet preach to the Jaguars and Lexuses waiting to leap ahead at the green.

"What, the addicts?" I said. "Or the apocalypse?" I jerked my chin at the homeless guy wearing a mood T-shirt that flashed "It is written. The end is near. Prey."

"The part about it being written." Shin flashed me his gap-toothed grin. "God should have streamed a visual if he wanted people to catch on."

Minutes later, we were slamming the car doors shut in front of a boxy high rise near the Red Line Metro station on Lankershim.

Only one slack-jawed teen wandered down the street, aimless as a broken toy, that vacant stare of the plague-stricken in his eyes. Nobody knew why Alzheimer's suddenly started to hit the young. All we knew is that about five years back, it did. And while Alz-X isn't contagious, there's no treatment for it either, let alone a cure.

But every intersection was a sea of green crosses promising relief. The acrid smell of burning sage and ganja hit my nose hard.

"Don't you know?" Shin said. "Burning skunk-weed's supposed to purify the spirit or something, Eddie."

"Purification stinks." I grinned.

Inside the building security cameras loomed from on high in the hallway corners—cheap units put in to scare away low-rent burglars.

Outside unit 313, black letters on yellow holo-crime-scene-tape screamed Keep Out in four languages, Spanish and English chasing Chinese and Korean characters round and round.

"Detectives Piedmont and Miyaguchi," I said, badging the uniform as we walked through the tape. The warning rippled and vanished, reassembling as soon as we passed.

"Robbery-Homicide?" As soon as he'd spotted our gray suits on the perimeter, first officer on site Jesus Velazquez had scurried over, the green light of his helmet-cam twinkling.

"What do we have?" Shin asked the P-1, groaning as he leaned over to slip paper booties on over his size ten brogues.

"Looks like accidental overdose." Velazquez cocked his head towards the bathroom opposite. "No sign of forced entry. DB's in the bathtub. Britney Devonshire, twenty-seven, one prior for soliciting." With squat fingers, he handed me the plastic bag holding the dead woman's California driver's license. "No family. Mother was an addict. Died from Covid-19 during the 2020 pandemic. No father or siblings on record."

I stared at the holo-photo. Britney Devonshire's skin was white as rice paper. Her big brown anime eyes, framed by hair like a red flame, stared back at me. "Another system kid?"

"Left Social Services at eighteen," Velasquez confirmed with a nod. "She was an exotic dancer at the Sandy Beaches Gentleman's Club for the past three years."

My turn to nod. I'd spent a year in the system myself. Not a pleasant memory, but I'd landed on my feet. Britney Devonshire hadn't been so lucky.

"Who called it in?" Shin said.

"Next door neighbor. Name's Ava Wu." Officer Velazquez gestured towards the open door of the apartment. "She had a key. She's got the vic's cat too."

Directly across the hall stood a dazed Asian woman of indeterminate age cradling a morbidly obese cat in her arms. The cat's talking collar kept repeating "Meow, I'm Cocoa Puff," over and over, each time reciting a phone number that matched the number on the driver's license. I guessed the recorded voice belonged to the victim too, a hollow echo of the now dead girl with no family.

"Wu and the deceased traded off on cat care," Officer Velazquez read from his notes. "Britney told Ms. Wu she was going on vacation last night. So the old lady stopped by around nine this morning to look after the cat. That's when she found the body."

Through the open door I saw the neighbor across the hall absent-mindedly shaking her head. The cat's yellow eyes flashed, and his tail swished a warning.

Shin and I shared a glance. "Your call," he said.

"I'll take the body."

"Why do I even ask?" Shin said. "I get the plump old neighbor. You get the girl."

"Dead girl," I mumbled to Shin's retreating back. He ambled off across the hall.

"The log," I said, turning back to Officer Velazquez. "You call SID and the coroner?"

"Coroner's on route," Velazquez said, eyes suddenly locked on his toes.

"Call SID," I said as I walked the place. "Maybe it's what it looks like. Maybe not. Don't lock yourself into a theory till the facts are in, Officer Velazquez. You found her phone?"

"Not yet."

That was odd. "Keep looking."

Britney Devonshire's apartment was a one-room studio with

thin walls and low ceilings. At 6'2" I felt the roof pressing down on us. There was a big open living area with a kitchenette and bath off to the side. No framed family photos, digital or old-school, no knick-knacks graced the shelves or countertops. The place was sparsely furnished. It read like Ms. Devonshire had been marking time, not really living there.

And the place was very neat for a junkie. Too neat—no half-empty containers of peanut noodles or pizza boxes strewn about, no wreath of scum and mold in a sink piled high with dirty dishes.

On the sofa bed opposite a wall-screen television, jeans and a green silk blouse were carefully draped over two little factory-issue throw pillows. A partially crumpled travel brochure announcing the launch of civilian trips to the moon next month stuck out from under an e-reader on the floor. Next to the brochure stood a pair of black ankle boots.

"Nice boots, huh?" Velazquez said. "My girl would go for those, big time."

"Till she found out where they came from." I popped my head into the bathroom. The sickly-sweet vanilla aroma rode the wave of voided bowel and bladder stench pooled in the cramped space like a fetid swamp.

Nothing lies as still as the dead. Wearing only an untied green silk robe and a thong, the redhead lay on her back. Her legs jutted awkwardly half-out of the empty tub—a marionette dropped suddenly by a bored puppeteer. The belt, used to tie off her arm, was still knotted round her left bicep. One green satin slipper dangled off her motionless right foot.

At first glance, the redhead's body showed the perfection of a porn star, surgically sculpted and hairless.

As I stared, however, the little imperfections beneath the artificial surface began to reveal themselves in death's grisly striptease: the chipped peach-colored nail polish, chewed cuticles and callous on the middle finger of her left hand, the tiny pale worm of scar tissue circling the aureole of a breast.

In life, Britney Devonshire had been beautiful, even if some of her attractions were manmade. Now her auburn hair already had that flat dull look of the dead.

No sign of the identity barcode I expected to see tattooed on her wrist though, standard issue since Homeland Security made the embedded chips near tamper-proof in 2030. However, a flick of my blacklight pen revealed the barcode hiding in plain sight. She had the upgrade—invisible without ultraviolet light.

Britney Devonshire's once luminous skin now looked like sallow wax. Death bleeds light along with the breath from the living.

"Hmm." I peered at the single fresh needle mark on the woman's left forearm just below the knotted belt and at the older tracks on her hips, peeking out from under her thong.

On the rim of the sink next to a tube of extra-whitening toothpaste stood a glass holding a toothbrush and a set of weirdly-shaped scissors. There was a toilet wedged between the sink and tub.

On the closed toilet lid a single e-cigarette lay in an ash tray crammed full of lipstick-stained empties. Vanilla Vapor. A set of works was propped up next to the ash tray—a pin prick of blood drawn up inside the syringe. Under the spike lay a sodden wad of Kleenex with greenish crystals tangled in the fibers.

"Green Ice," I spat. The synthetic opioid was twice as potent as fentanyl, itself fifty times stronger than heroin. Manufactured in Mexico and China, dealers mixed the drug with heroin. The doses were erratic; fatalities weren't. And Green Ice was flooding the streets of the city. I'd seen its epic-fail crashes first hand, courtesy of Eddie Piedmont Sr., another slave of the green angel, and not exactly my nominee for father of the year.

Outside the door, the voice of the Coroner's Assistant announced her arrival as she signed the e-log. A minute later Dr. Emily Bogardus was leaning over the tub beside me.

"The belt left the only ligature mark," the dark-haired Coroner's Assistant said, echoing my own conclusions, as she knelt down by the lip of the tub and examined the body. "No obvious external trauma. Or sign of a struggle."

A skinny SID tech named Marcos signed in after Bogardus. He did a cursory recording of the scene with his Handy. The image of the dead redhead shimmered in the glove phone's L-shaped space between his thumb and forefinger before vanishing. Marcos started in on evidence collection, bagging the set of works with long, latexed, fingers.

"Check for prints on the tub too, plus the light switches here and at the door," I said. "And get a reading on the microbial cloud before anybody else walks through."

Marcos arched his left eyebrow but nodded. Everyone who enters a space leaves telltale markers behind, a microbial fingerprint we can read. But departmental budgets are tight and overdoses common. A microbial reading isn't the norm for an overdose.

Shin was back from talking to the neighbors.

"Here's something," he said. "According to Ms. Wu, the deceased just lost her job at the club where she danced."

"Fired?" I asked.

Shin nodded. "But Ms. Wu said Britney wasn't all that broken up about it." Shin paused, cracking his knuckles.

Really. I shot my partner a look, then glanced back at the dead girl splayed out in the tub. Shin walked back to the living room and picked up Britney's e-reader.

"What about the hall security cameras?" Marcos said after a moment. "We haven't checked the memory yet."

"Sham-cams," I said, referring to the cheap fake hall units spotted on the way in. "We won't get anything off them."

"Nothing from the canvass either," Shin added. "Nobody knows anything. The cat's talking collar said more than the neighbors." He exhaled a long hiss of unsurprised disappointment.

"Anything else you can tell us?" I asked Dr. Bogardus, the Coroner's Assistant.

"Tracks here too." She directed my gaze from that single fresh needle mark to skin between the dead woman's toes. "Old tracks."

As I crouched down beside the tub, face to face with Emily Bogardus, two bright red spots the size of Yakima apples appeared on her cheeks. They blazed a brighter shade of crimson as I held her gaze. She looked away, smiled, then glanced back at me, a sideways glance, head tilted.

Emily was interested in more than her work. Before I met Jo, my live-in girlfriend, I would have gone for it. Now I just smiled politely.

Emily pointed at the darkened skin on the underside of the corpse where blood had pooled. "From the livor I'm guessing she injected herself and fell backwards from her seat on the lip of the tub." Emily's voice was all business again. Her smile faded along with the opportunity. "We won't know for sure until after the cut, but it sure looks like accidental overdose."

Shin nodded.

"Maybe not," I said.

"What then?" Emily's eyes narrowed, her black brows drawing together like the wings of a crow. "Suicide?"

"If she offed herself on purpose, Eddie," Shin said, rifling through Britney's e-reader, "why lay out that outfit on the bed? Not exactly funeral clothes."

I pointed to the tracks under her thong. "Why would a stripper who's careful to shoot up between her toes or anywhere else it won't show, put the spike in her arm all of a sudden?"

"Junkies will do anything for a high," Shin said. "She just lost her job. Poor kid was looking for a way out. She found it."

"But this hype was left-handed." I pointed to the weirdly-shaped pair of scissors on the sink and the callous on her left middle finger. "So why didn't she shoot up her right arm?"

"Maybe she couldn't find a vein," Shin said, peering at the dead woman's arms. Looking for the collapsed veins, a commonplace of the addict's life.

"Then we should see recent tracks on her right arm," I said.

That now-yellowing skin was clean.

"Well, Insta-tox tests positive," Marcos said, holding up the little disposable scanner to the light. "She has a ton of Green Ice in her."

"When's the cut?" I asked.

Emily Bogardus shrugged. "Monday. There were four bodies ahead of yours cooling in the fridge this morning—courtesy of the Zetas." Her tone was cool too. "Help me move her, will you, Marcos?"

As Marcos helped shift the body forward, the dead girl's silk robe fell to the side.

"Hold it," I said.

A fresh tattoo nestled just below the small of Britney's back—so fresh little scabs of clotted blood dotted the vivid green and indigo design like a macabre cartoon in a graphic novel. Her tramp-stamp featured strands of silk twisting round a lotus flower and the letters L and E.

"What's that?" Marcos asked. "Gang? Or a cult tat?" He leaned in and captured a close-up on his glove phone.

"A derma ad," I said. "Ms. Devonshire's been selling her skin in more ways than one."

Emily Bogardus nodded. "Lotus Eaters. It's a pot shop. Boutique, not your typical low rent place."

"Yeah?" I grinned at her.

"So I've heard," Bogardus said with an answering grin.

Once the deceased was loaded onto the gurney headed for the morgue, I followed Shin's shaved head out to the street.

"I'll file the report now," Shin said. "Cause of death, OD, accidental or suicidal, pending the coroner's report."

And one more system kid is tossed out like a piece of used Kleenex.

"Not so fast."

Shin glanced at me. "Eddie, no."

"C'mon. We'll swing by Sandy Beaches first," I said. "Be in and out in no time."

"The strip club . . . seriously?" Shin's voice had that strained quality, a tone I've heard before, so I flashed him a reassuring smile.

"Don't you at least want to know why they canned the girl?"

CHAPTER TWO

THE CALENDAR SAID OCTOBER, BUT AUTUMN HADN'T REACHED L.A. yet. A wet blanket of heat slapped us hard as we left the building's air conditioning and walked back toward the car. The sun's glare turned my contacts black before we'd taken two steps outside the dead woman's apartment.

Detective sedans are officially unmarked, but unofficially it's a different story. The ad for Firestone tires "Firestone—Protection to serve you" ran along the side of every sedan in the fleet: corporate tagging. The reflective ads made us as conspicuous as any black and white, but we were stuck with them. When overburdened taxpayers turned down another tax bump, Firestone had coughed up the cash for the city's new police sedans.

"Three o'clock," Shin said, checking his glove phone. "Too early for headliners, but we might catch the boss minding the store." He pursed his lips for a second. "Okay, ikimashoo." Shin slid his darkened glasses down on his nose and peered at me. His black eyes twinkled. "But, Eddie . . ."

"Yeah?"

"You back me up when I tell the wife the strip club was all business."

I wagged my head and grinned.

"I can't wait until you're married, you bastard." Shin rubbed his hands together and laughed. "It's gonna be payback—big time."

"You'll have your revenge soon," I said. "Picked up the ring yesterday. I'll ask Jo tonight."

Jo, aka Jocelyn Sloan, was the woman who made me realize the hucksters behind those love at first sight clichés aren't always lying.

"Women just fall at your feet, don't they?" Shin said. "I saw Bogardus hit on you back there. Must be nice."

Cars packed the streets as we headed south towards Sunset. I dodged the ever-present potholes and cracked tarmac. Stuck in gridlock a little further along, Shin put in a call to Vice for background on the Sandy Beaches Gentlemen's Club.

"Randy Bitches Strip Joint?" Detective Petra Miller's face appeared on the car's screen as we inched along in traffic.

"Call girl set up?" I asked.

"Allegedly." Miller's hands framed the word with air quotes. When she smiled, Miller's eyes almost disappeared in her chubby face like raisins in rising dough. "Sandy was an aspiring actress back in the day. Now she caters to big time clients with gutter type tastes—actors, studio executives, businessmen."

"Why no rap sheet?"

"Good lawyers, bad evidence." Miller winked.

"This girl Britney who worked for her wasn't so lucky," Shin said. "She had a prior from 2039—for soliciting and possession."

"Probably another ingenue who didn't make it," Detective Miller said. "Most of Sandy's girls get hauled in eventually. For hooking or holding. But none of 'em have turned on her—yet."

Shin and I turned east on Sunset Boulevard. Traffic started to flow more smoothly. Overhead, white pod-cars shaped like Tylenol capsules hummed along their monorails, ferrying tourists from posh hotels to Rodeo Drive. The interlinked LV Louis Vuitton logo glittered on the side of the white cars: more corporate tagging.

Shin and I thanked Det. Miller and finished the drive to the club. Located on the east side of Sunset, Sandy Beaches Gentlemen's Club was conveniently sandwiched between a drive-through spray tan boutique and a Dr. Tatt-Off ink removal. The club's façade was relatively low key and up-market. No flashing neon signs hawked naked girls inside. We parked in the underground lot.

A bouncer with twenty-inch biceps and the hint of a Santa Muerte tattoo peeking over his shirt collar checked I.D. at the door. At his side sat a black pit bull with a spiked collar that flashed the club's logo.

The club's less threatening beach motif immediately manifested itself in the central sand box where the girls danced, the inverted beach umbrellas hanging from the ceiling, and the patio loungers, scattered around the club on which clients reclined.

Blue light, endemic to all strip clubs because it hid flaws on the skin, gave the feel here of being underwater or surfing in the tube of a perfect wave. Sandy Beaches even pumped surf music with a heightened drumbeat pounding underneath. The thumping bass gave an erotic twist to the otherwise vanilla music. Judging by the clientele, they made a mean umbrella drink too.

The dancers weren't unattractive, but the best earners wouldn't be working for hours yet. The Latina with waist-length blue-black hair currently working the pole looked to be nearer forty than thirty.

I glanced round at the clients. A few drunk and cocky college boys, yelling and whistling, were peppered in amongst the silent, bleary-eyed middle-aged guys.

Most of the girls had that hard edge exotic dancers get once coke lines on the mirror start to carve lines on the face. But Britney had been in her late twenties. She'd have had a few years yet before reaching the sell-past age. It made me wonder again why she'd been fired.

The bartender was a burly Black guy in his late 20s, dressed in swim trunks, polo shirt and flip flops. Shin and I approached him, badges out.

The muscles told me he lifted weights religiously. His tats told me where and why. Blue ink from the earliest amateur work had been placed too deep in the skin, giving the tattoo a raised texture like a brand. A pro had re-inked over part of the design, turning it into an armlet of barbed wire. But I could just make out the five-digit number buried under that newer layer of ink–94974. San Quentin has its own zip code.

"We'd like to talk to Sandy Rose," Shin said as we both reached for our lapels and flicked on the body-cams.

The bartender's eyes did a slow-motion ricochet back and forth between our faces and the badges as he continued to wipe down the smooth surface of the bar. Peeking out from under the right sleeve of his polo shirt was the tattoo of a gun. Its barrel pointed straight out at me. Next to the gun was printed the initials "BGF." Unless this Q alum was declaring himself Sandy's best girlfriend forever, he was a shooter for the Black Guerilla Family. He hadn't tried to re-ink this little memento. Either Sandy Rose was a charitable citizen looking to help rehabilitate the city's felons, or she had some pretty serious security.

After a moment, the bartender reached out and flashed a hand signal to the wall sensor on his right.

"Yes, Deshawn?" responded a disembodied female voice. "What is it?"

His eyes darted from the security cams overhead back to us.

In no time at all the owner of the Sandy Beaches Gentlemen's Club made her appearance, slipping in from a previously hidden doorway in the back wall before the door was once again swallowed up by the seamless wall.

Sandy Rose looked like her name, tanned and delicate as a flower pressed in a heavy family Bible—except for the porn size implants standing at attention beneath her tasteful suit jacket. Her smooth face was flawlessly made-up to look dewy and makeup-free, her dark blonde hair perfectly cut to frame her face. I put her age at an early forty-something.

Sandy's head barely crested my shoulder, but she moved with authority. She didn't ask to see our badges.

"Detectives," she said immediately, smiling as she held out her hand to shake Shin's and mine in turn. "I'm Sandy Rose. Is there a problem? Our permits are up to date."

Her hands made me revise my earlier age estimate. Thin-skinned and riddled with thick ropey veins, they vibed a good thirty years older than the perfect, polished face and perky implants.

"It's about your employee," Shin said. "Britney Devonshire."

Sandy's sherry-colored eyes flickered. At the mention of Britney's name, those amber orbs glanced up from our body-cams to the security camera overhead. "Former employee," Sandy said. "I'm afraid we had to let her go."

"When was that?" Shin asked.

"A week ago, give or take." Sandy's upper-forehead puckered while her brows stayed immobile—the botox frown. "Has she gotten into trouble?"

"Why'd you fire her?" Shin smiled his easy-going smile and tapped his fingers to the beat of the music.

"We have a strict no-drug rule, detective. Enforced by random drug tests." Sandy fiddled with the bracelets on her arm. The golden charms tinkled with an agreeable music of their own. "Britney tested positive for Green Ice. I was sorry, but she left me no choice."

"So, you wouldn't be surprised to hear she'd died of an overdose," Shin said.

"My God." The news shattered the hard glint of those red-gold eyes. If she was acting, Sandy Rose was more talented than her critics let on.

"I'm sorry," Shin said, reflexively pulling up a barstool for her. He signaled to the bartender for some water.

"I'm fine," Sandy said, waving Deshawn away. But her hand trembled a little as she fidgeted with those bracelets again. "We weren't especially close, detective. It's just a—shock. I knew she used of course, on account of her test results. But still—she was so young."

"You said she tested positive for Green Ice?"

"That's right," Sandy replied.

"And that was a week ago?" Shin smiled gently. "When you tested her I mean?"

"Yes." Her voice maintained a steady calm, except for the wariness that crept around the edges.

"Had you tested her before that?"

"When we first hired her a few years ago. Of course, at that time she tested negative."

"Of course," Shin said. His glance told me Shin was ready to wind things up.

"When you fired her," I said, "did Britney seem unusually upset or depressed?" The cat lady neighbor had said Britney wasn't—which seemed odd.

"No one likes to be fired, detective." Sandy shifted her gaze to me.

I nodded. "Did she mention anybody who was bothering her? Maybe a customer? You've got some pretty heavy-duty security working here."

"My security team is here to discourage bothersome customers proactively," Sandy said. "Britney certainly never filed a complaint or raised an issue."

"Was she causing trouble with the customers or the other girls?" I glanced at the glassy-eyed girl. "Is that why you tested her?"

The Latina with the blue-black hair was watching us with interest as she gyrated round that pole.

Sandy's chin lifted a millimeter. Then she smiled thinly and shook her head. "Like I said, drug tests are random."

"Of course," Shin said in his affable baritone. "We won't keep you any longer, Ms. Rose." He turned to leave.

"I didn't catch your names, detectives," Sandy said, looking directly at me. "And here I thought I knew everyone from Vice."

"Detectives Piedmont and Miyaguchi." I made sure to pronounce every syllable clearly. Sandy Rose wasn't wearing a glove phone I could tap for contact transfer, so I handed her my card. "Robbery-Homicide."

The word 'homicide' hit home. Sandy's eyes narrowed to a squint as she stared at the card. Her lips seemed to pale under the neutral lipstick. For the first time, her face looked almost as old as her hands.

"So, the overdose," she said, "wasn't accidental? You think Britney was depressed because of—her job—and she . . ." Sandy Rose's words trailed off into silence.

"Can't say," I replied. "The case is ongoing."

She nodded. "Poor girl. If I'd known she was that close to the edge . . ." Sandy was sitting now, and her eyes were even a little moist. But I felt them burning holes on my back as Shin and I left.

"We'll probably never know for sure," Shin said as soon as we stepped outside the club and headed for the underground parking lot. "Accident or suicide, it's not always clear-cut."

I didn't say anything as we flicked off our body cameras. From one hundred feet away the car sensors read our barcodes and unlocked the doors with a chirp.

"You're not convinced," Shin said, getting in. "Why? You don't buy the boss's story?"

I raised and dropped my shoulders in a shrug. "I buy that Sandy Rose canned Britney and isn't happy Homicide turned up on her door."

"But?"

"A strict no drug policy? In a strip club? Half my salary and all of yours says a third of the girls there were high. Why no drug tests for them?"

"Everybody lies," Shin said. "Sandy probably only tests employees she already wants to can, but makes it just random enough to seem plausible. That way management avoids any potential discrimination charges. You saw the way she eyeballed our cameras and hers."

"Except, if the Devonshire girl had been using prior to getting fired," I said, punching the ignition and backing out of the parking space, "where were the fresh tracks on the body? And if she wasn't using, or causing trouble, why fire a hot young earner when you keep older users on the payroll?"

Shin paused. His chin dipped to his chest in a slow-motion nod. "When's that autopsy scheduled?"

"Monday." I drove us back out onto the street.

"Let's worry about it Monday then," Shin replied with a heavy sigh. "Log us out. I'm ready for a drink."

CHAPTER THREE

THIRTY MINUTES LATER, I'D PARKED THE CAR ON THE STREET a little way down from the Code Seven VR-Bar. Perched on the border between Hollywood and NOHO, the cop bar was an easy half-block walk down Cahuenga Boulevard.

As we strolled toward the entrance, Shin undid the top two buttons of his turquoise and ebony shirt.

"So, how're you gonna pop the question to Jo?" Shin said. "Drone ring drop, stadium marquee, or your basic grovel on the knees at an overpriced restaurant?"

He pulled his shirttail free, letting it hang loose over the belt of his 501 jeans. The weave of his shirt's solar-block fabric tightened in the heat of the sun's rays, making the palm trees on the Hawaiian shirt seem to sway in a breeze.

"Jo's not into big public displays." I pulled the ring box out of my suit pocket and held it open for him to see. "Will she like it, you think?"

Shin squinched his face against the glare and glanced appreciatively at the two carat emerald-cut diamond. "Set you back ten grand?"

"More."

Shin's low whistle was appreciative.

The ring did more than sparkle in that light. Sun, so hot it shimmered off the pavement, pooled in the air. Everything looked solarized—colors the bleached tones of Navaho blankets left too long in the sun.

"Jo'd say yes to zirconium," Shin said. "But even Ahn would approve of that."

Ahn, Shin's wife of twenty-six years, was almost as devoted to the finer things in life as she was to him. My partner pulled a Hanshin Tigers baseball cap out of his back pocket and jammed it on his shaved head without breaking stride.

I eyeballed his outfit and smiled. Shin habitually morphed to a casual-Friday look as soon as his shift was over, but I liked the gray suit and fedora of the RHD. A personal rebellion against the casual everyday world our fathers left us. Today the streets were a sea of hats. What started as another hipster fad had taken hold as necessary protection from the sun five years back.

"I gotta see that," Shin yelled, pointing up at the digital billboards for "*Batman vs. Dracula 3*." Digital bats chased each other up and around the sides of adjacent skyscrapers.

The billboards made my eyes burn. "You already have," I yelled back over the noise of the ads. "They just made it faster."

"Give in to the dark side of the Force," Shin intoned in a mock-serious voice. "Everybody else has."

Advertainment was everywhere. An eighty-ish woman with a parasol flashing a promo for Sun Salute solar panels passed us by. Faded sleeve tattoos blanketed her withered arms. I couldn't make out the design. Any red or green had long ago bled back into the body, leaving only the blue-black smudge. At least the deceased Britney Devonshire's rice paper skin was spared that degradation.

Once inside the Code Seven, the bar's sensors muffled the street racket. With its dark wood and crimson leather booths, the Code Seven was a high tech replicant of a 1940s cop bar. There were virtual reality booths along the wall where the occasional tourist could role play a crime scene with Bogart's Sam Spade, minus the half-open milky white eyes and stink of real death.

Cops just came for the whisky and beer.

Shin accepted a frosty mug of Moon Harvest Kirin 2040 from the bartender.

I signaled him to put Shin's beer on my tab and ordered a double shot of twelve-year-old Hakushu single malt for myself. There was a heavy satisfying weight to the glass tumbler in my hand. I took off my hat and set it on the bar next to a vintage bowl of fresh peanuts.

Shin tapped my glass with his frosty mug and gulped down a mouthful of beer.

The whisky burned my throat and left a warm happy glow.

"Piedmont, you drinkin' whisky?" a familiar voice boomed

from the entrance to the bar. "I thought you only sucked down wheatgrass lattes so you can keep that girlish figure camera-ready." The voice belonged to Detective Timberman from NOHO Homicide.

Timberman was a study in beige. His light brown hair, eyes, trucker tan, beige shirt, polyester jacket and Dockers all blended into a mash-up of bland on bland.

I shot a glance at his gut, spilling over his belt. "Looks like you could use a couple wheatgrass lattes." I signaled to the bartender, who set a glass of Johnny Walker Red on the polished oak for Timbo.

He smiled. Timberman had unusually small teeth of grayish yellow. "So, ladies," he continued as he ambled over to us and lowered his bulk onto the barstool like an elephant settling in at a watering hole. "What brings you to sit with us peasants in the 8-1-8?" He tossed back the whisky.

"Your lieutenant called us in to cover your ass." I grinned and filled him in on the dead stripper case.

"And here I thought RHD finally kicked out the Boy Wonder." Timbo belched.

Boy Wonder. Three years ago, I'd brought down a serial killer who'd terrorized the city. The department had promoted me and plastered my face all over L.A. in order to take advantage of the rare good publicity. So, at the age of twenty-six I'd moved from NOHO to Homicide Special, one of the youngest D-2's ever to make the unit. Timberman wasn't the only cop who had never stopped giving me grief.

"Have some peanuts, Timberman." Shin slid the bowl towards him. "They'll take away that taste of sour grapes."

Timbo smirked.

"You working the Zeta war?" I said.

North Hollywood was ground zero for the ongoing turf battle between the Zetas and AzteKas, two rival gangs tied to Mexican drug cartels. With profits from the marijuana market down since pot went legal, they'd flooded the city with Green Ice and other illicit drugs. As they fought for territory, the gangs were tearing big bloody chunks out of each other and leaving the chum for the police to mop up. Three of those bodies left behind were corpses the Medical Examiner had to finish before the Britney Devonshire autopsy.

An old song floated over the soft light of the dingy bar. Cigar smoke circled heavily around the guys' heads like a spectral cat, mocking the "no smoking" signs.

More cops migrated into the Code Seven, celebrating a birthday. Timberman joined them. Shin and I stayed at the bar for another round, chatting about his daughter Yasuko's second year at UCLA and the hit his bank account was taking. The small talk got smaller, and we stood to go.

"Haven't seen you in a while, Eddie." Jack the bartender handed me a Redbull for Shin and a ChillWater for myself before picking up glasses and wiping down the polished oak.

I nodded and held out my wrist—exposing the standard identification barcode tattooed there. Flashing his diamond studded teeth in an answering grin, Jack waved the sensor over the chip embedded under the skin of the tattoo, recording my purchase. I handed Shin the Redbull as we headed out the door.

Cacophony sounded the second I crossed the threshold back onto the street. The news was on the megathons racing up the sides of buildings on the boulevard.

"Six hundred fifty thousand more Americans underwent nano-cosmetic surgery this year, marking a sharp increase in profits from Magic Makeovers," trumpeted the blonde spokesmodel on the Fox WSJ Market channel.

NBC's *Tomorrow Today Show* interrupted with a promo for their special report on Alzheimer's X. "Early onset-dementia has claimed record numbers of victims under thirty this quarter," said a different blond commentator, a Latina. Images of blank-eyed teens, warehoused in special wards which had sprung up since the plague hit, flashed by on the screens.

"We should check for that Monday." Shin pointed at the newsfeed. "If a doctor told me I had early-onset dementia, I'd think about putting a spike in my vein."

"If you had it," I said, "it wouldn't be early onset."

"You hear that whoosing sound behind you, eight-pack?" Shin leaned in so close I could feel his hot beer-breath on my skin. "That's the sound of middle-age coming for you."

Shin reached out and grabbed a handful of air, stumbling a little. I grabbed his elbow and righted his stance.

"Breaking news today on a stunning reversal," said the Latina on CNN's *Crimecast*. "Convicted murderer Alfonso Nieto's sentence has been overturned due to irregularities in his trial."

I froze.

"Irregularities in his trial." Shin said. A Japanese native, he tripped a little over the r's when he drank. "They make it sound like a laxative ad."

I just shook my head. "The tiger," I said, flipping my wrist.

"Rolled over." Shin nodded. Years ago, he'd told me the ancient Japanese used to think the earth rested on the skin of a tiger. Whenever there was an earthquake or an event that rattled their world, they'd said the tiger rolled over.

"Two and a half years ago Alfonso Nieto," continued the *Crimecast* anchor, "a high-ranking enforcer in the AzteKa cartel, was convicted of the murder of Manuel Ortega, a rival in the Zetas. A minor dispute escalated into tragedy that left more than two families devastated and Alfonso Nieto in prison for life."

"Minor dispute," Shin scoffed.

"He disputed Nieto's right to blow his brains out," I said.

A photo appeared as the newscaster blathered on. With his affable smile and salt and pepper hair, Alfonso Nieto looked more like everybody's favorite brother than a stone-cold murderer.

"Nieto appealed the verdict when a supplemental police report from the first officer on the scene, Miguel F. Obrador, came to light after the verdict had been given." The newscast blathered on. Apparently, that supplemental report gave Nieto the hammer he needed to win on appeal.

"And they let him off." Staring at that smug face blown up to a hundred times its actual size, an angry red tide washed through me. It wasn't my case, but like every cop, I knew the basic facts. I wasn't all broken up about the death of another Zeta. But Nieto had set off a bomb that had taken out a detective and and more than a few innocent civilians. That was why every cop cheered when he was sent down for Ortega's murder. I remember that celebration well. That was the year I joined Robbery-Homicide.

As I stood gawking on the sidewalk, my hand curled into a tight fist. The urge to hurl something through Nieto's pixilated visage was strong.

Shin put his hand on my pitching arm. "Don't lose sleep over it, Eddie. Today's suspect, tomorrow's victim." Shin intoned the departmental mantra. "Karma gets them in the end."

I swallowed, trying to get rid of the sudden bitter taste in my mouth. "Problem is karma's a slow draw."

CHAPTER FOUR

IT WAS MAGIC HOUR. THE SETTING SUN STAINED THE SKY burnt orange as we headed back to our car.

Burning sage and that skunk stink of cheap marijuana wafting out onto the street redirected my attention to a life-size hologram of franchised psychic Cassandra as we passed one of her storefronts on Cahuenga. The parapsychological parasite promised ritual armor to ward off Alzheimer's X. Cassandra had hair the color of new tarmac framing glittering obsidian eyes. Her hologram shimmered like a heat mirage.

"Hello, Edward Piedmont," Cassandra said. The ad's "smart" sensor, embedded on the storefront behind her, read the barcodes of passersby and adapted the sales pitch to each. "Come inside. I'll tell you your future."

I know the future, Mama Cass. My thoughts flitted back to the reversal of Nieto's verdict. It's the past that keeps changing.

Shin and I walked on. The car's sensor clicked open with a chirp as we approached.

Shin ambled towards the driver's side, swaying a little.

"You only want to drive when you're toasted," I said, blocking the door.

"I'm not drunk," he protested.

"Exhale." I held out my glove-phone and clicked on the breathalyzer app.

Shin's breath would have caught fire if I'd held a lighter, not a phone.

"The Japanese have many virtues," I said, "but holding your liquor isn't one of them."

"That is a lacist srur, Eddie," Shin said, grinning and wagging his forefinger at me.

"Mock all you want," I said. "You're still not driving."

"You drive then, hakujin." Shin inclined his head in a fake bow. We got in and the car switched over our phones. The Nokia glove phones, called Handys, were courtesy of yet another corporate sponsor in search of a marketing bump. In five more years my guess is all city employees will be wearing suits plastered thick with corporate logos like NASCAR drivers.

I was behind the wheel as we drove south towards Nokia P.D., police headquarters, on our way to turn in the sedan. Though our shift was officially over, the car called in our position automatically.

Shin flipped on the radio and tuned into the last country music station in L.A. Some rhinestone cowboy began to wail.

"Tell me," I said. "Why is a guy from Osaka so hot for soap operas sung with a twang?"

"You just don't know what's good," Shin replied, crooning along in his off-key baritone. "She done left me on the bullet train, a bullet through my heart."

We took the 101 Freeway south, colors blurring as I hit the gas until we exited at Temple.

A few blocks down I stopped for the yellow light. Scanning the intersection as we waited for the green, I spotted two pairs of shoes dangling over the phone lines opposite, one a pair of black high tops with a white Z sewn on the dark fabric, the other a white tennis shoe with the letter A inlaid on the rubber sole. The Zetas and AzteKas marking turf. Sneakers were an improvement. Last month they'd strung up headless corpses on the Vincent Thomas Bridge in San Pedro.

"Look at that," Shin pointed to a rundown branding-tattoo-piercing parlor with a sign outside hawking its wares. Pete's Piercing—With or Without Pain.

"Wonder which costs more," I mused.

Then, the day and my life switched gears.

It started with a small violation. A black Excalibur SUV with illegally tinted windows ran a red through the intersection. Veering wildly all over the street, the SUV rocketed by. The radio dispatcher was already calling out . . . 503—stolen vehicle . . . 505—reckless driving.

A black and white pulled out from a side street, attempting to cut the Excalibur off and force a stop. The bar of colored lights on top of the police vehicle flashed like a Christmas tree. The Excalibur didn't even brake. It rammed the black and white, hurling the squad car into a cell phone tower. The black SUV careened past us.

Shin glanced at me. "We're off duty, Eddie." Shin was a stickler for protocol.

That's when we heard shots from the vehicle. I hit the siren and slapped the portable strobe on the dash. The light pulsed arterial red.

Shin sighed, but he activated the Traffic Light Expediter.

With the TLE changing the timing of traffic lights, how long they hold and how fast they turn, we sailed through green lights.

Shin answered the dispatcher's call. "Detectives Piedmont and Miyaguchi in pursuit. We have a visual . . . shots fired."

We took a corner fast. "You got strips up yet?"

"Affirmative," the dispatcher replied. "Spikes down two blocks away on Grand and First."

The sirens' wail got louder. The Excalibur accelerated to eighty, fishtailing around the corner. Staying well back, I cut through an alley. Now flanking his left, we herded him towards those steel spikes.

He slowed for a second then pounded the gas again. I blocked his left. Two black and whites appeared up ahead—cutting off his escape. So he made a sharp right on First and raced for Grand. Brakes squealed as he turned the corner. Too late. Two more black and whites stood waiting in ambush just past the Music Center. Then the SUV's tires blew. We'd corralled the Excalibur over those waiting spikes. The black behemoth on wheels lurched. It bumped and rattled and crawled to a stop. Excalibur's only escape now was backwards the way it had come. Slipping our Glock dual action semi-automatics out of holsters, Shin and I exited the vehicle. The red light on the laser option turned green. We kept our car between us and the SUV—blocking its escape.

"Police," I yelled to the occupants of the Excalibur. "Come out of the vehicle with your hands in the air."

That's when the first civilian left her little roach coach perched on the sidewalk outside the Music Center and ran out into the middle of the street, glove phone camera at the ready. She wore a T-shirt with the words Kill the Masters printed on the front. Her camera flashed and the Excalibur punched the gas hard in reverse.

Shin leapt from the cover of our vehicle. “Get Down!” he yelled. Shin shoved the girl, sending her flying wide-eyed to the sidewalk, out of the path of the Excalibur. But that put Shin directly in the line of the speeding behemoth on wheels.

“Stop!” I yelled. The driver didn’t. He turned and raised an arm. I saw the faint outline of the suspect’s head through the rear window. And a gun. No passengers or civilians in the line of fire. The suspect had already fired shots. So I did what I had to. I emptied the mag—fifteen shots in the time it takes to exhale.

My shots punched holes in the car’s metal skin and took out its rear window. Glass shattered and fell in a glittering mist. The Excalibur lurched, then meandered right into a yield sign and stopped. The horn suddenly blared. The uniforms covered me as I made my way to the driver’s side. I opened the door, gun at the ready. The driver, slumped onto the wheel, spilled out of the car onto the pavement. Crudely done gang tats covered the back of his neck. He didn’t move again. His .9 millimeter lay on the passenger seat, an extra magazine beside it. There was no other occupant in the vehicle. Just the strains of a new cover of an old narco-trafficker ballad, “Silver or Lead,” bleeding into the air.

Two uniforms moved in now, guns on the suspect as I checked his vitals. Two fatal shots had severed his spinal cord and punched a quarter-sized hole in the back of his head. I turned him over and saw the exit wound through what had been his left eye. Peach fuzz framed his pudgy baby chin. Shit. He was just a kid—some baby-banger.

The woman started to scream. She ran back into the middle of the street. Kneeling, she picked up a smashed telephoto lens attachment for her glove phone, cradled now in her outstretched palm. A hoard of camera-toting civilians were already taping. When Shin had knocked the first civilian to safety, the Excalibur had run over her phone-cam. Maybe the shooter had seen her as the diversion he needed, or maybe it had been pure coincidence. We’ll never know. Now this kid was morgue meat.

One of the officers on the scene scanned the dead kid’s prints into his Nokia and sent the dark swirls to the crimecom lab. They’d correlate his past and see if he had a record. Others put up the tarps to screen the victim from the cameras of more lookiloos.

Another bluesuiter picked up the shell casings from my Glock and those from the kid's weapon too. By law all registered guns imprinted the owner's identification on the bullets when fired. It was for the record. This time we already knew who fired the fatal shot. I forced deep breaths into my solar plexus.

My heart still pounded in my ears. Gradually, the pounding quieted, other sounds starting to register, as time sped back up to normal. That's when my hands began to shake. Adrenaline shakes are part of the job. You never really get used to standing there shivering like a wet dog in the wind, as the hormone works its way out of your system. But that's the inglorious reality of all gunfights.

By the time the shakes stopped, a new moon hung in the black sky. Lab techs had already taken blood samples and officers had statements from the witnesses. Paramedics were zipping up the body bag and lifting it onto the stretcher for that long ride to the morgue. Another paramedic swabbed liquid bandage on my hand. I hadn't realized I'd scraped the shit out of it dropping into position.

Shin came over. "Insta-tox confirmed he was higher than Jupiter," Shin said. "You okay?"

I nodded. "Did they run his barcode through the scanner?"

"Prints too," Shin said, nodding. "Paco Ramirez, age fourteen."

I winced. He obviously wouldn't have a license to drive, let alone a permit to carry. But Jesus, he was just a kid.

Shin looked at his notes. "They're correlating his past now but judging by his tats I'm figuring he was a baby banger for the AzteKa 17." It was a local street gang tied into the AzteKa organization and the Juarez Cartel down south.

"And I thought today was a good day."

"It's a pretty good day for me," Shin said. "Thanks to you, Eddie. I owe you." He handed me an Altoids breath mint.

"Don't thank me yet." I popped the Altoids into my mouth. The strong peppermint flavor burned my tongue. Until this moment, adrenaline had driven from memory the drinks we'd had at the Code Seven. The mint could mask any hint of alcohol on my breath, but both of us knew it wouldn't hide the booze in my blood.

"Right," Shin replied. "As my grandmother always says, "deru kuga wa utareru."

"The nail that sticks up gets hammered. I know. Looks like I won't be popping the question to Jo tonight after all."

Before I could say another word a swarm of cops, including both the brass and internal affairs, surrounded and separated Shin and me.

All officer involved shootings require an investigation by the team of the same name. A detective from a special section of Robbery-Homicide already strode across the tarmac to tape my statement and relieve me of my body cam and gun so that it could be checked by ballistics. He took my departmental glove phone too. Reflexively, I looked up at the ever-recording surveillance cameras on overhead billboards and traffic lights. It was starting to rain. Clouds of steam rose from the hot pavement. I just hoped the cameras caught the whole story, not merely the bloody end. I braced for the storm.

The day I was born I made my first mistake,
and by that path have I sought wisdom ever since.
—*The Mahabharata*

CHAPTER FIVE

The storm hit the next day. Captain Tatum wanted to see me right away.

The story as spun: white cop shoots fourteen-year-old Latino honor student, had made the late-night news and gone viral on the web in a heartbeat. Paco's smiling middle school photo with his big Bambi eyes played non-stop on the news cycle. Pictures of him shooting the .9 mm at that black and white, and us, didn't.

I hadn't slept a wink. Now as I wended my way towards Nokia P.D., an angry throng of people crowded the steps of the new police headquarters, calling for blood, my blood.

Nokia P.D. is a ten-story edifice of steel, metal glass and stone planted on the Second Street site of the former police headquarters, which in turn had replaced the crumbling Parker Center in 2010.

After the work of a suicide bomber had turned the new headquarters into a coffin for a hundred cops in 2029, the wireless company stepped in with the cash. The re-christend building looked like the architectural love child of the Getty Museum and a high-security fort.

"Once again police brutality is out of control in L.A.!" shouted a lean middle-aged man on the steps. He had razor cut hair and eyes that leaked bitterness into the waiting camera of reporters from *Crimecast* and the news blogs covering the story.

It was Ira Natterman spouting his usual diatribe. Natterman was a civil rights attorney whose entire career centered on suing the police for alleged violations. The joke among cops was that the most dangerous beat in L.A. was between Natterman and a microphone. And here he was, moist red lips hovering over the mike, a ravenous junk yard dog about to grab that bone.

Community policing, body-cams, huge increases in diversity

hires, sensitivity training, none of it ever changed Natterman's spiel. Whatever else ailed society: fatherlessness, mental health issues, drug addiction, poverty—to Natterman police were always the problem. Well, we were his meal ticket after all.

"We demand justice for this child's death, and his mother's pain." Natterman pointed to the red-eyed woman at his side.

Keeping my eyes on the ground, I moved ahead. That was low, using the mother's grief like that. Still, Natterman's spiel was old news to me. But halfway up the steps the lawyer's next line made me pause.

"We demand jail time for the reckless cop who put an end to the life of this fourteen-year-old honor student," he continued, grabbing the mike of the *Crimecast* reporter for emphasis. "Past reforms have not worked. Let's make an example and end racist police brutality this time!"

The crowd behind the reporters roared approval. Would these people screaming for my blood even have registered a complaint if events had gone the other way, and Shin or I were the ones lying in that steel drawer of the morgue today? I didn't feel very confident about the answer.

But I slipped through the crowd unnoticed and made my way inside Nokia.

RHD took up most of the third floor. Comprised of approximately one-hundred and ten sworn and civilian personnel under the command of Captain III Cheryl Tatum, RHD housed five sections: Robbery, Homicide, Special Assault, Cold Case and Special Investigation. As I passed RSS, my footsteps echoed on reinforced concrete. Digital frames hung on the corridor walls under energy-efficient fluorescents. The images changed every few seconds, displaying black and white wanted posters of suspects at large. Entering the Homicide Special Section, I glanced at the large digital "on-call" board, which dominated the front wall of the squad room. The board listed detective teams available for dispatch to new homicides. My name wasn't on it.

An aisle split the large room into two halves—Homicide I and Homicide II. The squads alternate by the week, with two-person teams often working independently. Walking past the two rows of twelve metal desks flanking the aisle felt like walking a gauntlet. I nodded to Shin, sitting next to my empty desk in Homicide I.

He flashed me a wan smile and a thumbs up. Making my way past the silent detectives planted behind those gray metal desks, and the doors to the offices of the two lieutenants who oversee each squad, I'd slid my barcode over the security scanner outside the captain's office. The door opened and I went in. LCD crystals on the privacy screen darkened the windows and muffled the sound almost before I'd closed the door. It didn't matter. Every detective in RHD knew what was going down.

Tatum didn't get up. She sat behind her desk, glaring at me. Captain Tatum had over twenty-seven years with the LAPD, and every year showed. She was a fifty-year old African-American with a body gone soft around the middle. Her eyes, however, were liquid steel.

"You wanted to see me, Captain?" I took off my hat, smoothed my hair and sat in the chair fronting her desk. I could see my face floating in the air before her. The open file on her computer was my jacket and ten card.

"Carmen Ramirez, mother of the deceased, has filed a complaint against you, citing wrongful death."

"I saved two lives."

"But you shot and killed her fourteen-year-old son."

"He shot first." I clenched the brim of my fedora hard enough to turn my knuckles white but kept my voice steady.

She nodded with narrowed eyes. "You're one of my best detectives and most decorated officers. So why is it you keep drawing fire?"

"Captain, that kid was a tweaked-out baby-banger. He fired shots and drove a three-ton stolen vehicle straight at my partner and a civilian. What was I supposed to do?"

"Let someone who didn't have a blood alcohol reading just under the legal limit take the call," Tatum snapped. "Thank God the uniform who tested your BAC had enough sense to wait."

I sat back in my chair. .08 is the legal blood alcohol limit. The officer, who had administered the breathalyzer, had done so an hour or more after the crash, giving my system time to wash some of the alcohol out. Legally, I hadn't been drunk, but I had been drinking.

"Our shift was over. I was off duty." I was careful to edit out all mention of Shin.

"You responded to the call. In a police vehicle."

"Because the suspect slammed into the black and white already in pursuit. Right in front of us. Ramirez disabled them, then shot at us."

"Piedmont, we're RHD. We investigate officer-involved shootings. We're not supposed to be the subject of the investigation. Maybe we promoted you too fast." She leaned back in her chair, peering at me.

A chill crept along my spine.

"Then there's the racial element," she continued, leaning forward again, placing her elbows on top of the desk and folding her hands together.

"Racist? The driver wasn't even visible." I explained that even if it hadn't been dark, the Excaliber SUV had sported illegally tinted windows.

"Racial, not racist, detective. Take it from a Black woman in a White world, there's always a racial element."

"The cameras should back me up," I said. "I was within policy."

The Captain put both her hands flat on her desk and pressed down as if she was either about to hoist herself up or keep the desk from levitating. "Civilians don't read police policy. They see the video of a dead child. You know the spotlight the department's under. Ambulance chasers are just looking for an excuse to tie our hands. Here you hand them another viral video."

"This was a righteous shoot."

"Your second in five years." Tatum jabbed her index finger at my floating file. The black hair and faded denim eyes rippled into pixels, then coalesced into my face once more. "I have cops who've never pulled their guns their entire twenty on the force."

They must work Pacific Palisades. We both knew those cops waved and drove by trouble so they wouldn't have to have this conversation.

"You want cops," I said, "or politicians out there?"

"Policing is political." Tatum exhaled a long, exasperated sigh. "Why didn't Miyaguchi drive?"

An eighteen-wheeler sat on my tongue.

Those steely eyes bored into mine for a few seconds before they softened a micro-millimeter. "Still not good enough," Captain Tatum said. "Not for RHD. Go home. You're on modified-administrative duty pending O.I.S. investigation. But Piedmont, if O.I.S. rules against you, you're out. We're not baseball. You don't get a third strike. Now get out of here."

The privacy screen lifted; I stood and jammed my hat back on my head. Eight pairs of eyes met me on the way out. As I walked through that gauntlet, nobody said a word. Shin's arched eyebrows framed his unspoken question as he mimed a hammer pounding a nail into his desk. I nodded and went home.

CHAPTER SIX

HOME WAS THE HOUSE ON HOWLAND AVENUE IN VENICE THAT belongs to my girlfriend Jo. I moved in three months ago. It's a contemporary smart-home design with an open floor plan and huge picture windows looking out to the canal. I still felt like I was the one piece of cheap furniture held over from a college dorm room amongst a house full of designer collectibles.

I walked in with the fingers of one hand curled around the neck of a bottle of good champagne. With the other hand, I tapped the little velvet ring box secure in my left suit pocket. The day before yesterday I'd picked up wine along with the ring with plans to pop the question. But the day before yesterday I didn't have a new case stalled and an OIS investigation looming over me. I stashed the champagne in the back of the Sub-Zero, and the ring in my gun safe.

Then I turned off the bathroom's smart-home technology. The last thing I needed today was Tommy the Talking Toilet giving me the rundown on my deficient vitamin levels.

Kicking off my shoes, I ambled back through the house to the kitchen area. Jo's cats appeared one by one, trotting along in my wake—yowling off-key like a bad garage band. I touched the menu screen of the auto-chef, and the 3D printer started to churn out their tuna dinner. The yowling stopped as the cats swarmed the stinky fish paste I emptied into their dishes.

Jo was a magnet for stray cats. She had a weakness for the ferals—wild warriors missing teeth, ears, and patches of fur. Eddie and the Ferals; we could start a band.

I poured myself a drink. OIS Investigation was routine for any shooting—no matter how justified. That's the song I was singing as the whiskey's slow burn blotted out the pictures in my head and smoothed out the rest.

"Fade to black," I said to the home monitor, and the walls went black. LCD crystals darkened the windows too. I sat down in the dark and let my eyes close.

I was too exhausted to open them back up, even when the face of system kid Britney Devonshire flashed into my head and morphed into Paco Ramirez. Then it was too late. The black hole where Paco's eye should have been dragged me down like a riptide. He'd been fourteen: just one year younger than me when I'd left home for good.

And suddenly I was back there—back to that day sixteen years ago with all the details clear and crisp as ever.

The black eye my fifteen-year-old self had worn to school that day had won me another trip to the nurse. Nurse Winters and I were getting to be old friends.

"I fell," I'd mumbled before my ass even hit the seat. I'd hoped the lie would pre-empt questions. The nurse's office always smelled like lemon air freshner and cleanser, but that day the scent of the freshly baked blueberry muffin she slid toward me made my stomach growl. Sunlight angled in from the window overlooking the street. The light made my swollen eye hurt.

"You fall a lot for such an athletic guy, Eddie," Ms.Winters said. The middle-aged nurse had a smiley mouth but sad eyes. "I have to report this." She put her hand on my arm. "We need to get you out of that house."

"Can't." Who'd look out for my Mom? I glanced down at my feet. The left Nike still had a spot of blood on the toe. I tucked it behind my right.

"If we don't," Ms. Winters said, "it doesn't take a prophet to predict your future."

I met her eyes as she continued. "Either your dad kills you or you kill him. My money's on you, Eddie. You're taller already. Getting stronger every day too. He's not."

I'd been counting on that myself. That part about me getting stronger.

I looked at Ms. Winters with her sad eyes. "I fell," I said again.

She shook her head and wrote something in my file. Chances

are she'd have catapulted me out of there anyway. But what happened later that night sped everything up. By the next morning with a bloody foot and a face like a patchwork quilt of bruises, I'd lit out from my parents' house in San Diego and trekked north to L.A.

I'd never gone back.

I must have fallen asleep during the trip down memory lane, because when I woke, Jo was leaning in to kiss me, a curtain of her pale blonde hair brushing my neck. I hadn't even heard her come in.

Tall, blonde and blue-eyed Jocelyn A. Sloan was a California girl, but she came from old money, east coast money. I didn't know much about her history except she'd gone to college in the east then moved to California, where her brother Craig was already well-established, to take a law degree. Craig, who'd set up a corporate security business flush with high profile contracts, had offered his sister a place to stay until she finished school.

Despite the heat, Jo wore a long-sleeved blue silk blouse that hid the row of small white scars on on her wrists. Those old scars told me Jo's history wasn't all unicorns and rainbows, but unlike so many women I knew, she didn't jabber on about herself or her past. So, I didn't press.

"Rough day?" Jo took a seat on the arm of the sofa.

I shrugged. For a couple beats neither of us spoke. "That feels good," I said as she started to massage my feet. I drank in the subtle floral notes of her perfume as she leaned in close.

"Anyone ever tell you, you have scars in weird places, Eddie?" Jo's fingers pressed the white worm of scar tissue on my left foot.

I let my eyes dart from her wrists to her deep blue eyes, waiting to see if this was Jo's way of signalling she wanted to talk about her own past. It wasn't and she didn't.

"I don't show my scars to just anyone." I kept my tone light.

"I'm flattered. How'd you get this one again?"

Kerchunk! The sound of the nail gun in my father's hand hammered in my head.

"Stepped on a nail." I pulled my foot in and pointed to the bag of groceries from Mizuma Market she'd set on the table. "What'd you get?"

"They had Kobe beef," she said, standing and heading to the kitchen. "I'm going to fix all your favorites tonight."

"Special occasion?" I stretched.

Jo took a slow twirl. "You are looking at the newest partner of Wen-Ho, Schwartz and Sloan."

"My Sloan ranger got her name on the door," I said.

Jo had been a senior associate in the firm. This was a major upgrade. On another day, it might not have felt like the sucker punch it did then. I was happy for her, truly, but with the sting of my own set-back still fresh, I had to work a little to inject the right enthusiasm in my voice.

"I'm proud of you, Jo."

She smiled. "The news won't be announced until the week after next. Assuming I don't do anything between now and then to mess it up."

Jo had a low, sultry voice that sounded like dark wood and cellos. She could read the back of a box of cat treats and the soft music of her voice turned trivia into a titillating promise of secrets for me alone.

"You won't. You're perfect." The muscles in my back kinked. Elbows out and hands behind my head, I stretched. "Kudos on making Partner with Tax Masters of the Universe."

Jo came back over and perched herself on my lap. "I don't think you really listen to me or you'd know I'm now heading up intellectual property. The—

"—hot arena. I listen. I just get distracted by the visuals." I kissed her again.

"You're not too hideous either," she said, lightly tracing the outline of my mouth with her index finger before she kissed me.

I put my arms around her and let my eyes wander appreciatively over her face with its pale blonde hair framing dark blue eyes. So different from my own black hair, black moods and faded denim eyes. Being with Jo just felt right, and had from the first moment I saw her.

"Give me a minute to reboot," I said. "I'll take you out to celebrate."

"And waste the Kobe?" Jo's eyes widened with mock alarm. "Never. You can do the honors on the grill. By the way, what's the champagne for?"

"Hmm?" I kissed her neck.

"The champagne in the back of the fridge."

"For you, of course," I said. It was only a tiny lie of omission any lawyer would appreciate. "The newest partner with her name on the door."

"You're amazing," she said. "So, you want to take a ride before dinner?"

Now that can mean a lot of things, and I admit I pictured other more exciting options, but ten minutes later we were paddling a canoe down the Howland canal in front of the house. That is to say, I was paddling. Jo, seated opposite me, leaned back, and inspired me to paddle.

Venice, California is a dream made from a memory. The dream was real estate entrepreneur Abbot Kinney's vision of a resort by the sea recalling the floating Italian city. It's an unfinished dream. In 1905 Kinney had sixteen miles of canals dug to drain the swamps of the area, but the grand complex of canals was never completed. By 1929 all but a handful of the canals had been buried under concrete and the city incorporated into L.A. Dreams written on water will drown one day.

We paddled under a pedestrian bridge of white wood laced with night jasmine. The agreeable scent filled the air.

"We need to weed the side border," Jo said, looking back towards the house at the tangle of weeds. "Remind me to tell the gardener."

"I'll do it."

Jo's hand trailed in the canal, leaving a wake. The city had cleaned up the water on the existing canals in 2035. These days it was good enough to drink.

"It's so peaceful here." Jo smiled. "Like nothing ever happens."

"Sometimes it's good to stir things up," I said, dipping the oar back into the crystalline canal water.

"Sometimes it's not."

I cocked my head and waited, focusing on the sound of the water lapping against the boat.

"I heard you were put on administrative duty," Jo said. "What happened?"

She knew. Of course she knew. Her brother Craig's security firm had feelers everywhere.

I stared at Jo. From the first moment I saw her, I'd wanted to sleep with Jo because of the way she looked. But I fell in love with her because of the way she saw. Only sometimes that had its drawbacks.

"Craig has too many friends downtown," I said.

"He's just worried about you."

"He should mind his own business."

"He's my brother. You're my guy. He thinks that makes it his business."

My guy. I wanted to be more than just Jo's guy. But it was suddenly crystal clear that diamond ring would stay stashed in my gun safe for a while longer. At least until I'd cleared the OIS Investigation.

"You should get a medal for yesterday, Eddie, not a complaint," Jo said.

"You don't get a medal when a kid dies."

Jo leaned forward and touched my knee. "Not your fault. Why put up with all the grief?"

"I thought you liked me being a cop." I kept my tone playful. Jo had never been a badge bunny, but she'd liked the thrill of dating a detective.

"I did," Jo said. "I do. What do you want, Eddie?"

The truth was, like most cops, I didn't like to talk about the job with civilians, even Jo. Try explaining sex to virgins. Being a detective wasn't something I chose. It chose me. Like family. Only . . .

"Every day I wake up wanting to make a difference," I said. "Some days I do. Days like today, I'm not so sure."

"If you want out, there are lots of options in the private sector." Jo dangled that suggestion like an expert fly fisherman flicking a tasty lure. "Craig would be happy to help."

I bet he would. "I'm a cop, Jo. I never wanted to be anything but. The right kind of cop." Not like my father, who'd been the wrong kind. Taking bribes to pay for his addiction. And worse. I shifted my eyes to the oar. "I'm already living in your house . . ."

". . . our house," she corrected.

"Our house, which you own. Security doesn't pay much."

"Corporate security does." She kept her tone light too.

Jo already out-earned me five times over, and that didn't

count her trust fund. And how much more would she rake in as a partner?

"It's not about the money," Jo added quickly. "I want you to be happy."

I looked at her earnest face, wishing she'd yelled instead.

Our canoe was drifting off course. I realized I'd stopped paddling and started again.

"Tell me the truth. You worried my being a desk jockey is going to reflect poorly on you, Madame Partner?"

She sighed. "I'm worried you're unhappy unless you're off by yourself digging up dirt somewhere."

"I have the weekend off," I said. "Maybe I'll tackle those weeds."

Jo smiled. "Maybe." She sighed. "Maybe we're both working too hard." Her tone of voice went from wistful to playful. "What do you say we quit our jobs and run away together? Some place calm—with a beach."

"The Greek Islands," I said. For our honeymoon. After I ace that OIS Investigation, close the Devonshire case and buy another bottle of champagne.

"All the way home I kept thinking." Her tone had gone all serious again. "What if things had gone the other way yesterday? What if you were the one who got shot?"

"They didn't," I said. "I wasn't."

"It's just . . ." She leaned forward. Her knuckles grasped the sides of the boat so hard the flesh was white. "Let somebody else be the hero for a change, Eddie. I need you."

"I'm not going anywhere," I said. "I promise."

Jo took a deep breath and leaned back again, her face inscrutable. I rowed a few more strokes in silence.

"What about that vacation?" Jo said. "You won't get bored with this partner if life does get peaceful. Will you, Eddie?"

I looked at her for just a second. Then I capsized the canoe. Jo squealed, and I swooped up the soaking wet woman in my arms. I kissed her. A long kiss. By the time I put Jo down the water had settled again, and I saw our reflection in the canal—the happy couple. I suddenly knew it wouldn't be long before I'd dig that ring out of my gun safe. I wanted to hold that picture in my memory forever, but I had to deal with less pleasant thoughts.

The Devonshire autopsy was set for Monday at eleven-thirty. Shin would be there—without me if my interview with the Officer Involved Shooting Team didn't go well. My interview was scheduled for Monday at nine.

CHAPTER SEVEN

AT EIGHT FORTY-FIVE MONDAY MORNING I WAS WALKING along the fifth floor corridor of Nokia P.D.. Jay Espinoza, the union rep I'd met moments before, scurried along on my right, rattling off a stream of advice as we approached the OIS interrogation room, unofficially known as the See Cave. The Use of Force Review Board is convened on all Officer Involved Shootings. The board submits its findings and recommendations up the chain to the Chief of Police. If they found me at fault, I was out of a job. Or worse.

"Now remember, I can defend a mistake, but not a lie."

"I'm telling the truth," I said. "It was a righteous shoot."

"Still best you don't say anything. Let me do the talking." Espinoza ran his hand through thinning hair. Fifty summers of sun and disappointment had etched deep trenches in his face.

I nodded.

The door to the See Cave popped open as we passed our barcodes over the sensor on the wall to the right.

"Counselor Jay Espinoza, Police Union Representative," announced the robotic voice of the smart-room as my rep stepped over the threshold. "Edward Piedmont, Detective II, Homicide I," droned that same metallic voice as I took off my hat and followed him into the room.

The See Cave was a bare room with green walls set up for hologram re-enactments. In the little back chamber, five gray chairs stood empty behind a long table of burnished steel, and two in front meant for Espinoza and me. A tall man with skin the color of café au lait and eyes of seaweed green was already seated in another chair off to the side. He nodded as we entered and handed me a holo-viewer. Robbery Homicide Detective Dewayne Jefferson was a familiar face, but I didn't really know him. A special section of RHD does all the preliminary investigations on Officer Involved Shootings. Jefferson had already taped my statement at the scene and submitted his findings to the committee.

Espinoza and I were just about to sit down when the door to the right of the last chair opened. Three cops and one civilian filed in and took their seats. My rep and I followed suit. One seat behind the steel desk remained empty. The panel members leaned in towards each other for some last pre-hearing pow-wow.

Espinoza took the opportunity to brief me on the players. Opposite me on my far left sporting a really bad haircut was Sonny Chung, a pudgy ballistics expert from the crime lab. Sonny knew guns and ammo cold, rattling off their stats like a rabid baseball fan discussing the RBIs of his favorite players.

"Sonny," my rep whispered, "knows his stuff, and he's fair."

Next to him sat a sergeant named Scott Black. He had the tough lean body of a much younger man with a veteran soldier's posture and an affable face that reminded me of Steve McQueen. The impression quickly faded. The sergeant's face, especially the eyes, had the opaque look of somebody who'd seen more than his years, way more than any actor.

"Black's a twenty-year veteran from Metro," continued my rep sotto voce.

I nodded. If Black had been on the front lines himself, he'd bring that understanding to my case. That's all I could ask.

Dead center in the row was the team leader, Lt. Marcella Figueroa, a handsome woman with high cheekbones, skin the color of expresso and an aura of gravitas.

"She's a recent transplant from Cuba by way of the Bronx," said Espinoza. "The word circling the department is she's smart and ambitious." My rep looked at me with special emphasis. "Don't give her a reason to go political."

I nodded again.

Next to Lt. Figueroa sat another officer I didn't know with hair the color of an Irish setter. His nametag read Rob Plotkin, and he had smoke-stained fingers and a drinker's nose. That could play for or against me. My rep shrugged. He didn't have any inside scuttlebutt about Plotkin.

Trouble in the form of an auburn-haired woman so thin her collarbones could slice sushi came through the door and took that empty seat at the far right. She was literally the last person I expected to see. Claire Kidder was a civilian like Sonny, but that's all they had in common.

"She's a top corporate attorney and a brand new appointment to the civilian oversight committee," Espinoza said, nodding towards the woman. "She might not be sympathetic . . ."

"I know her," I said.

"That's good," Espinoza said.

"Not really."

Claire lived in an upscale gated community on the Westside where crime was something you watched on your home entertainment center. From the safety of her Herman Miller chair she knew all violence perpetrated by police was excessive no matter what the provocation. I knew that for the same reason I knew she hated my guts without any helpful commentary from the union rep.

Claire and I had had one drunken hook-up a year ago. After that she'd left a series of texts and video-messages on my voicemail. I should've called her back. I didn't because the next day I'd met Jo, and all other women faded away like old photos left in the sun. I was kicking myself for that mistake now.

Sitting there at the end of the table, tapping her Mont Blanc laser pointer, Claire glared at me like I was a rabid pit bull off leash. Shin was right. Karma does get you in the end.

I leaned towards my rep Espinoza, starting to tell him about my history with Claire, and her obvious conflict of interest, but he gestured for me to save it. The proceedings had started.

The hearing began pretty mildly. Lt. Figueroa had Detective Jefferson enter the recorded testimony of Shin and two uniforms who'd been on site into the record. There was little difference in the facts of these three official statements on glove phone.

Next we heard the corroborating testimony of two civilian witnesses. The muscles in my jaw relaxed a little.

Then Jefferson played the contradictory statement of another civilian named Jody Trahn into the record.

"I got cuts and bruises all over my hands and knees from where the one cop shoved me to the ground," Ms. Trahn said to the officer who recorded her testimony, shoving her scraped palms towards the lens of the Nokia smart phone.

I recognized her and shifted in my chair. She'd been the woman with the camera Shin had knocked out of the way. He'd saved her life and put himself in danger.

"And the other cop, the good-looking one, who shot that kid in the SUV? He should have fired like a warning shot or something. Or maybe just wounded the kid in his arm. He didn't need to kill him."

"If I was the Sundance Kid," I mumbled. Civilians who've never picked up a gun always think cops should be able to replicate movie magic.

My rep stepped on my foot under the table as Detective Jefferson finished playing her taped statement into the record.

"As we will see in the holo-record momentarily, Detective Piedmont did warn the suspect," my rep Espinoza objected as he sprang to his feet. "That warning was ignored. The suspect discharged his weapon. For the benefit of the civilian, he explained how firing warning shots into the air, in a city as densely populated as Los Angeles, would likely kill or injure innocent parties, and was therefore not departmental policy.

"Nor is it policy for police to fire their weapons unless there is a lethal threat," he continued. "However, when a suspect creates that kind of threat, as did Mr. Ramirez, an officer must respond."

Claire looked up from her copy of the digital photos. "Yes, counselor, when there's a lethal threat. However, in this instance, the threat was exaggerated. Detective Piedmont overreacted to the actions of a scared honors middle school student. He responded with excessive force."

The room seemed to go even quieter than before.

I'd vowed not to look at Claire, but the sound of her voice made me turn my head. Her eyes were hard black beads. Three-timers determined not to head back to San Quentin for life had leveled eyes just like those at me over the barrel of a .45.

Espinoza was already on his feet objecting again. "We will show there was a lethal threat in the holo-record. For the moment, however, please note that the honor student story is media spin. I refer you to Detective Dewayne Jefferson's testimony."

"That's right." Detective Jefferson's deep baritone resounded as he read his background report on the dead kid into the record.

"Paco Ramirez was a marginal student at Adidas Middle

School with AzteKa 17 gang tats and one prior for dealing," Jefferson said, referring to his notes. "Not an honor student. He borrowed his brother's car and drove without a license. The gun was an illegal street purchase. Paco's whole family's tight with the AzteKas."

The knowing nods around the table told me we'd scored a point in my favor. Detective Jefferson finished his testimony without objection.

Then Sonny introduced the ballistics evidence, including a dissertation on the merits and debits of the Glock 20Z dual action laser semi-automatic. The registered number on each casing from all the bullets in the magazine discharged was read into the record in turn. Each had been found imprinted with a number from the gun registered to me as required by law. I never disputed that the fatal bullets shot were mine.

But Sonny proved Paco Ramirez shot bullets too. Ramirez' bullets came from an unregistered 9mm, which matched the gun found in his Excalibur. Now we only had to prove his bullets were shot before mine.

The See Cave went black as we put on our holo-viewers. Sonny revved up the holoplayer. Three cameras on site plus the footage from two officers' helmet-cams had captured the incident from various angles. When the holo-function was added, two dimensions sprang into three as the walls receded.

It was like reliving the scene as an out of body experience. We saw the incident from several points of view, unfortunately, none of them mine. Things had happened so fast I hadn't had time to turn on my body cam.

Bang! Shots fired from the Excalibur before it rolled to a stop. I saw myself shout "Police!" to the occupants of the SUV in a voice I didn't recognize as my own. "Come out of the vehicle with your hands in the air."

Once again the civilian, Jody Trahn, ran out into the middle of the street—just at the moment the Excalibur punched the gas hard and went in reverse. Rob Plotkin flinched, jumping back. I shut my eyes, tight, and sat quiet in the dark. I didn't need to watch to know what came next.

"Stop!" I heard my digital clone yell again, followed by the sound of my shots and a laser chaser reverberating through the room. I heard the Excalibur lurch and bang into the yield sign. The horn blared. There was the sound of feet scrambling across pavement, my feet, as I'd made my way to the driver's side and opened the door. There was a pause and the muffled thud of something soft and heavy falling out—Paco's body. Jody Trahn, the woman Shin had saved, started to scream. I opened my eyes. My stomach was a hard knot.

Sonny backed up the action and played the whole thing all again, freezing when the shots went off. Bang!

My union rep drew the group's attention to my image. "Note the clear indication that Detective Piedmont has not yet fired his weapon when the subject fires."

The clear indication was Shin diving for the ground in slo-mo this time, taking the clueless civilian with him, as I took cover and aimed. I yelled for the suspect to put down his weapon and exit the vehicle with hands up. He accelerated instead. My digital doepplegaenger fired.

"Can we see it once more, please?" Claire aimed her laser pointer at my image.

They played that shooting twice more. My head throbbed more with each replay.

"I'm forced to concur with the testimony of Jody Trahn," Ms. Kidder said finally. "Clearly Detective Piedmont used excessive force in this situation."

Scott Black, the Sgt. from Metro, shot her a look of disbelief. "It's a righteous shoot," he said, rubbing a hand over his short-clipped hair. "The suspect precipitated events. Detective Piedmont gave warning. The suspect didn't desist. Piedmont had no choice."

Lt. Figueroa asked for a show of hands on the ruling of my actions being within departmental rules. Four right hands rose into the air. Claire's arms stayed glued to the top of the table.

The vein throbbing on my temple eased up a bit. Maybe I wouldn't need to raise the alarm about my previous history with Claire after all.

Smiling slightly, my rep introduced the motion to adjourn the hearing. Then came the kicker.

"Wait," Claire said in a voice of deadly calm. "What about Detective Piedmont's blood alcohol levels?" There was the killer instinct for which corporate clients paid her big bucks.

Espinoza started to take furious notes, muttering under his breath as my blood alcohol readings from the scene were introduced into the record.

I'd had a BAC level of .045%, and .08% is the legal limit.

"Detective Piedmont was off-duty and returning the vehicle to the police lot when the 503 came over the radio," Espinoza argued. "The suspect rammed and disabled the squad car already in pursuit. Another cop might have waved and driven by, but Detective Piedmont had a direct visual on the suspect, and shots had just been fired. He did his duty and responded. He wasn't drunk. His BAC levels were well under the legal limit."

"It is a matter of record that even small amounts of alcohol impair reaction time and performance in general," Claire countered, her eyes boring into those of each of the panelists in turn.

Plotkin lowered his eyes first, his face reddening to a shade of crimson that matched his drinker's nose.

"But I see here that Detective Piedmont's blood alcohol test was administered a full hour or more after the incident," Claire continued. "That means there was time for his system to metabolize a considerable portion of the alcohol. So how drunk must he have been during the incident?"

"Not so drunk he couldn't hit a moving target," Scott Black muttered loud enough for the record.

Claire gave him a withering look. "Maybe because he's habituated to alcohol. And we all know how alcohol precipitates violence." She turned her gaze back to me. "Detective Piedmont's record shows quite a history of violence. This is his second officer involved shooting."

"That shooting was ruled within policy, counselor," my rep said.

I guess it didn't matter that shooting had also prevented the murder of an innocent civilian targeted by a serial killer looking to up his body count.

"I would remind you," Claire said, locking eyes with Sonny now, "that it is the job of this panel to address public concerns regarding our city's law enforcement policies, and to bolster public confidence in the men and women of the LAPD."

Sonny held her gaze, but his fingers started to beat a tattoo on the table top.

She moved her sights to the next target, focusing on Lt. Figueroa.

"If I thought Detective Piedmont's drunken behavior was the departmental norm, I'd say we need to look more closely at police protocols, so the LAPD could learn from these incidents. As a matter of principle."

When lawyers stand on principle, cops watch their backs.

Figueroa kept her expression blank, but her eyes smoldered and the muscles in her jaw tensed.

Black's face had hardened into a mask of dislike. A few bad apples in the brotherhood had tarnished the reputation of us all forever. Nobody wanted another Christopher Commission and more federal oversight.

Teeth grinding, I had to hand it to Claire. She knew all the departmental pressure points and where to lean.

"But I do not want to tar the entire department for the actions of one rogue cop," Claire said, winding up for the final pitch. "Instead I recommend a five year review of Detective Piedmont's record to determine the extent of his alcohol-related incidents. The safety of L.A.'s citizens demands it."

"I'm not a rogue cop," I said, keeping my voice calm as I locked eyes with Claire Kidder. "And I wasn't drunk. But sometimes you have to do things you wish you didn't." I hoped she'd hear and accept my apology for past sins.

Claire's face flushed. The panel turned with questions in their eyes from me to her.

Lt. Figueroa leaned over to Scott Black, and then to Plotkin and Sonny, whispering sotto voce, before conferring with Claire. Claire looked at me, then slowly shook her head.

Figueroa delivered the verdict. "Detective Piedmont, the Officer Involved Shooting team has determined four to one the shooting of Paco Ramirez was within departmental policy." He slid my gold shield back across the desk to me.

I wanted to pump the air with my fist, but I stayed planted in my chair.

"But we have ruled three to two," Figueroa continued, "that some of your actions prior to the gunfire were questionable. Therefore, it is our recommendation that the Chief of Police refer this case to the IAC for further disciplinary hearings, pending a five-year review of your record. You will remain on administrative duty pending mandatory psychological evaluation."

I nodded, clenching my fists under the table.

IAC rose out of the ashes of the Internal Affairs Division, when the latter was disbanded and re-established in 2020 after a series of battles with the civilian Police Commission and federal oversight committee over allegations of racial profiling. The IAC investigates all citizen complaints against the department. Ms. Ramirez, mother of the deceased, had made one. This OIS ruling meant the chief would refer my case to the IAC with a big black mark on it. I was still a Homicide Special Detective, but any hope I had held out for immediate redeployment had evaporated like fog in a high hot wind.

Jay Espinoza thanked the OIS for their time and tapped me on the shoulder. We walked out. Once in the hall with the door closed behind us, he said, "What was that about? I told you let me do the talking."

"Ms. Kidder and I have a little history together," I said. "It didn't go the way she wanted." I told him about the hook-up and her subsequent series of calls.

"Why didn't you tell me that before?" he sputtered. "That's conflict of interest."

"I was trying to tell you when the hearing started. I didn't know she was on the panel till then. Can't we use that?"

Jay cocked his head to the side, nodding slowly as the wheels visibly turned in his mind. "She should have recused herself and didn't. But we can't pre-emptively derail the IAC hearing now. So, prepare yourself. Put a lid on those outbursts and get through your psych eval. I'll see you at the hearing."

I thanked him as he hurried off to another appointment.

That's when the door opened and Claire Kidder strode into the hallway. Any impulse to mend fences died when she looked at me like she'd just won the heavyweight championship.

"Happy now?" I said. I looked forward to that IAC interview about as much as a public prostate exam, and she knew it. But while I had obstacles ahead of me, she at least was no longer one of them.

"You're lucky I didn't request an investigation into possible discriminatory conduct," Claire said pressing her lips into a smile thin as a razor blade.

"Sometimes discrimination's a good thing," I said. "We both should've remembered that back in the bar where you tied one on." I walked past her without another word. Her mouth opened and snapped shut like a baby bird expecting the worm that didn't come.

CHAPTER EIGHT

"So?" Shin was waiting for me at his desk on the third floor, nervously cracking his knuckles as he elbowed aside the evidence bags from the Devonshire case. "How'd it go?"

I flashed him my badge. "But you're going solo to the autopsy." As I glanced at the bag holding the contents from the deceased's purse, I filled him in on the O.I.S. verdict.

"Could be worse," Shin said, clearly relieved. "They benched you. They didn't kick you off the team." He handed me a flash-dot. "The Devonshire girl's phone records just came in. Have fun with the read through."

"You're actually enjoying this," I said.

Shin's grin and waving fingers were his reply as he headed out. The news feed playing on my computer was grim. More kids stricken with Alz-X, more bodies turning up on the streets since Nieto had been been released.

I turned off the newsfeed, put my feet up, and started the slog backwards through three months of phone records.

An orphaned foster kid, Britney had nobody in the way of family. I was hoping to get a sense of who she was and looking for patterns or anything unusual.

A glance at the log of calls from July through the first week of October showed Britney Devonshire had made over 1,500 texts to a local number that the system identified as belonging to a Mercedes Delblanco. A quick search revealed Delblanco was another stripper employed by Sandy Beaches. From her photo, I recognized the Latina with the blue-black hair I'd seen at the club.

Flipping past the phone log to the transcription detail, I started in on the cache of texts. The fifteen hundred back and forths between the girls confirmed Mercedes Delblanco as Britney Devonshire's BFF from work. I slogged through texts debating the merits of various makeup tips, including passionate discussion of favorite lip and nail color complete with emojis and multiple exclamation points. The deceased favored a shade called Apricot Dream. I remembered her chipped, bitten nails from the crime scene.

Neither woman was a fan of their boss Sandy Rose. Complaints were frequent. There was a spike in the number of texts at the end of August. The uptick in volume apparently centered on Sandy's decision to cut Mercedes' hours and move her to the afternoon shift at the beginning of September. Britney had stayed on prime time in the evenings. Sandy had merited a few choice epithets, but there was no mention of drug tests, random or otherwise.

There was, however, girltalk about clients: shared advice on who was a good tipper and who failed to observe the look don't touch rules of the establishment. But none of the clients seemed to be anything but minor nuisances.

Barring the litany of complaints Mercedes had about her ex-husband Raul, the usual chatter about boyfriends was surprisingly thin on the ground for a woman as attractive as Britney Devonshire. Mercedes dated, but her friend was either less forthcoming, or had less to report. Until a few weeks before her death when a few references to somebody Ms. Devonshire had met recently popped up, including one elated text complete with emoticon: *he said yes Merc!!!* ☺

Timecode showed Britney had fired off that text the same week Sandy Rose had canned the now dead stripper—just a week prior to her death.

Britany Devonshire's last text to Mercedes, sent only a couple hours before her estimated time of death, read: *Bye-bye to the 818. Movin on up.*

I switched back to the main log listing phone calls. Scanning timecode of incoming calls, I found one number that matched the timeframe for both texts. Moreover, Britney Devonshire had made three additional outgoing calls to that same number earlier in the month. The system showed the number she'd called only a couple hours before her death belonged to a Dr. Gabriel Lee.

Another quick search told me Dr. Lee was a sixty-three-year-old microbiologist employed by Genesys, a biomed research facility in Sun Valley. He was married with one teenaged son. I sat back in my chair and stared at the data. Why had the stripper contacted a microbiologist old enough to be her grandfather once, let alone five times in three weeks? Was he a client/john from the club, a friend, or something else, something more?

Her glove phone camera roll turned up mostly selfies and badly-framed shots of her cat. But there were a couple pics of a woman in a purple bikini I recognized as Mercedes Delblanco. In the picture Mercedes squinted at the camera as she stood on Zuma beach near the lifeguard station nearest the parking lot. I scrolled through the rest of the photos, but there was no Dr. Lee. No men at all in fact, which once again pointed to a black hole in the boyfriend department.

I put down the log and picked up the evidence bag of some of the deceased's effects. Her purse held the California driver's license I'd already seen, but no wallet. Like most people, she'd apparently charged all her purchases to her barcode. A small pink bag of makeup held some lipstick, mascara and a half-empty bottle of the apricot nail polish she favored. The only other item in the bag was a little pocket Bible.

Britney Devonshire's apartment had held an e-reader stuffed with gossip rags and travel magazines, but no books or religious paraphenalia. The title page told me the Bible had belonged to her long-dead mother. I started to flip through the pages and something fell out.

A grimy print out, it looked like a fuzzy identity barcode—then I turned it on its side.

"A blood spot?" I said the words aloud.

Blood spots, the colloquial term for genetic partial prelims, were a standard part of my job. The down and dirty genetic analysis of a single drop of blood revealed enough about the donor to make for an economical identifier that was nonetheless accurate to over ninety-eight per cent. Thirty years ago, blood spots had been confined to the criminal population where blood or saliva was harvested upon arrest. Once big data companies saw the potential, however, the pool of registered individuals had expanded. The fastest growing market had been neo-natal.

Many prospective parents wanted to know the medical forecast for their progeny, and fetal partial prelims were tailored to indicate undesireable genetic traits, both existing and potential.

This blood spot wasn't from the crime lab or the outside lab the LAPD used for its genetic contract work. That meant it hadn't been harvested from Britney Devonshire's prior arrest for soliciting. That also meant it likely was neo-natal.

I texted Shin to call me straightaway.

CHAPTER NINE

SHIN'S PIXILATED FACE FLOATED IN THE L-SHAPED SPACE OF my Nokia Handy. He was walking out the door from the downtown morgue on his way to the detective sedan. They had just finished the cut.

"Missing me already?" Shin sat down behind the wheel and cranked the AC.

"What did the M.E. find on Britney Devonshire?" I said.

"No real surprises. Probable cause of death—accidental overdose. But she had Blue Lotus in her blood as well as Green Ice."

"Ice and Spice." Blue Lotus was a synthetic marijuana often smoked by fans of Green Ice. "Was she pregnant?"

Shin raised his chin. The smile vanished as he shook his head. "No. Why?"

I held up the blood spot I'd found tucked in her pocket-Bible. Then I told Shin about the texts to her friend and the calls to microbiologist Dr. Lee. "So if she wasn't pregnant . . ."

"Maybe it's from an earlier pregnancy," Shin said. "The M.E. said Devonshire never delivered a kid. That doesn't mean she never miscarried or aborted. Maybe she held onto the blood spot and used it to pressure the reluctant boyfriend."

"Dr. Lee's not her boyfriend." I told Shin about the noticeable lack of texts and pictures from Britney Devonshire's phone. "More likely she feigned pregnancy to shake down a married client with a lot to lose."

Shin listened intently. "That's a bold play, Eddie. Risky with a guy who knows his science."

"Yeah." The kind of desperate ploy a systems kid who'd run out of options might try. "Any sign of sexual assault?"

"None, Eddie." Shin ran his hands over his face. He looked tired. Shin knew the stats as well as anyone. If a woman is killed, nine times out of ten her husband or boyfriend pulled the trigger.

"No sign of foul play at all? You sure?"

He nodded. "I think you're making too much of those texts."

"Hmm." There was no way the department would spend the cash for DNA tests unless Britney Devonshire's death was ruled a homicide.

"Eddie," Shin said, cracking his knuckles. "I see where you're going with this. Just between us, I agree the OD might not have been so accidental."

I waited.

"She'd just lost her job. She had money problems. Most likely—this girl accidentally on purpose took a one-way trip with the Green Angel. But homicide—you're too far out over your skiis."

"You check her accounts?"

"Of course." Shin looked a little put out by my question. "She made good money but spent more. Tracked down that derma ad too. Britney made peanuts on it. The cookie jar was bare. No cash deposits or record of money transfers from this Dr. Lee. If she tried to pressure him and that went south too? No surprise she wanted out, is it?"

"You're gonna write it up as suicide?" I said.

Shin shook his head. "We can't prove it wasn't accidental, so I don't see a reason to contradict the coroner. No next of kin is listed, but somebody might turn up. Why make it worse if they do, you know?"

I nodded, reminded again of why I liked Shin so much.

A lopsided grin spread across Shin's affable face. "Eddie, it's this desk-duty. You're like a Terminator-terrier chewing the ball to bits. Get cleared for active duty. We need you."

I thought about the newscast I'd seen, the higher body count since Nieto's release. Maybe Shin was right. Maybe I was just guilt-tripping myself over landing us in all the shit with the OIS.

Britney Devonshire's death was a non-starter for the department. The overdose of a stripper wasn't exactly a high priority in a city with three hundred odd homicides—courtesy of the Zeta war. But the fact this system kid had suddenly put a spike in the wrong arm so soon after that happy-talk text to Mercedes ate at me. Especially given the timing of phone calls to Dr. Lee and that blood spot.

"I'll send you her final autopsy report soon as I have it," Shin said.

"Do me a solid," I said, "and don't close out the file yet. Nothing adds up on this. That's interesting, don't you think?"

"You crazy hakujin," Shin said, shaking his head. "I'm raising three kids and juggling a full caseload. I don't have time for interesting. I hardly have time to eat. You feel me?"

"Meet me at the dojo," I said. "We can grab a bite after. I'm buying."

CHAPTER TEN

Every Monday night after work, Shin and I played kendo, Japanese fencing. The dojo was on Corinth Ave., a block south of Sawtelle in little Osaka. When I got there, it was magic hour. The dying light of the sun poured through the windows lining the long wall of the Japanese Community Center.

Slipping off my shoes, I bowed before entering.

Kendo is Japanese for "the way of the sword." There were no colored belts or changes in uniform to signify rank. Everyone wore the same midnight blue gi, the long-sleeved padded karate shirt, and hakama, floor length Japanese culottes. Protective armor, or bogu, shields the head, torso and hands from the full contact blows delivered by the opponent's bamboo sword. It made us all look like Darth Vader in blue.

As I knelt and strapped on my own bogu, Shin warmed up—doing suriashi across the expanse of the bamboo floor. He seemed to glide across the blond wood like a Noh dancer.

We bowed to each other, then began kiri-kaeshi, the traditional choreographed opening drill. Kiri-kaeshi, or cross-cutting, is both a warm up, and at higher skill levels, a chance to practice timing, footwork, breathing, and the recognition and creation of the right moment to strike.

Like a seasoned cop reading a threat on the street, an experienced player quickly sizes up the level of his opponent, adjusting to the level of the novice. An adept has practiced moves so many times his brain synapses fire faster than a novice's. His body acts on its own. I've played against a couple of masters. It's like moving in slow motion against an opponent in fast forward.

Shin and I started to spar. Shin remained nearly motionless, holding his sword steady. Then he lowered it a couple centimeters and slowly raised it again. It was a feint, an attempt to force me into a rushed attack. Edging in warily with my feet, I felt for that moment when the energy of the opponent shifts and the action goes down.

Shin was an advanced player, but not yet a master. Born in Osaka, he'd started playing in school, but when he left Japan, he dropped kendo and the banking career his parents had mapped out for him. Shin had moved to the U.S. and become a cop, only to take up kendo again when he landed in the Koreatown station where he'd served before Homicide Special. Even with the gap, my partner still had twenty years of kendo experience on me.

It was Shin who'd gotten me started on the martial art three years ago when we first became partners. He played classic kendo, no tricky feints or fast barrages of multiple strikes. Just one shot—one kill. It's an elegant style and the hardest to master, but Shin was patient and willing to suffer losses until he was good enough to win the way he wanted. I had to rely on speed, height and tricky set ups planned in advance.

I set up a rhythm, then broke that rhythm, trying to force Shin off his center to score. In far better physical condition than Shin, I played that to my advantage, dancing around him, wearing him down. Keeping him on the defensive until he was breathing hard, I feinted left for a kote wrist lopping strike, but landed a blow to the head instead. That match went to me.

"Doh!" Shin won the next match with a clean strike to the gut when I went for a wrist-head combination and left my core open. If the swords had been real, my guts would be spilling out over the floor like spaghetti.

Now tied, we both felt intensity build on the third match. This time I left off the dancing around and kept my eyes focused on Shin's whole body. I started to cheat the distance, right foot stealing ground under the hakama. He felt the feint as a move and went for my head. I beat him. He bowed, conceding.

"Most men your size aren't that fast, Eight Pack," Shin teased as we cleaned up after practice.

"You almost had me."

"Almost is still dead. But you rely too much on height and speed, Eddie. It's a young man's game. Let the sword move on its own."

I laughed. "I use what I have. You've got the edge in technique."

"You over-think things too," Shin said. His slow grin lit his face then dimmed. "Like the Devonshire case." Shin folded his hakama into its neat origami-like square for storage. We put our bogu and shinai back in their bags.

I stood and stared at Shin. "I just want to talk to this Dr. Lee."

"You can't until you're cleared," he said. "And since the coroner's ruling doesn't support your theory, Lieutenant Rodriguez is not gonna sign off on the overtime for me. I'm not going against policy, Eddie. Rules are rules."

"If I pass my psych eval, I'll be back on active tomorrow. All I'm asking is that you take your time on the paperwork till I've had a chance to talk to this guy."

Shin tapped his knuckles on the car's hood. "Come on, buy me dinner. I'm starving." He stored his bogu at the dojo. I stashed my bag of kendo armor and practice swords in the trunk of my car. Together we walked up Corinth and over to Sawtelle to grab a beer and some food at an izakaya tucked away there.

The light from the pulsing Kirin sign over the bar stained Shin's face red. A sweet sad J-pop song played softly in the background. Over a Kirin beer and a bowl of well-salted edamame at the bar, we started in on the file again.

Shin popped an edamame into his mouth. "What do we know about this guy?"

I read Shin's casual "we" as a hopeful sign and told him about the sixty-three year old microbiologist. "I only had time to google him. I'll run in-depth background on Lee later."

"Why wait?" Shin's glove phone came out while we waited for our food. He logged onto police biodata and checked out Lee's criminal history. "No priors, nada."

"Born Lee Gyeong-su in South Korea," I said, looking over his shoulder. "Some sixty-three years ago. Got his doctorate in genetics and microbiology at UC Berkeley at the age of twenty-four."

"A rising star like you, Eddie," Shin teased, switching back to the biodata page. "The university hired him before the ink on his diploma dried."

"Looks like he didn't stick around for long," I said. "Took a job in the private sector in 2008."

"Maybe he didn't have a choice."

Nestled amongst an impressive list of publications were a couple of weblinks to newsstories from *Science Today* and *The Lancet* dating back to the early 2000s. Shin had pulled up one of the articles. Dr. Lee had been shelved in 2011 for juicing the results on some experiments involving somatic cell nuclear transfer.

"I remember reading something about that," Shin said. "There was a little scandal in the Korean papers."

"Didn't stop him for long, though. Looks like he found a soft landing."

There was a two-year gap in Lee's publications, during which time he seemed to have dropped out of sight, only to reappear a few years later working on stem cell research in the private sector this time.

"He must be good," Shin agreed. "He rode out the news cycle."

A sizeable list of publications followed, most of them on Alzheimer's and Alz-X, and a bunch of links to related websites.

"What's his family like?" Shin said.

Biodata showed Lee had married anesthesiologist Merideth Kim in 2022. They had one son, Raymond, aged nineteen, currently a junior studying engineering at Cal Tech. The family resided in Pacific Palisades.

"Sweet," I said. "What's he look like?"

Shin pulled up Lee's DMV portrait from 2030 and more recent photos of the scientist at a conference held late in 2039. Lee had an oblong face with a serious expression framed by black hair that fell just shy of his collar. He was a lean guy of medium height who could have passed for a man in his late 40s.

"Geez, grandpa looks better than I do," Shin said, glancing at Lee's photo, and patting his own paunch. "You think the stripper was his first side dish?"

"At sixty-three?" I shook my head. "Maybe she was just the first to try and pin him with a kid."

"The blood spot," Shin said, nodding. He dipped another edamame pod in citron soy sauce and popped it in his mouth, tossing the empty casing on a cocktail napkin. "If he bought the scam, he'd see the price tag for twelve more years of private school and another half-million Cal Tech education coming straight for his wallet."

I could see Shin's resistance starting to crumble. The father of two college-aged Miyaguchis, and one daughter still in middle-school, Shin had the overtime hours to show for it.

"I wonder what his wife thinks about all this," I said. "If she knows."

"Speaking of wives." Shin glanced at his glove phone.

During his four-day shift, Shin bunked in the L.A.P.D. group barracks—bare bones sleeping pods with communal showers set up downtown at the Nokia P.D. There were similar arrangements for the nurses, firefighters, paramedics and teachers who worked where they couldn't afford to live. At the end of his shift, Shin took the bullet train home to his family.

It was late. We logged off and powered down, then I drove Shin to Union Station in my ten-year-old Porsche. We walked to the platform and waited. The sonic boom sounded from the east, herald of the bullet train exiting the last tunnel before arrival. The slowing train still moved so fast it pushed a reluctant bubble of air out of the mountain with a giant's roar. Gliding into the station, the train hovered, poised over the elevated silver track like a hummingbird. Any second it would shoot off towards the northeast at a speed that would top 310 mph.

The train, originally planned to run all the way to San Francisco, dead-ended about twenty-five miles north of Bakersfield when the money ran out. There was a short run of dead end track up north too. Shin lived outside Bakersfield with his family. The suburb had affordable housing, whole neighborhoods of marked down houses, abandoned in the last downturn of the housing market.

"I'm off three days, Eddie," Shin said as he hopped on the train along with the other passengers. "I'll keep the case open until then."

I nodded, looking down at my shoes. If I was wrong, no harm done. If I was right, well, every day a homicide goes unsolved makes it less likely it will be. So no time to lose. I looked up. Then Shin was gone, speeding off towards his family, and I was alone in the crowd.

CHAPTER ELEVEN

After I dropped Shin off at Union Station, I took my time driving home to Venice. Jo worked late, and I didn't want to rush back to an empty house.

Once darkness blankets the city, the same drive I made twelve hours earlier feels different. Freeways hum at a lower frequency, but time moves faster. Home in forty-five minutes, I pulled into the garage behind the house and walked through the door linking the garage to the yard. The pale moon, veiled in cloud, floated across the night sky like a bride on her wedding day.

An answering light glowed from the bedroom on the second floor. Jo must have beaten me home after all. I was feeling optimistic, but that moon decided me.

Letting myself into the house, I fished the ring out of my gun safe in the pantry and pulled a bottle of champagne out of the fridge on my way to the bedroom. Jo was dozing upright in bed, a book on her lap and German opera playing in the background. Standing in the doorway, I made a face at the opera, but admired Jo. Asleep in a silk teddy with one of my old shirts draped round her, she looked more beautiful than ever. I wanted to wrap her in my arms and stay here forever.

The shirt had slipped off Jo's right shoulder. Leaning down, I rubbed the cold champagne bottle on her bare skin. Jo stirred, sleepily. I bent to kiss her.

"Mmm," she said.

I spotted a tiny red dot marring Jo's forehead. I kissed the dot too. "A mosquito bit you," I said lightly. "Dr. Mosquito and the nano-bocoll?"

Nano-bocoll was the new combo of botox and collagen delivered via nanotechnology to the skin. It repaired any dermal damage. Ads for the drug were plastered all over the city.

I should have kept my mouth shut. Jo never talked about her age, but she was sensitive about it.

"Just a little injectible," she said, two red spots appearing on her cheeks.

"You don't need it." I backpaddled as fast as I could. "You're flawless."

I handed Jo a glass and filled it with the champagne. Gesturing at her book, I asked, "What are you reading?"

"The future of intellectual property law. Interested?"

"Only in you. I came to take you dancing. But we need real music."

"Are you dissing Senta's ballad from *The Flying Dutchman*?" Jo teased as I pulled her up to her feet, turned off the opera, and flipped on the radio option. "I'll have you know that's Joan Sutherland singing. One of the greatest sopranos of the twentieth century."

"Just broadening your horizons," I said.

Palomino Fire was playing a hypnotic love song.

Jo let me dip her in time with the music.

Champagne glasses in hand, we slow danced in the half light of the reading lamp and the reflected moonlight off the canal.

"Here's to your future, Madame Partner." I breathed in the scent of her hair and felt my eyelids close halfway, and a broad grin spread across my face.

"To our future."

"I like the sound of that." I spun her around and dipped her again.

"Craig said you had a good day." Jo squeezed my shoulder.

The boxed ring in my pocket suddenly felt heavier. Regroup.

"Way better than expected," I said. "And the night's young."

We spilled a little golden juice of the grape. Jo laughed. "If this is going to be a thrill ride, I'd better put down the glass."

"Think of it as christening new ventures." I nibbled Jo's neck. Her skin smelled faintly of vanilla and jasmine. I twirled her again. "You know in all the time we've been together we've never seriously talked about the future. Our future."

"The relationship talk?" She smiled. Then Jo's face got more serious. "I never felt the need. Things just felt right with you from the beginning."

I nodded. "Ditto. Ever since I met you, I can't see myself with anybody else." I took a deep breath but kept it light. "I'll even get down on my knees if you want."

Jo kept dancing, but one blonde eyebrow arched. "That is tempting," she said, "but rein it in cowboy. I just made partner. We don't want too much change all at once, do we?"

"Don't we?"

Still in my arms Jo leaned her head back and stared at me.

"Are you serious, Eddie?"

I slipped the little velvet box out of my pocket and opened it.

She took a sip of the wine. Her eyes widened, and she swallowed hard. "I don't know what to say. It's a huge step."

I felt hesitation in her every muscle. "A step you don't want to take?"

"I didn't say that."

"Didn't say, or didn't mean?" I felt my face redden. Had I misread her feelings? I was beginning to be sorry I'd brought up the whole idea tonight. The song changed, but we marked time, not looking at each other.

"Neither," Jo said, breaking away and refilling her glass. "Eddie, there's nothing I want more. Nothing. It's just . . . This is so hard to talk about." She fingered the tiny white scars on her left wrist reflexively.

I'd stopped dancing too. "Just say it." My jaw clenched and I steeled myself for the words I didn't want to hear. Words like "I've met somebody."

She took a deep breath and continued. "You know I'm older than you."

"So?"

"Well, you want children, don't you?"

"You don't?"

"No. I mean, yes. I do." Jo bit her lip. "But if we didn't have kids—would you be okay?"

"I don't understand."

"I never told you," she said, "but I had a—miscarriage. A long time ago."

I blinked, and stared at her worried expression, relief starting to trickle through me. Then other emotions started to rush in like a second wave that sneaks up on you. Here was a part of Jo's life

I knew nothing about—a part of life before I'd even entered the picture. "Jesus. Who was the father?"

"It was a long time ago, Eddie." She took another sip from her glass.

Jo sighed and walked over to the window, looking out over the canal, her back to me. "You're not the only one with an asshole relative." Jo plucked earnestly at her brow with her long fingers.

I let her talk, watching Jo's back and the reflection of her face in the picture window opposite. I moved close behind her.

"When I found out I was pregnant, I panicked." Again her fingers grazed those telltale scars. "The miscarriage was a lucky break really."

I was standing right behind her now, close enough that I could feel the heat from her skin. "What a bastard," I said, wrapping my arms around her.

"Really, it's nothing," she continued. "I only brought it up now because you mentioned children."

Cutting your wrists wasn't nothing. "And these?" I kissed the scars on her wrists.

"A cry for help," she said. "I got it. Ancient history."

I hugged her tighter, and the tension melted away. We started to dance once more.

"Lots of women have miscarriages and still have kids," I said as gently as I could. "We could try."

"I've been trying, Eddie," Jo said.

I stared at her.

"I should have told you that too," Jo said. "You see, I was fourteen when it happened. The miscarriage. There were complications I won't bore you with. And I did some things later—to pay for college. Long story short, I might not be able to have kids."

"Fourteen?" I was reeling. In my head this guy who'd hurt Jo was a dead man, but I stuffed down the anger and let Jo talk.

"I was afraid to tell you, but when you asked me to marry you, I had to." She took the ring in its little box and held it out to me. "I'm not saying it's impossible, but if we never had kids, would you be okay with that? I'd . . ." She paused again. "I'd understand if you wouldn't."

I heard the courage it took to ask in her voice, and the fear tucked behind it. The truth was I hadn't thought much about kids. I wasn't even sure how good I'd be as a dad. I didn't exactly have the best role model. But I guess I'd assumed Jo would want them at some point, and that was okay with me. And if we didn't?

"Yes," I said. I left the ring in her hand.

"You say that now, but you're only twenty-nine."

"In cop years," I said lightly, "that's close to fifty."

Her playful smiled returned. She cocked her head to the side, regarding me. "And when you're forty? What then?"

I took her chin in my hand and looked straight into her eyes. "Live for today, Jo. I could be dead by forty."

She flinched, but I didn't let go.

"Don't even joke about that." Jo lightly pressed two fingers to my lips."

I wasn't. "I'm all in," I said. "Don't you know that yet? Sure, kids would be nice, but I want 'em with you. I don't see that changing."

"Still," she said. "You should take a while and really think about it."

"I know what I want." I wrapped her fingers around the box. "I can wait for you. Just don't lose the ring."

Jo smiled and took a deep breath. We danced for a couple minutes without speaking.

"Do you wonder if life was easier when people didn't have so many choices?" Jo said.

"No." I kissed her neck. "They had problems too. Just different problems. Shit doesn't just happen. We make it happen, or we don't stop it from happening."

Jo nodded. Her smile turned mischievious. "What do you say we make something happen right now?"

I grinned and pulled her back into a fast spin. We lost our balance and fell on the bed, laughing.

"Bottoms up," I said.

Jo dimmed the light. The cool green reflection of our moving bodies appeared in the window opposite, and then I was too busy to see anything clearly. All questions about the past and the future and the dead girl with the derma ad could wait until tomorrow.

CHAPTER TWELVE

THE NEXT MORNING SUNRISE WAS A THIN STRIP OF APRICOT stretched along the horizon—like Jo's silk lingerie still lying at the foot of the bed. Jo left for the gym before six.

I jumped out of bed and padded around the kitchen, making coffee with a smile on my face until a glance at my calendar reminded me of my psych eval with Dr. Tyler Reese Sears. A quick Google search showed he had an office on Sunset Boulevard. I'd already weathered the physical exam and eight hours of diversity training plus simulations. The sooner I cleared the next hoop, the sooner I got back on active duty. My appointment was for four-forty-five.

I walked into his waiting room at 4:30. The door to Sears' office opened at 5:15. Maybe the wait was part of the test. His walls with their framed diplomas from CSUN and UCLA were pale lemon.

"Come on in, detective." The balding middle-aged man jumped to his feet from behind his desk and held out his hand. His voice flowed with the slower music of Virginia or one of the Carolinas as he gestured to the well-worn leather club chair opposite his desk.

"You must be present to win." I pointed to the wooden sign mounted on the wall next to the diplomas as I took the proffered seat. "Your mantra?" I recognized it as a sign from an Indian casino and wondered if Sears took a flutter now and then.

"Words to live by," Sears said. "Along with 'know thyself.'" The psychologist looked soft and frayed as an old stuffed toy, but his eyes were youthful and alert. There were a few more preliminaries as he sat back in his chair and folded his hands in his lap. Then he launched into it.

"I have the results from your tests," Sears said. "You're in excellent physical health, detective, and you handled yourself well on the simulator. Blood tests were negative for drugs and alcohol. But . . ." He brought the palms of his hands together in a prayer-like gesture, fingers touching lips.

I waited.

Sears' hands rotated, fingertips pointing at me now. The prayer-like gesture became a gun about to fire. "Your cortisol and testosterone levels are unusually elevated and you scored .085 on the depression and PTSD inventories." He smiled. "I think I can help with that."

"If you want to help, clear me to go back to work."

Sears smile twisted into a pained grimace. "I'm afraid .085 is well over the normal range, detective. I recommend you take at least a few days off."

"And let my partner shoulder all the work?" I shook my head.

"I thought you might say that." Sears lifted his hands, palms out in a gesture of surrender. "Then let's go through the checklist, shall we? How are you sleeping? Any unexpected bouts of insomnia, night sweats, that sort of thing?"

"Nothing out of the ordinary." For two days after the shooting I'd woken at three, covered in a sheet of cold sweat. But little recaps were to be expected. Stress was an old friend. Why give Sears the ammunition to shoot me down?

"Are you experiencing any unusual aches or pains since the incident?"

"No," I said.

"How much do you drink?

"A glass or two."

"Has your alcohol consumption changed since the accident?"

"I'm drinking less." In case of any unscheduled blood or Breathalyzer pop quizzes.

Was it my imagination or was Sears searching for the broken blood vessels and swollen nose of an alcoholic? There wasn't anything like that on my face to find. Still, I silently cursed Claire Kidder, the civilian lawyer from the OIS interview who'd put me under extra scrutiny.

"Are you experiencing any changes in your interaction with your partner since the incident?"

"Other than my being on the desk?" I repeated my desire to get to back to active duty.

"Patience, detective. We're almost done." Sears glanced at his glove phone, and then his eyes drifted up to the left corner of the room.

Were there cameras? A hidden feed for the panel reviewing my actions?

"I see from your file your father was a police officer too," Sears said. "He's had some trouble with anger management."

Ker-chunk! The sound of a nail gun slamming a four-inch steel nail through the flesh of my left foot echoed in my head. The hand on the nail gun had belonged to Piedmont Sr. The mere memory sent a shiver down my spine. I shoved the memory away.

"Have you been able to talk to your father about managing the stress?" Sears steepled his hands on the desk. "Maybe he could be a helpful resource."

I suppressed the laugh, but not the memory of how the Glock had felt in my fifteen year-old hand. Or the smell of cordite in the air. The nail gun on the floor and my father's used syringe on the kitchen table. The lamp over the kitchen table swinging round and round like a chopper with a spotlight flying overhead.

"If you've read the file on my father," I said, "you know he can't even help himself." Anger management and Green Ice weren't his only problems. It was an open secret my father was dirty. He'd taken drugs, and money for drugs, in exchange for turning a blind eye to some pretty bad actors. Eventually, he'd gotten caught and sent away for a three-year stretch in prison. That was another thing we didn't talk about, my father and I.

Sears said nothing, just held my gaze with a steady appraisal of his own.

And I suddenly knew he'd made up his mind before we'd even started the evaluation. Sears had expected resistance, and I'd given it to him.

So, I pivoted and jumped down a different rabbit hole.

"You know what, doctor?" I said. "I will take that vacation you recommended. I could use a couple days off."

Sears slowly lifted his head and beamed. "I'm glad you see that on your own, detective. That's a very hopeful sign. A little time to unwind can make a world of difference."

“When will you be making your report?” I said.

“We’ll be in touch.” Sears looked at me with a calm genial expression. “Get some R&R, Detective Piedmont.”

“I’ll head straight to the beach,” I said, not waiting for the door to slam behind me on my way out.

CHAPTER THIRTEEN

As soon as the door to the psychologist's office snapped shut behind me, I put in for three days of vacation—effective immediately. Then I called Shin.

"I'm off duty," he said by way of greeting. "So, what does it mean that I'm happy to hear from you already?" Shin was sitting cross-legged on the roof of his house making repairs, a messy stack of white, sun-reflective tiles to his right.

"You're a good cop and a bad roofer," I said. "I called to say go ahead and close out the Devonshire file."

Hammer in hand, he peered hard at me then slowly shook his head. "Every door that closes opens a window, as my grandmother used to harp at me. Is that it?"

"Your grandmother was a fount of wisdom."

"And you're a crazy hakujin." Shin put down the hammer and stared at me again. "Don't do anything stupid, Eddie. I mean it. I don't want to break in another new partner." He sighed, but I watched as Shin closed the Devonshire file via phone and went back to his roofing.

With the case closed, there was nothing that said I couldn't have a friendly chat with Dr. Lee during my vacation. My glove phone told me it was already past seven. Too late to head out to the Valley given L.A. traffic, but I might be able to catch him at home. For the first time since the shooting, I felt a sudden rush of optimism.

Pacific Palisades, with houses that dot the mountains as they spill down to the ocean, is utter suburbia for rich people who call themselves middle-class. Unlike gated communities for the ueber-rich, places like Beverly Park, no security guards control access to the Palisades. Its leafy streets fan off one feeder boulevard—Sunset.

Lee's home was a gray Cape Cod McMansion crammed onto a small lot not far from Sunset. Freshly painted white trim on the house matched the low white picket fence that ran along the edge of the line between sidewalk and lawn. Tidy borders of Mexican sage clustered near the fence.

A late model white Mercedes SUV sat parked in the drive. Last night's research with Shin told me it belonged to Lee's wife Meredith. There was also a high-powered Yamaha job standing next to it. The bike was registered to the teenaged son, Raymond.

No sign of Lee's Lexus E3, so I parked a little way up from the house and waited. Even from fifty feet away, I could spot cameras and sensors that covered the front and side doors of the house. A glance up and down the street at the neighboring homes told me they weren't standard for the area.

There'd been no police reports of illegal activity of any note in the vicinity of Lee's home either. Yet Lee's latest model Smart Sensa-guard security with its drone patrol and fast response time cost about fifty grand. Was Lee typically hyper-vigilant, or had something spooked him recently? Like a troublesome girlfriend making threats?

Past eight now, and still no sign of the Lexus, so I rang the front door bell and waited. The flat slapping sound of bare feet on hardwood floors told me someone was approaching, but the door didn't open. I flipped my coat jacket open, letting my gold shield wink at the invisible watcher behind those CCTV cameras.

"Yeah," said a bored teenaged voice that I guessed belonged to Lee's son Raymond. The face matching the voice appeared on the security screen to the left of the doorbell. He yawned. His hair stuck out at strange angles without benefit of product and he had sleep in the corners of his glassy eyes.

"Detective Piedmont," I said. "I'd like to talk to Dr. Gabriel Lee."

"He's not here."

"Where is he?"

Raymond shrugged.

This time there were no telltale footsteps before the door abruptly swung open. Meredith Lee stepped slightly in front of her son and regarded me with wary concern.

"Can I help you, detective?" Her eyes were black stones set in an unsmiling wrinkle-free face. Meredith Lee's ink-colored coiffeur showed no hair out of place. She wore an expensive beige sweater set with a single strand of black pearls and coordinated trousers.

"Dr. Lee," I said, remembering she'd been an anesthesiologist before taking early retirement. "I need to talk to your husband."

"It's Mrs. Lee. What's this about?" Her voice betrayed the barest hint of a Korean accent.

I could see past Mrs. Lee to the foyer. A row of white orchids anchored by smooth gray pebbles in square glass vases sat on a stone bench next to the wall to the right. A few pairs of shoes lined up with military precision stood under the bench, including neon-colored sneakers and a variety of women's shoes.

"I need to ask him about a woman named Britney Devonshire."

The name sparked no sign of recognition from Mrs. Lee.

"He may be able to help us out with some information."

"Why would my husband know anything about this woman?"

I shot a pointed glance at her son. "Could we speak in private, Mrs. Lee?"

Her spine stiffened. "I'm sorry. I think you've made a mistake. I can't help you." Mrs. Lee started to shut the door.

The door caught on my foot as I pulled up a picture of the auburn knockout and held it out for her and her son to see. "This is Britney Devonshire, an exotic dancer at the Sandy Beaches Gentlemen's Club."

Raymond's glassy eyes popped wide open. Mrs. Lee's narrowed.

"She's dead," I said. "You didn't know her?"

Two angry red splotches bloomed on Mrs. Lee's cheeks. She shook her head. Questions were already gnawing at her. Good.

"Ms. Devonshire made a number of calls to your husband. Including her last call right before she died. That's why I need to talk to him."

Mrs. Lee's jaw hardened as she lifted her chin. "I don't want any trouble."

"Neither do I. When do you expect him home?"

She pressed her lips into a thin line of disapproval, but said nothing. I let my silence push her.

"My husband and I are taking a little time apart, detective." Those wary black eyes met mine in a level gaze.

Trouble at home only made my interest in Dr. Lee tick up a notch higher.

"When you hear from him," I said, "would you ask your husband to call me right away?" I left my number.

A curt nod followed by the slamming door was my answer.

I lost no time getting back to my car. Mrs. Lee seemed to be telling the truth. The shoes under the bench corroborated her husband's extended absence. No matter—I didn't expect to hear back from Dr. Gabriel Lee either now or in the future, but in about thirty seconds I did expect his wife to call her husband and read him the riot act. Any wife would want to know what her husband was doing with some stripper young enough to be his daughter, and worse, what he had done to bring the police to their door.

I had my StingRey ready. The scanner mimics a cellphone tower, luring a phone to connect with it. Then it measures signals that phone puts out. Legally, I couldn't pull the call out of the air and de-encrypt it like a paparazzo tracking a celebrity scoop. I was just hoping for the "ping" and a number for Lee's glove phone.

A minute later the ping came. But not to Lee's glove phone. Mrs. Lee placed a twenty second call to a land line in Sun Valley. Genesys, the pharma research company where Dr. Lee worked, was situated there. Twenty seconds wasn't long enough for Mrs. Lee to have read her husband the riot act. It was, however, long enough to leave a voicemail. Was he still at work?

I put in a call myself and got voicemail, so I hung up and tried the main reception. The recorded message informed me Genesys was closed and gave the office hours. I guessed Lee had left for the day but was at least checking calls. It was worth the drive tomorrow. Singing along with latest Indigo Panthers-narco-corrida, I turned the car around and headed home.

CHAPTER FOURTEEN

EARLY THE NEXT MORNING, AS I MADE MY WAY THROUGH THE traffic gridlocking the 405 freeway that linked Venice and the San Fernando Valley, questions buzzed in my brain.

Lee had moved out. It seemed likely his trouble at home was linked to Lee's involvement with the now dead stripper. Had the new security system he'd installed at his Palisades home been aimed at keeping a hot little blackmailer away from the family? Had Dr. Lee done more than just install security? He wouldn't be the first guy to panic at blackmail and shove an inconvenient girlfriend into the void. For that matter, Mrs. Lee wouldn't be the first wife to back her cheating husband over a rival even if she did kick him out temporairily by way of payback.

In any event, Britney Devonshire's overdose was looking less and less "accidental." I needed to talk to Lee himself and see what I could see.

Sun Valley is a sunny name for a bland gray industrial section of the city. Genesys took up half a street block in this unassuming part of town, opposite a Psychic Franchise, and an Herbal Care, the drive-through boutiques that sell Lipitor, marijuana and other pharmaceutical antidotes to the pain of living.

The three-story burnt sienna-colored building could have housed an insurance company, so nondescript was its boxy façade. But the bland impression was quickly dispelled by the band of protestors spilling over from the sidewalk and blocking my entry through the gated Genesys parking lot. Tapping the horn, I waited in my idling Porsche, a rock in a stream as activists protesting the biomedical research company slowly flowed around me.

Their signs featured slogans in dripping red. Subtle slogans like: Genesys means Genocide: No to GMO, and Yes on Personhood, No to Murder! An equal opportunity offender, Lee's company had managed to alienate both sides of the political spectrum.

Security guards posted just inside the gate were hardbodied guys with that ramrod straight posture you see on ex-Marines—heavy duty for corporate watchdogs. The Genesys brass must have been worried about the protestors.

All the politics and protest were also unwelcome reminders of the police bond in the upcoming election and Captain Tatum's warning to me. I had to tread carefully.

As the sea of red paint parted and I threaded my way into the parking lot, one obvious hype caught my eye. He had the greenish pallor, rotten teeth and loose skin hanging off his emaciated frame so typical of long-time ice addicts. An addict with a cause though, that was different. Mumbling, the hype pressed a flyer under my car's windshield wiper. Others followed. They papered my car with flyers as I inched past.

"Shame on You, Yes on 2!" shouted the crowd, now safely in my rear view mirror. "Nature's Way, Not Corporate Play!"

Disease is nature's way too. I dumped the flyers in the circular file just outside the main entrance to Genesys.

Just inside the door I stopped at the security desk in front of the metal detector that blocked entry into the main lobby.

"Detective Piedmont," I said and flashed my badge to the security guard. "I'd like to talk to one of your employees."

Technically, I shouldn't have used the authority of the badge while on vacation, but one glimpse of that gold shield and the guard's bored demeanor instantly changed into something more respectful.

Eyes wide, he looked up from my badge and scanned my gray Brioni jacket for the telltale bulge where my Glock was tucked. It was my personal sidearm. The department issued Glock was still impounded. But he nodded me through and signed out a visitor's badge.

At the reception desk I asked to see Dr. Lee.

The hologrammed receptionist informed me Dr. Lee was not on the premises and asked if I wanted to leave a message.

"When will he be back?"

In no time at all Ms. Som, Director of Human Resources, appeared at my side wearing a silk dress in muted green and black along with her helpful smile. She informed me that Dr. Lee had taken sabbatical two weeks ago.

That made me perk up. Dr. Lee might be homeshored, but he wasn't home. So why had his wife called him here? Were things between them so cool she really didn't know where her husband was?

"When was the last time he logged in?" I said.

Emily Som tapped her authorization code into the personnel log and scanned a more restricted roster. "October 1st."

A couple days before Britney's death.

"Do you have a sabbatical address for him?"

She gave me the number for the Palisades place.

Another query told me Lee's salary went to direct deposit—another dead end.

"I need to talk to Lee's boss," I said. "Mr. Maclaren."

"The CEO?" Ms. Som's voice crept up half an octave.

"Would you call him." It wasn't a question.

"That might . . . take a while."

She gestured towards one of the chairs clustered around a squat coffee table in the lobby. "It will be at least an hour. If it's even possible for you to see him on such short notice."

Cut from marble, the squat table stood rooted under a central skylight. A square glass vase filled with waxy white orchids anchored in smooth black stones sat on the surface of the marble table. Across the way near the elevator, a screen played ads for the company's products. New meds in the pipeline included a treatment for erectile dysfunction. The screen changed.

"Genesys is on the cutting edge of Alzheimer's X research," a spokesmodel in a lab coat intoned.

Glancing at people walking through the lobby, I spotted a derma ad tattooed on the inside of a trim left ankle. The ankle belonged to a blonde in a white lab coat heading for the elevators.

Britney'd had a derma ad on her too, albeit for a marijuana boutique. Shin had said she'd been paid peanuts for it. In her file Shin listed his visit to the tattoo-parlor where Lotus Eaters' human billboards were inked. Britney's ad had been done only four hours prior to her estimated time of death. After that she'd texted or phoned only two people—her friend Mercedes and Dr. Lee. That gave a pretty tight timeframe for a last visit from Dr. Lee—if he'd made one.

Ms. Som was still on her phone, back towards me. If I had to wait an hour to see the CEO, I saw no reason to waste it sitting here.

I popped the tracker off my visitor's badge, flicking the dot to the ground near the foot of my chair, and headed off down the hall. But I got no further than the marketing kiosk when raised voices caught my attention. I stuck my head around the corner and saw Emily Som, the HR director with a security guard standing next to the squat table in the lobby. The guard was kneeling on the ground looking for something. Then, he hoisted himself up, and with thumb and forefinger, held aloft what I assumed was the tracker I'd just dislodged from my visitor's badge.

With an easy-going air, I headed straight back toward Emily Som and the security guard. "Guess the CEO can squeeze me in after all?"

A look of relief washed over their faces as they wheeled around and saw me with the visitor's badge still prominently displayed on my lapel. Emily Som inhaled sharply. "Mr. Maclaren said to bring you right up."

"Great." I had lots of questions. Maybe Lee's boss would have a few answers.

CHAPTER FIFTEEN

THE SECURITY GUARD USHERING ME AWAY FROM H.R. DIRECTOR Emily Som and toward the CEO's office was a wiry South-Asian with restless eyes and a perpetual frown.

He handed me over to Chiara, Maclaren's polished assistant in a cream-colored suit. Via private elevator, she led me up to the third floor. We passed a set of bullet-proof metalglass security doors with an iris scan. The offices got bigger as we walked down another corridor towards the mucky mucks.

The door to Chris Maclaren's office stood open.

"Come in, detective," Maclaren's steady deep voice sounded from across the room.

High tech contemporary, his office was the size of my dining room and kitchen combined. A coffee table with a sculptured base of black coral under floating glass fronted the soft leather sofa against the wall near the door. Mounted on their horizontal frame atop the table lay a pair of Samurai swords, the dai-katana on top and the short sword below. Museum quality. Maclaren's desk and two ghost-guest chairs stood all the way across the room. A straight flush of Harvard diplomas was in full view on the wall behind his desk. CEO Maclaren had an M.D., Ph.D. and MBA.

Even leaning against his glass desk, Maclaren was tall. From the tips of his handmade shoes to the black hair flecked with silver, I put him at about my height—6'2", maybe an inch shorter. He was dressed in that cashmere casual only the uber-wealthy can afford—with designer jeans that cost a fortune and a V-neck sweater in pale blue I was guessing cost even more.

"Thank you, Chiara." Maclaren smiled his polite dismissal after we both refused drinks. His assistant handed him a brown paper bag containing something compact and rectangular, and disappeared on cue. Maclaren's calm baritone had the assurance of a man who never raised his voice since his every suggestion was taken as an order. He placed the bag down flat on the surface of the desk behind him and gave me his full attention.

I figured I had about five minutes before I'd be ushered back out too.

"Chris Maclaren," he said as he waited for me to approach for the obligatory handshake. Maclaren had the toned physique of a man twenty years younger than his age. But the shadows pooling under the intelligent pale blue eyes told me he wasn't getting much sleep lately.

"Have a seat." Maclaren gestured to one of the clear plastic ghost chairs fronting his desk. I caught a glimpse of my own face hovering over the glass and steel desktop before he shut down the file. He remained leaning against his desk.

"Thanks for seeing me on such short notice," I said.

"Actually." He flashed a bright smile at me. "I've wanted to meet you for a long time, detective."

Flattery from a CEO only meant one thing.

"The Sphinx case," Maclaren said on cue. "My wife and I followed that in the news. Especially your work, detective. Impressive."

Sphinx was the codename for the serial killer whose arrest had gotten me my fifteen minutes of fame and my promotion to Homicide Special three years ago.

"My staff tell me you were looking for one of my employees?"

"Dr. Lee." I pulled up Lee's picture on my glove phone and held it out towards Maclaren.

The CEO barely glanced at the photo. "Gabriel," he said, looking genuinely concerned now, "is more than just an employee. He's a brilliant scientist. One of our stars. If there's any justice in this world, he'll get the Nobel prize."

"Do you know where he is?"

"On sabbatical." Maclaren's eyes widened a little. "Why? Has something happened?"

"Do you have an address for him? Besides the house in the Palisades?"

Maclaren slowly shook his well-groomed head. "He's due back within the month. What's this about, detective?"

I pulled up the picture of the stripper and held it out to him. "Do you recognize this woman?"

Maclaren studied Britney's picture before turning back to me and shaking his head. "I think I would've remembered if I had. Who is she?"

"She's dead. Her last call was to Lee."

Maclaren looked at me for a full second before responding. "Surely, you don't think Gabriel Lee had anything to do with . . .?"

"You said he was on sabbatical. Did he have personal problems? Maybe girl trouble?" I cocked my head at the stripper's image.

Maclaren's eyes widened just enough.

"You seem surprised."

Maclaren fumbled about for words. "Gabriel Lee isn't that kind of man."

"The kind to cheat on his wife?"

"The kind to waste time," he said. "We're all workaholics here, detective. I make it a point not to get involved with my employees' personal issues, unless it affects their work. And whatever he was going through, Gabriel's work never suffered."

"Then why is he on sabbatical?"

Chris Maclaren gave me an appraising look. "We're all under a lot of stress with this plague. As team leader for the Alz-X group, Gabriel's felt it more than most. He's a conscientious man. And then the death threats started."

"Death threats?" I kept my voice neutral, but my senses had snapped to high alert. I'd run Lee's record. There was no history of death threats or any reported incidents on file.

Maclaren gestured to the window. "You must have seen the protestors outside. Those are the moderates." His smile had turned grim. "The fanatics," he said, "are Pro-life—except when it comes to killing scientists. They're not fond of our company in general. But they practically issued a fatwa against Dr. Lee. I thought he might have a breakdown if he didn't get some rest away from here."

The security hardware on Lee's house suddenly took on new meaning. "Did they ever do more than threaten?"

Maclaren nodded. "At first it was just vandalism, graffiti, that sort of thing. Then somebody lobbed a rock through his living room window. Lee upped security. That's when a 'stray' bullet from a drive-by hit his front door."

"Why didn't Lee file a police report?"

"No one was hurt, and he didn't want to fuel publicity and further endanger his family. Radicals have fire-bombed the homes of other scientists, you know."

I did. "Why was Dr. Lee specifically targeted? Did it have anything to do with that business up at Cal? I read he got in trouble faking research."

"Not faking," Maclaren said, eyeing me cooly. "Running insufficient trials. A youthful mistake, but one our protocols here at Genesys would prevent in any event. Fanatics don't care about that. They targeted him because he invented a test to detect the genes responsible for Alzheimer's during pregnancy or IVF. The test resulted in unintended consequences."

"Abortions spiked?"

Maclaren nodded. "People don't want to bring a child into the world with the curse of dementia looming if they don't have to. But a lot of people view genetic testing as an invasion of privacy. With the increase in abortions . . . well they went after Lee. But they'll all want his cure for Alz-X when he nails it."

"If Lee's test screens out Alzheimer's in the womb," I said, "how has the dementia spread so fast to young people?"

"Traditional Alzheimer's, even the early-onset variety, and Alz-X aren't the same disease. There might be a mutation or more genes involved in Alz-X. We think something's triggering the Alzheimer's genes to turn on very early."

"Like marijuana and schizophrenia," I said. "Or smoking and lung cancer?"

"Exactly." Maclaren nodded. "It's complicated. But we've narrowed the possibilities. Dr. Lee's current work," he said, "is key to finding that cure for Alz-X. If we do, we'll save millions, possibly billions, of young lives. We're close." Maclaren grabbed fistfuls of air with both hands. "Very close. That's why we need Dr. Lee rested and back at work as soon as possible."

I thought about those blank-eyed kids wandering the streets or warehoused in clinics—casualties of this plague.

"Any of those protestors personally threaten Dr. Lee?"

"Harvey Pink." Maclaren spat out the name like it had a bad taste. "We have a whole file on him."

"Pink?"

Maclaren moved to the window and pointed out the skanky hype I'd seen earlier. "He's out there practically every day. But security ranked him as a nuisance, not a serious threat." Maclaren's expression told me he might be revising that threat assessment.

I looked out the window at the protestors stilled massed there. Pink stood a little apart from the others, chin lifted. He stood still—staring up at the building, at us.

"I'd like a copy of that file on Pink," I said.

Maclaren nodded. "I'll have security send it along."

"Thank you for your time. I hope you find that cure soon."

"So do I." Maclaren stood and shook my hand again as his assistant magically appeared to get my contact information and lead me out. "Very nice to meet you, detective. And I hate to ask, but . . ." Maclaren smiled a sheepish smile as he reached for the brown paper bag and extracted a brand new copy of *Riddle of the Sphinx*, the ghost-written book the LAPD was still hawking as a joint publicity-fund-raising effort. He held it out to me. "Would you mind? My wife Paige would love an autographed copy."

"If you hear from Dr. Lee . . ." I scrawled my best wishes to Paige over my face and handed the book back.

"I'll be sure to contact you," Maclaren said. "And would you let me know if you find him first? I'd like to know Gabriel's all right."

I nodded. Time to move. Unanswered questions about Britney Devonshire and her connection to the MIA scientist kept snowballing. I walked out of there with a jumble of new information and the name Harvey Pink etched on my dance card.

CHAPTER SIXTEEN

I DIDN'T WASTE ANY TIME. SPEEDING OUT OF GENESYS, I scanned the pack of protestors through the lobby's picture windows, looking for Harvey Pink. Protestors still massed outside the building. But the hype had disappeared into the wind.

A long stream of profanity followed. Still, it's a rare ice addict without a record. Even without Maclaren's file, I'd find Pink before long.

Right now, Dr. Lee was my person of interest, and in order to locate him, I'd need to track his barcode for recent purchases. That required special skills.

With Genesys in my rear-view mirror, I weighed options. The case was closed, and I was on vacation, so technically I hadn't stuck my toe over the line. But my foot was right at the edge. If enough evidence turned up to reopen the Devonshire case as a homicide, repeat visits would be necessary for the record. I didn't want my online activity to flag the attention of Captain Tatum, or cause trouble for Shin or me if and when the case came to court.

Shin could find out if Lee's barcode had registered new activity, but until I'd played out my hunch, it was better if I didn't involve my partner any more than I had to. After all, I had asked him to close out the case.

So, at 1:15 I pulled into the Starbucks on Camarillo and Tujunga in North Hollywood.

I spotted her immediately via the electric-kiwi stripe in her otherwise inky black hair. Denver Lakshmi was a nineteen-year-old Ex-hacktavist, now gainfully employed with the LAPD through the ex-con employment program I'd hooked her up with. She had awesome I.T. skills, a killer memory, and never skipped her lunchtime java. Moreover, where Shin was a straight arrow whenever regulations were concerned, Denver liked to bend the rules.

Denver's hands moved like the conductor of an invisible, inaudible symphony as she sat at one of the little outdoor tables. From the way she swiped back and forth with her right hand and directed her gaze towards the left, I knew she was scanning code in one window and viewing images in another. But I couldn't see the files. She must have been wearing a Solo Shell VPN that blocked both the audio and visual to all but the user. When she touched the glimmer of silver embedded in both her brow and left ear, I knew I was right.

Denver's head bobbed back and forth in time with inaudible music. Circling around in back, I touched the edges of her I-Brow and ear wearables simultaneously. The strains of some upbeat Bollywood tune spilled into the air.

Fear morphed into a scowl when she saw it was me.

"You will meet a tall dark man soon." I read aloud from the now-visible psychic dating website Denver'd been checking. "Hey, is your parole officer tall?"

"No, she's not," Denver said in her snarkiest tone. She inclined her head. "I've already met somebody, Piedmont, but you keep visiting me, and people will think you're in love."

"The sooner I get the information I need, the sooner we save your reputation," I rapped in time to the Bollywood tune.

"I'm busy."

"Yeah," I said. "I can see that."

She swiveled around in her seat and I saw her mood T-shirt with the one word question WHY? change from black to magenta with the shift in body temperature.

"Go ahead and laugh." She pointed at the floating horoscope with short square nails painted kiwi and mint green to match her hair. "This is my future we're talking here."

"If you want clues to your future, look at your past."

"That's depressing. My past sucks."

"Trying to game the government will do that."

Denver had been arrested as a minor for trying to hack into DARPA via backdoors in MIT's Artificial Intelligence Department. She thought all cool gadgets should be free to the public. What she got was a visit from the FBI. Denver'd been on the verge of a long stay in juvie and possibly a stint in Federal prison after she turned eighteen. Fortunately, her excellent legal team gained

Denver a much shorter sentence in a local juvenile facility. There she'd come to my attention as one of those kids whom it might still be possible to turn. We needed talent like hers on our side. And Denver was basically a good kid. So, I helped her get the job.

"They never would have caught me if those corporate sellouts hadn't punked me out. It's all a conspiracy rigged against the little guy. Corporations own the universities and government. They make the rules."

"Before you're drafted for the Hunger Games," I said, "I need a current address." Pulling Lee's barcode and credit card numbers from Britney's file, I slapped them down on Denver's table. "Not the Palisades place. Cross check with retailer and credit report files for recent purchases."

"Pitiful." She rolled her eyes, her expression the platonic ideal of teenage distain. Denver was already entering the info in her search engines. Using the latest analytical formula, she needed only three bits of information—metadata such as location or timing—to identify the unique signature purchasing pattern of ninety-per cent of people. And Denver had much more than three bits for Lee.

She sliced through paywalls, those websites restricted to paying users only. Financial information was supposed to be encrypted, but many companies sold client information to other companies. Companies that used old software. That information was easy for any reasonably computer savvy user like me to access. But Denver could move through this stuff like a laser cutting paper.

"Any useful cookies on him?"

"Like maggots on old meat," she said. "There's code here from like 2038."

"What's he been buying?"

Swish, swish, swish. Denver's fingers swiped and minimized floating images back and forth on the air in front of us. "Digital scratchers, big ATM withdrawals at a couple casinos, and a lot of high-premium gas. He shops regularly at a Whole Foods north of Santa Barbara. He eats non-hydrogenated almond butter and organically grown veggies. Your basic high-tech-upper-middle class-wheatgrass-scientist demographic."

"Except for the scratchers and casinos. Sounds like he likes a flutter at the tables. What about money problems?"

"He's overdrawn his checking account a few times," she said. "Missed the mortgage payment twice. Looks like his wife took over the bills about a year ago."

"Give me dates and locations on all Lee's purchases in the last six months," I said. "What about a billing address?"

"He charged his barcode. No shipping address either," she said, "so don't ask."

"Medical?"

Her fingers swiped the air again, making Denver look like a conductor of pixels.

"Lots of visits to shrinks in the past few years. Anti-anxiety meds, but who doesn't take those? Hello." Denver mimed a snipping motion. "He had a vasectomy a while ago. And he's burned his social networking sites. There's nothing there but an empty wall."

Like Britney Devonshire's.

"Gambling and a vasectomy," I said half under my breath. "What about legal fees? Anything?"

"You link vasectomy to lawyers? You're really weird, you know that?" Denver kept searching, then cocked her head and turned to me. "But not totally insane. Meet Pang Kim and Jacob Lester, both attorneys at law."

"Divorce?" I stared at the two smiling lawyers Denver'd linked to their respective websites. "Or tax?"

"One each." She cast me an appreciative glance. "The psychic website should hire you."

"I'm not psychic," I said. "Just a cop."

Lee'd been talking to a divorce lawyer but hadn't filed for divorce. "When did he get the vasectomy?"

"Five years ago," Denver said. "Why?"

Five years ago, but Britney Devonshire hadn't known Lee then. So, if she'd tried to pin paternity on him with that blood spot, Lee would have known it was a scam without a DNA test. Contradictions kept mounting.

"Everybody lies," I said. "And hides stuff."

"Like you doing searches on the Q.T.?" Denver's mood T-shirt now read WHY NOT? in green.

I winked. "I'm on vacation. And I'm one of the good guys."

"Not that good." With a knowing grin, she downloaded the

information. These days most people store whatever data isn't on the cloud in their DNA. Thumb drives have become literal since that's where the USB port is. But I don't like using even my junk DNA for storage, so I go old school. Denver handed me the flash-dot, the miniature memory stick the size of a pinky fingernail. For just a second, the lagoon green of Denver's T-shirt bounced off the reflective surface of the Starbuck's window. The question flickered on her glasses. Then it vanished like a rainbow in full sun.

Lee's favorite new hang-out was an Indian casino just outside Clara Vista, one of those little beach towns on the coast north of Santa Barbara.

"This is me saying good-bye, Piedmont." Waving her hand in dismissal, Denver flipped back to her horoscope.

I wagged my finger at her good-naturedly. "The fault, dear Brutus, is not in our stars, but in ourselves." The line from high school Shakespeare was still in the mental hard drive.

"Who's Brutus?" Denver said.

"Backup singer in an old death-metal band." I watched as she touched the edge of the I-Brow wearable again and retreated back into her Solo-Shell.

I was in a good mood. Clara Vista—the search had given me my next move.

As I walked out, Denver whirled back around, her head and heart already focused on her stars caught in the web.

October afternoon sun beat down on the city. Beads of sweat trickled down my spine by the time I reached my Porsche. In the car's cool interior, I voice-activated the number on my glove phone I still knew by heart.

Frank Waldron, my former partner from NOHO homicide answered on the ninth ring—pretty good, considering. Frank appeared, floating in the Nokia Handy's L-shape between my thumb and forefinger. He had a face like a dried apple, but the eyes were still bright and lively.

"Hey, Frank, it's me," I said. "You look like shit."

He'd turned fifty-five last year. Frank had bad knees and a cheap animatronic arm that gave him chronic pain. He'd lost his left arm when the Sphinx collar turned ugly. While the Sphinx arrest got me promoted to Homicide Special, it had permanently retired Frank on disability. And disability didn't pay enough for one of the deluxe animatronic arms. I'd offered to make up the difference, but Frank was allergic to anything even close to a handout.

"And you still dress like you're going to a photo shoot, not a homicide scene." He was grinning now though, not wincing. "I knew you couldn't drive a desk for long."

"You saw the news."

He laughed. "Lots of lightning. Thunder hit yet?"

Lightning to thunder was our code for the time delay between the shit that goes down on the street and the emotions that flood in, sometimes days after.

"Still standing," I said. "You busy?"

"You know." He wasn't.

Now a licensed private investigator, Frank got by on disability payments, pension, and whatever his buddies threw him in the way of work. He and his wife Ruth had moved inland, up north of Oxnard where property values were cheaper.

"Listen, if you're free," I said, "I need you to put some eyes on a Lexus SUV out your way."

After all, there was nothing in the regulations that prevented Eddie Piedmont, private citizen on vacation, from hiring a licensed private investigator to find Lee.

"Roger that, house mouse," Frank said.

He was never gonna let me live down desk duty. But I was glad to hear him breaking my balls. It meant he hadn't given up.

"Ta ma-de, Frank," I said with real affection for the old guy.

"I see your vocab hasn't improved," Frank said. "Just gone global."

I walked him through what I already knew about Lee before ending the call.

With Frank on the job, I looked forward to my first night of real sleep since the shooting. I hoped it'd be dreamless.

CHAPTER SEVENTEEN

AT 7:30 THE NEXT MORNING, DOG WALKERS AND SQUAWKING tourists had barely started their morning perambulations round the canals of Venice when Frank called. I left the deck, where I'd been staring out over the water, and headed back inside. The smart home shut out the noise with the click of the sliding glass door.

"You find Lee already?"

Still shirtless in sweat pants, I leaned back against the kitchen counter, feeling the cool touch of granite on the small of my back as I stared at Frank's floating face in my Nokia Handy. I could hear gulls in the background. Frank's glove phone had that shaky-cam effect. He was walking back to his blue Toyota Corolla, parked on a tony Clara Vista side street, somewhere near the beach.

"Spotted his Lexus at the Whole Foods you tagged," Frank wheezed as he stopped to scrape beach tar off the soles of his shoes. "Chipped it while he was inside. Take a look."

The lean Asian man in the first pic Frank sent had on Dockers, a worn blue Oxford shirt, and New Balance sneakers along with his unkempt beard and mustache. His once black hair was longer and scruffier than Lee's had been on his driver's license. Now dyed a mousy brown, he'd combed it over his ears—like a man on the run keen on hiding a major security bio-identifier. The bones under his hangdog face were more prominent too, and the skin round the jaw had softened. It looked like Lee's skull was pressing up through thinning skin even as gravity tugged the flesh down towards his chest. The combination of time and stress had not been kind to the scientist. But it was Lee all right, leaving the grocery store and getting in the Lexus. The next couple snaps showed the same man exiting the Lexus and entering a small beach bungalow.

The bungalow was one of those places built for the Hollywood overflow the first decade of the twenty-first century, when even wealthy people looking for ocean front property found themselves out-priced by the tech billionaires in the Malibu market.

"What's the word on the beach house?" I said.

"Rental leased to a trust. But it looks like Lee's not moving back anytime soon. The wife may be his next discard."

"He's been talking to divorce lawyers," I said, nodding, "but hasn't filed."

"Maybe the ax is just about to fall." Frank sent me a little streaming video over the phone. "This happened yesterday around four."

In the video, a woman wearing a beige sweater set and black pearls I instantly pegged as Mrs. Lee got out of her white Mercedes. She stormed Lee in the driveway of the Clara Vista bungalow. I paused the video and checked the time code: 5:14 p.m. yesterday.

"That's the wife, isn't it?" Frank said.

"Yeah." I did a rough calculation. "She must have headed up north right after I left her door."

"She's hopping mad," Frank said. "You tell her the husband was bonking a stripper?"

"I may have given her that idea."

I let the video play through this time. Lee and his wife held themselves stiffly at first, but as their conversation escalated into a heated argument, the gesticulations got wilder. Then, Mrs. Lee slapped her husband hard and started pummeling him like a windmill on overdrive. Dr. Lee covered his face, warding off the blows. Finally, Mrs. Lee whirled around, and ran back to her car.

"I couldn't make out a single word," Frank said. "Korean?"

I nodded and replayed the argument with the audio up this time.

I flicked on my phone's translation app. Divorce popped out. Police and shame repeated several times, but the rest of the translation was more gibberish than English.

"The dialect's too thick," I said. "I'll get Shin to translate."

Shin's wife Ahn was Korean, and his time in K-town before his transfer to Homicide Special had made Shin's already good Korean fluent.

I watched the argument replay once more. Divorce, police, shame. Their conversation seemed more linked to my questions about Britney Devonshire than any beef with protestors, but two things were clear. Dr. Lee was in meltdown mode. And he was hiding all right, but it wasn't from his wife. She'd known exactly where he was. She'd lied to me.

"Stay on Lee," I said to Frank. "I'm coming up north."

CHAPTER EIGHTEEN

I LEFT WORD FOR JO NOT TO EXPECT ME BACK EARLY. FOUR hours later I met Frank outside the Clamshell Casino in Clara Vista.

The casino lay in an outgrowth of urban sprawl just a little further north of Clara Vista proper. It was one of those smaller operations that catered to the senior crowd, a place and time the developers momentarily forgot. Centered in a large patchwork of parking lots, the casino was flanked by the green cross of a marijuana outlet at one end and a drive-through Chinese-Mexican joint at the other. Two big north and south facing entrances and exits gaped like giant maws gobbling up and spitting out gamblers into the traffic of the surrounding streets.

Dr. Gabriel Lee's Lexus was parked two aisles down from the Casino's main entrance. Frank was already stationed near the north exit. Upon arrival, I'd driven through the Take a Bao and Burrito and picked up food for us both, pepper chicken for me and spring rolls with black beans for Frank.

When I rapped on his window, Frank startled. His face was squashed pink from the door. It was obvious he hadn't been to bed since I'd first called him yesterday, and he looked even worse than he had over the phone.

But Lee's Lexus hadn't budged from its parking space since the scientist pulled in three hours ago, and we had the tracker on him, so I let the nap ride. After dropping off Frank's food, I returned to my car, parked near the south exit so Lee couldn't slip past us unseen, and waited. I called Frank up on my Porsches' vid-phone.

"What does your fortune say, Frank?"

"I should have bought gold in 2007."

Grinning, I set my fortune cookie aside and dug into the pepper chicken.

As we watched and ate, Frank launched into one of his golden oldies.

"Remember that moke who got out of prison and the same day he's back into B&E? Only he forgot he already ripped off that house? The old guy inside, however, has not forgotten. So when the moke goes in this time, he has a close encounter with a double barrel shotgun." Frank chuckled. "Fate caught up with him."

When we'd been partners in NOHO, Frank hadn't been one to dwell on the past. He was reveling in it now though, laughing and gesticulating with gusto. I let him relive the old days.

Frank chattered on. I finished my chicken and tossed the remains back in the bag. "What you say we expedite and wrap this up?" I said after he'd finished another story and started to repeat his recitation of the first golden oldie. "Lee should have lost all his money by now."

"Sure. Let me make the approach." Frank clipped the little body camera onto his lapel. "That's what you hired me for."

It killed me to take the back seat, but Frank was right. Besides, the camera would give me a front-line view of Lee. "Okay, I'll stay back in case he slips out."

Frank headed in, and I watched from my Porsche.

The casino had a big open floor with ten rows of clanging slot machines closest to the door. Beyond the slots were the roulette and blackjack tables. Three additional rooms branched off the back, a small area for poker, and a larger space for sports betting and bingo. Bright lighting and unobtrusive cameras stood sentinel overhead. No clocks anywhere distracted customers with unwelcome reminders of time slipping away, along with their money.

Frank didn't even have to circle the floor once. Dr. Lee sat, shoulders hunched and elbows planted at the blackjack table, a squat glass of whisky and a small stack of chips to his right. He looked even thinner than he had in the video, shrunken. The shadows pooling under his eyes were darker and his complexion had taken on a dull grayish cast. But his lips were curled in a hopeful smile. Lee must have won a hand.

There were several open seats around the blackjack table. I watched Frank take the one on Lee's right.

"Excuse, me, Dr. Lee?" Frank signaled to the server to bring Lee another round. "Could I talk to you for a second?" Frank kept his tone light and polite. He held out his private investigator's license and introduced himself.

Lee's head tipped to the side like an inquisitive dog. The smile disappeared, but his face remained calm as he accepted the drink. "What about?"

"I'd like to ask you a couple questions about Britney Devonshire."

The eyes widened the second Lee heard the name. "Sure. Would you excuse me for just a second though? Too much whiskey." He slowly rose to his feet and turned as if to go to the can.

Watching from my Porsche, I felt it before it happened. I punched the ignition as Lee whirled round and knocked over his chair onto the seated Frank. As Frank untangled his animatronic arm from the chair, Lee bolted for the front door, leaving his pile of chips on the table.

Red-faced, Frank recovered and followed, but Lee had a head start.

I had Lee's Lexus up on the screen before the scientist made it out the door.

I called Frank as Lee scurried to his car.

"Don't sweat it, Frank," I said. "We've got the tracker on him. Besides, his reaction told me half of what I wanted to know." The deceased's name alone was enough to make Lee run. He was scared, and he looked guilty as hell. Shin would have to reopen the case and pull Dr. Lee in for questioning.

As I followed Lee from a distance, I hit the satellite map and traffic system, scanning options.

Frank was back in his Toyota. I could hear his labored breathing and mumbled self-recriminations.

"Lee's heading to PCH," I said. "Take the shortcut on Vista Drive to get ahead of him. You're front. I'm follow. But give him room. Let's just see where he lands."

"Roger that." Frank raced ahead, managing to pull out onto PCH three cars in front of Lee.

There we were driving along the strip of coastline—Frank in the blue clunker up front, staying well ahead of the speeding silver Lexus SUV, and me bringing up the rear in my black Porsche—hugging the curves as we headed north, a sheer drop to the left. I kept to the speed limit.

We drove for about forty-five minutes. During that time, Lee calmed down enough to slow the Lexus to 70 mph. Where was he heading? Did he know, or was he just running?

As Lee calmed down, Frank ramped up. His mumbling stopped, and I could hear the adrenaline surge in his voice. "Just like the old days, huh, Eddie?"

That's when I noticed fluid leaking from Lee's car. There'd been no sign of a leak back in the parking lot, but now liquid trickled out and left a clear trail.

"Frank," I said. "Let him go." I told Frank about the leak and pulled way back.

"Your show," Frank said. "But I think we should play it out."

"It's not a chase, Frank. The last thing I need is another black mark on my jacket."

"Just let me push him a little. I can nail this." Frank slowed down just as Lee sped up, boxing the Lexus in.

That's when Lee must have suddenly realized the old guy in the poky Corolla was the same guy from the casino. Lee's answer was to try to pass Frank in a no-passing zone. Just as the two lanes going north narrowed into one. A construction zone. Frank sped up.

A widening plume of fluid from Lee's car painted the road now.

"Frank," I said, speeding up too. "Get out of there now."

With Lee sandwiched between Frank out ahead and me coming up from behind in my Porsche, we cornered another turn, tires screeching now. The road grade grew steeper. That's when Lee started to panic. He punched the gas and jerked the wheel, veering onto the shoulder of the road.

I heard a small bang and saw a plume of greasy smoke rise from under Lee's car. Suddenly the leak gushed like a severed artery. I drove over a mare's tail of spilled fluid.

Lee opened his windows. Careening wildly over three lanes of highway, Lee reached over and grabbed something from the glove department. I saw the black shape as Lee sat back up and drew parallel with Frank's car.

"Taser, Frank! Punch it!" I yelled and braked hard, but Lee fired into my partner's open passenger-side window.

The taser's harpoon whizzed through the open window and stuck in Frank's animatronic arm. His seat belt kept Frank pinned to the car seat. The sharp jerk of the fifteen-foot line wrenched the taser out of Lee's hand, sending it whirling out the window. It spun around Frank's Toyota like a steel tether ball until it smashed into the rear window screen.

A golden halo encircled Frank's dark blue Toyota. Frank slumped over the wheel, his animatronic arm ripped off his shoulder and wedged in the frame of the car door.

Lee punched the gas and wrenched his steering wheel to the right. But his tires slid on the leaking plume of greasy fluid, skidding into the dead Corolla at 70 mph. Lee sent Frank's Toyota hurtling off the cliff. I heard the explosion as Frank's car hit the rocks below.

I swerved, riding two feet up the lip of the mountain on the passenger side, and steered hard to avoid the collision. It was a miracle I didn't flip or hit anything but rocks.

The texting driver in the southbound BMW wasn't so lucky. Other drivers stopped or swerved in time, but the distracted BMW guy looked up from his phone just in time to see the Lexus sitting there in the middle of the road, facing him.

The BMW rammed Lee's Lexus and sent it spinning into the telephone pole on the mountain. I pulled over and raced out of my Porsche. Frank's Toyota was swallowed in flames, a fireball raging twenty feet below. I'd only scrambled a couple steps down the cliff when the hot blast from the second explosion hit me like a force field, slamming me up and back into the cliff.

"Frank," I croaked. But there was no way to get down there. I stood watching—helpless.

That's when I heard Lee's strangled yell for help up above.

I scrambled back up the cliff. A little river of gasoline slithered out from under his car. I hit the auto-emergency icon on my glove phone.

The BMW driver sat in his car without moving, eyes wide and round, white-knuckled hands gripped tight around the steering wheel.

"Get out and get back!" I yelled at him, slamming my hand on his car door to jolt him out of his shock. "Way back!" I yanked his arm and propelled him towards safety.

The BMW driver stirred and stumbled back two hundred feet. I raced to Lee's Lexus and forced open the driver's side door, but he was already an accident cyborg—a big spear of telephone pole, metal, and flesh melded into one bloody mess. The airbags had inflated, but he hadn't been wearing a seat belt. There was no way I could get Lee out without disemboweling him.

"Hang on," I said. "Help's coming."

Lee was still conscious. He stared at me with a puzzled, almost vacant look. Shock. He closed his eyes, chin falling to his chest.

"Please identify yourself," the maddeningly calm emergency services voice on the other end of my phone said. She asked for details.

"Detective Eddie Piedmont." I gave coordinates and requested ambulance and firetruck. ASAP.

"Piedmont?" Lee tried to sit back up. His eyes went wild like a terrified horse. He grabbed my arm hard with his bloody claw. "They got to you too?" His voice was a hoarse croak. "Like Fuentes."

I locked eyes with him. "Who's Fuentes?"

"Since their talk? A dead man."

"Who's they?" I said, taking hold of the arm that grabbed mine. "What are you talking about?"

Lee's mouth opened, but the strangled sounds were no longer intelligible. Choking out syllables, he struggled to speak. He wouldn't make it to the hospital, let alone the interview room.

"Tell me about Britney," I said, grabbing his shirt. "Britney Devonshire. Did she blackmail you?"

His face was ashen now. He nodded.

"Did you kill her? Is that why you ran?"

His mouth opened and closed. "3.3.3 . . .1.1,1,0." Lee pointed at me. "Fa-ther . . ." The rest of his words drowned in his own blood. I ripped off my suit jacket and wadded it up, trying to staunch the flow. Lee was rambling, but held my arm in a death grip.

"Did you kill Britney?" I pressed. "Did you?"

Lee shook his head. He opened his mouth to say more, but all that came out was a gush of red. His head drooped like a cut flower wilting in a blast of heat.

The smell of spilled gas was sharp. I pried off his arm and ran back to my car for the first aid kit. Maybe I could find something to keep him alive. But before I could open the trunk of my Porsche, Lee's Lexus exploded.

The blast hurtled me five feet into a close encounter with the tarmac. Skin skidded on pavement. When I dragged myself upright, there wasn't much to do besides watch in horror.

The wall of flames from Frank's car matched the fireball in front of me. I couldn't breathe. But it wasn't the pain of the fire that doubled me up.

I heard a long, drawn out animal scream. The stranger howling was me.

CHAPTER NINETEEN

AN HOUR LATER POLICE SWARMED THE AREA LIKE ANTS ON AN anthill. Detective Rubinov of the Clara Vista P.D. took my statement and released me under my own recognizance with an order to appear in his office at nine the next morning.

My first call was to Shin.

He took one look at my face. It must have been bad. "Jesus. What happened?"

"Lee confessed to Britney Devonshire blackmailing him." I filled him in on the essentials of the crash. "Listen," I said. "The case was closed. You were off duty. If the Captain asks, you didn't know anything about anything until I called you. This call."

"Eddie," Shin said, rubbing his shaved head. "I'm primary on the Devonshire case. I should have been the one to run it down."

"Shikata ga nai," I said. *It can't be helped.* It was one of Shin's favorite tag-lines. "What good does it do for us both to take the hit?"

"We're partners." Shin screwed up one side of his face. "I can't leave you holding the bag."

"I lost one partner today," I said. "I won't lose another."

Shin went silent. Then he nodded slowly.

Next I called Jo, my finger hovering over the video option on this one. The phone rang on her end. Shin had recoiled at my appearance. I took my finger away, leaving the phone on audio only.

"Eddie?" she said. "I can't see you. Are you there?"

"Yes," I said. "Don't worry. I'm north of Ventura County. There's been an accident, but I'm fine."

"Thank—God." The relief in her voice suddenly shifted to anxiety. "Was anybody else . . .?"

". . . Frank. And the guy we were tailing. Somebody else was after him too. He panicked and things got out of hand. I just wanted to tell you before you hear about it from someone else." There was a long pause.

"But you're okay. And you weren't drinking." Jo dropped the last words casually, like adding ice to a soda.

When I didn't reply, she continued. "Were you?"

"Clean and sober," I said, "and two people are still dead. I gotta go." Hanging up, I started the car. My foot crunched on something under the accelerator. Leaning down I found the crumbled remains of my unread fortune cookie from the Chin-Mex place. It must have dropped out of my pocket. I picked it up.

Count no man happy while he still lives, it read. I dumped that cheery fortune in the trash and drove to a motel nearby.

I'd barely checked into my room and tossed the overnight case on the bed when my phone rang. It was Captain Tatum. With the vid option on my phone still off, she waited for me to confirm I was in one piece. Then she lit into me.

"We gave you vacation so something like this wouldn't happen, Piedmont. What were you thinking?"

I came clean—about the blood spot, Lee's confession that Britney Devonshire had blackmailed him, and how he'd spooked because somebody else was after him. "We didn't chase him, Captain."

Tatum took a deep breath. "You know this is still going to play badly with the IAC."

I knew. The hole I was standing in had gotten deeper.

"It's not just the press and the public," she said, her voice softening a hair. "I don't have any leeway on this one. If the IAC doesn't rule in your favor, you're off the force. Without pension."

Yesterday that would have mattered. Today Frank was dead.

When I didn't respond, Tatum continued. "I'll do what I can. I don't want to lose you, Piedmont. Make sure you keep your therapy appointments going." And she was gone.

I dreaded what I had to do next, but Detective Rubinov had agreed to let me be the one to call Frank's family. I couldn't tell Frank's wife that she was now a widow over the phone. Every cell in my body cried out for the drink everybody thought I'd already had. I took a shower instead, holding my head under the pounding water. If only the whole day could've washed off with the blood and grime.

My suit jacket was stiff with Lee's blood. I pulled out a second suit of a darker shade of gray from my overnight bag and let the steam from the shower do its work on the wrinkles. I dressed with care. Frank's words when I'd just gotten my gold shield came back to me as I tied the knot in my tie a little tighter than usual.

"Telling people their loved ones are gone forever's the worst part of the job. The suit shows respect."

Hell of a thing to be wearing the suit for Frank.

In slow motion, I drove over to the house where Frank had lived with Ruth, his wife of thirty-one years. She met me at the door. It was the first time I'd seen Ruth's short brown hair uncombed, her normally ruddy face ashen and without makeup. The local news must have covered the bones of the story. I took a deep breath and began.

Two hours later I was still sitting with Ruth at her kitchen table. "It's funny," she said, running her hand over a face which now looked much older than its fifty-two years. "All those years, every time Frank stepped out the door, I was afraid he wouldn't make it back. When he retired on disability, I could finally breathe." She tried to smile, but it was a thin effort. "And now it happens."

"I'm sorry, Ruth," I said. I'd lost track of my apologies—and regrets. There were too many to count.

She waved me to silence, then took my hand. "Not your fault. Frank hated retirement. When you called, his whole face lit up, Eddie. Frank was alive again in a way I haven't seen since he was first diagnosed."

I looked up at her in surprise. "Diagnosed?"

"Cancer," she said. "Pancreatic. Got the diagnosis three months ago."

I sat there stunned. "He never said anything."

Ruth nodded. "Frank made me promise not to tell you. Didn't want you to worry, did he." She patted my hand. "Maybe it's better he went this way. Beats dying by inches. Frank hated hospitals almost as much as you do." Ruth took a sip of the now lukewarm coffee. "And good-byes."

Frank had cancer. How could I not have known?

I felt Ruth's eyes on me. Frank's widow was looking at me

with pity and concern. And I thought I couldn't feel worse.

"Can I do anything for you, Ruth?"

"Would you see to Frank's things at the—morgue?" Ruth stumbled on the word morgue. "I—can't."

"Of course." A glance at the time on my glove phone told me even on an expedited schedule, neither Frank's nor Lee's autopsies would be done for another few hours.

On the drive back to the motel, I turned on the car's automated GPS. I didn't need directions—just wanted to hear the sound of a calm human voice that seemed to have all the answers. Back in my motel room, I fell onto the bed and into a dark dreamless sleep.

CHAPTER TWENTY

A COUPLE HOURS LATER, THE VIBRATION OF MY NOKIA HANDY woke me. It was Shin with the official report from the Devonshire autopsy, complete with the toxicology follow-up. As expected, massive amounts of Green Ice were found in her blood, but not her urine. That was typical for fatal overdose. The deceased had died before the drug had been metabolized.

"Blue Lotus in her system too," Shin said. Ice and spice was as lethal as it was popular.

"Any evidence of Gabriel Lee on or in her person?" I scanned through the report.

Shin ran his free hand over the stubble on his head. "It wasn't his semen in her, but SID matched his thumbprint to one on the light switch in her bathroom." Shin's gap-toothed grin beamed. "Captain Tatum already reopened the case herself—suspicious death, possible homicide. We're canvassing neighboring buildings for surveillance footage to lock down times for Lee's entrance or exit. And I sent a copy of the crime scene's microbial cloud to the coroner doing Lee's autopsy."

"Thanks." I should have felt a wave of relief. The thumbprint put Lee at the scene. His admission that she'd blackmailed him established motive. More would follow. And the fact that my hunch had played out in the reopening of the case gave me additional cover for the IAC hearing.

But when Shin hung up, I didn't feel relieved. My head was stuffed with thoughts of Frank and cancer, and the signs I'd missed. His wheezing and the ashen skin. His recycling the golden oldies on an endless loop and tossing protocol.

I forced my thoughts back to the case. Straddling a chair opposite the motel bed, I stared at Britney Devonshire's autopsy report. Questions kept multiplying, but the two people I was sure had the answers were both dead.

It was 5:00 a.m. when I drove to the Clara Vista morgue. Even if the autopsy on Dr. Lee wasn't done yet, I could at least pick up Frank's things for Ruth.

A full moon still hung in the dark sky, the image of a Nike Swoosh projected on the lunar surface. I could just barely remember what the moon looked like before it became a billboard for athletic shoes and glove phones every month. But that image was already ancient history. Easier to imagine the city at night without electricity.

My footsteps echoed as I walked down the hallway of the Clara Vista morgue. Hard bright light chased shadows from the corners. Ten feet away I heard strains of Mack the Knife, in German, bleed through the door to the autopsy room. There could only be one forensic pathologist who played that during an autopsy in the wee hours.

Pathologist Dr. Sidney Heller, elbow deep in a charred corpse, looked up. He was a pale New England variation on one of those rough-hewn faces you see carved on totem poles. Gaunt to the point where he was all gristle and sinew, Heller was oddly graceful with his long hands and fingers, and the stretched legs of a spider. He moved slowly, but deliberately.

"Hey, Sid," I said. We'd worked together on the Sphinx case.

"Well, well, well." He turned that lined face with its deep-set eyes to me. "Been a while, Eddie."

Sid took his gloved hands out of Lee's charred corpse as if to shake hands, but dropped something on the metal tray at his elbow instead. The hands were coated in blood.

"Yeah." I took a deep breath and regretted it. The air reeked of disinfectant and charred human hair. "Ruth sent me for Frank's effects."

Dr. Sid Heller took a deep breath too. Almost a sigh.

"Over there." He gestured towards the box of items on the table opposite. "I'm truly sorry, Eddie. I gave Frank VIP treatment. You knew he had cancer?"

I nodded, walking over and picking up the box of Frank's personal effects. Such a small box for the man.

I turned to the other body Dr. Heller was currently working on. Dr. Lee's corpse was a charred mass barely identifiable as human, utterly unrecognizable as the man who only hours before had spat out his last words in a river of blood.

"Anything you can tell me so far?"

"His cloud's degraded and fire-scorched," Dr. Heller said, "but it's compatible with the bacterial cloud your partner sent over."

Everybody who entered a crime scene left detectable, and identifiable, traces from skin and gut bacteria behind. This was additional evidence that put Dr. Lee in Britney Devonshire's apartment the day of her death.

"Could you verify if Lee had a vasectomy?" I said, nodding at the corpse on the table. "Or check his DNA against this blood spot? I need to rule him out on paternity."

Pulling up a picture of the fetal partial prelim from the file, I held my phone out for Heller's inspection. "I'll pay to expedite."

Heller leaned close and peered at the partial prelim. "Save your money." He pointed to the blood type listed on the corner of the page with the fuzzy barcode. "I can tell you right now Dr. Lee isn't the father. Blood types are incompatible. And yes, he did have a vasectomy."

I let that information rattle around in my brain for a second. "Father"—that was one of the last words out of the dead man's mouth, but Heller's findings confirmed what Denver had told me earlier. Lee had to have known he wasn't the father of any stripper's kid when she tried to blackmail him.

According to his boss, Lee had been under a lot of strain from work and the protestors targeting him. Maybe when he'd confronted her with the truth about his not being the father of her child, they'd argued, and things had escalated. Next stop—murder and a panicked run. I called up the Devonshire autopsy results on my glove phone next and held them out for Sid's inspection. "What about her? Is she the mother?"

"Her blood type doesn't rule out maternity," Heller said, craning his neck. "But you'll need a DNA scan to confirm. No equipment to do that here, Eddie."

Thanking Sid, I picked up the box of Frank's effects. The pathologist's choice of music continued to play in the background. The torch singer wailed like she had glass shards and blood in her throat. I couldn't understand the German lyrics, but rage and despair needed no translation. The door swung shut as I left to drive back to my motel in the murky dawn.

CHAPTER TWENTY-ONE

HILLS IN THE DISTANCE WERE ETCHED IN INDIGO AGAINST A red-orange dawn as I left the morgue. By the time I unlocked the door to my motel room, the robo-maid had come and gone, leaving a stale mint on the pillow and a trail of dust in its wake. But sleep wasn't an option.

I started to sort through the box of Frank's effects, jettisoning things that were scorched or bloodied beyond repair. No point in having Ruth see all that. Frank had his case file for Lee on flashdot, the fingernail-sized portable memory chip. I kept that for a detailed read later when I was less exhausted.

It took me three attempts to open Frank's phone. On the third try I entered the year of his anniversary as a password. Bingo. Flipping through the photos, I spotted lots of current family shots and a few old pictures, including one of Frank, Ruth and their daughter Susie at Disneyland. Frank's unlined face looked so happy—and young. Of course, I knew Frank hadn't sprung from the womb at age fifty. But in my head, he was always gruff and middle-aged. I never pictured him as a guy my age.

Shit-shit-shit. I carefully tucked the phone back in the box and tidied up the package for delivery to Ruth later that day.

I turned on the local news at 7:30. *Crimecast* was already running the story.

"Detective Edward Piedmont," the news reader said, "known to many for his starring role in apprehending the Sphinx Serial Killer who terrorized the city of L.A. and Ventura County five years ago . . ."

The media had already released my name. Protestors would be doxing me soon. Or worse. I changed the channel. And the hits kept coming.

". . . Piedmont, put on administrative duty for shooting middle school honor student Paco Ramirez two weeks ago, was involved in a hair-raising auto accident that took the lives of two people earlier today."

"Shit."

"The other surviving driver in the accident," said the newscaster, "is reality T.V. star Jordan Huang from the show *Xe*.

Jordan Huang turned out to be the texting driver of the BMW. Great. Celebrity involvement meant even more scrutiny. A different face spoke, but it was the same story on the next channel. Then they cut to aerial video footage of the drive along PCH just prior to the accident.

"How the hell?" I blinked at the footage. I didn't remember any traffic cams on that part of PCH.

The ugly face of Ira Natterman popped on screen next. "Detective Piedmont was suspended for reckless behavior in the Ramirez case," the civil rights attorney said. "And not two weeks later he's involved in this crash? Why is this murderous officer still on the force and not behind bars?"

Murderous. As usual Natterman had his facts wrong, but it didn't matter. I was responsible—for Frank.

I couldn't listen anymore. Picking up my jacket, I drove back to the crash site.

The acrid smell of burnt brush hung in the air, and the skid marks and oily residue still painted the tarmac like some crazy Jackson Pollack.

With my car parked on the shoulder of PCH, I verified what memory'd told me. Unlike virtually every corner of L.A. and the more crowded areas of Oxnard, there were no traffic-cams installed on this thinly populated stretch of PCH north of the city.

I scrambled up the hillside. Perched high over the Pacific Coast Highway, I had a good view of the whole area. But there was no way anyone standing anywhere here had the bird's eye view that matched the news clip. It had to have been taken by a drone or chopper-cam.

I checked messages. Jo had left two. She picked up on the second ring.

"I'm flying up north," she said. Jo gave me her ETA.

"What about your partnership?" I said. "Don't risk your promotion."

"I can multi-task," Jo said. "I'm hiring you a PR firm."

"The department already has one."

"They have their own agenda too. We need to get ahead of this."

Jo had a point. While Captain Tatum's recent reopening of the Devonshire death was reassuring, the release of my name in the Ramirez shooting was not.

"Tell him Nokia PD is already wall to wall cameras." The male voice in the background was only too familiar.

"Put Craig on," I said.

The image in Jo's glove-phone shifted and a sleek, well-preserved fifty-something businessman in an impeccable dove gray suit and lavender shirt appeared. Craig Sloan always looked like the biggest challenge he had was rectifying an accounting error at the country club.

Like his younger sister Jo, Craig had good genes, but the silver in his blond hair reminded me of the age difference between them. They shared the same father, but Jo's mother had been the second wife.

"Somehow, Eddie," Craig said in his superior drawl, "trouble always seems to find you."

Craig had Jo's straight nose, full lips and blond hair. It was odd how the same features differently arranged created an entirely different effect in the faces of the two siblings. Where Jo radiated refined sensuality, Craig looked like Caligula all cleaned up after one of his orgies.

I was looking down on the crash site from the hilltop. "Take a look at this." I angled my phone to show the road. "No traffic-cams on this part of PCH. So how did the news get footage before the crash?"

"Right," Craig replied. "PCH is part of Titan's police contract."

Titan was Craig's high-end security firm that handled a lot of government contracts.

"But we haven't installed cameras that far north yet," he continued. "Besides, the footage isn't a typical traffic cam."

I nodded. "Any idea who would tail me or Dr. Lee?"

"Who even knew you were there?"

"Besides Frank and Jo, nobody I told," I said. "But somebody knew." I remembered how spooked Dr. Lee had been. Somebody'd been after him besides me.

Craig paused before speaking. “Lie low for a couple days,” he said. “Maybe I can find a way to spin it in our favor.”

“Thanks,” I said. “Call me paranoid, but this feels more like an ambush than an accident.”

Craig had dropped his snarky tone. “Watch yourself, Eddie.”

CHAPTER TWENTY-TWO

As I stood on the Clara Vista hilltop overlooking Pacific Coast Highway, I replayed options in my head. The road and the ocean beyond were clearly visible from this spot. At least they would be after the morning fog burned off. Anyone with access to choppers or drones could have taken the footage. That covered a lot of people, including my own department.

I took a deep breath, letting the scent of wild dill, sea air and rosemary fill my lungs.

Helmet, drone, and chopper-cams were a standard part of police work. Since their introduction, charges of police aggression had plummeted. The cameras put both police and civilians on our best behavior. But this was undercover surveillance, a very different kind of record. Still, if the IAC had had me watched, the last thing they'd want would be for the footage to go public. Besides, L.A.P.D. jurisdiction didn't go this far north, and Ventura County didn't have the budget for the birds.

I called the televison station where the news report of the accident had first played.

"This is Detective Piedmont from Robbery-Homicide," I said.

They put me straight through to the station public relations director.

"How can I help you, detective?" The forty-something's smile was as striking and as fake as her red hair.

"The footage you aired last night," I said. "The crash on PCH that played on the eleven o'clock news? I want to know who sent it."

Her sherry-colored eyes glinted. "Are you the same Detective Piedmont who was in the black Porsche?"

I nodded.

The PR woman pursed her lips and reflected. "Listen, would

you consider giving us an exclusive interview? Your side of what happened?"

"I'd consider it," I said. "Who sent the clip?"

"A tourist filmed it on phone-cam," she said. "It's logged as anonymous. No name, no number."

Sure. Who wants to go to Disneyland when you can tape traffic? I stared down at the road from the hilltop. There was no way anyone with just a glove phone could have taken that crystal-clear bird's eye footage, even if helicopter tours had run overhead.

"Did anonymous cash the check too?"

"We didn't have to pay for this one. But we'd pay you of course," the PR director added in a rush.

I let the offer hang in the air for a second before asking, "You get many anonymous submissions like that?"

"Not in the two years I've been here," she said with a chuckle. "We caught a lucky break."

"Yeah." If the tipster hadn't left a name or number, there was no way now to trace the call short of a subpoena of the station's phone records. At the moment I didn't have that authority. One more to-do item for Shin.

"So what about that exclusive you said you'd consider?"

"You find out who sent that footage," I said before disconnecting, "and we'll talk." Maybe I'd hear back from her. Maybe not. Right now I had to pay a visit to Detective Rubinov at the Clara Vista station.

CHAPTER TWENTY-THREE

THICK MORNING FOG STILL BLANKETED THE COAST AS I HEADed towards the Clara Vista police station.

The road brought on flashbacks of Frank: cases we'd worked, things he'd said over the years. But all the good memories ended with the crash and my visit to his house yesterday. I kept seeing Ruth's broad grateful face on every mile marker. Her gratitude made me feel even worse. Only pulling into the station pushed the pause button on the recriminations.

The Clara Vista police were housed in a small one-story station built in the Spanish colonial style. After checking in with the desk sergeant, I was escorted back to Detective Rubinov's office.

Rubinov was a thin, hawk-nosed man. He rose to his full height of five foot eight as he shook my hand. Gesturing me to a seat, he settled back once more behind his desk. With his hat off, Rubinov's balding pate reflected the overhead light, and his brows were wiry tufts of gray that framed hooded hazel eyes.

Rubinov hit the privacy screen before I was seated. The windows darkened and dampened the sound to the outside.

"Never expected to host a detective from the Glass House up here," he said.

I gave him a slight nod.

The Glass House had been the nickname for Parker Center, L.A. police headquarters, in the way back when. Parker Center had been torn down and replaced with the new headquarters in 2010, but the nickname was resurrected after the terrorist bombing of 2025 shattered the windows of the new building in a rain of glass. These days the newly renovated headquarters, which housed Robbery-Homicide, was more concrete bunker than glass, so the old name was resurrected—an ironic touch. Cue the emojis.

"Sorry to hear about your partner, Detective Piedmont," Rubinov said. "That's a tough break."

I nodded and stared at my feet.

Rubinov tapped the cursor on his wall screen, and the public service screen saver disappeared as the holographic recreation of the accident site appeared, floating in front of us. With fingertip sensors Rubinov detailed the trajectories of the three vehicles. Blue for Frank, green for Lee, black for my Porsche: he painted the light trails of the three vehicles from the start of the accident to their final positions. Then Rubinov clicked through some additional frames. They had a shot of me after the accident standing by the side of the road looking like I'd just taken a sucker punch to the gut.

"This is just a formality," Rubinov said. "Lee's precipitating use of the taser, and the forensic reconstruction of all vehicle trajectories, have cleared you of fault. No charges have been filed. The widow's letting it go. Bottom line: it's officially ruled an accident."

The skin on my face was suddenly cold and clammy.

"What?" Detective Rubinov said, leaning back in his chair. "I thought you'd be relieved. This—"

"—wasn't an accident." I pointed to the wake of that spilled fluid on the screen. Pink like transmission fluid.

"Lee's car was leaking fluid," I said. "And there was a small explosion before Lee pulled the taser. Something that turned the leak into a gusher."

I pointed to the line of leaked fluid on asphalt. It was harder to see after all the fireworks, but definitely there. The trail got darker and thicker—as if a kid with a black crayon had traced over a thin ink line.

"Did you get samples of the trail to forensics?"

"Transmission fluid." Rubinov tipped his head to the side like an elderly kestrel. "Tech said it's probably due to pre-collision features on his Lexus."

Rubinov was referring to the millimeter wave radar and stereo cameras. The features sound an alarm to warn the driver when they sensed an imminent collision, automatically putting on the brakes and tightening the seatbelts in case the driver was incapacitated, or just slow to react.

I glanced at Rubinov's report. Tony Gomez was listed as automotive tech advisor. I made a mental note of the number.

Rubinov looked down at his report. "His seat belts retracted like they're supposed to. But Lee didn't have his belt on, so it didn't matter."

"What about the brakes?" I asked. "ECB?"

"Yeah," Rubinov said. "Brake calipers on electrically controlled brakes are aluminum. The taser probably shorted them out too. Like they did Frank's arm and his Toyota's steering. That taser on cloth and aluminum could also explain the smoke you saw."

It was almost a reasonable theory. Almost.

"Tasers don't have enough juice to short out that much. Besides, Lee was already losing control before he used the taser," I reiterated. "Any sign of tampering?" I peered more closely at the image floating before my eyes, tracing the lines through the scorch marks back down the highway. I could just make out the faintest trail of black, thin as a hair stuck on the lens. The trail seemed to connect Lee's car and mine like beads on a string.

Rubinov shrugged, the corners of his mouth tugged down into a frown. He gave me the dead eye stare. "Just this on the underside of the Lexus." Rubinov plunked a burned and twisted hunk of metal on the desk. "Looks like a tracker. Yours?"

I nodded. "We were tracking the Lexus, like I said. Nothing else?"

"Not that we found," Rubinov replied, running his hand over his balding pate. "Unfortunately, both Lee's Lexus and Frank's Toyota are completely incinerated. There's no way to find the leak itself—let alone prove whether it was caused by tampering or just a fluke break."

I started to say something. Rubinov stopped me.

"This is courtesy visit, Detective Piedmont. You mind if I ask the questions? Seeing as how it's my jurisdiction and all?"

I sat back in my chair with a shrug.

"Tell me again why you and your partner were tailing Lee in the first place?"

I recapped what I'd told Rubinov yesterday—about the stripper's blackmail scheme that Lee had confirmed after the crash. I added the news about the calls to Lee and his thumbprint found in her apartment.

"And the microbial cloud," Rubinov said. "I spoke to the pathologist too. As I see it, if Lee killed the girl, he got what was coming to him."

"Yes and no." I told him how Lee had said "they" were after him. Rubinov looked skeptical as I laid out the dying scientist's cryptic words about Fuentes.

"He was bleeding out, detective. People say weird shit at the end. You know that."

"They also truth-tell," I said.

"What are you saying? You think somebody tried to kill him as well as the girl?"

"Tried? Last time I checked both were dead."

"Look, if this girl was blackmailing him," Rubinov said, "I get why you wanted to talk to Lee about her death. And why he might have offed her. But who would have wanted to kill him?"

I shrugged my shoulders. "Maybe the same person who videotaped a traffic accident before it happened? Let's start with his wife. Maybe she has a reason for not filing charges."

Rubinov laughed. He pushed away from the desk and started to rock back and forth in his chair. "What, this Palisades housewife with no priors rigged some high-tech gizmo to turn her husband's car into a fireball and filmed the whole thing? What is she—ex-special forces?"

"I'm not making accusations," I said. "I just want to ask her a few questions. You do too, don't you? Otherwise you wouldn't have checked her priors."

"And found nothing, detective." Rubinov's bushy brows arched now. "His boss said you knew Lee was on sabbatical for stress. Maybe he was so preoccupied he forgot to take his car in for servicing. Suddenly he finds police on his tail. He panics and his bad transmission springs a leak."

I let Rubinov talk.

When he finished, Rubinov leaned forward, elbows planted on the desk, chin cradled in his hands. "What I don't get is why you're fighting this? It's ruled an accident. You're in the clear."

"Because it wasn't an accident. Somebody went to a lot of trouble to make it look like one."

"Maybe you're not the best judge of that right now." Rubinov switched off the hologram.

I looked at him, at his face bland with controlled concern.

"Don't tell me you buy the media spin?" I said.

"No." Rubinov didn't elaborate, but his face spoke volumes.

"What did Captain Tatum tell you?"

"What everybody but you already knows," he said. "God knows the job takes its toll on us all. It's easy to blame yourself for things that go sour—even things you weren't responsible for."

I blinked. "Now you're my therapist?"

Rubinov sighed, massaging his temples with gnarled fingers. "Look, I'm doing you a favor," he snapped. "Your partner's dead. You're not gonna bring him back. Drop this crazy talk before IAC starts asking whether you concocted these wild allegations to cover your own sorry ass."

My turn to stare at him. Rubinov had done his homework on me. Too bad he hadn't been as thorough on the crash.

"You're free to go," Rubinov continued in a softer tone, "but you should take that vacation for real. You're lucky to be alive."

"Yeah." I stood up and jammed my hat back on my head. "Desk duty for a righteous shoot. A routine call on an overdose turns into three homicides. Now Frank's dead and I'm facing possible forced retirement without pension. Everybody thinks I'm a whack job and there are no answers to anything. I'm lucky all right." I headed for the door. "I should head to Vegas and bet the house."

BOOK THREE

The fault, dear Brutus, is not in our stars,
but in ourselves, that we are underlings.
—Shakespeare *Julius Caesar*

CHAPTER TWENTY-FOUR

WHEN DETECTIVES LOOK BACK AT A CRIME, WE OFTEN SEE MIStakes the victims made, mistakes that made the crimes, if not inevitable, inevitable for them. Innocent little missteps nobody would peg as mistakes at the time appeared—lingering at the bar for just one more martini, stopping to help the wrong stranger on the road, taking a call that should have gone to voicemail. On another day they might not have mattered; the very same actions could have trickled away into nothing, but on this day, they ended in blood.

But this time the mistake was mine, and Frank had paid the price. I'd made the call and brought him into the case thinking I was doing him a favor. Instead I'd set my old partner up to crash and burn like a human meteorite.

The sun was starting to burn through the thick gray mist shrouding the parking lot as I walked out of the Clara Vista station. I made my way to my Porsche on autopilot, the vein in my left temple throbbing.

I sat in my car and gripped the steering wheel hard. My pounding head seemed stuffed with cotton wool. I opened the window, letting the engine idle and the sea breeze wash over me. The sky was the color of a mottled trout belly. The scent of eucalyptus and wild dill mingled with the tang of salt air.

Rubinov had nailed me on my regrets about Frank, but he was wrong about the crash. Forensics may not have found the cause, but this was no accident. When coincidences pile up like one royal flush after another, someone's dealing from the bottom of the deck.

Yesterday I'd thought Lee, who'd been under pressure from his work and the threats from the protestors, had killed Britney when she'd tried to blackmail him. But what if somebody else had killed them both?

Only a sliver of steel-hued sky pressing down on the strip of gray-green ocean was visible from the parking lot. A flock of honking geese flew overhead. One goose fell further and further behind the tight V-shaped flying formation of the others—like a black pearl thrown to the ground when a string of pearls breaks from a white neck. Black pearls—like the ones Mrs. Lee wore.

She wouldn't be the first jealous wife to take out a cheating husband and possibly his girlfriend.

But there I agreed with Rubinov. Mrs. Lee was a cool customer, but she had no priors, and there's usually a learning curve for homicide. I called up the argument Frank had captured on his phone and watched Mrs. Lee pummel her husband again. Could she have hated him enough to murder in cold blood? Because if this was homicide, it was no crime of passion. Was Mrs. Lee really the type to rig a cheating husband's engine to explode? It was a leap, but I've seen far worse in my time on the force. And Mrs. Lee was well-off. She could have hired someone else to do the dirty work.

Rubinov had said Lee's car was so fried that forensics couldn't find any evidence of tampering, or even of the leak itself.

Tony Gomez was the automotive tech expert who'd conducted the forensic evaluation on Lee's Lexus. The gearhead picked up on the fourth ring, his square furrowed face with Cocker Spaniel eyes appearing on my glove phone.

"Tough break about your partner, detective," Tony said after I'd introduced myself. "What can I do you for?"

"Lee's Lexus."

"Yeah, I went over it myself." With his free hand he took a rag from his jeans pocket and wiped a smear of grease and sweat from his face. "Total crispy critter."

"Do me a solid and check the underbelly once more." I reiterated the particulars of the leak. "There's gotta be something near the fuel line. If you didn't find chemical residue or a timer, it's something else. Something the average tech won't find."

Tony squinched his spaniel eyes and sighed heavily.

He seemed to be weighing the challenge against a good review for a tight budget, so I put my finger on the scales. "For a fellow officer."

"Aw, geez." Tony Gomez pursed his lips and sighed again. "All right. I'll take another look. Can't do it today though."

"As soon as you can. I owe you one." I left him my number and sat there in the parking lot minutes after Tony'd already signed off.

Whoever tampered with the car had needed access to Lee's Lexus and time to rig the explosion. The leak couldn't have started much before the chase, or Frank and I would have seen the telltale signs in the casino parking lot. That narrowed the window of opportunity. If somebody'd tampered with the car, they'd have had to have done it at the casino.

Nobody but Lee had approached the Lexus while I'd been there, but what about earlier? Frank had been stationed near the scientist's car the whole morning Lee had been inside the casino, and Frank'd said no. But given what I now knew about his deteriorating health, the cancer he'd worked so hard to hide, could I even trust Frank's account?

Plus, when I'd dropped food off with Frank upon my arrival, I'd caught the old guy napping. It hadn't seemed important then. But it was just possible my partner had dozed off long enough for somebody to tamper with Lee's car unseen.

It was eleven: autumn sun rode high in the now crystalline blue sky overhead. The vanished cloud cover would have been more appropriate for the day's coming attractions. Frank's funeral was scheduled for later this afternoon. I had to change. But first I'd head back to the casino parking lot and see what those security cameras had to say.

CHAPTER TWENTY-FIVE

JO HAD FLOWN THE RED EYE UP NORTH LAST NIGHT FOR FRANK'S funeral—bringing my dress blues with her. Leaving her to sleep in a while longer, I stepped into the bathroom of the dingy little motel room and put on the uniform.

"Hell of a thing, Eddie." Adjusting my hat in front of the mirror, I heard Frank's voice so clearly, I turned my head, half expecting to see him standing there behind me. There was nothing but steam and silence.

Writing a hasty note to Jo with a promise to pick her up for the funeral, I slipped out of the room and headed for the Casino parking lot in search of those security tapes.

Shin called before I'd closed the door to the Porsche. He was about an hour's drive south on PCH.

"Hey, Eddie." Shin's voice was missing its usual optimistic vibrancy. "Holdin' up?" His concerned face floated in the L-shaped space of my Nokia Handy.

Avoiding his eyes and questions, I raised one shoulder and let it drop in a shrug.

"Eddie, about Frank . . . I—"

"Yeah," I said. "Me too."

Shin started to say something and stopped. "See you there." His pixilated face dissolved as I closed my hand and started the ignition.

Yesterday, Lee's Lexus had been parked in space 003 in the Clamshell Casino lot. A gray Honda with a vanity plate GR8 WON sat there now. I was hopeful. Even casinos as low rent as this one tend to be vigilant on security. Stepping out of my car, I looked up. Sure enough, cameras were mounted on all the parking lot security lights. I noted those with the best angles on all sides of space 003. Climbing up on the spool-shaped concrete bases of each light, I read the serial numbers etched into the metal on the cameras' underbellies into my phone.

The security guard's cubbyhole was squeezed into a corner near the public rest rooms. Smelling of new paint and stale cat piss, the industrial gray office featured a long low desk with a bank of screens mounted on the wall above.

The fifty-something security guard sat hunched in a swivel chair in front of that desk wolfing down an Egg McMuffin. He had hair like a frightened porcupine, and glasses with thick black plastic frames that could have been cool, but weren't. The guard kept his eyes moving intently between two of the screens.

On one of the screens a server in a skintight micro-mini skirt bent to dispense drinks to the gambling guests. The guard angled his whole body down to the left in hopes of getting a better view.

"If she's skimming from the till," I said, "she's not holding on her person."

The guard whirled his chair around towards me. "What you want?" A blob of thick glutinous yolk from the McMuffin dribbled onto his tie.

"Detective Piedmont," I said, and flashed him my badge.

He perked up as he took in the badge and my dress blues.

"Pete Simpson," he replied, dabbing at his tie with a paper napkin. His pudgy fingers only smeared the yellow paste. "Two years retired from twenty on the Santa Barbara Police Force." He reached out to shake hands, then retracted the proffered yolk-smeared paw with an embarrased shrug.

I forced a smile. Given the way things were going, next year I might be the one squirreled away in a gray cubbyhole spying on girls in skirts with more buckles than fabric and dribbling food all over myself.

"Have a seat," Pete Simpson said, smiling as he pushed forward a small metal seat with his foot. "Wedding or funeral?" Simpson gestured at my dress blues as he sat back in his rolling chair and took another bite of breakfast sandwich.

"Not a wedding."

My words wiped the smile off his face. Simpson held the McMuffin suspended in mid-air in front of his open mouth for a second without taking another bite—just like a frozen holo-screen.

"How long do you keep the footage? I said.

He set the sandwich down on the paper napkin and wiped crumbs from his mouth with the back of his hand. "A week, give or take," he said. "You lookin' for something in particular?"

"My partner and I were tailing a silver Lexus yesterday," I said. "It was parked in your lot for a while before things heated up."

"Whoa," he said. "That chase on PCH I saw on the News? The one with the old Porsche?"

"The old Porsche," I said, thumb pointing at my chest.

Simpson shook his head and clicked his tongue with a slightly sympathetic ruefulness. "Shit, man. I'm sorry—about your partner and all."

I gave him the serial numbers of the cameras. "Late afternoon."

He jotted down the numbers. "Man, that was some bad luck you stepped in."

I nodded.

Pete Simpson swiveled back around so he was facing the computer and bank of screens once more. Watching Simpson type in the serial numbers with one finger was like waiting for the water in a stopped-up sink to drain on its own.

Eventually, he found the footage for the first camera. We started skimming through, looking for anything out of place. Simpson said nothing, but his attention kept wandering back to the pretty servers on the other cameras.

"Listen," I said. "I don't want to hold you up. How about you make me a copy, and I get out of your hair?"

Simpson squinched his face. "We're supposed to get permission and fill out a bunch of paperwork," he said.

"But for a brother in blue . . ." I wheedled.

He gestured to me to have at it and scooted the swivel chair back over in front of his preferred viewing.

I wasn't as nimble as Denver on a keyboard, but five minutes later I had a copy of the security disks from all three cameras for that entire day on flash-dot in my hand.

Heading back to the Sierra Madre Motel, I shelved intrusive thoughts of an unwanted future staring back at me in the form of a pudgy nearsighted peeping Tom as fast as possible.

CHAPTER TWENTY-SIX

THERE WASN'T TIME TO REVIEW THE SECURITY FOOTAGE FROM the casino parking lot before Frank's funeral.

When I pulled up into a space behind the motel room, Jo was already out front waiting, dressed in a little white dress and black pearls: fashion forward funeral attire. On an ordinary day, I'd have told Jo how the dress was anything but ordinary on her, and she would have criticized my choice of accomodations. But today was the day I had to bury my friend. We drove to Frank's funeral in silence.

The service was held at St. Michael's Anglican Church one street over from Vista Drive, the small town's main thoroughfare. The church itself was a simple whitewashed Mexican structure with bougainvillea framing the heavy bronze doors. The thorny bushes erupted into violent fuschia and orange-colored blossoms shimmering in the heat. From the street, it almost looked like the church was on fire, flames licking at the white plaster as they ran towards the tiled roof.

I parked next to the old green Volvo that belonged to Frank's daughter Susie. Wreaths of blue and white spilled out from the altar to the doors, their sweet perfume heavy in the heat as Jo and I walked inside.

"Hell of a thing, Eddie," said a familiar voice. Detective Timberman stood in the aisle next to Frank's and my old captain from North Hollywood station. They'd been talking shop. Something about a struggle for power in the AzteKas ever since Nieto left prison. Timberman gave me a stiff-armed bear hug. Lieutenant Dixon with his bald pate and military bearing just shook my hand and clasped my right shoulder with his left hand, shaking that bald head in wordless sympathy.

There was a jumbotron up near the altar, playing a continuous loop of pictures of Frank. Baby Frank cut to a ridiculously young Frank at his wedding, to Ruth, then Frank getting his gold shield.

There was a shot of him and me celebrating the Sphinx collar at the Code Seven. I was looking out at the camera. Frank was looking at me. He had an expression on his face like a Little League coach beaming when his player knocks one out of the park.

I don't remember much about the actual service. In my head, I was back in NOHO working cases with Frank.

"Eddie?" Jo was squeezing my arm.

The next thing I knew, I was walking up to the podium on legs as heavy as leaded steel. I'd carefully prepared a speech. Taking the folded pieces of paper out of my pocket, I smoothed the creases with my hands, trying to make the papers lie flat. I cleared my throat and looked out at the congregation.

Seated mourners in blue were peppered liberally amongst those in black and white. Since Frank was retired at the time of his death, there'd be no missing-man chopper formation or a gun salute to pay tribute to his years on the force. But he'd have been really proud to know the thin blue line stretched so far north to see him off.

I refolded my speech, tucking the pages back in my breast pocket.

I heard my voice start to speak.

"People change you," I said. "If you let them in. So, you want to make sure the people you let in are good people. Frank was one of the good guys."

Several uncomfortable looking teens in ill-fitting blazers and ties bunched together in the back of the church like a murder of crows. One kid sat hunched by himself off to the side in the very last row. I could guess who they were. Frank had taught a Drug Abuse Resistance Education class continuously for the past twenty years.

Most of the kids stared at me red-faced, but one head in a dark nanoskin hoodie tilted down towards the black chopper helmet cradled in his lap. The neon colors from some streaming download were bright enough to see from the podium. The twerp was futzing with his glove phone—at Frank's funeral.

"'Serve and protect' weren't just words to him," I said. "He lived them. Frank was my partner and my mentor. He was the father I never had, and I'll miss him every day of my life."

There was more I'd wanted to say, but I walked back towards my seat feeling like I'd swallowed a hot coal scorching its way down to my guts.

I was just about to squeeze back into the pew when the kid with the black hoodie stepped out of the church.

I slipped out the side door and followed him to the parking lot. He was just about to lower that helmet onto his head.

Approaching from behind, I yanked his hoodie back hard. He dropped the helmet and it fell, clattering hard on the tarmac.

"What the fuck?!" the kid spat at me. He'd dropped his glove phone too.

I took a step forward and heard the satisfying crunch of computer chips and leather under my right foot.

"Next time, show a little respect," I said. "Especially at the funeral of a guy who tried to help you, you miserable little git."

Eyes on his back, I retrieved the dropped helmet with my foot, and kicked it into my hands.

"I didn't even know that old fuck," the kid spat. His voice was familiar.

As he turned around and took a step towards me, I caught my first good look at his face. He wasn't one of Frank's D.A.R.E. kids. It was Raymond Lee—the son of the scientist who'd tasered Frank's car that day everything had spun out of control. That was a surprise.

"Why are you here, Ray?"

"None of your business." He reached out for his helmet.

I pulled the helmet into my chest fast, and he had to let go or lose his balance. He swore again. Maybe Ray had come north with his mother to identify his father's body. Maybe he slipped away for some air while she made arrangements for the funeral and ended up here.

But Ray's nose was running. He wiped it on the sleeve of his hoodie. Raymond's skin didn't yet have the greenish-yellow tinge or the stench of dirty socks, but when you live with an addict as long as I had, you know.

"You're hurting," I said. "On your way to make a buy?"

"No. What the fuck." His eyes narrowed to blazing slits. "Why couldn't you just leave him alone? My dad."

"He was caught up in the murder of a young woman, Britney Devonshire."

"I don't know anything about those women. But you killed my dad!" Ray's face was a patchwork of angry red blotches. "I wish it was you who bought it," he said. "Not your friend."

Me too, kid. I looked at Ray, and for a second, his father's face pushed through the kid's features. Father—333-1110.

When Gabriel Lee had said father after the crash, I'd assumed he was referring to Britney Devonshire's blood spot. What if he was trying to tell me something about his son?

"I'm sorry about your dad," I said. "But I didn't kill him."

"Chumonio!" Ray grabbed for the helmet again. This time I chest-passed it to him like a basketball. Ray jammed the helmet on his head, and pulled the visor down over misting eyes.

The bronze doors of the church clattered shut. I looked up to see Jo on the steps with Shin hard on her heels.

I needed more than a feeling to hold Ray for questioning. I let him go, watching his back as he sped off on the Yamaha.

"Everything all right?" Jo spoke in that voice she reserved for calming squalling cats or clients. "Father Valdez is starting the interment."

With a curt nod, I followed her and Shin back inside, vowing to pay a little visit to Raymond Lee and his mother at the first opportunity.

We interred Frank in the columbaria opposite the Mary chapel. When it was over, Ruth squeezed my hand.

"This terrible accident would have been even worse if you weren't here, Eddie. Thank you."

Head lowered, I examined the cracks in the pavement. This wasn't the time to tell Ruth Frank's death wasn't an accident.

CHAPTER TWENTY-SEVEN

SHIN LINGERED WITH ME IN THE SHADE OF THE CHURCH PARKing lot as the mourners departed. He waited until Jo headed to the ladies' room before speaking.

"Eddie," Shin said, "wasn't that Gabriel Lee's kid? What was he doing here?"

"He wanted a look at his dad's killer." I pointed my thumb in towards my chest.

"Shit," Shin said. "Kids." He mopped away the beads of perspiration strung along his brow.

Even in the shade, the sun was hot enough to melt tarmac. I felt sweat trickle down between my shoulder blades.

"Captain Tatum called again this morning." Shin kicked the tarmac with his toe. "Lee's fingerprint was enough for her to reopen the Devonshire case as a suspicious death, but we need more in the way of solid evidence to prove you're right."

I filled him in on what the pathologist had said about Lee's microbial cloud. It was one more piece.

"How's your Korean?" I said.

Shin cocked his head and shot me a quizzical look. "Better than my Japanese, if you believe my mother." Shin's marriage to his Korean-American wife Ahn had been a sore spot with both families initially. "Why?"

As I filled him in on Lee's last words and cued up the footage Frank had recorded while surveilling the now dead scientist. I played the argument between Lee and his wife for Shin.

A slight frown replaced Shin's habitual smile as he watched the scene that ended with Mrs. Lee pummeling her husband in the driveway of Lee's Clara Vista rental. Shin replayed it, this time with the volume up as he leaned close to the phone.

"What did Mrs. Lee say? The translator app was a little vague."

Shin winced. "She hammers him. Lee's a bad husband, and a bad father. He gambled away their retirement and the money for Ray's senior year of college. Now this. Something else about the son I couldn't totally make out."

"What?" My thoughts raced back to Lee's last words—father, 333-1110. "Could you get any of it?"

"How it was all Lee's fault," Shin said, shifting his weight back and forth between right and left foot. "But she doesn't say what."

"Anything else?"

"He's selfish. Brought shame on the family and put them in danger," Shin said. "Can't say I entirely blame her about that."

"What's Lee say?"

Shin replayed the section where Lee fired back at his wife. "Says she's happy to spend the money when he has it. She knew what he was doing all along."

"Then she starts to speak with her fists," I said. "Could go to motive."

"I don't follow."

"What if Gabriel Lee didn't kill Britney? What if somebody who knew they were involved took them both out?"

Shin stared at me as I filled him in on the leak and Lee's last words. "Somebody worked hard to make both deaths look accidental."

"Somebody like Mrs. Lee?" Shin's tone was skeptical.

"Mrs. Lee was an anesthesiologist," I said. "She'd know her way around drugs and needles. Her son's up here with her. He's an engineering student. He could finesse some sort of detonator for his mom. The tape you just translated goes to motive."

"I'll go to the mat for you," Shin said, "and not just because I owe you. But you're pushing air here. It was Gabriel Lee's print and microbial cloud we found at the Devonshire girl's place, not his wife's. Do you have anything solid to back this up?"

"Not yet." I told him about Gomez doing another check on Lee's car, and the security footage from the casino parking lot. "And don't forget the surveillance video on the accident itself."

Shin's expression stayed skeptical. "I put in for a search warrant on the Lees' Palisades house as soon as we found his print in Britney's place. We should be able to prove the Devonshire girl blackmailed him."

"I'll go through the security footage for the casino parking lot."

"Okay." Shin dug the toe of his shoe into the tarmac. "But keep this between us. You can't be spinning wild conjectures now, Eddie. Promise me you'll be smart and keep your head down through the IAC hearing."

"Who's asking, Shin? You? Or Tatum? Did she ask you to tell me that too?" It stung that they might have been talking about me behind my back.

"You know you can be a real asswipe sometimes," Shin replied.

"So I've been told." I walked him to his car. "Sorry, Shin," I said, when he slammed the door shut. "But it's not just wild conjecture. I saw that leak. Lee's death wasn't an accident. Who else wanted him dead?"

He sighed. "Keep it to yourself for now. Let's see what pops from the search. Otherwise you know what the IAC will say."

"I'm chasing ghosts."

Shin stared at me. "More than that. The real connection between these deaths is you. You're tired, you let yourself get involved personally, and you're fucking up."

I balled my fists, but nodded.

Shin's face brightened at my unaccustomed tractability. "I almost forgot," he said, the corners of his mouth twitching with surpressed glee. "Did you need me to translate Raymond's parting words to you?"

"Chumonio?" I shook my head. Even my Korean was good enough to recognize the word for motherfucker.

CHAPTER TWENTY-EIGHT

SHIN SPED BACK SOUTH TO NOKIA PD. JO WAS FLYING PRIVATE back to Ciudad L.A. right after the funeral reception, so I drove her to the airport.

"You worried about the hearing?" Jo said before we'd turned the corner away from the church.

"Hmm."

"It'll be fine." She squeezed my knee. "I've hired your PR rep too. Sasha Gilels. She's good. We do a fair amount of business with her at the firm."

"If you think it's necessary." The streets blurred as I accelerated.

"I thought we already settled that." Jo pushed her Raybans down on her nose as she gave me that appraising look.

I nodded. She didn't need to remind me that my name was already all over the news, and not in a good way. I updated Jo on my recent conversation with the PR woman at the television station, detailing the anonymous caller who was listed as having sent the crash footage.

"We'll find anonymous," Jo said, smoothing a few wayward tendrils of blonde hair. "Don't worry."

I knew "we" included Craig, and I wasn't too keen on owing him a favor, but Jo was family. Maybe it wasn't all bad to have her brother around.

I pulled some music down from the cloud for our drive: The Glass Leopards' electro-version of Lou Reed's Pale Blue Eyes. The original on vinyl had a home in my collection, and I liked it better. Reed's flat, untrained voice, and the scratches on the vinyl gave the song about remembering an old love a rawer haunted quality. But this wasn't bad.

I dropped Jo at the airport and waited until her plane

skimmed the sky. Then I turned the nose of my Porsche south toward C.L.A. I planned on going straight home and getting in gear for Monday's IAC hearing, but I found myself driving past Gabriel Lee's Clara Vista beach house.

Lee's body had been cremated with an "immediate family-only" funeral and no memorial service. That was unusual for Asian families and unfortunate for me. I'd wanted to pull a Raymond and see who else turned up at the scientist's funeral. I especially wanted to keep a sharp eye on the grieving widow.

Mrs. Lee was the only person of interest who'd had an obvious reason to want both her husband and Britney dead, and she'd lied when I'd questioned her earlier about Dr. Lee. She had opportunity and motive, but Shin was right. I had no hard evidence to connect her with either death.

Still mouthing the song's lyrics under my breath, I slowed outside Lee's gray Craftsman style bungalow. A "For Lease" sign had sprung up on the lawn overnight. Mrs. Lee's Mercedes and Raymond's Yamaha were gone. Stacks of neatly tied garbage bags were piled high on the curb next to overflowing trash bins set out for pick-up.

Mrs. Lee had moved fast on closing out her husband's life.

A couple of hastily tied bags on the top of the pile of discards had spilled open, disgorging pops of color and shiny bits in the afternoon sun. Maybe Raymond had packed these.

In any event, trash on the curb is public property.

I parked and got out of my car to investigate. The first open bag held Dockers, a few outdated silk ties, button-down shirts, and toiletries. Another entire bag was crammed full of Berkeley and Genesys company T-shirts and New Balance sneakers in different stages of wear.

Nothing that hinted at any relationship with Britney Devonshire.

I pushed aside an old shirt with the toe of my shoe and felt my pulse race. I reached down for the discarded phablet peeking out from under the pile of clothes. The screen was smashed, but the phablet body was intact, minus a few scratches.

My excitement evaporated when I saw the memory chip had been lifted. I tossed the phablet back on the pile and started to nose through some of the other discards on the off chance that the chip had fallen in there somewhere. It hadn't.

An old homeless scavenger at the end of the street caught my attention. The woman was dragging an overstuffed garbage bag toward an empty shopping cart somebody had upended and abandoned. Scars on the metal near the wheels showed where the pilfered carts' GPS monitors had been knocked off.

As I headed over, she stopped at the back of the cart and reached down to touch the metal. Then, still dragging the garbage bag, she circled round to the front of the cart and stopped again. She stared at the cart and reached out again, touching it like it was something she should know how to use but didn't. Then she circled round again. The woman made two more rounds in the time it took me to close the distance. She was stuck in a loop of endless rotation.

On approach, it hit me the woman wasn't old. She just moved with that hesitant shuffle you see on the elderly. Up close I could see her full lips and unlined skin. With a shock, I revised my estimate of her age down to somewhere between late teens and early twenties.

Which led to one depressing conclusion: Alzheimer's X.

Her gray sweat pants were stained, and her tangled black hair hadn't been cut in a while. Makeup free, the woman wore a faded purple plaid shirt under a green Genesys tee that was two sizes too big. Discards from Lee most likely.

"Hey, Miss, you all right?"

She was mumbling something over and over. The girl looked at me. Confusion in her eyes gave way to fear, and then a sudden expression of recognition.

"Jesus, mi hermano!" She grabbed my arm like a drowning child clinging to a lifeline.

I didn't try to correct her. Better to play along than try to convince an Alz-X victim I wasn't her brother, let alone the Lamb of God. Her stolen cart wasn't the only thing without a tracker. Alzheimer's robbed the brain of its GPS. Whoever she was, she was lost, and her fear was real.

I had no sooner scanned the girls' barcode into my phone to see if I could find a home address, when a beat-up Buick scratched the curb as it came to a screeching halt. The car disgorged a forty-ish woman wearing a frantic expression.

This woman had dark pouches under her worried coffee-colored eyes. Her black hair was streaked with silver like the tinsel on a discarded Christmas tree a week after the holidays ended.

"Isobel," she yelled, putting herself between me and the girl as Isobel dropped my arm.

I already had my badge out.

As the older woman looked from the gold badge to my face and back at the badge again, the muscles of her face relaxed. She closed her eyes and exhaled a deep breath that was more like a sigh.

"Gracias," she said, taking my left hand in both of hers and pressing her face to it.

I felt the warm salt tears streaming down her face on my hand as she held it.

"I work two jobs, officer," the woman said. "Sometimes I get so tired. I fell asleep."

"It's okay," I said, patting her hand, and gently pulling back my own. "It's okay."

"No." She shook her head. "It's not. Isobel." Her voice trembled on a higher note. She tenderly pushed a stray strand of tangled hair out of the girl's face. Shifting her battered pleather purse onto her other shoulder, the mother started to peel her daughter's hands off the shopping carts finger by finger.

I stared at Isobel with her mismatched clothes and uncombed hair. The ghost of a pretty girl was just discernible in the frightened ruin that stood before me. God, I hated this plague.

Grooming was one of the first things Alzheimer's X patients forgot. Day by day, the disease was stripping her of memory. She was forgetting what ordinary things like keys and phones and grocery carts were for. Soon she'd forget how to speak altogether, and finally how to swallow. Her personality would empty out with the memories, and only the vacant husk of a ravaged body would be left behind. Most families prayed their loved ones caught pneumonia before the end game. It was a better death.

I reached into my jacket pocket where I squirreled away contingency cash. I stuck a twenty into the mother's purse as she helped her daughter into the Buick and drove away. They needed more than prayers and my twenty, but that's all I had.

I stood there on the sidewalk long after they'd disappeared

around the corner. Then I turned back to the abandoned garbage bag and started to rummage through the junk. Sure enough, Isobel had played magpie with the Lee discards. Under the pile of pilfered Genesys T-shirts and crockery, there were some of the scientist's souvenirs from various casinos. I pushed aside a little blue and white ceramic clamshell. It rattled. I picked it up and turned it over, weighing it in my hand. There was a coin-sized slit along one of the seams in the back. I shook the figurine and smiled when it rattled again.

I dropped the clamshell on the tarmac and let it smash. There in the midst of the shattered bits of clay, a little silver disk shone bright as a mirror with an Apple logo. It was the flash-dot jacked from Lee's phablet. Bending down, I pocketed the silver circle of memory.

CHAPTER TWENTY-NINE

WHAT HAD GABRIEL LEE HIDDEN ON THE FLASH-DOT? I snapped the dot into my own phablet and glove phone. When neither worked, I tried the car's computer. The files were unreadable. Either the memory chip was damaged or encrypted. I punched the starter button on my Porsche and headed back south towards L.A.

By six that evening, I was pulling into the parking lot behind Vapor Time 3, the hookah lounge on Santa Monica Denver Lakshmi frequented after work. With any luck, the ex-Hacktavist could recover whaever information the scientist had squirreled away.

In the parking lot, I stepped on a playing card, the queen of hearts. There was another card ten feet away. The parking attendant, who'd apparently been playing solitaire, scurried after them. The remaining cards were scattered all over the lot like a giant fortune cast to the wind.

I made my way inside and headed past the low tables clustered in the front to the booths in the back. There was a digital sign announcing a special on Blue Lotus, the synthetic marijuana called spice. The air was heavy with the scent of cloves and cinnamon, and just enough of that telltale skunk underneath that told me I'd have a contact high if I stayed too long. A buzz of chatter mingled with the sound of water gurgling in the hookahs planted at each table. I spotted Denver's hair first—big bubble gum pink stripes against the sea of black today.

"Hey Security Princess." I moved aside an expresso cup and plunked the flash-dot memory disk down on Denver's table as I took a seat. "Fuentes, Father Fuentes, 333-1110, or just father," I said. "See if you can find a reference to any of them in the dot."

"Father?" Denver said, grinning. "Like who's your Daddy, or pervert priest?"

"You tell me."

Denver was bubbling like a freshly uncorked bottle of champagne. Her pink streaked hair bobbed up and down.

"You vaping purple haze now?" I said. "What's got you so damn happy?"

She held out her left hand with a flourish. The nails were painted to match her hair, and a blinding sparkler weighed down the third digit. It was at least two carats bigger than the two carat stone I'd given Jo.

"You recovered the iceberg that sank the *Titanic*?"

"Diamond Dog just gave it to me last night," she squealed. "I met him on Heavenly Matches."

"That psychic matchmaking site?"

"Yeah. D-Dog and I, we're engaged!"

"Congratulations," I said. "Diamond Dog, huh?" I pictured some skanky alternative rock geek with hair like a gel-spiked dandelion. "Did your fiancé rob somebody for the bling ring?" The sparkler was seriously massive.

"If he did, in three months I'll make him an honest man. Clear your calendar. You're giving me away." Denver's father had died of lung cancer five years ago.

"Rushing things a little, aren't you?" I said.

"The heart wants what the heart wants." Denver's voice took on a dreamy air as she twirled a strand of fuchsia-colored hair on her finger. "Why wait?"

I stifled the twenty reasons that immediately popped into my head. "I always wanted to be a Daddy," I said, smiling. "I just pictured a smaller bundle of joy my first time out."

"Where's my glove phone?" Denver searched through her bag and shoved aside a pile of napkins and the expresso cup and saucer on the table, looking for the phone. "I want your help."

I lifted her phone out of the bag's open outer pocket and handed it back to her.

She flipped me off as she took the phone and brought up a file displaying three wedding dresses in traditional white, Hindu red and Goth Black. "Which?" she said, holding each under her chin in turn so I could picture the bride.

"I like this one." I pointed to the white gown. "But my wardrobe works with any of them."

"It's sick," she said, beaming as she stared at the dress. "D-Dog and I have our blood test this week. I'm so happy I could puke."

California didn't require blood tests, but families like Denver's often did. Full genetic scans to sniff out potential health problems down the pike.

"Let's hold on our toast then," I said. "Call me ASAP if you find anything on the flash-dot. When you're not high."

She flipped me off again, but with a big smile this time. Denver's happy mood was infectious. I left the girl with a smile on my face too, and checked messages on the way to the car.

There was one from my mother that instantly killed the happy feeling. I didn't have to hear it to know what it said. My father's birthday was in a week. Every year my mother tried to broker peace. Every year marked another epic fail.

I could not face that prospect right now. And the reminder of other coming attractions drowned any remnants of my happy mood. The IAC disciplinary hearing awaited me Monday morning at ten.

CHAPTER THIRTY

Over the weekend, I called every name with a 333-1110 phone number in the country. Nothing and no one appeared tied to Dr. Lee. I also ran down every Fuentes in California listed in the computer's search engines—to no avail. Jo came in late Sunday night. She must have found me with my head cradled on the dining room table.

"Wake up, Sleeping Beauty." The flash from her phone-cam chased away the shadows.

"I liked it better when you woke me with a kiss." I lifted my head with a start to see Jo holding out the picture of me, floating words and the numbers 333-1110 from the case file projected on my forehead like a derma ad.

"No problem." She bent down and bestowed the requested kiss. "Good news. You remember that PR rep I hired?"

"Somebody your firm worked with." I stretched the cramped neck muscles my catnap had given me.

Jo nodded. "Sasha Gilels. She phoned with the update on the Clara Vista crash footage."

Jo had my full attention.

"Forensic analysis confirmed the footage was taken via civilian drone," Jo said moments later, kicking off her heels and pulling a bottle of wine out of the fridge. She poured us both a glass of pale gold Viognier.

"How'd she get the footage so fast? The warrant hasn't even been served."

"Remember the texting BMW driver?" Jo curled up on the sofa and patted the seat next to her. "Jordan Huang is a client of Sasha's. He was going to tell his story as soon as he was cleared from all charges anyway. Sasha arranged for him to give an exclusive interview to KTCV in exchange for the footage. You're a hero, Eddie."

I took the proffered seat on the couch as Jo pulled up a news clip of the now voluable BMW driver. He was standing on that stretch of PCH, arm extended as he chattered on about the crash to the riveted reporter on his right.

"It all happened so fast," reality star Jordan Huang said. "I didn't know that driver of the Porsche was a cop. But he saved my life, man. I was like frozen until he snapped me out of it. I would have been toast in that explosion. Wherever you are, Detective Piedmont, thanks, man."

"The clip's gone viral," Jo said. "It's already made a big dent in the number of protestors from the Ramirez shooting."

"What about the phone anonymous used to call the crash footage into the station?"

"Ah." Jo pressed her lips into a frown. "That was a burner. It's dead."

"Another ghost trail." I drank in the clean spicy notes of the wine's aroma. It tasted fine too. "Unless." I leaned over and nibbled Jo's neck. She tasted even better. "Any chance the phone number on that burner was 333-1110?"

Jo shook her head. She gave me the number. It was an 818 and I made a note to check it against' Britney Devonshire's phone logs.

"But you can go to your hearing tomorrow with a win in your corner."

"And knowing it definitely wasn't the LAPD who launched that spy drone." I smiled. It helped to know Jo had my back, and the department wasn't spying on me.

Jo made me promise we'd not mention work again until the morning.

We went to bed without another word and made love without speaking, the passionate tension-release of partners who know each others' bodies well and don't want to think, let alone talk.

That night I dreamt of an interrogation room with black walls and a ceiling that started to lower with the sound of scraping metal.

I woke to the clatter of a garbage truck rattling down the street at six o'clock the next morning.

A blanket of pale gray cloud cover was visible though the skylight overhead. I lay on my back listening to the sea gulls and mourning doves outside our bedroom window and watching the shifting skeins of cloud in the sky overhead. They seemed to form meaningful patterns, only to lose shape and dissolve in the morning breeze.

Jo lifted her head, shifting her body so that her chin rested on both slender arms crossed over my chest. I lightly stroked her hair. The pale strands smelled faintly of vanilla. She traced invisible circles on the skin of my chest with a teasing smile.

I could've used a replay of the night before, but Jo had to get to the office by nine, and I had to gear up for the IAC hearing. So we hauled ourselves out of bed and into the bathroom.

"Mirror," I said, and the wall above the sink transformed. My face stared back at me from the mirror, which had been a blank wall. Lathering the shaving brush until its soft bristles were covered with a head of white foam, I started in on my jaw, and frowned. I leaned in close to the mirror. My mom's unanswered phone call shot straight back into memory. And that prompted thoughts of my father's birthday.

Every day I worried I'd see my father's features pushing their way up through my skin, like some extinct monster rising up out of the black ooze of the La Brea tar pits. Somedays I thought I did, mostly when I was tired or pissed off.

As I leaned in, the light suddenly shifted. It was Jo standing behind me now, watching me shave.

"What's the matter?"

"Nothing." I angled my head and lifted the razor for another run down the side of my jaw. "Phantoms. My mother logged two calls. I haven't called her back. She'll be after me to visit my father again."

Jo leaned in close, her cool hands on my deltoids. "You look nothing like him," she said, reading my mind. Jo ran her hand through my hair. "But you could use a trim."

"I'll make an appointment later." Today it was true I saw no trace of my father on my face. The black hair, faded denim eyes, the set of the shoulders, the uncurled lips—even the scrapes—all I saw were my own familiar features staring back at me.

By nine fifty, wearing my favorite blue Brioni suit, I'd made my way to the fifth floor of Nokia P.D. and settled myself into one of the three little gray chairs in the corridor outside the See Cave.

My interview with the Internal Affairs Committee was scheduled for ten.

I checked messages. Shin left an encouraging voicemail. Jo had texted me—"Break a leg—somebody else's."

I loved this woman.

If things went according to the best case scenario, I'd be officially reinstated. If the hearing went the other way, I'd be fired with no pension and no prospects to look forward to but a law suit and my own recriminations.

The IAC wasn't a jury. That's why they were interviewing me under compulsion with a union rep instead of a criminal attorney. So, if they ruled against me, they could hold me personally liable and fire me on the Q.T., sparing the department a court trial and any further embarrassment.

But I had a play too. I planned to inform the IAC that Claire Kidder, the OIS civilian board member who'd pressed for this further investigation, and I had shared a drunken hook-up five years ago. Kidder should have recused herself from the OIS hearing in the first place due to conflict of interest. She hadn't. Now if the IAC canned me, I'd have grounds for a lawsuit of my own.

The door to the Sec Cave opened. Geared up for battle, I leapt to my feet. But before I could enter, Jay Espinoza, my union representative, scurried out in a breathless rush. The creases in his lined face seemed even deeper since our last meeting.

He was practically vibrating with energy.

"Should I make my statement on Claire Kidder right at the start?" I said. "Or hold it for the end?"

"No need," Espinoza said, a broad grin splitting his tired face. "Hearing's over, detective. I submitted your statement ahead of time and made them see that Ms. Kidder's actions tainted the whole proceeding. It's not court, but fruit of the poisoned tree still applies."

I stared at him as the implications of his words sank in. "So I'm reinstated?"

"With caveats." Espinoza's grin faded a little. He rattled off the four deployment periods I'd be fined and the periodic blood or breathalyzer tests I could look forward to in my future. "The bad news is," he continued, "they may move you out of Robbery-Homicide."

I felt that sinking feeling in the pit of my gut.

"But trust me," Espinoza said. "They don't want a counter-lawsuit. That will only give fuel to agitators. I'm guessing you'll stay put."

"So I can work cases?"

He nodded.

It was irony on steroids. The same drunken hook-up that had gotten me into trouble with OIS boardmember Claire Kidder had been my ticket out of trouble with the IAC. Things could definitely be worse. I shook Espinoza's hand and thanked him.

Deputy Chief Garber was exiting the room now, the same metallic twang of a computerized voice intoning his name as the door sensor read his barcode. Overly tanned and lean, he looked like the human equivalent of beef jerky. He walked past without a glance in my direction. IAC Detectives Andy Tarr and Mary Redhawk flanked him like book ends. Tall, fit, and blond Tarr resembled an actor playing a cop. Redhawk wore oversized glasses with thick black frames that matched her too-black-for-nature hair. The hair was pulled into a tight bun at the back of her neck.

When she saw me, Redhawk paused and peeled off from Garber. She gestured to Tarr to continue, but asked me to wait a minute. "It's not official, Mr. Espinoza," she said to the union rep, "or I'd ask you to stay too."

"You want me to stay?" Espinoza shot me a worried look as if to say "Did you sleep with this one too?"

"It's okay," I said.

He shuffled off with a worried backward glance.

I entered the See Cave after Redhawk and took a seat in another uncomfortable little chair facing the big table. The lights were hard and bright against the black walls, and there was the stale tang of sweat and disinfectant in the air.

Detective Redhawk half stood, half leaned on the long table opposite. She waited until the door closed, then turned her gaze on me. "Nice play, detective," she said. "Waiting until after the OIS ruling to raise the conflict of interest."

"That wasn't how it went down."

"Can I ask you something off the record?" she said.

"You can ask." We both knew "off the record" didn't apply to IAC.

"I worked with your father on a couple cases back in the day. Before I moved to C.L.A. He used to put away a drugstore worth of Oxycontin before breakfast. That was before he took to green ice and heroin."

I stared hard at her, realizing she was older than I'd guessed if she'd worked with my father. Nano-surgery probably—it was getting harder and harder to gauge a woman's age these days. Was she one of those police officers out to get me because I was the son of a dirty cop? Or had he rubbed a little dirt on her too?

"I'm half Black Irish and half Navaho," she said, leaning back on the desk. "Six out of ten of my family members are drunks, and three out of the remaining four probably would be if we started drinking. You can carry the genes for alcoholism, but if you manage to push away the bottle, you won't trigger the disease. Have you had your genome checked?"

"Let me save you some time," I said, standing. "I don't do drugs and I don't need a DNA scan to know I'm not my father."

She squinted a little at me. "Family history is a predictor of future problems. Everybody has something."

"Thanks for the advice." I took a step towards the door.

"Do you have nightmares yet?" Her words hit my back.

Everybody's worried how I sleep these days. I paused at the door and looked back, saying nothing, but she knew.

Nodding, Redhawk took off her thick lenses and rubbed her eyes. She looked older without the glasses, the pouches under the eyes more pronounced. "Your father was a different man before the drugs got him," she said. "He helped me out of a jam once. I can't pay him back, but maybe I can help his son. You're still young. It's not too late to think about a career change."

"Are you saying the department will find a way to fire my ass?"

"I'm saying maybe you should quit. Before you turn into one of those cops who's already dead but just hasn't laid down yet."

"Consider your debt paid," I said. "But I have a job to do."

CHAPTER THIRTY-ONE

LEAVING THE SEE CAVE, I TOOK THE STAIRS TWO AT A TIME back down to the third floor and HSS. I tried not to think about the possibility of the Department brass moving me out of Homicide Special, but the tick-tock was palpable. How long would I have to find out who'd killed Frank, Britney, and Dr. Lee?

This time the gauntlet of detectives as I walked to my desk was a series of nodding heads and tentative smiles.

Shin wasn't back yet. He'd taken the search warrant to the Lees' Palisades' home. Once I'd logged the flash dot with the security footage from the Clara Vista Casino in as evidence, I sat down at my desk across from Shin's empty seat and started to slog through the footage.

An hour later I'd finished scanning one disk when the clatter from the hallway announced Shin's return.

"How'd it go?" he asked, laying his suit jacket over his chair.

"My bank account's lighter by four more deployment periods, but you have your partner back. For now." We knuckle-bumped over the desks, and I explained the fallout from the hearing. "They may move me to Traffic by 2042."

"That'll never happen," Shin said. "Anybody who's seen you drive knows you'd be a menace in Traffic."

"That's reassuring. Anything turn up on the search of Lee's place?"

"We found this." Shin reached down and pulled an evidence bag from his jacket pocket with a flourish worthy of a Las Vegas magician. The bag was filled with green ice, the same drug that had killed Britney Devonshire. "And these." Shin held up another bag filled with syringes still in their packaging. "We're running a check on all phones and phablets."

Until we found another copy of Lee's work on a home machine, the flashdot I'd lifted from Lee's trash in Clara Vista and left with Denver had just tripled its value.

"We're a long way from proving Mrs. Lee's involvement, let alone a murder charge. Still, between the drugs," Shin continued, waving the bag of ice, "Lee's bacterial cloud and the print we found at the Devonshire girl's, we have cause for a formal interview with Mrs. Lee about her deceased husband."

The casino footage continued to play as Shin spoke. What I saw out of the corner of my eye made my shoulders slump. I let out a low hiss.

"What?" Shin ambled over and stood at my shoulder.

The feed from Camera Three of the Clara Vista Casino parking lot focused on the area where Lee's Lexus had stood. Camera Four featured the area where Frank sat on stakeout outside the casino—in the car he'd died in.

There was Frank, huffing and puffing as he walked back to his Toyota to wait.

At the sight of my old partner sitting himself down in his own car like it was any ordinary day, I felt icy invisible hands grab hold of my guts and twist.

Before long, Frank's head bobbed.

"So you were right about Frank nodding off," Shin said. "How long until you show on the vid?"

"My call woke him up here." I fast-forwarded to the point on the dot where Frank woke. "I pulled into the lot about ten minutes later," I said, noting the time code into the record. "Let's see what happened during that ten minute gap."

I toggled back to Camera Three. As if on cue, a skinny guy wearing Nike-3000's, jeans, and a hoodie entered from the left side of the screen. Under the hoodie he wore a Dodgers baseball cap pulled low over his face. Hello, hello.

"Do you have a closer angle on him we can run through facial recognition?" Shin said.

"No need." Baseball cap or no, it was a face I recognized. "His name's Harvey Pink. He's an addict and an agitator at Genesys where Lee worked. I saw him there myself." I filled Shin in on what the Genesys CEO had said about Pink's history with that company.

Shin read my mind. "If he's an agitator, maybe this could be tied to their cause."

"Activists don't hide their actions," I said, "and make them look like accidents. They want credit to advance the cause."

"Depends on the action," Shin said.

On the vid, Pink held a brown paper bag with something rectangular-shaped inside. Shin and I watched as Pink approached Lee's Lexus. He had a slight twitch to his step, and his tense shoulders were hunched up near his ears. Pink walked round the car, stopping near the rear passenger door on the driver's side—next to the gas tank. He knelt suddenly as if to tie his shoe, but Nike 3000's fastened with Velcro, not laces. He reached under the car.

"There." I froze the frame and printed it.

We couldn't see what Pink had put under the chassis. His angled body blocked the view, but there was no doubt he'd tampered with Lee's car. When he stood back up, the paper bag in Pink's hands was empty. Asleep, Frank had missed it. And that tiny lapse had cost my partner his life.

"Well," Shin said. "That's solid evidence Lee's death wasn't an accident. But it blows a hole in your theory that Mrs. Lee was behind her husband's death."

"Unless she hired Pink," I said. "According to Lee's boss, he had it in for Lee. She might have met him outside Genesys. Let's see what Pink has to say before we talk to the widow."

CHAPTER THIRTY-TWO

I SPAT THE NAME HARVEY PINK INTO THE CALIFORNIA DEPARTMENT of Justice voice-activated information network and got a hit. Pink'd been popped three times before 2030. Like many an addict in need of cash to fuel his habit, he'd strewn criminal breadcrumbs all over town, jacking money from an unlocked car here, perpetrating a little B&E there. On collar number three, Pink had spent some time behind bars.

That must have been where he found God. Pink was paroled September 1, 2041. Upon release, he'd suddenly demonstrated an obsession with pro-life activism, practically taking up residence outside Genesys. Pink already had a protest-related citation for rock throwing and a recent restraining order against him.

"The rock throwing fits with what Maclaren told me about somebody exercising his pitching arm on Lee's windows," I said.

"We'll need to get hold of those Genesys security disks too," Shin said. "We have to at least consider the option this Harvey Pink is behind it all, but I don't buy it."

"Agreed. He vibes too small time for a double-homicide perpetrator," I said. "And a guy who gets caught on petty theft and B&E isn't smart enough to engineer these two deaths."

I linked to the county probation department and traded Pink's name and DOJ number for his current address.

Shin nodded. "Plus, why would he target the Devonshire girl? If he did."

I paused. "Let's ask him."

An hour later we found Pink's address on a converted garage tucked away on a rundown street in Van Nuys. The street had peeling paint on all the houses and multiple cars spilling out of the driveways. Other vehicles sat on blocks on the parched lawns.

The bell on the house with Pink's address didn't work. Shin

knocked, but Pink didn't answer. He hadn't bothered to put any curtains on the windows, so I walked around the place and peered in. A sagging couch with stains on the faded green fabric, and a folding card table with scratched legs, were the only furniture in the living room—except for a 2041 4D virtual reality wall-film television so new the sticker was still on the bottom corner. Some ultimate caged fight was playing—Apollo Silver versus some other steroidal wonder. This set up would put the viewer ringside—close enough to feel the streams of sweat and blood shooting off the fighters.

The goggle-eyed Oculus VR helmet that made a viewer look like a black lacquered praying mantis had fallen to the floor. Pink was slumped on the couch in front of the screen. His head had fallen back. His mouth was open, and there was drool all over his already none too clean T-shirt.

A smear of greenish white powder lay on a piece of cardboard next to the spoon and matches he'd used to cook the drug and the dirty syringe that must have injected it not long ago. Pink had the sickly greenish yellow pallor, loose skin, and rotting teeth that brand all long-time slaves to the Green Demon.

"Green Ice," Shin said. "That explains the minimalist décor. The furniture probably went to pay for his habit."

I nodded. "So, where'd he'd get the cash for the TV?" I activated my glove phone and shot a little footage of Pink at home, making sure he was clearly visible in the same frame as the drugs. Drug use was a major parole violation. That gave us probable cause to enter. I turned the knob. The door wasn't locked, so I let us in.

"Hey, whaddya doing?" He raised his bleary-eyed head and struggled to get up, but the drug in his veins pinned him down. "Who the fuck are you?" Pink yelled in a slurred voice. Recognition slowly swam through the glaze in his eyes. "Oh shit."

While Shin went through the rest of the house, I pulled Pink to his feet, shoved him up against the wall, spreading his legs with my foot, and patted him down. "Wake up, Harvey," I said, spinning him round. "We've met before. Outside Genesys. Remember? I've got some questions for you."

When I spun him around again and released him abruptly, Pink thumped back into his seat on the couch and oozed back down into his former semi-recumbent posture.

I loomed over him. "What were you doing in Clara Vista last Friday, Harvey?"

"Clara Vista?" Pink's face showed a lot of rapid blinking and a mouth gaping open like a fish. "I doan know what you're talkin' about."

"I have security footage from the casino parking lot if that'll help jog your memory," I said. "So, let's try again. What were you doing there?"

"None of your fuckin' business." He rubbed his eyes.

"My case, my business. And you violated parole here, Harvey." I reached down for the piece of cardboard under Pink's used syringe on the table, flipping it over. The cardboard serving as the base for Pink's works had been torn from a box housing what looked like the TV remote. Only half a picture of something black with the words "titanium alloy" remained.

I picked up the remote. It was black plastic inside what looked like a titanium casing. "Nice TV," I said. "Expensive, huh?"

"Hey, give that back." Pink grabbed for the remote.

"You've got a real bug problem, Harvey. Cockroaches. Let me help you with that." I let the remote drop to the floor and stomped on the black plastic. The image on the screen of the two fighters froze.

"Aww—fuck!" Pink groaned. With difficulty, he pulled himself up to an upright sit and shot me an angry glance.

No way this guy had taken out Lee on his own. Not to mention Frank. I ground the broken plastic with my heel. "Last Friday, Harvey. Clara Vista Casino. Your memory coming back yet?"

That's when he rushed me. And somehow managed to smash his balls into my fist. Pink shrieked, sank to his knees, and groaned again.

"Everything okay, Eddie?" Shin's voice called out from the back of the house.

"Fine, here." I waited for Pink's eyes to roll back into place and his breathing and color to resume.

"We're talking homicide of a retired cop," I said, "and murder one of a world-renowned scientist you're on record for harassing. You'll never see the light of day again, Pink."

"What?!" he cried. "I didn't kill anybody!"

The image on the casino security disks played back in my head—Pink kneeling down to put something under the chassis of Lee's car—dissolving into the fireball that had been Frank's Toyota.

"You tampered with that Lexus in Clara Vista," I snapped. "You caused that crash. That's murder, Pink."

"That's right." Shin nodded from the doorway.

Pink was looking confused now. Anxiety was mounting on his face.

"We don't want to charge you with murder, but we will." I shoved him deeper into the cushions of the couch. "What did you put under the chassis?"

"I didn't mean for anybody to die," he whined, eyes richocheting back and forth between Shin and me. "I swear I didn't."

I stepped back and regarded him. Pink's defiant posture collapsed like a balloon losing air all at once.

"You know what, Harvey? I believe you."

"Me too," Shin echoed. "You're just the fall guy."

"But unless you tell us what you put under that car," I continued, "and the name of the person who hired you to put it there, you're going down anyway."

"Don't make me go back," he pleaded. Pink leaned down, arms over his head. He wiped the snot from his nose with the palm of his hand.

"It's looking bad for you, Harvey. Help yourself here."

"I didn't even know whose car it was until I saw the news that night," he whined, wringing his hands, tears streaming down his filthy face. "It was supposed to be a joke—you know. He said the owner of the Lexus was screwing around on his wife, and they wanted to catch him in the act, and put it on the net."

"He?"

"The guy who paid me to stick a GPS tracker under the car."

Pink pointed to the bagged remnant of cardboard box that had been under his works, the one that looked like a television remote. "There's the box for the tracker. Part of it anyway."

"Who's the guy?" I said, eyeing the cardboard. The brand name had been torn off too. There was no identifier on it. "What's his name?"

"I don't know his name," Pink wailed. "Not his real name. His tag's Apollo."

“Right.” I glanced back up at the television wall screen with the frozen image of the caged fighters, one of whom was named Apollo Silver. Pink wasn’t even a good liar.

“How’d you meet this Apollo?”

“At an NA meeting,” Pink stammered. “I was clean. I swear. He’s the one got me started using again.”

“Describe him,” I said, “this guy you met at Narcotics Anonymous.”

“Young, Asian, not so tall as you. I think he’s prob-ly a med student cuz of the T-shirts,” Pink said, his head moving up and down like an antique bobble-head toy. “He always wears these T-shirts with equations and shit. And he’s got money. Rides a nice bike. A rice rocket.”

Shin and I exchanged a glance. Then I pulled up a sixpack of pictures on my glove phone, swapped one out for another shot, and held it out for Pink to see. “Any of these guys Apollo?”

He blinked a few times and peered, eyes narrowed. “Him. I think it’s him.” Pink pointed to the headshot on the bottom right.

“You think, or you know, Harvey?”

“It’s him. It wasn’t me. I swear.”

I looked down at the picture of the surly kid Pink had identified. I showed it to Shin. The picture was Raymond Lee.

CHAPTER THIRTY-THREE

CUFFED AND TUCKED INTO THE BACK SEAT OF THE DETECTIVE sedan, Harvey Pink slumped against the window as we took the 101 back downtown to Nokia P.D.

God, Pink stank. I raised the soundproof barrier between the seats.

Pink had identified Raymond Lee as the guy who'd given him the gizmo he'd put under Ray's father's car.

"Raymond's an engineering student at Cal Tech," Shin said. "He'd have the savvy to engineer a remote explosive of some kind."

"Yeah. And Pink's little narrative about how they'd wanted to catch Dr. Lee cheating on his wife hints at the involvement of more than just Ray. I'm guessing Mrs. Lee roped her son into it."

We rode in silence for a few miles. Then I put in a call to Tony Gomez, the automotive forensics expert on the Clara Vista crash.

"You find something on the underside of Lee's Lexus?"

"What, are you clairvoyant?" Tony shouted, wiping grease and sweat from his other hand on his green coveralls. "Hold on." The clanking din inside the automotive forensics unit was muted as he moved outside for the call. "This model Lexus chassis is comprised of carbon fiber," Tony said, standing on the tarmac outside the forensics garage now. "Or should be. But when I did a metallurgic analysis, I found an anomaly. A metal that shouldn't be there. Titanium."

I glanced at the evidence bag on the front seat between Shin and me. Shin lifted up the bag with the piece of cardboard from Pink's place and tapped the letters "Titanium alloy." I sighed. "Thanks, Tony."

Harvey Pink was snoring now, his mouth open, his cheek pressed flat against the glass.

"You don't sound as surprised as I was," Tony said, "or as happy as I thought you'd be."

Shin and I drove on in silence. In some remote corner of my mind, a tiny window of irrational hope I hadn't even been aware of closed. It was official. Lee's death was no accident. Which meant neither was Frank's. Sometimes you don't want to be right.

CHAPTER THIRTY-FOUR

RAYMOND LEE WAS REGISTERED AT CALTECH FOR ADVANCED mechanical engineering, robotics, and fluid dynamics this term. Engineering some sort of IED to rupture the fuel line to his dad's car should be in his playbook, but I needed confirmation and specifics. So while Shin charged Pink and got him seated in an interview room, I went to get it.

Attractive and surprisingly human-scaled, the CalTech campus boasted lots of low-slung off-white buildings and plenty of places to sit outside under old oaks with a cup of coffee as you pondered the mysteries of dark matter.

Professor Paul Reiter had agreed to meet me at one of the tables planted next to the campus Starbucks under a cluster of old oaks. The thirty-something man who matched Professor Reiter's online photo barely looked up from his glove-phone as I flashed him my badge and introduced myself. I sat opposite him across a worn table with several generations of students' names scratched into the white paint. Immortality on the cheap.

Reiter was a thin hollow-chested man. His lank reddish-blond hair was pinned atop his head in a man-bun, anchored by thick black plastic glasses with a kind of geek-chic. He wore a plaid shirt older than he was over faded black jeans. The robo-server read our barcodes and gave us our orders, a shot of coffee snuff for him and a cup of bad java from burned beans for me. I waited as Reiter peeled the foil top from the little silver shot cup of espresso crystals and raised it to one nostril. He took a snort as I navigated away from the obligatory small talk to queries about Raymond Lee.

"Was Lee in class on October 6th from two to five p.m.?" I asked.

Reiter called up the attendance roster on his glove phone. "The auto-roster doesn't show him logged in that day."

"Does he miss a lot of classes?"

"Lately he does." Reiter nervously tapped his steepled fingers against his lips. "His work has fallen off. I understand there are some problems at home."

I nodded. "He talk to you about that?"

"No. After midterms and before final exams, Student Health sends us notices about students struggling with severe anxiety and depression. With student permission, of course."

"You got a notice about Ray?"

Reiter's turn to nod.

"Did you see signs that he was self-medicating?

"I don't want to speculate. And he's a good student otherwise," Reiter said hurriedly. "One of my best, actually."

"Good enough to alter a GPS tracker?"

Professor Reiter pulled his glasses down from the top of his head and peered at me. "Alter how?"

"Into something that could cause a fuel line on a Lexus to rupture?" I pulled out the piece of cardboard Harvey Pink had given me. "This is the equipment we're talking about."

Professor Reiter picked up the piece of cardboard and examined it from several angles. Reiter slouched so much that when he angled his own body to examine the cardboard in the dappled sunlight streaming through the oak leaves, he looked like a backlit question mark.

"You wouldn't need to alter much," Reiter said. He tapped the words "titanium alloy" on the box. "I can't be sure without more detail, but I don't think this is a GPS tracker."

"What is it—exactly?"

"We call them disrupters. DARPA declassified them a few years ago."

DARPA was the research and development group that worked on top secret defense technology and scenarios for the government.

"They resemble GPS trackers externally," Reiter continued, "but they release nano-bots you control remotely or via a timer."

"The microscopic robots used in surgery and construction?"

Reiter nodded.

"So somebody could release these nano-bots and direct them to cause a fuel leak or shut down transmission, if this disrupter was affixed to the underside of a car?" I flashed on the pink trail of fluid spraying from Dr. Lee's Lexus.

"They can perform multiple functions," Reiter said. "That's what makes disrupters so useful. Very versatile. They were initially designed for remote control of rovers on Mars."

"You said they were declassified. How would a civilian get hold of one?"

"Oh, they're available in a limited way now," the professor said. "We use them."

"In robotics?"

He paused. "Some of my students do work at JPL for the Mars and lunar rovers. When parts break down on another planet, we can't just send a repair team. We use remote control nano-bots to do repairs."

"That's a pretty powerful tool. Do you take precautions about access?"

Reiter nodded. "Disrupters are registered like explosives or poisons. Homeland Security keeps track."

"Do you keep a copy of that log? For your robotics classes? I'll need to see it."

He nodded and began to root through his glove phone files. "Here we are." The professor bumped the information to my phone.

His face told me even before I looked that Raymond's name was on the list.

"Of course, I collect them back from the students at the end of term," Professor Reiter said. Or deactivate those we can't recover. We've never had a problem."

There it was: the perpetual refrain cops hear when we're mopping up after a tragedy. He was such a nice guy, a quiet neighbor, kept to himself. Nobody can believe that silent cypher could—fill in the blank—rob a friend, murder his father, or blow himself and half the city to smithereens. But the evidence says different. That's the dark matter in the human soul.

"I don't think you'll be getting Ray's disrupter back, Professor," I said. "But let's put the request on record. Text him now and let me know if he responds."

The flesh on Professor Reiter's face sagged as he watched me leave moments later.

Raymond Lee didn't pick up Reiter's text about the disrupter. Further checks with the rest of Ray's professors told the same sad story.

As I walked back across campus to my car an hour after that, I spotted students perched on the roof of one of the taller buildings chucking a giant pumpkin to the ground where it splattered with a satisfying thunk. It was a Caltech Halloween tradition. I found myself humming a remix of the Smashing Pumpkins' alt-rock anthem "Disarm." The killer in me is the killer in you. What I choose is my choice.

It was time to bring Raymond Lee in.

CHAPTER THIRTY-FIVE

INITIAL QUESTIONING OF RAYMOND LEE WENT NOWHERE. We had seventy-two hours to hold him before charging or releasing him in connection with the murder of his father. Witness testimony and circumstantial evidence linked him to the nano-bot that caused the crash, but a good lawyer, like the one Raymond's mother had hired, could poke holes in that easy. We needed Pink to pick Ray out of a line-up.

My phone pinged. I looked down to see the floating face of the desk sergeant.

"There's a Mercedes Delblanco wants to talk to you, detective," the sergeant said. "Should I put her through?"

Mercedes Delblanco—the name pinged too. She was the Latina with the raven-wing hair from Sandy Beaches Gentleman's Club and Britney Devonshire's best friend.

"Put her through."

"Detective Piedmont?" Her voice was a hoarse whisper. The base from some pop song pounded its way through the blue-gray walls littered with graffiti behind her head. She was speaking on her glove phone from inside a stall in the ladies' room of the club.

Mercedes leaned in so close to the phone's wide angle lens that the face floating before me was suddenly distorted like it had been stretched tight—over a globe. Under the fluorescents of the ladies' room, I saw her eyebrows had been plucked to oblivion and redrawn with a single arch of black ink like a butterfly's antenna. Mercedes' lips were painted violet, but there was a gap between the edge of the natural lip and the hard outline of deep purple. It reminded me of little girls who couldn't color within the lines.

Mercedes scrutinized my face too. What she found satisfied her enough to continue. "You're the cop who came to the club. The one handling Brit's case. Britney Devonshire?"

"How can I help you?"

The image shifted vertiginously as she leaned down and peered out from under the stall. Hers were the only pair of feet in the bathroom.

"You know the Lotus Eaters in East Hollywood?" she asked, jerking the camera up again as she stood up.

"The vaping lounge on Vine and 3rd?" That was the boutique marijuana shop that had paid Britney Devonshire for her derma ad.

She nodded. "Meet me there in a half-hour."

"Come downtown," I said. "I'm in the middle of . . ."

She shook her head violently. "If Sandy knew I talked to you . . ." She glanced at me, then turned her eyes away. "I could be next."

"Make it an hour," I said. "See you there."

Forty minutes later, I strode into The Lotus Eaters, a vaping lounge with clouds of steam twirling in pirouettes overhead and Wi-Fi at every table.

It took me a second to recognize the woman sitting in the back was Mercedes. She wore a gray hoodie over black yoga pants. The garish makeup was gone, the blue-black hair pulled straight back from her face tied into a knot at the nape of her neck. Makeup-free Mercedes looked ten years younger. She spotted me right away and gestured to the seat opposite with a sidelong glance.

I took the seat and ordered a cup of expresso from the auto-server on the table. "You want anything?"

Mercedes shook her head and took a hit from the dragon-headed hookah planted at her feet. When she pursed her lips and exhaled a cloud of cherry-vanilla-scented steam, she looked like a cute baby dragon herself.

"What is it Sandy doesn't want you to tell me?"

Mercedes took another quick hit and wrapped the edges of the hoodie around her a little bit tighter. "That Brit didn't O.D. on Green Ice like they said. She was murdered."

I waited until the human server suddenly at my elbow set my expresso down on the table and left. The coffee's aroma did battle with the sweet cherry-vanilla. "I know," I said, tasting the dark rich liquid. "But I need proof."

"I'm telling you," Mercedes said, her face flushed. "No way she O.D'd. No way. Brit didn't use. Not for a long time." Mercedes crossed her short but shapely legs, the knee bobbing up and down in counterpoint to the rhythm of the trance music playing in the lounge.

"Proof," I said again. "How can you know for sure she didn't inject the ice herself?"

"Cuz Sandy got us both drug tested every month. Brit was clean. She wouldn't have been cleared to sell if she failed the test."

"Sell?" I leaned forward, cupping my hand tight round the expresso's white ceramic. I wasn't surprised that Sandy Rose had lied to Shin and me about the club's drug tests being random, but this was something else again. "Was Brit hooking for Sandy?"

Mercedes opened her mouth to say something, then closed it. Her knee started to bob faster. She looked round the lounge like she expected her employer to pop out at any moment. "Not hooking, just selling. Eggs."

"Eggs?" The trance music in the lounge wasn't that loud, but I thought I must have heard her wrong.

"Yeah," she said. "There's good money in the fertility biz. It's legal, mostly, but Sandy's not down with us doing side deals." She paused and shivered, turning her head back towards me.

"Britney was an egg donor." I sat back in my chair. "The tracks," I said, remembering Britney Devonshire's dead body draped in her bathtub. "The tracks on Britney's hips. Fertility drugs?"

Mercedes's knee stopped bobbing. "Yeah," she said. "Brit showed me how to shoot up the hormones so the marks don't show when we dance."

There had been three sets of tracks on Britney's corpse—the red dot on her forearm that marked the latest, lethal shot, the recent tracks on the dead girl's hips versus the older ones between her toes or under her toe nails. Finally they made sense.

"So you girls were the egg donors," I said. "Sandy made the arrangements. Who's the buyer?" At Frank's funeral Raymond Lee had said something about not knowing any of those women. His cryptic line started to make another kind of sense.

"That fertility clinic," Mercedes replied. "Baby Mine."

The company's inane smiling baby logo flashed to mind. Baby Mine sat next to Genesys Pharma in Sun Valley. Genesys—Dr.

Lee's employer. Lee was a genetic researcher, a guy who needed eggs for his work. One stop shopping.

"How much does it pay?"

"Depends," she said. "Smart pretty Asians get the most. Blonde college girls after that." Mercedes snorted in derision. "Everybody who isn't Asian wants that Ivy League prom queen look."

"Ballpark, how much money are we talking?"

"Depends on how many good eggs you make that month with the drugs," she said. "Girls eighteen to twenty-four get sixty to one hundred K each cycle. Less for older girls. You can't donate more than twice a year though."

If ten or twenty girls from the club were paid sixty to one hundred thousand for two cycles, how much did Sandy clear? I started the rough calculation. "You mentioned a side deal."

She nodded. "There was this guy, the scientist."

"Dr. Lee?" I pulled up a picture on my phone and held it out for her.

Her chin jerked up and she nodded. "Yeah, that's him. He approached me and Brit about doing this deal on the side. Said he'd pay cash up-front and our boss would never be the wiser. I told Brit not to cross Sandy. That she's in bed with some bad people, gangs, but Brit didn't listen. She needed money, and she said she had insurance."

"Insurance?" Britney had blackmailed Lee. With what exactly? Had she threatened to tell his employer about the off-book deal?

Mercedes shrugged. "She wouldn't explain. Just smiled like that cat in *Alice In Wonderland*. Brit agreed to do the deal. The next thing I know she's dead, and you show up at the club asking questions." She took another long deep pull on the hookah and exhaled a plume of steam long and full as a mare's tail. "Sandy can't know I told you."

I reached over, took her phone hand, and bumped my direct line into her contact list. "Call me anytime, day or night. Do you have someplace you could go? If you need to move fast? Family or friends out of town?"

She nodded.

"Now would be a good time to visit them." I paid the bill and started to leave.

Mercedes remained sitting for a second longer. Her eyes had

gone steely. “I hope you get them,” she said. “Those murdering bastards. Britney was my friend. I don’t have many friends.”

I nodded. At the door, I paused and looked back. Mercedes had already disappeared out the rear exit. The door closed behind her with a soft click.

What had Britney and Lee gotten themselves into? And how did Harvey Pink, Raymond Lee and his mother fit into this mess? Another rabbit hole had just opened up.

CHAPTER THIRTY-SIX

I HEADED OUT OF THE LOTUS EATERS PARKING LOT WITH more than cherry-vanilla steam clouding my thoughts. I'd driven around for several minutes without really tracking where I was going, my foot as heavy on the accelerator as a steel diving boot.

My conversation with Lee's employer came back to me as I turned onto Vine. Maclaren had told me how difficult it was for scientists to get viable embryos for genomic research. Dr. Lee had been an ambitious man, and he was under enough pressure to produce results that he needed a sabbatical for nerves.

My own research showed he'd also cut some ethical corners in the past. Say Mercedes was on the level and Sandy Rose had provided Lee with a way to cut through that bureaucratic red tape. She'd furnished him a hassle-free and virtually endless stream of viable blackmarket eggs he could use in his Alzheimers X research. Sandy would charge a hefty fee on top of the other expenses, and Lee was a man with a gambling addiction and money problems. Enter Britney undercutting her employer with a discount side deal.

If Sandy, or the people she ran with, had found out that one of her girls and a client had cut her out? Some people would kill for a lot less than that.

Then Britney had taken that step too far, blackmailing Lee. More pieces started to fall into place.

I pulled onto the 101 South and headed back towards Nokia PD.

The green and white off-ramp sign for Benton Way had just flashed by when my call to Shin went through.

"Bad news," Shin said before I could update him. "We've gotta cut Raymond Lee loose."

My foot came off the pedal. The car hiccoughed until I eased my foot back down on the accelerator. "Pink recanted in the line-up?"

"Suddenly all Asians look alike," Shin said, pulling a face and nodding. "We can sweat him, but the D.A. doesn't think any jury would convict Raymond on Pink's word at this point. Even with the nano-bot info and the Green Ice we found in his room."

"Let Raymond go for now," I said. "We've got a new scenario to consider."

Shin stared at me, head cocked, eyebrows raised so high they almost brushed his hairline. "I'm all ears."

"Maybe the reason it's so hard to make the pieces fit is that we've been looking at the picture from the wrong angle. What if Britney wasn't blackmailing Lee about an affair at all?" I filled Shin in on what had gone down in my interview with Mercedes Delblanco.

He sat there cracking his knuckles as he took it all in. "So Britney goes against Sandy to make this side deal with Lee," Shin said when I'd finished. "Then she turns around and uses the deal to blackmail him. So he kills her."

"Or he turned around and came clean to Sandy Rose," I said, "and she took care of the problem." I remembered the gang tats on Sandy's security personnel. "Mercedes said Sandy ran with a rough crew. Once Britney was dead, Sandy figured everything would go back to normal; Lee has learned his lesson, and she holds the whip."

"Only the scientist is so shaken up," Shin said, "he panics and runs."

"Or makes a bigger mistake," I said. "Tells Sandy he's gonna come clean to his employer and the police."

"O-kay," Shin said. "But how does that tie in with Harvey Pink, Raymond, Lee, and the nano-bot detonator?"

"Somebody had to take the fall. Harvey's tailor-made for the job. And she can use him to implicate Lee's son Raymond. That gives her even more leverage over the Lees. You've got to hand it to Sandy. She's a strategic thinker."

"So, tell me," Shin said. "Is all this just a hunch, or do you have actual proof?"

"When you put it that way, it sounds mildly insulting."

He sighed. "Looks like another long night researching Sandy

Rose and the Baby Mine clinic. Let's make sure this Delblanco girl isn't pulling our chain."

"I trust you to handle it in your usual excellent fashion," I said, turning off the freeway.

"Me? Where are you going?"

"To see a girl about a file."

CHAPTER THIRTY-SEVEN

Given Mercedes' new information on Lee's true connection to Britney Devonshire, access to his research files had inched up even higher on my list of priorities. So twenty minutes later, I eased the nose of my Porsche into a spot opposite the café two doors down from the Bradley Building on Broadway and West Third.

The Scratching Post was one of those downtown pet cafés where people who live in animal-free zones come to get their fix. People like Denver Lakshmi. From the door, I saw felines sitting on the shoulders of the red leather booths and winding their way through the forest of human legs under tables.

Denver was seated in a booth on the right. Her black hair had cobalt blue streaks today. They matched her iridescent nails and the fitted dress that looked like something from a digital ad for some new flavored vodka. Somehow the look suited her.

"It's a good thing I'm not allergic," I said, gesturing to the fat orange tomcat sprawled on her lap.

"You're the one wanted to meet on my therapy night," she replied. "Besides, they're mostly animatronic. Or bred allergen free like Tomaso here. So stop your bitching. We have to make this quick. Diamond Dog is meeting my parents at Vegan Heaven tonight at eight." She petted the cat. He purred on cue.

"Your show." I pulled out a chair from the neighboring table and straddled it. "Just give me the update on Lee's files. You able to salvage anything?"

"Most is damaged and almost all is encrypted."

"Tell me something I don't know. Did you break the encryption?"

"Don't tell them, but I networked our computers in with UCLA's for a brute force assault. It should have been enough to break through."

"But it didn't?" I didn't hide my disappointment.

"I don't think Lee used any typical encryption program," she replied, pushing the cat off her lap and straightening her dress. Then her hair. "He may have gone old school, used a key."

"One of those words I gave you before?" I thought back to the cryptic names and numbers Lee had blurted out before death: Father, Fuentes, 333-1110.

She pulled a long face and shook her head.

"You said almost all is encrypted," I said. "What's not?

"His vid-diary." She grinned. "Something he did for rehab—one of his twelve steps. I tried to watch, but it's boring as hell. Depressing too. Lee was such a lonely old guy."

"I'll watch it later. Did anything connect with—"

"—3331110?" Denver's broad smile lit her face. "Watch this. File menu," she said, loading the memory dot. A list of files popped up, floating in the air before us. "This encrypted stuff over here—" She pointed to a column of symbols and numbers, pulling them over with her fingers so the electric green digits swam closer. "—has been damaged." She touched one of the encrypted files with her right index finger. "But take a look at the file save option." As I followed the dance of her fingers in air, the name of the file to be saved came up, clearly legible.

3331110 wasn't a phone or serial number, but part of the name on Lee's encrypted file—AI3331110.doc.

"Awesome," I said as we knuckle-bumped. "What's the AI for, artificial intelligence?"

"Like I know. That's your department."

Grinning at Denver, I didn't stop her going on about the vocal command software connection being damaged and defaulting to the original keystrokes. All I cared about was that the name of the file we were staring at matched the number Lee had muttered at his death.

"Great. Now all we have to do is break the encryption on the file itself to find out what's in there."

"We?" Denver said in a tone dripping derision.

"I provide the pertinent questions, necessary incentive and moral support. Copy me on the vidlog."

"You're too predictable," she said, holding out a flash-dot, the fingernail-sized memory stick with the vidlog already loaded.

"Don't ever try to hack. You'd be toast."

"Reliable," I countered, pulling her into my arms for a quick hug. "Not predictable."

"Hottie that you are, you're too late, Piedmont." She waved her left hand, engagement ring flashing at me. "I'm already taken. Remember?"

"Diamond Dog's a lucky guy." I winked and released her. "Let me know as soon as you break that encryption." I started to head out.

"Yeah," she said, yelling at my retreating back. "I got a life now you know, Piedmont. You should get one yourself."

I smiled all the way to the car and headed home, eager to pop Lee's vlog into the computer and see what answers it held in its digital keep.

CHAPTER THIRTY-EIGHT

JO'S CAR WASN'T IN THE DRIVEWAY WHEN I ARRIVED HOME forty-five minutes later. But my phone pinged before I'd turned off the engine.

The caller wasn't Jo. I stared at my mother's face without picking up, listening as she left me a message. My junkie father was in the hospital again. No surprise there. They don't parole a prisoner on compassionate leave unless he's pretty much circling the drain. He wanted to see me. I deleted the message and went inside the house.

I turned my glove phone to vibrate and sank down into the butter-soft cushions of Jo's white leather couch with a bottle of Kirin Lime and a bowl of blue corn chips and salsa. I started to watch Lee's vlog, searching for a flesh-out of his connection to Britney Devonshire and the Baby Mine Clinic, Sandy Rose, or any reference to Fuentes and the file number AI333-1110.

According to the time-code, the diary stretched back ten years, but it was sporadic with big gaps in some years. Lee had compartmentalized the vlog into discreet sections—like his life. At a later date I'd watch the whole vlog frame by frame, but the answers I needed now were most likely sown in the last few entries before his death. I fast-forwarded towards the end.

As the image skidded ahead towards the present, the office in Lee's vlog maintained the same bland background, but computer format changed with the years. I whirred through earlier entries lacking the holographic function with its 3D form, stopping once more in 2041 to let the vlog play in real time. His image now floated before me like a digital ghost.

Lee had grown out his hair long enough that it brushed the collarbone beneath his unbuttoned shirt. The dark circles under his eyes were pronounced. He carried himself differently from the guy glimpsed at the beginning as well, shoulders curving inward toward his core.

Denver was right. It was depressing stuff. He yammered on about his gambling addiction, money problems, and arguments with his wife and the alienated son.

Just when I was beginning to think the entire vlog was nothing but an endless litany of complaints, the scientist made another entry. Two weeks before his fatal crash.

"I can't believe it," he'd wailed. "How could this happen? All I ever wanted was to help people." He paused, knuckles white as he grasped his left hand with his right. "Sure, I hoped my name would be up there with the giants one day. When I earned it. Was that so terrible? I made one little mistake and the next thing I know, things have gotten completely out of hand. Now they've gone and paroled that asshole. Oh, my God. What have I done?"

I paused the vlog and took a deep pull on the bottle of Kirin.

Harvey Pink was paroled September 18th of this year. The timing fit. I sat up straighter, leaning in toward the digital image as I hit play again.

Lee's voice sounded like his throat had been scraped raw. "I have to put it right. For my son, if not for me. I should have put a stop to things a lot sooner."

The last entry was short. "Fuentes is dead," Lee said, his face expressionless. "There's no way out. They'll come for me next." He paused.

Fuentes again. I stopped the vlog. It was the same Fuentes Lee had said was a dead man right before Lee himself died in the crash. But the time-code pushed this reference three weeks earlier. Who the hell was this Fuentes? I rewound and let it play through this time.

"Fuentes is dead. There's no way out. They'll come for me next. Then Piedmont. It will end like it began." Lee's image vanished.

"What the . . .?" Thinking I'd heard it wrong, I rewound and played that last bit back. No mistake. Piedmont.

I rechecked the date. No mistake. How the hell had my name dropped into Lee's world over a week before I'd first shown up at the door to his home in the Palisades?

I sat there motionless, mind racing, staring at the empty blue screen as the vlog went to white noise.

BOOK FOUR

The sins of the father are visited upon the son.
—*Exodus* 20.5

I was much too far out all my life /
And not waving but drowning.
—Stevie Smith

CHAPTER THIRTY-NINE

THE SHOCK OF HEARING LEE MENTION MY NAME IN HIS VLOG rooted me to that couch. Only the sound of another voice, emanating from my phone, shook me free. My mother was crying. I was just about to pick up the call when she said my father was in the hospital. Again. I left my finger hovering above the "accept call" icon.

"Please come, Eddie," she said. "I know you have issues with your dad. But he's your dad."

Issues. I took slow, even breaths, but fatigue and everything else must have weakened my internal firewalls. My fifteen-year-old self shoved his way through and tapped me on the shoulder. He dragged me back fourteen years.

The thermometer had topped 112 degrees by noon that July 4th, 2026. The fridge had been empty at breakfast—except for half a can of tuna and some moldy cheese.

I'd spent the day working next door. My neighbor, Mr. Santiago, was putting on a new roof. He threw me some cash in exchange for my help. Hot and sweaty, my stomach growling, I'd staggered home with a bag of groceries after a ten-hour day. My mom was lying down upstairs. I started to unload the carton of milk, some sandwich meat, and bread into the fridge.

I smelled him before I saw him. My father plopped down on a chair at the dining room table, readying his works for a hit.

His sweat stank of dirty socks and acetone even then. He'd been at the Green Ice all week.

I carefully set the nail gun and tool belt on the table along with some Fritos, then plopped down in the chair opposite him.

As I pulled off the heavy steel toed boots, one by one, I watched my old man calmly tie off his arm, make a fist, then casually tap a vein as he prepared to shoot the hot load of ice that would take him to Emerald City. I still had a black eye from our last "chat," so I just sat there, munching Fritos, and watched.

Then I stood up real slow and walked over to his side of the table. The past few months had added five inches and twenty pounds to my frame. I towered over him.

The spike was millimeters from his skin now. He glanced up at me, a quizzical look in those brown-black eyes.

"Do you even think about your family?" I said. "Do you?" The next words spilled out before I could stop them. "You fucking junkie."

His fist hit my face. I forgot how fast he could move—when he wasn't yet high.

Everything slowed down then—like over-cranked film running in super-slo-mo.

My head snapped hard to the right, and I heard the dull thud of cracking cheekbone before I felt it. I crashed hard on the table. The cheap plywood cracked in two. My heart pounded. My dad had his Glock out before I knew it.

That's when my mom ran in from upstairs. She threw herself between us, trying to shield me.

The blow meant for me landed on her. He slugged her so hard she crumpled to the floor. The sunglasses she wore to hide a fresh set of bruises flew off.

Something shifted in me then. I don't remember standing up, but I must have. I slugged my father—hard. He reeled like a drunk staggering backwards. He stared at me with this stunned look on his face. I'd never hit him before. More stunned than pissed off at first, but his rage followed like a tsunami chasing an earthquake.

"You ever hit me again, you snot-nosed little punk, you better kill me," he hissed, and slugged me again, the Glock in his hand this time.

I fell once more, knocking the saucer-shaped lamp we had hanging over the table. My father dropped his piece with the impact of the blow. I grabbed his hand and bit down hard. The taste of his blood filled my mouth. He grabbed the nail gun and nailed my foot to the floor. *Kerchunk*.

I screamed like a little girl. He came after me with fists and his steel-tipped boots after that.

About to land that steel in my liver, he kicked but hit only air. He found himself staring down the barrel of his own gun, in my hand this time.

I shot him. Blood and flesh spattered the wall with a sick wet sound. The old man crumpled into a sitting position on the floor opposite me, holding his bloody arm. The bullet tore a big chunk out of his shoulder. His face turned paper white under his sunburn, and he looked at me like I was a stranger. And for the first time I saw fear on his face.

I ripped the nail out of the floor, then out of my foot, leaving a bloody chunk of my flesh behind.

My mother screamed and screamed. The hanging lamp swung round and round, casting its circle of light like the spotlight from a police chopper thrown over a perp on the run. When I close my eyes, I can still see that lamp circling.

Not long after, my mom called 911 and reported the accident.

That's how it was recorded—an accident. My father never pressed charges, and he never hit me again. The tiger had rolled over.

"You all right?"

I flinched and looked up to see Jo kicking off her heels as she took a seat next to me. "What?"

Jo's eyes had that worried look as she drew up her feet under her. I hadn't even heard her come in.

"Your mother called me from the hospital when she couldn't reach you. Your father's in ICU. Eddie, you never told me your father was so ill. She mentioned compassionate leave. I didn't even know he was out on parole. How long have you known?"

Paroled: that one word richocheted round my head and sent other thoughts spiraling with it. Maybe Lee hadn't been referring to Harvey Pink on that vlog at all. Maybe the reason Lee knew my name before I'd ever shown up at his place was that it wasn't my name alone. Piedmont Sr. had it first. And he'd dragged our name through the muck when he'd gone on the Zeta payroll. Now they'd gone and paroled that asshole.

"You want me to go with you to the hospital?" Jo put her hand on my arm in a reassuring manner.

I cocked my head and just looked at her.

"You are going?" she said. "Eddie, you have to—for your mother. For yourself. You'll regret it if you don't."

"Don't worry. I'm going." Jo started to stand when I did. "No need for you to drive over there too," I said. "Might be a false alarm."

"You sure?" She settled back down on the couch when I nodded. "I'll be here if you need me."

I leaned down and kissed her. "Get some sleep. I'll call you if there's any news."

I checked the laser clip Glock 17 and re-holstered the weapon.

"Home security, alert level orange," I said into the smart-home receiver on the wall nearest the door to the driveway. The sensors clicked on, one by one, little pin lights on the console beaming like a myriad of amber-colored insect eyes. Then I stepped back into the night.

A couple minutes later, I turned onto the Santa Monica freeway.

My skin felt cold and numb. A part of me still couldn't believe what I'd heard on Lee's vlog. It had sounded insane. But now the insanity made sense.

I headed south towards San Diego and the KP Med-Center, gas pedal pressed to the floor.

For some people, San Diego means Sea World and Comi-con. For me, it's the home you don't want to go back to. Two hours later, my gut had already tightened into a hard little ball as I pulled into the lot at the downtown KP Medcenter.

I hate hospitals. The last time I'd been in this one, the doctors had stitched up my foot and the skin near my mom's eye. That memory wasn't helping. Taking a deep breath of the night air, I headed in.

The brightly patterned curtain that served as a door to my father's room was pulled to the side. My mom had fallen asleep in the chair by his bed, her head nodding with each breath like a wilting flower in the breeze. From ten feet away, I could see the old scars on her face and hands peeking through thick makeup. At least there'd be no fresh bruises anymore.

The stink of sweaty socks and dirty diapers assaulted my nostrils as I crossed the threshold. No nurse could wash away that characteristic stench of a long time Green Ice addict. The stink crept into my mouth and made me want to retch. He looked shrunken, with tough yellowing skin. His eyes were closed and his breathing shallow and raspy. An oxygen tube snaked into his nose. Computer monitors reduced his vitals to numbers and sharp jagged lines, and an intravenous line ran into his veins. That I.V. should feel like auld lang syne to my father.

Dr. Tabandeh, my father's oncologist, spotted me first. Standing at the foot of his bed, she gestured for me to follow her out to the hall. Dark shadows pooled under her eyes—almost matching her hair.

"Detective Piedmont?"

I nodded.

"I'm glad you're here." With hands still bearing fading henna designs, the kind you see on Indian brides, she pushed a few errant strands of black hair behind her ears. "Unfortunately, your father has been diagnosed with stage four leukemia." She paused. When I didn't say anything, she rattled on some more about the disease and its complications, given my father's addictions and generally poor health.

I couldn't even pretend surprise.

"The only option is a bone marrow transplant from a compatible donor," she added. The expectant look on her face told me she was waiting for me to volunteer. When I didn't, the doctor tried again. "I apologize for my bluntness, but the transplant has to be done as soon as possible. Can we test you for compatibility right away?"

I laughed. I couldn't help it.

The doctor's eyelids fluttered—three rapid blinks—as her startled brows shot up. Followed by an awkward silence. When I didn't apologize, the startled look gave way to a frown.

"I expect you need to think it over," she said. "But don't take too long, detective. Your father's a fighter, but he doesn't have a lot of time."

In every cloud a silver lining. "Thank you, Doctor." My father didn't need a lot of time. Just enough to answer a few questions. I watched Tabandeh's retreating figure stride down the hall to yet another patient circling the drain. Then I headed back inside the old man's room.

Without waking my mother, I pulled up a chair from the other empty bed in the room and sat down by her side.

A dying plant stood on the nightstand, and the corner of a contraband pack of Marlboros peeked out from under his pillow. The skin on his spindly arms, pitted with scars and needle tracks, looked like a railroad map. One side of his hospital gown had fallen down, revealing another scar on the shoulder, a deep one. That was the one I'd given him—back when his arms weren't spindly.

I must have closed my eyes for a minute. When I opened them, Mom had slipped out, but he was awake, staring back at me. The whites of my father's coffee-colored eyes were jaundice-yellow—like his bladder had burst and piss had flooded his body. I shifted my gaze to the dead plant.

"You always did have a black thumb," I said, fingering the dried-up leaves.

"Takes one to know one. Heard you got suspended. Shot up a banger."

"Good to know you keep up with current events, even if you got the facts wrong." I grabbed the cigarettes tucked halfway under his pillow and dumped them in the trash. "So lame. If you want to kill yourself, couldn't you manage it with less wear and tear on Mom?"

"Don't, Eddie." My mom entered the room with two cups of Medcenter java and handed me one. The aroma of burnt coffee mingled with the smells of the room.

"Why'd you come?" he asked. "I know you don't give a shit I'm dying."

"Ed!" my mother pleaded, eyes bright with tears.

It was always the same. Five seconds with my dad reduced us both to circling sharks tearing big bloody chunks out of each other while my mother wept.

I activated my glove phone, pulling up a picture of the now dead scientist, and shoved it in front of my father's face.

"Recognize him?" I watched my father's face closely.

"You in K-town now?" He narrowed his eyes and leaned in close, his stench nearly gagging me as he examined the picture hovering in the air.

"Just answer the question," I said. "How do you know Lee?"

"Who says I do?" He sank back into his pillows and leisurely started to scrape thin black slivers of dirt out from under his nails.

"He did." I scattered the pixels momentarily into a brightly colored soup as I jabbed at the picture with my right forefinger. "Not long before he died." The pixels realigned and the face of the dead scientist coalesced once more. "I need to know your exact connection."

My father's eyebrow rose a millimeter. He smiled. "I need a bone marrow transfusion." My father crossed his arms and lifted his chin defiantly as he leaned back into his pillow. "Didn't the doctor spell it out for you? Without it I'll be dead in a month."

"I'll donate," my mom said, her voice quavering. "We don't need to bother Eddie."

"The doctor said a blood relative," he replied. "I don't have any siblings."

"So, if I agree to test," I said, "you'll give me a straight answer to all my questions?"

"That's the deal."

I didn't trust him as far as I could throw the whole Medcenter bed with him on it, but I didn't have time to tease out answers. "Deal. How do you know Lee?"

"Not so fast," he replied. "Blood test first."

"How do I know you'll keep your word?"

"Goddamn it, my life's on the line here!" His face turned red, then white. He wheezed and started to cough. My father sucked deep drags on his oxygen line until his color returned.

Neither of us had time for bullshit.

So, no sooner had the needle left my skin, and the Medcenter robot rolled off to the lab carrying tubes brimming with my blood, then I repeated my questions about Lee, as I rolled my sleeve down and put my jacket back on.

"Maybe I saw the old guy making a buy when I was in vice some ten years back." My father mentioned a spot near the wharf, a favorite haunt of drug dealers and prostitutes on the prowl.

This time I didn't even need to see the hesitation, the twitch at the corner of his eye. "Lee never lived in San Diego," I said, "and he doesn't have an arrest record. Period."

"Didn't arrest him, did I?"

"Why not?"

"Better things to do than fill out paperwork on some fresh off the boat user," he said.

"Yeah." Like scoring ice and hookers for himself. My father had taken cash from the Zetas until they started paying him in other ways. That's what finally got him kicked off the force. "What about Fuentes?" I watched his face intently to see if this other name from Lee's vlog triggered any telltale micro-expression.

"Be specific, Eddie. This is San Diego. You can't turn around without hitting a Fuentes or a Sanchez."

Proximity to death hadn't killed off his racism either.

"Did you kill this Fuentes?" I said. "Or look the other way when somebody else did? Like one of your Zeta compadres?"

"Sure," he answered, scratching the dry skin on his left forearm where the I.V. was attached. "I killed him if that's what you want to hear. What you gonna do about it now? Arrest me?" The glimmer in his eyes matching the crooked grin that split his face.

The anger drained away, and all I felt was this sick empty feeling. Putting on my hat, I stood up.

"Where you going?" he said. "If you're a match they'll be back any minute to schedule the donation. You do it, I'll swear to anything you want."

I paused at the door. "The deal was I'd give blood, and you'd give me some straight answers. Not obvious bullshit."

"I said I'd answer your questions. I didn't say you'd like the answers."

"You do you," I said. "But when you code blue? Don't call me." I turned to go.

"I'm sorry," my father said. His voice even sounded like he meant it. "We always end up fighting, you and me. Oil and water. Why is that? You're my son."

An apology from a man who never apologized for anything. My feet stuck to the floor.

My mother grabbed me and held me back. "Eddie, don't be that way. Your father's sick."

Excuses—the old refrain. I could actually feel my heart harden along with my spine. "Listen to me, Mom." I leaned in and held her face in both my hands. "He's sick, but not the way you mean.

He has a gun in his mouth, and he likes the taste of the metal. Run. Come live with Jo and me."

My father's laugh was a hacking smoker's croak. "You can't run from who you are, Eddie. We're blood. That's all there is. You think that girl you're with now is going to stay with you? Haven't I taught you anything? People with money marry people with money. Sooner or later, she's gonna flush you down the toilet."

I clenched my hands into tight fists so he wouldn't see them shake from the anger flooding through me.

"I hope I am a match," I said. "Because this is me walking away."

I rested my hand on my mother's shoulder. "Think about my offer, Mom." I left her sitting there by my father's bedside as the old man turned the air blue with profanity. As I walked back the way I'd come, my father's ranting turned to a desperate whine. "I'm sorry, Eddie. I've always been proud of you. I have."

Funny how words I'd always longed to hear could hurt worse than a nail through flesh. When I didn't turn around, my father's verbal abuse resumed.

But his voice grew fainter and fainter until I'd turned the corner and the distance finally buried the now muffled abuse.

Tick-tock, tick-tock—another hour gone, but I had learned something. I shivered despite the warm breeze that hit me when I exited the hospital. The old liar in the hospital bed had no idea who Lee was. Or Fuentes. So the Piedmont referenced in Lee's vlog, the Piedmont still in the crosshairs of a killer at large, couldn't have been the burnt out addict who sired me. As I headed to my car, I could almost feel the target settling on my back.

CHAPTER FORTY

I PUT THE CAR ON AUTOPILOT FOR THE RIDE HOME. LEE'S DIGItized voice was the refrain I couldn't get out of my head. Piedmont—it will end as it began. But if I was the Piedmont in Lee's vlog, that meant not only was I in the crosshairs, the connection between the deaths of Britney Devonshire and Lee ran through me. How?

Every cop has a mental list of perps most likely to carry a beef. I ran through mine, but none of them seemed likely to be tangled up in this. So how? Had I set the dominoes tumbling simply by refusing to write off the Devonshire girl's death as an accident? Had my stubbornness been enough to trigger Lee's murder? And ensure Frank's death as well? Each green and white exit sign flashing past my window felt like a slap. That sick empty feeling in my gut grew denser, pulling everything into it like a black hole.

Jo was asleep when I got back around 3 a.m. Still stretched out on the couch, she wore a shirt of dark blue silk, but her long legs were bare. *All About Eve* was playing on the wall screen. Without makeup in that light, Jo's face looked like a teenager's. I waited for Bette Davis to buckle her seat belt for a bumpy ride and turned off the movie. The sudden silence woke Jo. She yawned and stretched.

"What's the news?" That concerned face again.

"Nothing good." I leaned down to kiss her, then gave Jo the brief rundown of my visit to the hospital, editing out the ugly bits.

She nodded and squeezed my shoulder. Wordlessly, Jo sat up, pulling her knees in toward her body as she patted the soft cushions of the couch in front of her. I sat down, leaning my back against her smooth legs, feeling the cool silk of her shirt brush against my skin as she started to knead the knots out of my shoulders and neck.

"I did something bad," I said. "Can you forgive me?"

Her fingers barely skipped a beat before continuing their rhythmic kneading. "What's the offense, and how do you plead?"

"Guilty. By reason of insanity. I just invited my mother to come live with us."

Her fingers stopped altogether.

"Even though, your mother, being your mother, turned you down." She paused. "Right?"

"Naw, she's moving in next Tuesday."

Jo landed a playful punch to my shoulder.

"Ouch."

"That's what I love about you, Eddie." She continued her massage. "One of the things. Underneath all the macho bluster? You're kind. That's rarer than you know."

One of the things I love about Jo is she thinks I'm better than I am. But that scared me too. Screw my father and everything he'd said in the hospital. I pulled one of Jo's hands away from my shoulder and kissed the palm.

"Hmm." She kissed my neck. Jo playfully pushed me away with her feet and turned around, leaning against me this time. She placed my hands on her thighs, under the long silk shirt. "Maybe we should do something bad together."

And all the thoughts of Lee and Fuentes and my part in this tangled up mess were put on hold as Jo pulled me upstairs to the bedroom.

When I woke with a start, the clank of the garbage truck moving down the street rattled away. For a second it was just another day. The sun was rising, working its ancient magic, light once again turning the flat black silhouettes of dawn into the three-dimensional world.

But the skin on the backs of my forearms prickled. Neither the sun nor the clanking garbage trucks had ripped me from sleep. The silent flashing red of my phone confirmed my internal alarm.

So did the home security system. Its silent alarm had triggered. Someone without clearance was trying to gain entry. I listened on high alert. But the house was quiet. My phone vibrated.

The security company—asking for authorization to send a car or stand down.

"What is it?" Jo's voice was still sleepy.

"Probably nothing." I zipped my fly and pulled up all the security cameras. They flashed onto the wall screen opposite the bed.

We had cameras on every door and window, plus the driveway behind the house. Houses on the canals are tightly squeezed together. Anyone approaching from the sidewalks out front is highly visible. There was nobody at the front door.

But the screen covering the back was black. Pitch black. A short of some kind? No. The kitchen camera went dark next. I activated the stealth alert to the security company.

When I holstered my Glock, all sleepiness left Jo's face.

The door to the bedroom was steel reinforced. "Stay here," I said, locking it behind me.

Glock out, I headed downstairs.

The back door gaped open. The entry code panel was smashed. The blow that smashed it had to be what had woken me. Black spray paint dripped down over the lens of the retina scanner. The empty can lay just inside the door.

The sharp acetone smell of the spray paint lingered near the dripping mess that blocked out both retina and thumbprint scanners. Paint still wet. The perp Picasso could still be inside.

Back-up was on route. But a squad car would take ten minutes to get here. Minimum. This was Jo's home. My home. Jo was upstairs. I clicked the laser function on my Glock to hot.

There's a reason cops call doors vertical coffins. Even with back up, there's always a blind spot as you move through. My back-up was ten minutes out. Glock out, I went back through the house the way I'd come. Pivoting the gun in an arc in front of me, I cleared the room. Nobody. The next doorway—the same procedure—the same result.

Crack! Smashing glass and metal sounded from the next room.

As I rounded the corner into the living room, the pungent odor of aftershave mingled with adrenaline and stale sweat hit my nose.

"Police," I yelled, "Freeze!" Wheeling around, I aimed at the blur of black and white streaking past.

The black and white blur coalesced into a lanky guy in baggy jeans and oversized white T-shirt. He held a metal baseball bat over his head—frozen before he could deliver the second blow to one of the cameras he'd smashed moments before. There was a spiderweb of cracks through the floating glass tabletop too. My home computer was toast.

He slowly turned around to gawk at me. The face, excepting his dark eyes, was entirely concealed by a black balaclava.

A drawing of the wings of a headless angel covered the front of the oversized Ed Hardy T-shirt he wore. The brand was a favorite of both the AzteKas and the Zetas. But they usually accessorize with a nine-millimeter—or an AK.

"Put the weapon down on the ground," I said. "Slowly. Keep your hands where I can see them."

His baggy black jeans puddled on the floor as he knelt in slow motion, setting the metal baseball bat down on the ground. No telltale bulge of a concealed firearm in the pockets.

I walked over and kicked the bat out of his range. And ripped the ski mask off his face.

A twenty-something Hispanic face. A stranger's face.

He had a goatee and wore a green bandana with the number 7 tucked over his dark hair. The green, the number 7 and the headless angel T-shirt told me his life story. All I needed to know anyway. He was from the Loco 7's—a Venice chapter of the AzteKas tied into the Juarez Cartel down south. But not a shooter. He was missing those distinctive gang tats.

From far off in the distance sirens wailed. Back-up.

The sound startled Headless Angel. His eyes darted around the room, ricocheting between the barrel of my Glock and the back door. He went for it, sprinting past me for the door.

I could have shot him. But he wasn't armed, and I didn't want another hearing. So, I sprang after him. Grabbing the tail of his shirt, I yanked hard.

The banger spun around and threw a right at me, wide, and missed. I slugged him hard, once to the gut, followed by a sharp righ jab to the nose with my Glock.

His head snapped back. Blood gushed. He fell backwards to the ground and lay panting. I reached for my cuffs with my left hand. And remembered I didn't wear them at home. I pushed my right foot on his chest. Pinning him to the ground, I reached for his belt.

Headless Angel froze as I lifted and started to turn him round. He looked up, but not at me. At something over my shoulder. Not something. Someone. He smiled.

I pivoted right. Fast—but not fast enough.

The bullet skimmed my side, shredding its bloody wake in red.

Headless Angel seized the moment. He grabbed his bat and slugged me. I heard my ribs crack. The impact slammed me back a couple steps, lifting me onto my heels.

Shooter stepped in and hammered me with the butt of his gun.

I fell backwards, dropping my Glock, the wind and sense knocked out of me. With each breath a searing pain shot through my chest.

"Cameras." Shooter's voice was calm as he delivered orders to the junior banger. "Ahora."

I struggled to pull air into my lungs. My sides screamed. My gun. I forced myself up onto my elbows.

This second guy, the guy with the gun now pointed at my heart, slowly shook his head as he kicked me back down. The flat black eyes of a practiced killer stared through his balaclava as he stood over me. Sleeve-tats blanketed the arms under his T-shirt. A gun, the barrel pointed out, was inked on his forearm—mirroring the real steel pointed at my head now.

Headless Angel raced around the room like a squirrel on speed, pulverizing every visible camera, plus smart-home control panel, family pictures, and anything else he could smash. He wrenched the large contemporary painting off the wall and dropped it onto the floor.

Once the cameras were smashed, Shooter calmly peeled off his own ski mask. A black tear was tattooed by his right eye. He wanted me to see him. He wasn't planning on leaving any witnesses. He moved the gun closer to my head.

But Headless Angel had missed the auxillary cameras, concealed and protected behind bendable metal glass barriers.

"Facial recognition match." Close-ups of all our faces floated free in the room. "Carlos Salazar," boomed the mechanical voice.

"Age 22." Under the mug shot of the little guy with the bat, his priors scrolled: B&E, vandalism.

Headless Angel saw his own face before him. He squealed again and raced around the room. Trying to avoid the cameras, he scrambled to find his mask. Fingers fumbling to yank it back on. Futile.

Shooter slipped his own balaclava back down over his face. Too late.

"Enrique Ramirez. Age 31," droned the mechanical voice as the floating close-up of Shooter's image froze. Two priors for armed robbery and GBH. One arrest for manslaughter. My murder could earn him another tattooed tear, but he wouldn't be mourning.

Ramirez shrugged and took slow aim at my head. "Por Paco."

Ramirez. Enrique Ramirez. For Paco. Paco Ramirez. I was looking at a relative of the baby banger I'd shot three weeks ago.

A shot rang out. Blood and brains splattered me. But not mine. I rolled.

Jo stood in the doorway, arms out the way I'd taught her, both hands on the Glock I'd given her last summer.

And Enrique Ramirez' faceless, lifeless body fell where I'd been seconds before.

Salazar screamed and rushed Jo. I tackled him first and heard his knee pop as his fell. I grabbed the bat. His hands reached for his ankle. The knife was just a blur as I smashed the bat down on his head.

His head hit the floor, out cold.

"Eddie!" Jo ran towards me. Her hands were shaking. Our eyes met for a split second. Then I saw the knife sticking out of my upper thigh. Blood gushed. And the world went dark.

CHAPTER FORTY-ONE

When I came to, I was lying in a hospital bed. Jo sat in the adjacent chair, holding my hand. A young blue-suiter with sandy hair stood guard outside the door.

My chest pinched with each breath, and my head felt as big as a beach ball. I sat up, or tried to, a little too quickly. Searing pain shot through my side. I eased myself back onto the pillows, sucking air through clenched teeth.

"He's awake," Jo said.

"I'll get the doctor." The uniformed officer hurried off.

"I'll say this," Jo said as soon as he left. "Life with you is never boring, Eddie." Her tone was light, but her hands were trembling.

"I did tell you to stay in the bedroom." Jo was all right. I mouthed a silent prayer of gratitude and squeezed her hand. Even that pressure made the room pulse.

"I never was good at taking orders." She rose from her chair and sat facing me on the side of the bed.

"Lucky for me. I owe you. Big time." Gingerly, I lifted the blanket. My chest was taped and my thigh was covered with a thick bandage. "One more inch to the left and no more talks about having little Piedmonts."

Jo leaned in and hugged me tight.

The sound of a throat clearing made us separate.

"I'd say get a room, but you already have one." It was Shin standing at the door, a thin smile on his face. The doctor, a middle-aged Asian guy a head shorter than my partner, strode towards me. Dr. Trahn—I silently pieced together his name letter by letter on his security badge as he neared me.

"You lost a lot of blood, detective," Dr. Trahn said. "Not to mention concussion and two cracked ribs. We took a bone splinter out of your lung too." The doctor took a pre-loaded needle-free syringe out of a vacuum pack and shot the pain meds into the pocket between my lip and cheek. "Don't try to swallow."

The bitter meds filled my mouth. The cold bright hospital light flared brighter and made me squint.

"We gave you something to regenerate the tissue faster too," Dr. Trahn said, pinning my shoulder to the bed with a gentle but firm hand. "You're mending quickly. But we're still keeping you overnight for observation." He entered a few notes on his digital medpad and left. Shin stayed, taking a seat in the chair Jo had vacated.

The meds made me nauseous. I focused on the faded blue green diamond pattern of the curtain surrounding the bed. The diamonds throbbed with every breath.

"Enrique Ramirez," I said. My mind was racing, but it was hard work to force words out of my mouth. "He's . . ."

". . . dead," Shin said. "And as for Salazar, it's a solid bust, Eddie. We have their retina scans and prints from your smart house. Not to mention the blood. Not all of it was yours."

"Aztekas," I said with difficulty.

"We know," Shin said in the reassuring tone he used to calm victims at crime scenes. "Salazar is looking at conspiracy to commit homicide, assault, and GBH just for last night. Plus, he's a person of interest in the Zeta-AzteKa war."

"No . . ." I said, frustrated that I couldn't get my mouth to force words out fast enough. "Ramirez. Paco—Ramirez . . ."

"We know, Eddie," Shin repeated in that patient voice. "Enrique was Paco's older brother. It was an ambush—revenge, Azteka style. Salazar smashed up your place so Ramirez could shoot you when you came down to investigate."

"Not just shoot," I said. "The knife."

Shin glanced at Jo, then just tipped his head in a shallow nod of acknowledgement to me. We both knew the Aztekas' M.O. Shooting was just the appetizer. They'd planned to deposit my severed head on the steps outside Nokia P.D. The meds were kicking in now, dulling the pain, but simultaneously making it harder for me to concentrate. There was something I was forgetting. Something important.

Shin picked up a little carton of juice on the table next to the hospital bed and started to peel off the plastic wrapping from the attached straw.

"There's more bad news. We had to let Pink go. His high-priced lawyer got him out on bail."

The stream of profanity I let loose only rattled my head more. "How . . . could that bottom-feeder af-ford . . . high-priced lawyer?"

"He can't," Shin said.

"Who?"

Shin shook his head. "The lawyer's on retainer for the Aztekas. And here's the thing, Eddie. He's not just repping Pink and Salazar. Salazar is talking. He confessed."

I stared at Shin. Salazar had run around my place like a crazed squirrel as he tried to hide his face from the cameras. But once arrested, even a junior Azteka would know enough to keep his mouth shut. Even before his lawyer told him to. Why hadn't Salazar?

"The D.A. . . . cut him a deal?" My words slurred a little. Or did he figure attempted homicide gave him street cred? And better tattoos.

"You're not getting the full picture yet," Shin said. "Salazar confessed to getting the nano-bot off Raymond Lee in exchange for drugs. He gave the bot to Pink. On Ramirez' orders."

"What?!" My throat went dry. This was not happening.

Shin nodded. "We've been looking at the case from the wrong end of the telescope, Eddie. According to his sworn testimony, Salazar is Ray's dealer. Lee was making noises about going to the police. So, according to Salazar, Ramirez took out Dr. Lee. But it was you he really wanted dead."

CHAPTER FORTY-TWO

THEY RELEASED ME FROM THE HOSPITAL THE NEXT DAY. THE crime scene team was just packing up as Jo and I pulled into the drive behind our house around 10:30: They nodded as we passed them on our way in. A blue-suiter stood guard at the door. Taking no chances, Jo had put in the call to her brother Craig on the ride home and ordered a joint security and clean-up team.

I bobbed my head to the uniformed officer. Even that took energy I didn't have. I felt weak as a newborn kitten.

"Probably be a good idea to stay someplace else for a while," Shin had said when we left the hospital. "Until we know what's what with the Aztekas." I glanced around at the mess in our living room. He might've been right.

The damage to the house was even worse in the light of day. The place looked like I felt. Broken glass crunched under every step. The home theatre wall film had been ripped off its organic mount over the fire place.

Hot spots embedded in the walls had been damaged along with the visible security cameras, so home holo-functionality was down, as was our default access to the web. We had only glove-phones.

At least the acute throbbing on the left side of my head had turned into a dull faint ache. I poured a glass of orange juice and tossed back two extra-strength aspirins.

"I'll pick up the cats on my way back," Jo said, heading for the front door. She'd packed up the felines and left them with a neighbor. All except for Woolsey the big tom. He'd hidden somewhere even Jo couldn't find him. "Is there anything you want from the store?"

I shook my head.

"Rest up, Eddie. The team will be here in fifteen." The door closed quietly behind Jo.

Very gingerly, I bent down to retrieve the now dented frame of a digital photo. The glass over the photo had shattered. The blow from Salazar's bat had broken the photo's digital function, too. The photo was of Jo and me—a goofy romantic shot we'd had taken on our first date down at the Santa Monica pier. Jo and I stood frozen in the now damaged picture.

Jo—the Aztekas had smashed her house and pointed the gun at her head. But it was me who'd pulled Jo into their crosshairs. Frank and now Jo. Protect and Serve. I felt like a total chump.

I couldn't wait for Craig's clean up crew. Digging out a broom, I started to sweep up the mess. Each brush of the broom hurt. I welcomed the pain.

When the promised cleaning crew arrived fifteen minutes later, I let them in and watched as they began their efficient clean-up operation. Feeling both underfoot and out of place, I surrendered the broom and headed outside to the deck, carefully lowering myself onto the chaise longue. The hot sun beating down from its position directly overhead made me feel drowsy. I closed my eyes and must have dozed off. I woke with a start when one of Jo's cats began winding around the legs of the chaise longue, yowling and nudging. Woolsey, the black tom built like a bull dog, had come out of hiding.

"Where were you when the bangers were here, huh boy?" I chuffed his fur, then pushed him off my lap.

Woolsey strutted back and forth, nudging my hand with his head.

"All right." As I got up to let him back into the house, I heard the front door open behind me.

It was Jo, back from the market with the cats in tow. I must have been asleep for at least a couple hours. She cast me an appraising glance when I offered to carry groceries into the kitchen. "Let your ribs mend."

"I'm fine. Those meds they gave me really work." I helped her carry in the cat carriers and released the furballs.

While I'd slept, the clean-up crew had cleared out the broken glass and put paintings back on the walls that didn't need repairs. The security team was starting in on the walls that did, rewiring the smart-home features, patching and painting the drywall. Drills whined and there was a sharp tang of new paint in the air. But there was still a lot to do.

"Shame about the house," I said. "It's gonna cost a fortune to get things back to normal. Even with Craig's crew, the place is a war zone."

Jo waved away my apology with a dismissive little wave of the hand. "You're okay. I'm okay." She smiled at Woolsey. "The cats are fine too. We can always replace stuff."

People with money. I nodded. I wasn't one of them.

I watched Jo's face as she spoke, almost tuning out her words. Jo's skin and that white blonde hair glowed. She was so alive, so smart and beautiful. If things had gone the other way—I didn't even want to think about that. But I had to.

"Maybe you should stay somewhere else—just for a while," I said.

"Me?" Jo closed the kitchen cupboard and turned around, leaning her back against the counter. "Don't you mean us?"

"The Aztekas aren't after us."

"We can talk about it later," she said.

I shook my head. "Jo."

She came over and laid her hand gently on my arm. "I know you worry about me. Her hand exerted just the slightest pressure as she squeezed my flesh. "Don't. I'm a pretty good shot." She kissed me. "Thanks to you. And I'm not letting those thugs drive us out of our home." Jo started to put groceries in the subzero. "Or spoil my news." Jo smiled a sly little grin.

I gave her the point, deciding to try again when I felt stronger. "Good news?"

"The city's lawyers settled the Ramirez suit out of court today." Jo continued in a breathless rush. "For two point five K." Two hundred fifty thousand—we both knew a typical settlement was in the seven figure range.

I stared at her. Opened my mouth to say something, then thought better of it.

Jo nodded, and in a giddy voice said, "I know, right? It's incredible. That figure's practically an admission of how groundless the suit against you was."

"Nobody said anything to me. Not Captain Tatum, not Espinoza. Not Shin."

"They probably don't know yet."

"And you do—how?"

Another dismissive toss of her head. "The judge in the case had a little too much Pinot Noir over lunch yesterday with one of the partners."

I stared at her, gleefully relaying the story. While I'd been napping, one of her partners must have phoned Jo to tell her the good news. Forces well beyond my control were in play, and my whole future had been a tasty little morsel of gossip shared over a casual lawyer lunch, nothing more. Piedmont Sr. had been right about one thing. Jo was part of a world I didn't belong to and never would.

"I thought you'd be thrilled." A muted note of disappointment played under her words. "Now that there won't be a public trial over the original shooting, the demonstrations will stop. The L.A.P.D. will want this investigation to go away quietly. You're home free. We can put this whole business behind us."

"It's good news, Jo," I said, pulling her close and breathing in the vanilla and lavender scent of her pale hair. "Really." I held her against my chest for a few seconds. Until she broke away, nodding.

"You sure? You don't look happy."

"That's just my face," I said.

"It's a nice face." Jo kissed me, then took a seat on the sofa, her smile enigmatic as she tapped the seat next to her. "I have more news." Jo kicked off her flats.

I sank back into the white leather of the seat next to her, waiting. "Good or bad?"

"Definitely good." She curled up close to me but glanced around the living room. "You know, you may be right about this place. We should look for a new house together in a few months. Someplace bigger."

My phone rang. The ringtone told me without looking it was my mother. I let the call go to voicemail.

Jo's phone pinged a couple seconds later.

"Don't answer it," I said, kissing her neck.

Jo glanced down at her phone. Her face paled. "Eddie, you need to take this."

I looked from her to the text my mother had sent. And as Shin would say, the tiger rolled over again. The cancer had won. My father was dead.

CHAPTER FORTY-THREE

I COULDN'T LIE TO MYSELF. MY FATHER'S DEATH WAS A RELIEF. There'd be no more screaming matches, no more bruises of purple and green suddenly blooming on my mother's face.

But I was surprised to feel a kind of hollow ache. Any hope for a real father-son relationship, however faint, had gone into the grave with him. And losing that sliver of hope I'd only half-known was there hurt a lot more than losing him.

The rest of the day I buried myself in work. Shin held the fort at Nokia PD interrogating Salazar. I busied myself in the paperwork, making sure the files on the Devonshire and Lee cases were up to date. The next day, Jo and I drove down to San Diego to bury my father.

Most of Eddie Piedmont Sr.'s funeral went by in a blur. Bits and pieces stood out though, like vivid shards of stained glass. Sky the color of bleached denim, frayed at the edges. Cut flowers, sun-wilted, laid out on neighboring graves. Digital faces, blinking portraits of the dead, smiled from the niches on their respective tombstones nearby.

My mother's face, pale and waxy under the white Sunumbra parasol Jo held for her. Like one of the wilted flowers.

My mother and her older friends wore traditional black. Jo wore white. As did several others seated in the four neat rows parallel to the grave. When had white become fashion-forward for funerals? Was it after the big melanoma scare of 2032, or had the surge in Chinese immigrants once the CCP put the screws on Hong Kong and Taiwan fueled the Asian trend? I tried to remember.

Most of the seats in the four rows were filled. I was surprised at the decent turnout until my glance around the faces confirmed most of the mourners were there for Mom. A few had braved the drive south for me, but I didn't see anyone who was there for the deceased. Every person graveside, including my mother, was dry-eyed. I hoped when I died, I would have lived the kind of life that makes mourners at my funeral actually mourn.

And there was Shin, a late arrival tip-toeing towards us. I hadn't expected him to make the drive all the way down here. I caught his eye, and we both edged our way to the empty seats at the back.

"Ashes to ashes." The words of the priest were a low hum in the background—the way other people's conversations sound in restaurants.

I leaned toward Shin. "Did Salazar cough up something worth the drive?"

"Why didn't you tell me about Lee's vlog?" Shin whispered back. "That he mentioned you by name?"

I turned face forward again. "Things happened so fast. My old man." I sighed and told Shin about the emergency visit to the hospital. "I had to find out if the connection ran through him." I jerked my chin toward the grave site.

"Which it did," Shin said. "Even if he didn't know it."

Familiar faces in the crowd suddenly seemed far away—faces glimpsed through the wrong end of a telescope.

"Salazar knew my father worked for the Zetas on occasion," I said.

"He confirmed it." Shin ran his hand over his buzz cut.

The attack against me wasn't just about the Ramirez kid. This was tied into the gang war—Aztekas battling the Zetas over turf, peddling Green Ice, Blue Lotus and the marijuana that made its way into the storefronts behind the green crosses on every corner.

"So, when they found out it was a Piedmont who shot Enrique Ramirez' little brother . . ."

Shin nodded. "The Aztekas figured it as part of a larger Zeta play. Don't forget the car the kid was driving belonged to the older brother. Enrique Ramirez was their top enforcer after Nieto moved up in the hierarchy."

"Nieto who just got out of prison," I said.

Shin nodded. "According to Salazar, Nieto thought the Zetas had put you on payroll to take out his lieutenant. That you tried to. And shot the kid by mistake. So, Ramirez and Salazar paid you a visit in turn."

I kept my eyes so tightly focused on the green blankets of fake grass draped over the newly cut earth. *My father's dead and I'm still getting fucked from his shit.* I hoped there really was a hell, and he had just checked into it.

Then Jo appeared at my side and handed me a white rose, and I was standing. Jo nudged me again.

I stood there looking down into my father's grave. I could have laser-cut that gaping hole with my stare alone. Shin, standing right behind me, leaned forward to whisper. "He's gone, Eddie. You can't kill him twice."

"No." But monsters should stay buried. I dropped the rose on the ground outside the grave. Grabbing a fistful of wet black dirt, I tossed it on my father's casket. The clods of earth made a dull thud as they hit the wooden coffin down in the darkness below.

Not longer after, the crowd began to disperse. On her way out, Dr. Tabandeh, my father's oncologist, walked up to me, her stiletto heels crunching on the gravel.

"I'm sorry for your loss," she said. Shielding her eyes from the blinding sun with her left hand, Tabandeh held out her right for me to shake. "Your father fought the good fight."

I focused on the little beads of sweat blistering up along her hairline to keep from grimacing. "It's nice of you to take the time, Doctor. I wouldn't have thought my father made the most popular patient list."

A sly little smile crept across her face. "Well, to tell the truth, he was a bit difficult."

"You're a diplomat."

Her smile transformed into a broad conspiratorial grin. "Maybe a bit. But not every patient agrees to donate organs or marrow either. It's a tremendous help to my research." Dr. Tabandeh smoothed her white silk coat-dress.

I'd nodded again, but her words jolted me. It was strange to learn the old man had done something right for a change. Not enough to change my overall opinion of him, but still, a nice surprise.

Tabandeh nodded, running her hand through her short dark hair. "Actually, I came today to apologize."

I shot her a quizzical look.

"For asking you to test the other night. Really, the chances of finding a match in donors who aren't blood relatives are slim to none. I wouldn't have put you through it if I'd known."

I stared at the doctor like she'd been speaking Hindi. "Are you saying I'm not my father's blood relative?"

A look of embarrassed shock flickered over her face. "I'm sor-ry," she stammered. "Truly sorry for your loss." Her ears had flushed bright pink at the tips. Dr. Tabandeh headed off to the left, then wheeled back around towards the cars. Taking short hurried steps across the manicured grass, she'd passed me again, her whole face burning red now.

The row of black limousines stood waiting with their doors opened singly, or a couple at a time, like a string of crows about to take flight from a phone wire.

I stood frozen in place until, with robotic steps, I followed Jo and my mother into the limo for the ride to the reception. What could Dr. Tabandeh have meant?

"Mom," I said, squeezing her arm after the behemoth ferrying us glided away from the curb. I relayed my conversation with the doctor.

"What?" My mother's eyelids fluttered in a series of rapid blinks.

"Dr. T. said the blood test showed I wasn't related to Dad. Not by blood. How's that possible?"

"Eddie," Jo said. "This isn't the time."

"There's never a good time for most of the questions I have to ask." I pushed the button for the privacy screen. The air between the driver's seat and ours froze into a clear soundproof crystal. I repeated my question.

I expected her to say the doctor had it wrong. That there must have been a mix-up at the hospital. Something like that. But she didn't. She didn't say anything.

"Mom?" I shot her an incredulous stare. She quickly looked away. Her eyes stayed fixed on the landscape floating by her window as the car glided past another block. Her hands shredded the Kleenex she held into soggy bits.

"Mom." I reached out and placed my hand over hers. She stopped shredding. Then she sighed deeply. Tears crawled noiselessly down her face.

"I know I should have told you a long time ago, Eddie." My mother's voice went strangely flat. Her eyes stayed fixed on the street. "But you two fought so much, and it was just a little white lie." She paused and turned her head. Mom glanced pleadingly at Jo and back to me again. "To keep the peace."

"Tell me about the lie," I said.

"I wanted you so much, Eddie. You don't know how much. I thought a baby would—fix things, you know, make everything all right between your father and me. But your father—couldn't. All the drugs, I guess. Anyway he couldn't. So—we got help."

"What kind of help?" I flashed on all those stories of kids who'd found out they were adopted. But those kids weren't me. I had my birth certificate. I'd been born in the KP-Medcenter back when it was called something else. Both my mother and father were listed in the appropriate parental unit spaces.

"Fertility treatments," Mom replied. "Dr. Singh helped us with the IVF."

In vitro fertilization. Dr. Singh had apparently been her fertility specialist as well as OB-GYN.

"Dad agreed to that?" It was hard to imagine my father admitting his swimmers needed any outside help. Admitting any weakness.

Mom's eyes brimmed, but she didn't answer.

I nodded. "So, he didn't know."

She fixed her eyes on her hands in her lap.

I nodded again. "You used a sperm donor."

Her tears slid down the creased skin, making her black eye makeup run. "I never wanted Ed to think you weren't his, Eddie. I didn't want him to feel different about you than he would about—his own biological child."

"I'm 29, Mom," I'd said. "When were you gonna tell me?"

More tears were her answer. There was the sick joke. I might not be his blood relative, but I still had one thing in common with Piedmont Sr. I'd made my mother cry.

The reception was held at Mom's church. It all went smoothly. I laughed and joked with guests, pouring drinks and balancing a tray of little sandwiches Jo had ordered up from some fashinonable new Brazilian restaurant.

"We have wait-staff to do that," Jo said. "You all right?"

"Don't I seem all right?"

"Better than all right," Jo said. "I can see your molars when you smile."

Six hours later, after we had seen the last guest out, driven my mother home and ourselves back to L.A., I pulled off my tie and shoes and collapsed onto the sofa in the Peninsula Hotel. Jo had booked us a room for a week until our place had been restored. She came over and perched on the sofa's back.

"You sure your mother didn't want to come stay with us?"

I shook my head. "Too tired. She wanted to sleep in her own bed. Maria, that friend from her church, is staying with her. I'll check on her tomorrow. You hungry?"

"Starving." Jo had been so busy with guests she'd forgotten to eat.

I checked my glove phone. "Come on." I leapt up and pulled Jo to her feet with me.

"Where we going?" she asked as we ran to the car.

"Little Havana." I backed the Porsche out onto the street. "Their food truck'll be in the parking lot behind Jorge's Liquor in twenty minutes. If we hurry, we can beat the line."

"Oh my God," Jo said, laughing with me as I cut through back alleys and side streets. "Use the Traffic Light Expediter!"

"No skill in that." Little Havana made the best Sandwich Cubano outside Miami or Havana. Even without the TLE we made pretty good time. In thirty minutes, the line of customers snaked through the parking lot and half way down the block, but we were leaning against the Porsche savoring Italian bread grilled to perfection and stuffed with ham, succulent roast pork, Swiss cheese, zucchini pickles, and mustard. I watched an elderly couple in NPR hoodies holding hands. Neither Jo nor I spoke until half our respective sandwiches were gone.

"We should tell them to pick a more scenic locale," Jo said, kicking an empty beer bottle, one of several strewn around the tarmac like party favors.

"That would just draw a bigger crowd." I popped the top from a bottle of beer and offered it to her.

Jo made a face. "No thanks."

I took a swig as we continued to chow down on our sandwiches. A forty-something ginger-haired father in a Dartmouth College T-shirt lifted his toddler son onto his shoulders as they waited.

Jo sighed. "What a day."

"Yeah. I always knew my family was fucked up. But you know what I realized today?"

"You don't have to hate your father anymore?" Jo said.

"Right, I can start hating Mom instead."

Jo playfully punched my shoulder.

I shrugged and smiled. "For as long as I can remember, my . . ." I paused. "I don't even know what to call him now. My father in name only? Anyway, we were at each others' throats my whole life. I was sure sooner or later he was gonna kill me, or I was gonna kill him. It was in our blood, like a curse. I left home at fifteen to keep that from happening. And all the time I've been living a complete lie."

"You're upset," Jo said. "Give yourself a break. You just buried your father."

"He wasn't my father. That's the point. I don't know who I am."

Jo's face darkened. "Eddie," she said. "Blood isn't everything. Don't you see? You're right. He wasn't your father. You're free. You can finally move on with your life." Jo met my gaze and held it. "I know who you are. You're my Eddie. You know you have me, right? We're family."

I took her hand and squeezed it tight. "I'll never leave you, Jo." I turned her hand over and kissed it. "That's a promise."

"I'm a lawyer. I want it in writing." She leaned into me and kissed me back—lightly brushing my lips with hers. Jo reached into her purse and, with a show of hesitation, pulled out a baggie. "As for moving on, this isn't how I planned to tell you, but . . ."

Jo turned her hand over. In her palm lay a white plastic wand inside the baggie. She held out her hand so I could see the wand close-up. The home pregnancy test had turned a vivid blue.

I blinked and stared at the wand. I was going to be a father. My stomach dropped about twenty floors. "When?"

"April. I'm almost four months in now."

"April."

She nodded.

"The thin blue line," I said finally. "Do you think that means he'll be a cop?"

Jo pointed to the technology readout on the side of the wand, detailing sex and general good health. "*She* might want to be an artist. Or a lawyer."

"Not a criminal defense attorney," I said. "Please." Picking up Jo's left hand, I held it out. "You still have the ring?"

She cocked her head and shot me a look. "Of course."

"Hold onto it." I ran into the liquor store and came out with a bottle of champagne and two plastic flutes. Jo was laughing as I walked to my car and popped the trunk. I pulled out my practice katana, the one I used for kata. I peeled the foil and little wire basket off the top of the bottle, felt for the seam in the glass and, with a smooth strike along the seam, popped the top off the champagne. The cork and its severed circle of glass shot ten feet across the parking lot.

"I'm not part of the Cassandra franchise," I said as the wine gushed out into the plastic flutes, "but I'll tell you your future, counselor. I see a wedding. A big one."

"I don't need a big wedding," Jo said, leaning into me as I downed the champagne. "But let's make it legal soon. I don't want to be fat when Craig walks me down the aisle."

I nodded. The tiger had rolled over again. I was going to be a husband and a father.

I couldn't keep the goofy smile off my face.

I'd never been so happy—or so scared.

CHAPTER FORTY-FOUR

THE NEXT DAY, AFTER JO HAD LEFT FOR THE OFFICE, I CALLED San Diego from our suite in the Beverly Hills Peninsula hotel and checked in on my mother. She and her friend Maria were finishing up breakfast. Sitting on the edge of the hotel bed, I chomped down on a piece of rye toast from room service and watched my mother brew her second pot of coffee. My mother's breakfast plate was untouched. Lit by the morning sun streaming in her kitchen window, she looked faded and thin, like a photo left too long in the sun. Whatever I thought of Piedmont Sr., my mother had loved him.

"I'm fine, Eddie," Mom's floating image said. "You don't have to worry about me."

"I know," I lied. "I really called to tell you the big news. You're gonna need a new dress, Mom. Get something nice. I'm buying."

She stared at me, frowning for several beats, before her expression lightened. "You're finally getting married!" It was the first time a smile had reached her eyes in a long while.

I nodded. "There's more." I told her the good news about the baby. By the time we disconnected, I was happy to see Mom deep into plans for making her granddaughter a wardrobe that would last the kid through high school.

As for myself, I planned to spend the day with the wrap-up on the Devonshire case files after I swung by the house to check on the restoration work. Barely an hour had passed when I rolled into the drive of the Venice house.

Craig's cleaning crew had been hard at work, clearing out detritus, re-hanging paintings and generally putting things to right. As I looked around the room, the painting hanging over the fireplace grabbed my attention. An abstract oil by Xervenka Zentos, one of Jo's favorite contemporary artists, the design was a patchwork of sea greens and grays with flecks of gold shrouded in the depths of receding plains. Staring at the canvas, something struck me. The abstract looked different—wrong.

There was a smudge on the lower right-hand side of the painting that didn't belong. Odd how the painting's jagged lines, the patches of green and gray, and ink black shadows suggested a different mood when the eye was drawn to the wrong focal point by that oily smudge.

Some soiled glove on a clean-up crew member, I thought. No art critic, he wouldn't have known what the abstract was supposed to look like. So, he hadn't noticed the smudge—right there in front of his face.

That smudge—I felt the familiar tingling on the back of my hands and neck I get when something overlooked suddenly comes together in a case.

Flipping my Nokia Handy on, I rushed to pull up the blood spot from the Devonshire 51 file. Leaning in so close my nose almost brushed the pixels, I scrutinized the tiny piece of genetic flotsam and jetsam.

The partial prelim resembled a standard identification barcode. But where the dark vertical lines of a barcode are sharp, the black lines of the partial were fuzzy—like smudged charcoal. Nothing odd there.

Then I saw it—a tiny dark line, almost a shadow, at the very bottom of the code that I'd never taken note of. Too small to make out with the naked eye, I magnified it fifty, then one hundredfold.

Each hair on the back of my neck prickled as individual letters in the smudge became legible.

I could just make out the letters and numbers: D-3331110. I felt the old rush.

Not an exact match—Lee's file name started with the letters AI, not D. But the block of numbers he'd choked out before dying, the seven-digit series I'd initially taken for a phone number, the same series repeated in Lee's encrypted file with a different prefix, AI, was right here staring me in the face. Serial number identifiers? Lee's file had to be linked to this blood spot, but how, exactly?

I pushed a call through to the crime lab, and left word for serologist Jim Mar, marking the message urgent. The case may have been cleared, but I still wanted to know how all the pieces fit.

Something kept nagging at me.

I texted Shin an update on my way back to the hotel.

I'd planned to spend the rest of the afternoon on the file, merging Frank's notes with Shin's and mine for the official record. I had just started to google the numbers with the AI and D prefixes when Jo walked in on all the excitement. I'd forgotten we'd planned to celebrate our future.

"Let me jump in the shower," I said. "I'll be ready in ten."

"Take your time. I want to change too." Jo's voice was lightly teasing. "Maybe I'll join . . ."

She paused in mid-sentence, shook her blonde head and smiled. "What do patents have to do with your case?"

"Patents?" I followed her gaze to my search.

With her well-manicured index finger Jo pointed to the numbers AI and D-3331110.

The air in the hotel felt electric.

CHAPTER FORTY-FIVE

"TALK TO ME," I SAID TO JO. FOR THE SECOND TIME THAT DAY a prickling sensation rippled up and down my skin. That feeling I get when a case starts to break wide open.

"Patents," Jo replied, leaning close from her seat next to me. "Standard format. Patents typically have seven digits and some prefix. 0 stands for a utility patent. X denotes patents dating prior to 1836. RE is a reissue and so forth." Jo pointed at the file. "D stands for design. AI means additional improvement."

"Additional improvement on the initial design?"

She nodded. "Probably—given that the series of numbers in both is the same. Eddie, what do these patents have to do with your case?"

"I don't know yet. Can you tell from the numbers what the patents are for or when the initial design or the additional improvement was made?"

"Medical research," Jo said after a quick check of her own on the public registry for patents. "Awarded to a Dr. Lee. Patents are valid for twenty years from the filing date. In the U.S., whoever made the invention first, and can prove it, is awarded property rights for those twenty years."

"Why would a blood spot, a genetic partial prelim, be tied up with a design patent?" I asked. "A human genome's not an invention."

"Now I have proof you don't listen to me," Jo said with a groan. "It was briefly outlawed about thirty years ago, but that changed about the time gene editing for humans was approved: around 2029. Genetics are one of the hottest areas of intellectual property."

"You can patent somebody else's genome?"

"Only a part of it," she said. "The part that would be useful as a building block for basic research in the field. Patent holding companies sequence the genes and convert them to another form called cDNA. Then a patent is sought on the cDNA rather than the gene itself."

"That's a shell game, isn't it?"

"Not if you're the one who put all the time and resources into discovering the useage." She shrugged. "It's common practice, and it's legal."

"So other scientists would have to pay the patent owner licensing fees every time they used your research to further their own."

"That's right," Jo said.

"How much money are we talking for a licensing fee?"

"Depends," she said. "If you have the rights to a common diagnostic, that can mean serious money over time. For example, back in 2001, an American company got a European patent for BRCA1."

"The breast cancer gene?"

Jo nodded. "That company can and does charge a substantial fee to test people in order to determine whether or not somebody carries the mutation that virtually guarantees cancer down the line. Six figures is a low estimate on value."

"But a big motive," I said, "for murder."

Britney's partial prelim had the D-3331110 identifier, so that had to be the original design. Since Lee's name was on the registration for the patent, the scientist had evidently patented part of that genome for his work on Alz-X. And his encrypted file with the AI prefix must hold an improvement of some kind. What was the improvement? A diagnostic that predicted the onset of the disease, or some form of resistance to it?

I leaned over and kissed Jo, then activated my phone. "This is big, Jo. Thanks."

It was four o'clock. As Jo went to shower first, I put in a call to Lee's boss, Maclaren. What patents did Lee's Alzheimer's X research entail, how much money was involved, and most important, what happened to the patents now that he was dead? Maclaren would know. Unfortunately, it also seemed to be the day that everybody I wanted to talk to was out of the office.

I called Shin again and updated him on what Jo had said about the patents. Shin listened with interest.

“Okay,” he said, his holo-image nodding. “I’ll pass it along to Vice.”

“Don’t,” I said, pulling up Lee’s vlog on the hotel’s giant wall screen.

Shin shot me a look. “Why not?”

“We’re not done with the case. Salazar’s statement is a web of lies.” The home invasion by Salazar and Ramirez had slowed me down, but my brain was starting to come back online, thoughts skipping ahead. The thing I’d forgotten, the important thing nagging at me since the hospital, had finally inched its way back to me. “About Lee’s vlog.” I pointed to the image on the wall screen. “Look at the timestamp, Shin. If my shooting the Ramirez kid was the trigger for everything the Aztekas did to me and to Dr. Lee, how could Lee have mentioned my name a week before the shooting happened?”

Shin’s eyes grew rounder. “Why would Salazar corroborate AzteKa involvement?”

“Sleight of hand,” I said. “He put the blame on a dead man.”

“Send me the whole vlog,” he said. “ASAP. I’ll go see the captain as soon as I’ve watched it.”

CHAPTER FORTY-SIX

THE PATENTS GAVE US BOTH A NEW POTENTIAL MOTIVE AND hard evidence that linked Lee's research to the blood spot I'd found in Britney Devonshire Bible. Both deaths were tied up in this mess that led back to Piedmont Sr. and the Aztekas. Maclaren could help me sort out what the patents meant to Lee and his heirs. But, since his company had an inherent interest in that research, it would be good to know as much as possible about Lee's work beforehand.

Jim still hadn't returned my call, so I put in a Hail Mary to Denver on my glove phone.

"Any news on the de-encryption of the Lee files?" I blurted out as soon as Denver's holo-image appeared.

She looked wan and was missing her characteristic spark. Denver's hair was a dull brownish black, minus her usual vibrant colors. Moreover, her black lacquered nails were chipped.

She didn't give me her usual grief either. Just stared at me with flat empty eyes.

I hesitated. "What's the matter? You look like you haven't slept in three nights—for all the wrong reasons."

Denver shook her head. "Nothing."

"What aren't you telling me?"

"Let's stick to the encryption."

"From your face, I'm guessing it's a no go."

"Guess again." In slow motion Denver synched our wireless projection modes so I could see the mathematical algorithms from the file she was reviewing floating in the air before me. "It's a matryosha encryption. Pretty fucking ingenious actually."

"Matryosha? You mean those Russian nesting dolls?"

Denver nodded. "Lee layered his encryption. Layers within layers."

As she started to speak, tears began to roll down her pale cheeks. Denver never cried, not even when she'd been arrested.

I leaned in towards her floating image. "What's wrong?"

"Nothing!" She wiped the tears with an angry swipe of the back of her hand, but they continued to flow. "Lee used a fucking complex labyrinthine encryption. By the way, the flash dot's really an external hard drive. He hid the data stored on the drive by changing the suffix at the end of the name of key files."

"Denver."

"He used the end part of the file address that tells the computer what software program it needs to open the file." Denver's words tumbled out of her mouth in a rush like somebody on a coke rant. "Lee used the suffix '.rar,' which relates to a type of software that reduces the size of a file. But they were actually created with a different program, Totally Private, which enabled each file to run as a separate, encryption-protected virtual hard drive. Without the correct password, the files were completely unintelligible."

"Denver." I reached out to touch her arm, but of course only managed to disturb the pixels.

"One of those numbers you gave me was the password and the other one was the file name," she said.

I let her babble on.

"You'd think that would be enough, but even when I cracked that, I couldn't read the shit 'cuz he enciphered the text again. It was all scrambled eggs. Totally unreadable until I unscrambled it. There was a disguised file on the external hard drive that looked like it was meant for viewing photos. It wasn't. The file really consisted of coded text with a set of instructions for using a spreadsheet containing a purpose-built formula to decipher the scrambled text. Once I saw that, I knew we'd passed go."

"So what was worth all this security?" I said. "What's the file say?"

"I cracked the code," Denver replied. "Doesn't mean I can read the shit. Look." For a second her usual snarky tone had reasserted itself. But the uncontrolled tears started again with her next breath. She opened up Lee's file for me to see. Words from the file floated in the air before us—

"Neurofibrillary tangles . . . beta-amyloid plaques . . . amyloid precursor protein gene . . . disintegrated dendrites . . ." I said. "His Alzheimer's X research." This had to be the patent material.

"The final nesting doll." Denver sniffed. "Isn't that ironic."

"Except," I said, smiling, "this time we've got people who can read the Russian." I sent the file to Jim Mar at the crime lab.

Denver didn't respond. I kept staring at her stricken face. "Tell me what's wrong. Is it Diamond Dog?"

Denver sighed and shook her head. She switched files. The new file consisted of a single sentence under the heading listing Denver's name. The sentence read "test results positive."

"My family insisted the D-Dog get a full genetic read-out before the wedding. So, I got one too, to keep him company. He passed with flying colors."

A pair of icy hands reached into my chest and squeezed all the air out of my lungs.

Denver had tested positive for Alzheimer's X. The diagnosis meant the twenty-one-year-old had three to five years before the disease turned her into one of those zombies walking the streets of L.A.

"Have you told Diamond Dog?"

"Can't," she said. "What if he dumps me?"

"He won't."

The tears had started again, silently sliding down her cheeks. "You're usually a better liar, Piedmont."

CHAPTER FORTY-SEVEN

THE IMAGE OF DENVER'S STRICKEN FACE ACCOMPANIED ME AS I made my way along Venice Beach to the Theban Grill. More than ever, I wanted to pick the brain of Jim Mar, the crime lab serologist, and I'd finally managed to track him down. Jim was just back from vacation, and he agreed to meet as soon as he got off work. The aroma of grilled calamari and rosemary chicken kabobs wafted towards me as I walked.

Sandwiched between a henna and hemp store and the parking lot filled with laughing thong-clad hover-boarders, the grill was the last stop on the boardwalk.

A girl about Denver's age sat on the beach directly in front of the café. She wore a ragged dress and rocked an imaginary baby in her arms as she stared at the waves.

I tried to focus on the case as I slid onto the seat behind a metal picnic table to the side of the grill. A showboating hover-boarder had barely circled around me twice flashing his porcelain veneers when I spotted Jim walking towards me.

Jim rolled his eyes at the hover-boarder as he showed off the fluorescent derma ad for a gay bar inked on his back before heading off.

Jim was over forty, but today he vibed a good decade younger.

"You look rested," I said with a little more edge than intended. "Good vacation?"

He dumped his bag on a seat opposite me. Jim turned his face, giving me exaggerated right and left profiles in turn. "What do you think? A little nano-fill here, micro-lift there, and goodbye mid-life crisis. Don't judge, Eddie. You're too young to know what it's like. Tell me about this file you've been pestering me about."

"Did you read it?"

He raised his left eyebrow almost as high as his Regenerexed hairline. "It's my first day back. I was about to when I got your very impatient call to meet."

"Read it now." I re-forwarded him the file from Dr. Lee, which Denver had decoded.

Jim sighed. "Why do all the really good-looking men only want me for my brain?" He started to read. What he read didn't take long to engross him.

Jim didn't look up even when the waiter returned with our drinks and plunked them on the table. He took a sip and kept reading.

I poured water from the pitcher into my ouzo and watched clouds form in the clear liquid. As I waited, I looked around. Everywhere I looked, vacant-eyed teens and twenty-somethings wandered aimlessly among the rest of us. There seemed to be more of them every day. But the weirdest thing wasn't the afflicted. It was the way they disappeared in plain sight. People just averted their eyes and went on with their lives like they do with the homeless. Would Denver soon be one of the hollow-eyed wanderers?

Suddenly, I wasn't hungry. When the server brought the food, I picked at my grilled calamari just to have something to do.

Jim dug into his lamb as he kept reading. "Wow," he said. "Is this for real?"

"What exactly did Lee discover? Be specific."

"Genetic research for Alzheimer's X, the genes that make people vulnerable."

"So, he could predict it years before the disease manifested." That had to be Lee's original D-design patent. That wasn't news. That was the test Denver had just taken.

Jim nodded. "It gets better. Eddie, I think this guy Lee found somebody whose DNA is resistant."

I sat up a little straighter. "Someone genetically immune to the disease?"

Jim cocked his head to the side. "Well, highly resistant to it at least." He took a big swallow of his Wine Dark drink. "Scientists have known for years which gene on the nineteenth chromosome makes people vulnerable to regular Alzheimer's. We've also known that a defective APP gene on chromosome twenty-one is associated with early onset Alzheimer's."

"Alzheimer's X, you mean?" I asked.

"The forerunner," Jim corrected. "According to this, Lee also discovered certain drugs create variations in the epigenome—causing inflammation and the wrong kind of protein manufacture in genetically susceptible people."

"Which drugs?"

"Green Ice and Blue Lotus."

I leaned forward. "So Alz-X is triggered by ice and spice—like marijuana turns on schizophrenia."

"Worse," he said. "They catalyze the disease in genetically susceptible people. People who might have gotten Alzheimers in their eighties now get a more virulent senile dementia in their teens. Welcome to Alzheimer's X."

Jim took a bite of the lamb and chewed thoughtfully before continuing. "But if this guy Lee's on the level," Jim said, tapping his forefinger on the metal table, "he engineered a treatment based on the resistant genome."

"A cure?"

"Better," Jim said. "Immunization would derail the disease before it takes hold. People don't even get sick."

That had to be the additional improvement Lee had registered with his AI patent. And Lee held the rights to both the diagnostic test for Alz-X and the patented cure. Or he did until he died.

"Who's the miracle resistor?"

"The source is identity blind." Jim pointed to a footnote in the article thick with unfamiliar numbers. No way to know whose it is just from Lee's file."

Jim's eyes met mine as we both stared at the Devonshire girl's blood spot in the case file. It wasn't much of a stretch to think the DNA we were staring at wasn't just a link in the chain, but the whole double helix, the source of the resistant genome.

"How long will it take you to compare the genome in this file with both the partial prelim and Britney's blood from the autopsy?" I said.

"A day. I'll want to run it twice to confirm."

"Make it half a day." I signaled the waiter for the check.

"Wait, Eddie." Jim leaned in towards me, his voice lowering to a whisper. "What company was this guy affiliated with? Are they going public?" Jim was already tapping his glove phone to start up a new search.

"Jim." I shut down his glove phone. "This has to be on the QT for now."

"This is a once in the lifetime opportunity," Jim said.

"It's a murder investigation."

Jim frowned. "I won't tell anybody. You have my word on that."

I knew I couldn't keep Jim from acting on the information for long. "How soon could this come to market? Soon enough to help somebody just diagnosed?" Somebody like Denver?

"Maybe. But the disease moves fast. FDA trials don't. Where are they in the process?" Jim made a clicking sound with his tongue as the server scanned my barcode for the tab. "It takes nine years for a drug to make it to market." We both stood to go.

"Hurry," I said.

I headed straight to my Porsche. Jim didn't even glance in Tan Hover-boarder's direction as he backed his gray electric Honda out of the parking lot and gunned it towards the lab.

A finding this big, a finding that led to immunization, could mean billions, not just millions. That kind of money caused people to do all sorts of desperate things. Like kill a stripper when she found out the true value of her genome and tried to muscle in on the profit. And anybody who got in the way, like Lee, Frank, or me, would also fall in the acceptable losses column. Especially with the Aztekas involved . . .

I punched the ignition, put the car on autopilot, and called Shin with the update. His floating image showed me Shin was still at Nokia, but had stepped outside for some air. He stood next to one of those headless torso sculptures of black steel standing sentinel round police headquarters.

"We'll have to subpoena Lee's will," Shin said. "Find out whether the family or the company inherits the rights to the patents."

"I have a call into Lee's boss. He should be able to give us some answers. And Jim should have the blood work done by end of day tomorrow."

"Good," Shin said. "I'll get the warrant for the Baby Mine clinic first thing in the morning." He paused2. "The AzteKas."

"Yeah," I said. "They wouldn't be too keen on word getting out that Green Ice and Blue Lotus catalyze Alz-X. Those are their top sellers. Maybe they hoped taking out Britney and Lee might delay or derail the news getting out."

"That explains why they deviated from their usual M.O. too," Shin said. "Making both deaths look like accidents draws attention away from their involvement."

"But taking out Lee also delays the cure. The cure would be good for them."

My partner cocked his head to the side. "Let's find out who gets those patents," Shin said.

Though still early, night was already closing in as I made the drive back to the hotel. The Santa Anas were wailing through the city like ghosts lost in high rise corridors and canyons. Halloween was just two days away, and decorations had sprung up everywhere. Little orange lights glowed; paper ghosts fluttered, and fake gravestones pushed up through the ground in suburban front yards.

"God, listen to those Santa Anas," Shin said. "Creepy. You know some people think Halloween's the time when the veil between the living and the dead is thinnest."

Listening to the wail of the winds, I thought they might be on to something. The city's chorus of ghosts seemed to be crying out louder than ever tonight.

Maybe that's just a homicide detective's view of the city. Whereas civilians navigated by landmarks like a new Starbucks or a familiar gas station, for me the streets were marked by the bodies found on the scene: a robbery homicide at that Arco, a domestic dispute that ended with two dead a block away. Blood shadows haunted me at every turn.

An irritating buzz from my Nokia Handy interrupted my reverie and the car vid-chat with Shin.

"Gotta take this." I angled the glove-phone so Shin could see the Caller ID on his screen.

The incoming caller was Harvey Pink.

CHAPTER FORTY-EIGHT

"DETECTIVE PIEDMONT?" HARVEY PINK'S THIN VOICE GRATED in my ear as I drove back to the hotel. He had the video option switched off, and his voice was pitched higher than usual, but a second glance at Caller ID verified the number was indeed Pink's. "I need to talk to you."

"What's that, Harvey?" I could hear the urgency in his voice, but if Harvey Pink told me the sun was shining, I'd check for rain. I set my scanner to triangulate his position.

"Not over the phone," he said. "Meet me at the Baby Mine Clinic."

Harvey had my full attention.

"You sound high," I told him, stalling. "When did you last use?" The scanner had one point nailed. Two to go.

"What's that to you?"

"It's a long drive out to Sun Valley. How do I know you're not jerking me around this time? You lied to me. You lied to my partner."

The only sound from Pink was his ragged breath. Then, "Do you want to know why I made Lee crash or not?"

When I jerked the car off autopilot, I barely braked in time to avoid rear-ending the BMW ahead. Why was Pink owning Lee's murder now? Salazar's lawyer had gotten Harvey off with a slap on the wrist, claiming the now-dead Ramirez had been responsible.

"I'm listening."

The scanner pinged the second point. One point left.

"The Baby Mine Clinic," he repeated. "Hurry." And Harvey Pink was gone.

Harvey was somewhere in the north Valley, but he'd hung up three seconds before the scanner could verify the call's exact location.

"Probably a wild goose chase," Shin said when I called him back. "To muddy the waters around Salazar."

"I didn't think Nieto and the Aztekas cared that much about the little weasel."

"They care less about Harvey Pink," Shin said.

"True." I punched on the Traffic Light Expediter and turned the nose of my Porsche around. "Only one way to find out." The TLE changed all lights to green as I raced onto the 405 south towards the Valley and the Baby Mine Clinic.

My brakes were squealing when I finally pulled up to the two-story sepia-colored building in Sun Valley thirty minutes later. No sign of Harvey in the front lot. A couple of amiable looking women chatted casually as they passed an oak tree, bent like an allen wrench to the right of the clinic's front door, and headed inside. The older woman wore blue scrubs. The younger wore green.

A small prickle of irritation needled me. Was the hype jerking my chain after all? As I circled round to the back of the clinic, I puffed out a sigh of relief. There sat a beat up old Toyota sprawled across the two handicapped parking spots crammed closest to the building. The familiar constellation of bumper sticker complaints told me it was Pink's ride all right. I started to turn into the lot, but a cream-colored Sebring convertible blocked the entrance.

The driver idled his engine, waiting for a twenty-something woman, who moved slower than old ketchup as she strolled to the car from the back door of the clinic. I honked for the Sebring driver to move out of the way. He got out of his car, stared at my Porsche, and flipped me off. Pulling out my badge, I opened my door and gestured for the knucklehead to move his car away from the lot entrance and into a parking spot ASAP.

That's when Harvey Pink ambled round from the front door, heading for his beat-up Toyota. About ten feet behind him trailed a familiar raven-haired beauty—Mercedes, Britney Devonshire's friend. Why was she here? She didn't glance in Harvey's direction. Harvey didn't slow his stride to wait for her. Both at the clinic, but not together. Why?

"Hey," I yelled.

Mercedes looked up with an anxious smile. But when Pink turned and spotted me, he scurried to his Toyota. The junkie looked surprised and confused, and not at all happy to see me.

He hadn't placed the call to meet. The little chirp of his car door unlocking flooded me with a sense of dread. I suddenly knew why the pitch of Pink's voice had sounded high on the call.

"Down!" I yelled and dove under my car, covering my ears.

Mercedes froze with a look of startled confusion plastered on her face. And Pink's Toyota exploded in a ball of flame.

The force from the explosion rocked my Porsche like a row boat in a typhoon. My head bounced off the chassis. When I crawled out, the world was eerily still. No sound for what seemed like an eternity. Then I heard a heavy rain on the windshield. Only it wasn't rain. A shower of blood splattered the reinforced glass and painted everything with a red mist, including me.

Where the clinic had been, there was only a shell now. The whole back of the building near Pink's car was a pile of refuse, shrouded with a cloud of greasy black smoke. Body parts lay strewn haphazardly around the parking lot. A woman's arm and bloody entrails hung in the blackened oak tree out front. The air felt thick and hot.

No sign of Pink.

And Mercedes—one second she was standing next to the tree by the door. The next, she was falling to her knees in the dirt, her crimson blood mingling with the dust.

"No. No. No." My ears were ringing. My eyes stung. I could feel sweat pouring down the singed skin of my face. I wiped my face with my sleeve. The sleeve was covered in blood. The skin of my face felt numb. I staggered a little before finding my feet. I made my way to Mercedes. She was supposed to be staying with relatives—safe out of town. I ripped off my shirt. I probed her wounds, trying to staunch the blood with the once white cotton. Pointless. Shrapnel had torn the life from her body. Her eyes were already glazing. I sat back on my heels and slowly draped the shirt over her face.

Standing, I called out under the rubble to any survivors. It was a fool's errand. Nobody in close could have survived the blast. The guy with the cream-colored Sebring convertible had toppled backwards—skewered with a hunk of metal and fragments of glass from the explosion.

"911." My voice was hoarse from the smoke. My glove phone couldn't understand my command. Trying to activate it manually, my numbed fingers felt awkward, making it difficult to punch the numbers. My ears were still ringing. The stinging smoke made me squint.

Staggering over to the seared remnants of Pink's Toyota, I made my way around the burnt-out hull of twisted metal and melted plastic. Plumes of smoke wafted their way skyward from the wreck. Around what had been the passenger side, I staggered. And found what remained of Harvey Pink. A burnt offering to a savage god.

The force of the blast had tossed him ten feet or more, landing Pink behind his Toyota. His head was smashed in, but his torso had burst open like a piñata in a horror movie. The stench of burnt hair and flesh filled my mouth and nose.

Not long after, approaching sirens blared. An EMT chopper car landed with a full medical team that rushed towards us. Some minutes later I texted both Shin and Captain Tatum about Pink, Mercedes, and the explosion, then watched as the medical team did their job. By the time the paramedic had glued the gash in my forehead, police scanners had been buzzing for a quarter of an hour. Shielded by the Sebring that had blocked the entrance to the parking lot, my Porsche was dented by falling detritus but still intact. I wiped the blood from the reinforced windshield and found the engine purred to life. White vans crammed with breaking news crews were pulling up, satellite dishes swaying, as I drove away.

CHAPTER FORTY-NINE

CAPTAIN TATUM REACHED ME AT THE HOTEL ABOUT AN HOUR later. I was fixing a bag of ice to put on my pounding head when she called.

"You okay?" she said, her forehead puckered in a worried expression.

I nodded. Leaning against the ice dispenser down the hall from Jo's and my hotel room, I gazed at Tatum's normally stern face. The cold steel of the dispenser felt good on my skin. "Anything at Pink's place?"

"We found a suicide note." Tatum tapped her fingers on the surface of her desk at Nokia PD. "He claimed responsibility for the deaths of all the clinic's 'baby killers' and, I quote, 'the cops that protect them.' I figure that last was meant for you, Eddie." She paused. "I'm glad you're okay."

I nodded. "Pink didn't rig his Toyota with the car bomb, Captain."

"It does seem way beyond his pay grade," she agreed. "But he did put the nano-bot under Lee's car. And claimed responsibility for Lee when he called you to the scene, right? That fits with premeditation."

"Check on that call." I told her about the surprised expression on Pink's face when he saw me outside the clinic and ran to unlock his car. "Pink was a pathetic mess, but he had no clue about the bomb. I'm betting somebody used a spoof card to set us up."

"And pretended to be Pink to lure you to the scene?" Captain Tatum cocked her head to the side, considering.

Tatum knew spoof cards were a useful ploy because we used them. With one of the prepaid cards you could buy in any supermarket and enough technological savy to set up a fake Caller ID, you could get a perp to show up at a hospital thinking his dear old mom had just checked into ICU. When he arrived, a pair of handcuffs waited for him instead of Mom. Totally legal.

I nodded. "Mercedes Delblanco was set up too. One less witness. Nieto's behind this. Explosives are his thing."

"The AzteKa enforcer?" Tatum said.

"He's been paroled." I filled her in on what I'd learned from Jim Mar about Lee's work and its relevance to the case. "The AzteKas are behind all this, Captain. We're getting close."

"Maybe too close. This is the second attempt on your life in a month. I'm thinking I should pull you off the case before the third."

"I have a better idea." I paused, shaking the bag of melting ice and putting it back on my head before meeting Tatum's eyes again. "Pink couldn't cook up anything more complicated than his next fix, but maybe we should let people think different—for a while."

Tatum's face took on the pensive look of a chess player planning two moves ahead. "Now you're starting to think like Robbery-Homicide, Eddie." She smiled. A wicked little glint lit up her eyes.

Later that night crime news broadcasts were still updating reports on the deaths from the blast. Six dead, all innocent victims, plus Pink.

Jo and I were sitting up in the hotel bed watching the news as Captain Tatum stood behind a podium of plain blond wood inside Nokia P.D. and gave her on-camera statement to waiting reporters. Silver stars gleaming on the black collar of her dress uniform matched the silver threads in her dark curls. Tatum's calm and serious expression was the picture of gravitas as she skillfully laid out the facts in a way that encouraged the press to leap to the conclusion that Pink was the bomber and he'd acted alone. With luck, Nieto and the AzteKas would believe we'd bought it too and back off.

Reporters shouted questions. The questions blurred into a river of noise.

Tatum held up her hands in a gesture that demanded calm. "We'll keep you apprised of further developments," she said, and left the podium.

Jo leaned her head against my shoulder and let the on-camera reporters drone on with their speculation about Pink. Jo had been so freaked out after the bombing, I hadn't told her the truth about the spoof card.

Then, Pink's picture filled the screen.

My head was filled with other faces though: Britney Devonshire, Lee, Mercedes with that puzzled look on her face, right before she sank to her knees and poured her life out into the dirt, and Frank. Always Frank. But the last face I couldn't get out of my head—that belonged to Nieto.

CHAPTER FIFTY

BY THE NEXT MORNING, ANOTHER CROWD OF SCREAMING CITIzens massed in front of Nokia PD. From a hundred and fifty feet out, I spotted a digital poster with my face on it. I hunched my shoulders, hoping to make myself a smaller target. Only when I got close enough to read the signs bobbing up and down on digital placards did I see the tagline under my printed picture: Local hero. The same hard-charging behavior, which had gotten me into trouble a couple weeks ago, had now gotten me out of it. News coverage on the clinic bombing had redirected the mob's anger away from me this time.

I took a deep breath. The city's ever-present stink of purifying burning sage and ganja filled my lungs. The smell was especially sharp and pungent today.

"Our hero," Shin said in a playful tone as he fell in beside me.

"Give me a break."

With my hat pulled down over my face and shoulders hunched, we slipped through the herd unnoticed and walked in the back entrance. Shin and I went through security, ran our barcodes over the elevator sensor, and hit the button for the third floor.

When the door opened, there stood my rep Espinoza, waiting for me just outside the elevator. He gave me the official version of what Jo had confided days earlier. I'd been reinstated with a clean record.

Irony be damned. A thousand pound weight had been lifted from my shoulders. The day was getting better and better.

"You're good police," Espinoza said. "I'm proud to have represented you, and don't take this the wrong way, detective, but I hope not to see you again." A quick handshake, a few more words, and he was gone, scurrying down the third floor corridor.

*

Captain Tatum met us right outside Homicide Special, her tired but smiling face appraising me. There was a familiar presence on Tatum's right flank. The dark-haired woman with a heart-shaped face and eyes like a raptor belonged to Anna Vargas, Head of the Technology Unit.

"I ran a trace on that call that lured you to Baby Mine," Vargas said. "You were right about the spoof card, Detective Piedmont."

Pink's mobile had not made the call—even though my Caller ID made it seem like he had. Vargas took my glove phone and personally issued me a new Nokia Handy with special latest edition encrypted security.

"Officer Vargas sent our best mechanic to scan your Porsche for any potential IEDs too," Tatum said. "Just in case."

"Jimmy Chung's going over your car right now," Anna confirmed.

I nodded thanks. "Good press release last night, Captain."

"Let's hope the AzteKas take the bait," she said, glancing at Shin and back to me. "The case is yours to close, detectives. Don't fuck it up."

Shin and I watched Tatum and Vargas enter the elevator before heading to our desks and digging in to the update on the explosion.

"Forensics found traces of large quantities of hexamethylene triperoxide diamine and pentaerythritol tetranitrate on the chassis of Pink's car," Shin said. "They're tracking the sale of the explosives."

"PETN: Nieto's brand of choice," I said, nodding.

"I'll get to work on the subpoena of Lee's will," Shin said, "and follow Pink's digital trail."

That left the terms of Lee's employment contract at Genesys, plus follow-up with Jim on the genetic work to me. I left an urgent message for Chris Maclaren, Lee's employer, and called Jim Mar about the blood work.

"I need more time," Jim said, his holo-image floating in the L-shaped space between the thumb and forefinger of my glove phone. His hair was unwashed, and he was wearing the same clothes he'd worn during our chat at the Theban Grill.

I was pretty sure he hadn't slept since then either.

"Is Britney Devonshire the source genome for the Alz-X treatment, or not?"

"I don't know yet," Jim said. "There's some damage on the file you gave me. We don't want to be wrong on this. I'll call you when I know."

We hadn't yet found the evidence that clearly linked Dr. Lee and Nieto. Salazar had claimed Raymond Lee's drug habit was the link between Dr. Lee and the AzTekas. The explosives were a Nieto signature, but we needed definitive proof. So, while I waited to hear back from Jim and the Genesys CEO, I pulled up Nieto's rap sheet and dug in. It was a long and bloody sheet, capped by the murder of a Zeta in 2036.

That's when I saw the name: Miguel Fuentes-Obrador. He was the first uniform on the scene of the Nieto murder. No way that was a coincidence; this had to be the Fuentes Dr. Lee had mentioned in his vlog and at the time of death.

It took another half hour to locate Captain Tatum again and get her to authorize my access to Fuentes-Obrador's confidential personnel file. Pins and needles pricked the pit of my stomach as I entered the access code and started reading.

Officer Miguel F. Obrador had not only been the first uniform at the crime scene. He was also the young P-2 who filed that supplemental report over a year later, claiming he'd had a lapse of memory about an unnamed potential suspect who'd fled the scene.

Since this new evidence had directly contradicted the sworn testimony of the only eye witness besides Nieto himself, it gave the defense attorneys the hammer they needed. The report necessitated another cross examination of the witness on appeal. The only problem was that the witness wasn't available for cross examination. She wasn't available because her dead body had turned up a month earlier in a Mexican ravine.

It took another year for the lawyers to game the system, but eventually Miguel Fuentes-Obrador's highly suspicious report got the conviction overturned on procedure. That first week in October of this year, 2041, the bad guys had won, and Nieto walked free. The announcement had been playing on the news that evening Shin and I left the Code Seven VR-bar. That news story had been the start of an evening I wasn't likely to forget, the evening that ended with the Ramirez shooting and my being put on desk duty. The pieces of the puzzle were coming together fast now.

I desperately wanted to talk to Officer Fuentes-Obrador, but a glance at his file told me that too was impossible. As Lee had told me, Fuentes was two inches in the obit column. The dead man's file listed the caulse of death as heart failure brought on by overdose of Green Ice. He'd died on September 15th. Britney Devonshire had overdosed on the drug too, and the 15th was only a couple weeks before her murder. The dates for Fuentes' death tallied with Lee's last words to me at the crash that had killed him. Ditto his vlog.

I read the files again. This new information linked Dr. Lee to Nieto through Fuentes. But the connection opened up nearly as many questions as it answered. Like how had Nieto gotten to the young P-2 when Nieto was already in prison by that time?

"Shin," I said as soon as he was off the phone. "I'm heading out."

"Where to?" Shin cocked his head to the side and took a sip of his Redbull.

I filled him in on Nieto's record. Shin spilled his Redbull over the front of his shirt when I showed him Fuentes' personnel file. I watched the genetically engineered cotton self-clean itself and wished the city could rid itself of filth like Nieto just as easily.

"Cause of death listed as heart failure due to overdose," I said, rereading the Fuentes personnel file again. "But in his vlog, Lee said they got to Fuentes."

"So." Shin cut me a glance. "Most likely not an accidental overdose." Shin turned away from the holo-screen. "I'll get the autopsy report and check with Obrador's supervisor. Then there's the wife and Obrador's partner."

I had already pulled a name from my computer and an address in Big Bear.

"Let me guess," Shin said. "You want to talk to his partner first."

I nodded as we shared a glance at the name I'd pulled: Dick Logue. "Partners always know."

CHAPTER FIFTY-ONE

I WAS WELL ON MY WAY TO BIG BEAR WHEN MY NEW HANDY vibrated. It was Jo.

"Eddie, did you forget to send me your schedule?"

I had. The case had pushed personal life off my agenda for the moment. "Sorry."

"Send it, okay? I'd like to get the wedding calendar settled before my trip to China."

Hong Kong would lose any remaining autonomy and be completely absorbed into the People's Republic of China in 2047, and Jo had a big intellectual property conference coming up in a month to deal with the anticipated repercussions. I smiled. My Jo hated any hint of chaos. She liked to keep things organized.

"I'm on it." By the time I'd followed through on that and called Shin back, my partner had finished checking out Fuentes-Obrador with his supervisor.

"As as far as his lieutenant knows," Shin said, "he didn't have any health issues. He was current on the rent and all his bills too. Other than that supplemental report, Fuentes-Obrador's jacket was as clean as an Eagle Scout's."

"No prior drug use?" I said.

"Nada," Shin replied.

"And he suddenly overdoses? Nobody checked it out?"

Shin's face screwed up into an apologetic expression. "His lieutenant said there was no sign of foul play, and nobody wanted to make a stink about a possible suicide. Fuentes had a wife and two kids."

"Three reasons I'm thinking he didn't check out on his own."

Shin nodded and hung up as I veered off CA-330N to CA-18. Time to talk to Fuentes-Obrador's partner and get some answers.

*

Officer Richard Logue had retired from the force two years ago and settled in Big Bear.

Pine-covered San Bernadino Mountains surrounded Big Bear Lake like a mother's embrace. But August wildfires had laid waste to much of the parched scrub and pine trees on the hillsides, and a hard rain had sent boulders and a sheet of mud hurtling down the naked mountainside onto roads. Ominous boulders stood as mute sentinels of natural disaster on the side of the cleared road.

The Grizzly Lodge, a three-story bed and breakfast perched on the edge of the lake, was a mud-colored, down-at-the-heels ski chalet. I spotted one dark-haired woman with a golden retriever and two little kids playing outside, but otherwise the place felt barren.

I parked in front and walked inside. The walls of the ski chalet were made of pine stained dark from wood-smoke. A walk-in fireplace dominated the wall to the right. A huge stuffed grizzly reared on its hind legs by the front desk opposite the fireplace.

Heading towards the man behind the desk, I asked to speak to Dick Logue. He gestured to an old bulldog of a guy carrying a stack of towels towards the kitchen off to the right.

Logue wore Levis, a plain white T-shirt, and a baseball cap with a grizzly bear embroidered on it. The jeans bagged around his scrawny legs, but Logue carried fifty extra pounds, all around the gut. It was as if somebody had picked him up by the legs and shaken all his muscle and fat to the middle like the filings in an Etch-a-Sketch, then set him back down before it reached his chest and arms. A small silver cross hung from his neck.

"Officer Logue?" I could smell the beer on him from six feet away.

"Just Dick Logue now," he said. "I'm retired."

"Some things never leave you." I badged him. "Eddie Piedmont."

"Ain't that the truth." Logue's rheumy eyes searched my face with the puzzled look of somebody trying to remember how they know you. "I never made detective," he replied, barely glancing at the gold shield. "I liked the street. What house?"

"Homicide Special."

His smile twisted into a smirk. "The golden boys in the Glass House." Logue gestured me into the kitchen. Then he stopped and pointed at me. "You're the one with his face plastered all over the city a few years back. What can I do you for?"

"I'm hoping you can help me out with some information. About your partner, Miguel Fuentes-Obrador."

Logue's dismissive stare instantly became wary.

The kitchen was thirty years out of date with its aqua subzero fridge and gray granite countertops. There were chips in the granite and nicks in the tile floors, but it was clean, and the air smelled of lemon scented Lysol. Logue set the pile of towels down on the counter and opened the fridge.

"You want a beer?"

I shook my head no.

He grabbed a can of Coors for himself and lumbered over to a wooden table with a couple chairs on either side.

Logue lowered himself onto the hard wooden chair with a thud and gestured to the chair opposite with a tilt of the head, simultaneously popping the top on his beer.

"About your partner," I said, taking the seat.

"What about him?" Logue lowered heavy-lidded eyes.

"I was wondering why a twenty-something guy with no prior drug use or health issues suddenly keels over from heart failure due to overdose."

"I'm not a doctor." Logue stared at me through those heavy-lidded eyes. "I'd say Mikey just had bad luck."

"What kind of bad luck? The kind the wrong friends bring? Like the AzteKas, for instance? What was he mixed up in?"

Logue's voice immediately bubbled up with defensive anger. "He was my partner, detective. Let him rest in peace."

I set my fedora on the wooden table top and smoothed my hair. "I lost my partner too. Frank Waldron, know him?"

Logue shook his head, no.

"Somebody took out Frank a couple weeks after you lost Fuentes. I know how it feels to want to do right by him."

Nodding, Logue shifted around in the chair.

"I need information about an old case," I said. "Remember the Nieto collar five years back?"

"What's that to you?" Logue said with a deep sigh. "You

weren't the detective on the Nieto case."

I pulled up copies of the two reports—Miguel Fuentes-Obrador's original from five years ago stating that Nieto was the only suspect spotted at the scene. The second was the supplemental, the report he'd filed after Nieto's conviction, in which Fuentes had suddenly added a false account of an additional unidentified man leaving the scene. Reasonable doubt in black and white—and the grounds for the killer's appeal.

"According to the file, your partner swore up and down he'd forgotten that key bit of evidence," I said. "But I think he falsified that supplemental report and got the scumbag sprung. From his jacket he reads like a good cop. So why would Fuentes do that? Unless Nieto or one of his crew got to him. What did they have on him?"

I'd expected Logue to bristle again. Instead, his defensive posture collapsed like an old boxer in the ring who suddenly gives up and accepts the blows.

"I always knew somebody'd walk through that door someday," Logue said, but instead of explaining, hauled himself out of his chair. "I got a delivery coming. Let me make a call and get Art to handle it." He lumbered over to the front desk and said something to the hired hand standing there. Art nodded.

With his back to me, Logue made a call on the land line. After a few minutes he hung up the phone and retrieved an envelope from a safe behind the counter. Slowly he made his way back toward me.

"Come on out to the dock," Logue said when he got closer. "I don't want Art involved in this." He cocked his head in the direction of the employee still standing behind the front desk.

I stood and followed him as he headed out onto the dock, Logue's steps heavy and hollow-sounding on the wood.

"Did I pass?" I asked. I figured Logue had made a couple of calls to check me out. I would have.

"Word is, you're an arrogant prick, but everybody liked Frank."

What they say about you is you took a lot of sick days. Coors flu. "About your partner," I pressed.

Logue took a while to start. Even though I felt like taking a cattle prod to the old guy to speed things along, I let him take his time. He wanted to tell me something. The sun was just beginning to set, the air cooling off fast. We watched in silence. As the dark lake slowly started to swallow the light of the sun, the sky bled a reddish pink. The horizon was a smudge of dirty brownish-black.

"The thing you have to understand about Mikey," Logue said finally, "is that his wife Maria was everything to him. They grew up together, and outside of her and the kids he didn't have any family. He would have done anything for her."

Logue activated his glove phone and brought up a picture of Fuentes-Obrador and a pretty, young, Hispanic girl-woman still in her teens standing against the backdrop of Disneyland's Sleeping Beauty's castle. Long waves of dark hair framed her delicate face as she hung on Miguel's arm and smiled a mischievious smile.

"I took that picture of Miguel and Maria in 2034," Logue said, before sliding another photo forward on the glove phone. "This one's from last week when I stopped by."

In this shot, twenty-four-year-old Maria perched on the edge of a chair in what seemed to be a nursing home. Her little bird wrists hung out of an orange plaid shirt two sizes too big and pillowed out over purple polyester pants several patterns too loud. Somebody must have brushed her dark hair too and pinned it back with butterfly barrettes appropriate for a little girl of six. No one home in those vacant eyes.

"Alzheimer's X?" I said.

He nodded. "She was diagnosed in 2037. She's been in the nursing home since 2038."

The year Miguel filed the supplemental report. "What did your partner get? Money? For his wife's treatment?"

"No." Logue handed me another slip of paper. "Not money."

He opened the envelope and pulled out a slip of paper. It was Maria Fuentes's admittance slip for a clinical trial. On the back Fuentes had written *May God forgive me* in Spanish. The admittance slip was stamped approved with GEN-333-1110, the corporate logo and a barcode. GEN for Genesys—Lee's company, and the patent number of the drug he'd pioneered.

There it was—the missing connection between Lee and Nieto that led straight through Fuentes-Obrador.

"Nieto got Dr. Lee to put Miguel's wife into a clinical trial for an experimental Alzheimer's X drug," I said.

Logue nodded. "At first Mikey lied to me, said he'd really forgotten to file that supplemental. You know. He only came clean after his wife's clinical trial was discontinued—about a year ago. Finally admitted they'd come to him with a deal three years or so back. They promised to slip Maria into the trial and give her the real meds, not the placebo.They were getting good results from that trial."

"Who approached Miguel about filing the report?

Logue shrugged his shoulders.

Nieto himself had been in prison at the time. I brought up my glove phone and showed him a digital snap of Lee. "Is this the guy?"

His face showed no sign of recognition. "I don't know."

"What about this guy?" I flashed to a shot of the Azteka lawyer who repped Salazar and Pink after they'd assaulted me. When Logue shook his head again, I flashed him a shot of Sandy Rose.

"I don't know who approached him, detective. I just know they said if Mikey would suddenly remember this other bit of business, file the amended report and say that it had allegedly been "mislaid," they'd put his wife into the clinical trial and make sure she got the real drug, not the placebo."

I waited.

"But after he did what they wanted," Logue continued, "they still discontinued the clinical trial, and well, you saw Maria. How she is now." He looked out on the lake. "It was all for nothing."

A couple of recreational fishing boats cut wakes in the water behind them—coming in from the last catch of the day. Their trails disappeared in the swell.

"Worse than that," I said. "Nieto didn't stop with the murder of that Zeta in '36. He's implicated in at least two more homicides—including my partner Frank's. That's just what we know about."

Logue took a deep breath, nodding. "You think he didn't know that, detective? At the end I mean? What Mikey did left a heavy wake in his life."

He stared out at a slower power boat with deep choppy water trailing behind. The woman, her two kids and the retriever I'd seen out front before were in the boat, laughing. "He couldn't live with it, could he?"

"Suicide?" My kid wasn't even born yet, but I couldn't imagine offing myself if Jo had what Maria had. And speaking of Fuentes' kids, where were they now that their father was dead and their mother worse than dead?

"No," Logue said. "Mikey threatened to come clean about the supplemental report. And suddenly he turned up dead. I didn't buy it, but there was no sign of a struggle on his body and nothing in the autopsy to suggest foul play."

"And if you raised a stink, and they ruled it a suicide, his widow might not get his pension." I nodded. "Did he mention who approached him about faking the report to get Maria into the clinical trial? Was it the same person who put her into the trial? Or somebody different?"

"I don't know," Logue replied. "For real. I wasn't there either day—when he got first got the call, or later when they came to him about the report."

I glanced at that Coors can in his hand. "You called in sick."

Logue looked away and nodded. I still had a lot of questions but found myself following his gaze. Logue's eyes kept circling back to the laughing kids in the power boat.

"Those are Fuentes' kids," I said with a nod of recognition. "They live here with you."

Logue nodded in turn. "I'm their godfather. After Maria was diagnosed, they made me legal guardian in case anything happened to Mikey."

He pointed to the dark-haired woman with them. "That's Carla, their nanny. None of us thought it would turn out like this."

"Yeah," I said, tucking Fuentes' paperwork back in the manila envelope. "You know you should have come forward with this. If you had, maybe my partner wouldn't be dead." I turned to go.

Logue reached out and grabbed my arm. "You gotta understand, detective. Sometimes you take the easy way out, and you don't know until later how hard it's gonna make it for you to live your life."

"I get that," I said. "Still doesn't change things. Fuentes was dirty. You knew it."

"You don't get it." Logue tightened his hand on my arm. "Except for this one time, Mikey was the straight arrow. I was the one who sometimes worked the gray zone, you know, but he always had my back."

"That morning I called in sick with the flu five years ago? I didn't have the flu. I had a hell of a bender the night before. Mikey covered for me and the shit came raining down on him. After Nieto was arrested, the scumbag's people hit Mikey's weak spot, and he caved. Two years after that, the clinical trial was discontinued. Maria's condition deteriorated. Mikey didn't have the money to keep her in a good place like she was in."

His grip tightened into a vise. "And then about a month ago, Nieto's conviction was overturned. Mikey came to me all upset. But when he finally came clean about the whole thing, I told him he fucked up bad. Said what was done was done, and he had to live with it. There's no going back. Man up, I said to him. Keep his mouth shut. This one time he stepped outside the line, and I let him down."

Logue looked out at the boats again, not meeting my eyes. "He died that same night. Mikey came to me for help, and I made it worse. And there's not a fucking thing I can do to change that."

I slowly unpeeled his hand from my arm and started to walk back towards the lodge.

He grabbed at my arm again. "You still don't know the worst of it, Piedmont. Why I couldn't come clean. Not now."

I turned my head and saw Logue staring out at the kids in the boat once more. Fuentes' kids.

"His kids live on his pension and benefits," I said. "You didn't want them to lose that."

"Especially the medical," he said, pressing his lips into a tight line of regret. "They'll need that. They have their mother's genes."

CHAPTER FIFTY-TWO

THE PICTURE OF MARIA FUENTES WITH HER VACANT EYES haunted me as I drove away from Logue and Big Bear, heading back to L.A. in the dark. Maria—and her kids with that genetic time bomb hanging over them, Fuentes, and the desperate steps he'd taken to protect them—all for nothing. So many things could go wrong for a kid, any kid. How would I protect my unborn child from all the bad out there?

I put the sedan on autopilot and made three calls as the car inched along in traffic.

Given what Logue had told me about the clinical trial, the first was to the Genesys CEO. Maclaren was in his office when we finally connected. I asked him about the patents to Lee's work.

"Dr. Lee's family owns the rights to the initial test," Maclaren said, his tall frame leaning against the desk.

"The test that detects susceptibility to Alzheimer's," I said.

"That's right." Maclaren's pale blue eyes looked tired. "We'll license the process."

"And the treatment for Alz-X itself?"

"The company owns that," Maclaren said.

"So your company benefits from Lee's death," I said.

"Hardly." As he drew his hand across his face, the skin seemed to sag. "The company has always owned that intellectual property. Dr. Lee's percentage will go to his family as it would have gone to him. If and when we get to market."

"How soon will that be?"

"Third stage of clinical trials are underway," Maclaren said, brow furrowing. "But we've had some problems."

"Like corrupting the results?" I told him I knew about Lee putting Fuentes-Obrador's wife into the clinical trial and giving her the real drug. He didn't look surprised.

"That was a serioius error of judgment on his part," Maclaren conceded. "As soon as I found out, I suspended the trial. It was one of thirty six. That's delayed our progress, but not completely derailed it, thankfully."

So, Maclaren had been the one to derail the clinical trial, not Lee.

"But you didn't fire Lee," I said. "You sent him on sabbatical."

Maclaren didn't deny it. His face fixed itself in a flat scowl.

"How did you find out about the tampering?"

"Dr. Lee told me himself." Maclaren ran his hand through his dark hair and sighed. "I thought it better not to ruin a man's life for a moment of weakness."

"Not his first lapse," I said, referencing the ethical problems he'd had in the past. "You needed Lee to finish the work."

"I don't deny that," Maclaren said. "But Gabriel Lee has paid for his mistake. If his work doesn't go forward, millions of innocent people will pay for it too."

"Probably," I said. "But did you ask yourself why Lee let this particular woman into the trial?"

"I asked him," Maclaren said. "Dr. Lee said he took pity on her. He told me she had small children and very little money."

"She also had a cop for a husband. The husband filed a supplemental report that got an AzteKa enforcer out of jail," I said. "Nieto and the AzteKas had to have leverage over Lee to make him do what he did. Are you aware, Mr. Maclaren, that your employee was using black market embryos in his research?"

Maclaren's face had paled under his tan. "That's a serious allegation," he said.

"Does that mean you didn't know about it? The black market embryos? You knew about his patient tampering."

"Of course I didn't know. I still don't believe it." The CEO was sitting down now.

"You better start," I said. "Because the AzteKas play rough. And if they had leverage over Lee, they'll use it on your company too. Is there anything else you want to tell me?"

Maclaren shook his head. "You've given me a lot to think about. I'll have to bring the lawyers in to sort through liability issues."

I cut him off. "Up security first. And the second Nieto or anybody else makes an approach, I want to know about it."

"Of course." Maclaren looked ashen as I disconnected.

As soon as we'd hung up, I put the second call through to Shin and filled him in on my chats with Logue and the Genesys CEO. Shin was still at his desk in Homicide Special. His suit was so rumpled the wrinkles had wrinkles.

"You think Maclaren's on the level? I said.

"He's hedging his bets." Shin cracked his knuckles. "But the terms of Lee's will corroborate his statement. So, we don't have any reason not to believe him."

"Nice to have a witness tell the truth for a change."

"What I want to know," Shin said, "is how did Nieto find out about the embryo sales in the first place? The Devonshire girl? Maybe a little pillow talk with some AzteKa she met at the club?"

"Too bad we can't ask her." I drummed a tattoo on the steering wheel. Glancing at the rear-view mirror, I watched the long black ribbon of highway spooling out behind me. "But there is somebody who might have wanted to punish Britney and tighten the vise on Lee at same time."

"Sandy Rose," Shin said. "But why would she bring in the AzteKas? She doesn't strike me as the profit-sharing type."

I thought back to Shin's and my visit to her gentleman's club, Sandy Beaches. There'd been a bouncer with a Santa Muerte tat at the door. AzteKas favor that design, and I don't believe in coincidence.

"Maybe they were already involved." I told Shin about the bouncer. "She needs security to run that kind of operation."

"If Britney Devonshire didn't spill the beans herself," Shin said, "one of their soldiers could have heard something and relayed the intel up the chain to Nieto's people."

"Let's bring Sandy Rose in and talk to her again. We're breathing down Nieto's neck, but I want to get ahead of him." Shin and I disconnected.

Traffic was moving now. The freeway's amber alert signs predicted another forty-five minutes to downtown L.A. I checked my voicemail. Jim Mar had logged a call while I was talking to Shin. My third call was to him.

"I took that fetal partial prelim you got from Britney Devonshire," he said from the crime lab, "and ran the comparison with the genome from Lee's encrypted file." His eyes had a feverish glint.

"And?"

Jim's face, floating in front of the car's green dash screen, took on a spectral appearance in the night. "There's data corruption in the blood spot," he said.

"Yeah, you said that before. How bad?"

"There are some gaps. Can't confirm the race or sex on the blood spot, for example." Jim smiled and his grin broadened. "But it might not matter. On the DNA we do have, the blood spot's a point for point match. Allowing for statistical error, I'd say it's gotta be the same genome."

I felt that little zing in the blood you get when a hunch pays off. "So, the person whose DNA is on that partial has to be the same person whose genome was the basis for Lee's Alzheimer's X vaccine," I said. "The highly resistant source genome."

Jim's head bobbed up and down in affirmation.

"But the genome isn't Britney Devonshire's," Jim said, repeating what he'd told me during dinner two days ago at the Theban Grill. "Not even close."

"Could Britney be the resistant source's mother, or egg donor?"

"No. Kids inherit one genetic marker from each parent at every location on a chromosome," Jim explained, holding two genetic barcodes up to the camera. "So, when we run a forensic DNA test, relatives will have lots of markers in common."

He pointed to several specific sections of what looked like fuzzy barcodes and a couple numerical charts showing the respective location and type of various markers for the two genetic samples.

"These don't. Sorry Eddie, no familia here. Ditto with Gabriel Lee. I ran that comparison too just in case."

"So, who?" Had the stripper stolen some other girl's partial from her boss, Sandy Rose? Was that why she ended up dead in that bathtub well before her time?

"I don't know," Jim said. "But whoever the source is, she's walking around with a goldmine in her blood."

And a target on her back. Unless she was already dead like Lee and Britney Devonshire. I had to find her.

I'd taken my eyes off Jim's floating face for a second and was staring blankly at the road. Amber dots and dashes against black tarmac flashed by—like Morse code I couldn't read. *Send me some answers from beyond, Frank.*

"You still there, Eddie," Jim said, "or am I looking at a frozen d-stream?"

I took a deep breath before answering. "Just thinking."

"Any news on when this vaccine's coming to market?"

"Go home, Jim," I replied. "And thanks." He groaned goodbye and disconnected.

The air in the sedan suddenly felt hot and clammy. I opened a window.

The vaccine and that vacant stare of Maria Fuentes-Obrador—Nieto and Lee—the entire case circled back to Lee's blackmarket embryo buys. And the identity of the vaccine's source genome. I had to find her, and fast.

By the time I neared Nokia P.D., a full moon hung high over the city like a fly ball that would never be caught. Ten o'clock. Wind howled through the nearly deserted parking lot.

I badged the security guard upon entering the station, and took the elevator up to the third floor. Shin was still at his desk.

"You find anything?"

"Served the warrant for Baby Mine today." Shin reached up and massaged the kinks out of his neck. "Some shell corporation fronts the clinic, but three guesses who's the real puppet master?"

"Sandy Rose," I said.

Shin nodded. "Right. Thirty odd years ago, she and an OB-GYN named Dr. Singh ran an outfit called Global Baby. That company folded seventeen years ago after they got in trouble selling extra embryos left in the freezer. One of the clients sued and the OB-GYN lost his license."

"So Sandy Rose shuts down Global Baby," I said, "and reboots the company under the name Baby Mine?"

"And this time she supplies her black market clients with a steady stream of eggs from girls who wouldn't be filing any charges."

"Or leaving any records," I said. "Let's bring her in first thing tomorrow."

CHAPTER FIFTY-THREE

WE BROUGHT SANDY ROSE IN FOR QUESTIONING AT EIGHT THE next morning, but she refused to speak until her attorney arrived. At 10:30 the desk sergeant informed me that lawyer Jason Goldblatt-Wong was seated with his client in Interview One.

So, holding two cups of java crystals in one hand and a new e-cigarette pack in the other, I headed into the small, spare room. There was a desk with two scuffed steel chairs on either side. I took my seat and slid the coffee snuff across the desk towards Sandy Rose and Wong.

Sandy Rose stood at the back of the room, staring at me through hooded eyes. She shivered and wrapped the black ends of her paper-thin sweater around her gaunt frame.

"You cold?" I said. "I can get you real coffee."

She shook her head, jaw clenched, and slowly lowered herself into the seat beside her lawyer.

"What's this all about?" Her lawyer ran his hand through gelled hair that resembled a pack of black lacquered ramen noodles. Wong had an imperious voice, and from the cut of his bespoke suit, it was clear he made a very nice retainer. "What are the charges against my client?"

I hit the privacy screen. The glass walls clouded and turned opaque steel gray.

I slid the new e-cigarette pack towards Sandy Rose. She pointedly withdrew her own electronic cigarette from her black lizard bag, and flicked it on, frowning.

"Your client, Ms. Rose," I said to Wong after entering our names and the time into the record, "has been operating a black market trade in human eggs and embryos out of her fertility clinic. That was the facility Dr. Lee worked at thirty years ago. But recently he discovered a cure for Alz-X based on the resistant genome of an egg donor or embryo he acquired illegally. With help from your client's clinic." I brought up a picture of the remains of the Baby Mine clinic on the wall screen to Sandy's left. It was all twisted steel, shattered glass and mangled limbs. Blood painted every surface.

Sandy Rose's lawyer kept his mouth shut about the charges.

I stared at her ruined face. "Ms. Rose's employee, Britney Devonshire, was one of the black market egg donors. But she was doing a side deal with Lee. Somehow she got hold of the blood spot that contained the resistant genome." I pulled up a close-up of the blood spot.

Sandy leaned close to Wong and conferred with her lawyer in a whisper.

"Former employee," Sandy Rose said. "Britney stole confidential files from the clinic. Legitimate files."

I nodded. "Okay. Then Ms. Devonshire tried to blackmail Lee. We have her phone and text records linking her to him. Dr. Lee got a little desperate. He knew he'd be ruined, and the researched derailed. He made a couple calls we traced."

When Sandy Rose took a deep drag of her e-cigarette, the blue light flickered and sputtered out. She sniffed and tried to relight, angrily flicking the battery-ignition on and off without success.

Lee had made those calls to a ghost phone, which are untraceable, but the display of angry nerves on Sandy Rose's face read loud and clear. She had been the one Lee had called.

"After those calls, you fired Ms. Devonshire."

"Coincidence," Sandy said. "She failed a drug test."

"Which you administered at whim," I said. "Then Ms. Devonshire turns up dead. Her death is made to look accidental so no investigation would derail the progress of Lee's research to market."

When I pulled up a crime scene photo of Britney Devonshire lying dead in that tub, Wong leaned over to his client for another sotto voce conference.

"But Lee panics and runs," I continued. "Then he's murdered too. Along with my former partner Frank. Again, everything is made to look like an accident."

I pulled up a photo of the Clara Vista crash that featured Dr.

Lee's burnt and bloodied corpse in close-up. The lawyer quickly looked away. Sandy Rose never looked at all.

"Now your client's Baby Mine clinic is a burnt-out pile of twisted steel—" My glance richocheted from Wong to his client. "—and Ms. Rose is the only one left standing."

I took the vaper, refired it for Sandy Rose, and handed it back. This time she grudgingly accepted my help.

"Interesting theories," the lawyer said. "But that's all they are. You don't have enough to make your case against my client. Not in court. From what I've heard here, my client was an innocent victim of two criminal employees. You push ahead with this, and we'll sue the city for harassment."

"I don't need to bring the case to court," I said and turned to stare at Sandy Rose. "I just have to charge your client. Sure, you'll get her out on bail, but she'll have a target on her back. Even a good lawyer doesn't mean much if you're dead, Ms. Rose. You're a loose end, and you know how Nieto ties up loose ends."

Sandy Rose leaned back in her chair and studied me coolly. But the moment I'd said 'Nieto,' she'd wrapped the loose ends of her jacket even more tightly around her gaunt frame, an ancient vulture tucking its wings protectively as it watched the other birds of prey circle overhead.

"And if he hears I cooperated?" she said. "How long do I last then?"

"Longer than you will if you don't cooperate. I don't want you. I want Nieto, and I need your information to get him. I know he's behind this. If you help me, I can take him off the street. Without your help, well, he'll have more time to get to you. And he will get to you."

The lawyer was just about to speak when Sandy Rose put her hand on his arm. While they leaned their heads together in conference, I tapped the app for Assistant District Attorney Garcia.

"We'll need assurances," Wong said a few moments later.

"Here's ADA Garcia now." I smiled as the heavyset thirty-something lawyer entered the room and closed the door behind her.

"Can I assume," Sandy Rose's lawyer said, mopping a slight sheen of perspiration from his broad forehead, "that the presence of Ms. Garcia means you agree to grant my client full immunity from prosecution in exchange for her testimony?"

"So long as her testimony is worth it." I glanced at Garcia.

Garcia had barely taken her seat and smoothed the wrinkles on her navy off-the-rack suit, but she nodded, her halo of dark curls bobbing. "And she tells the truth."

"Nieto's the one you want," Sandy Rose said in a cool voice. "But you already know that."

"I need to hear it for the record. How'd he get involved with your operation in the first place?"

A vein in Sandy Rose's temple started to throb through the papery skin. "I needed security. I hired some ex-gang members years ago, including AzteKas. That was a mistake. They brought him in."

She confirmed that the girls in her club had talked, and the information about the black market sale of human eggs and embryos had made its way up the chain of command to the AzteKa enforcer.

"He threatened to turn us in to the police unless I upped his security fee," she said, using air quotes around the last two words. "When he was sent to prison for the murder of that Zeta thug, I thought it would end his threats. But by then he'd figured out Lee had discovered the golden goose with his cure to the plague. So, Nieto's demands only escalated."

"He wanted a get out of jail card," I said, "and he forced you to help him get it. Who put pressure on Fuentes-Obrador, the first officer on the scene of the Nieto murder?"

"Nieto's people," Sandy Rose said. "In exchange for getting the officer's wife into the clinical trial for Alzheimer's X, they got him to file that supplemental report. That report sprang Nieto from jail."

"So he didn't force you to pressure Fuentes-Obrador yourself?"

"All I did," Sandy Rose said, "was to convince Dr. Lee to put Obrador's wife into the clinical trial. Nieto made the threats. I still kidded myself that I could control him. But he always wanted more."

"Did Nieto kill Britney Devonshire?"

She closed her eyes and nodded. "And Lee, through Harvey Pink. I'm sorry about your partner, detective. I don't think even

Nieto intended for that to happen. But you're right about him coming for me."

Sandy Rose pulled up a series of pictures on her glove phone and held them out. The first couple of shots showed the strip club. The office, squirreled in the back, had been tossed. Furniture was smashed. The last picture showed a black pit bull lying in a pool of blood—its severed head propped up on the dog's hind quarters. The dog's genitals were stuffed in its mouth. I recognized the dog as the mascot from her club.

"Nieto mess you up?" No bruises were visible, but Sandy's long sleeves and layers could have hidden them.

The tip of her electronic cigarette glowed ice blue as she took a deep drag of nicotine vapor. Sandy Rose shook her head. "I wasn't there." She took another drag. Little lines feathered out all along her top lip as she sucked in the poison. When she exhaled, the plume of vapor-scented air smelled like spearmint. "Nieto and his thugs broke into my office two days ago," she said.

"They left Angelo's body for me to find." She angled her head to indicate Angelo was the dog. Sandy Rose pressed her lips tight and looked away. But her eyes were brimming.

"Nieto tossed the place," I said. "Was it just part of his threat, or was he looking for something specific?"

"A password," she said. "For an off-shore account. My security plan—against him. He knew so long as I was—healthy," Sandy Rose paused, "deposits from that account would keep coming."

"Did he get the password?"

With a heavy sigh, she nodded.

I took the details of the account from her and shot a glance at Garcia. The money was most likely in Nieto's hands already, but the ADA immediately texted her assistant to get the warrant we'd need to freeze the account.

"How much does Nieto know about Lee's work?"

"Enough. He's a psychopath. He's not stupid. He saw a big opportunity for the drug cartel. An opportunity that would advance his own career within the AzteKas."

"Who's the source of the resistant genome for Lee's research?" Now more than ever we needed to find her and keep her safe until Nieto was back behind bars.

Sandy Rose shrugged. "Lee erased the name from the file.

Part of the new security system he introduced." She sniffed. "Security for him, the little cheat. He'd reorganized all the stock too. All I can tell you is that it came from the Global Baby inventory. 2010-2020."

"It's strange." I paused. "Nieto was released from jail last month. I'm surprised he waited so long to pay you a visit."

"He didn't, detective." The first hint of a smile turned up the corners of her mouth. "Nieto was there that day you and your partner came by to ask questions about Britney. He watched you interview me from the back room of the club."

I felt a sick, angry burn in the pit of my stomach.

"Nieto saw you didn't buy Britney's death as an accident. When you left," she rattled on, "he made it crystal clear I would have an accident too—if I didn't keep my mouth shut. I'm only alive because he didn't want a murder that could be linked directly to him. A murder that couldn't be made to seem accidental. But that's all over now. He knows the noose is tightening. Now he's got my money. When he comes for me, Nieto won't bother to make it look like an accident."

"Tell us where to find him." Nieto was a ghost. His last place of residence on file had been sold.

"He has my Mercedes," she said, giving us the the plate number: ROSE-2. "One of the club's cars. And he was staying at the Mandarin Oriental under the name of Duarte."

Hiding in plain sight.

"We'll get your statement ready for signing," Garcia said. She was already expediting the warrant to arrest Nieto.

"We can offer you protection," I said.

"No you can't." Sandy Rose turned off her e-cigarette. "I've already told you everything I can. I'm leaving town—today."

"Stay here for a few hours," I said as I stood. "You'll be safer. We're going to take Nieto off the street. And this time he's not getting back out."

Sandy Rose shook her head. "Nothing personal detective," she said, "but I don't want to be anywhere near you while he's free." She told us she had a private plane waiting at the airport and extra security to get her there.

I should have tried harder to convince her to stay.

CHAPTER FIFTY-FOUR

SANDY ROSE HAD BARELY LEFT THE INTERVIEW ROOM BEFORE I contacted the Mandarin Oriental. Her intel checked out. At 12:15 the clerk at the desk told me a man who matched Nieto's description was registered at one of their private residences under the name of Duarte.

"Let's go." I waved the warrant for Nieto at Shin.

A black and white and a heavily armed SUV were waiting in the parking lot to follow in our wake. In the first was a K-9 unit complete with sniffer dog. In the second, a unit of the bomb squad. Both were instructed to keep sirens and lights off.

As we climbed into the detective sedan, I told Shin that Nieto had been at the strip club when we'd interviewed Rose the first time. How I'd led Nieto right to Lee three weeks ago. What I didn't say was the part that ate at me. I'd led him right to Frank as well.

"It all fits," Shin said.

"How'd it go with Mrs. Lee and Raymond?" While I'd grilled Sandy Rose, Shin had interviewed the mother and son two doors down.

"I offered Raymond a stint in rehab," Shin said. "Not jail."

I nodded as my partner popped the flash-dot of the taped interview into the player.

Built on the site of a former parking lot directly behind the former Times Mirror Building, the hotel fronted Second and Spring Streets. Practically across the street from Nokia PD. Drumming an anxious tattoo on the steering wheel, I cut through traffic as we listened to the replay of Shin talking in soothing tones to Mrs. Lee and Raymond.

Ray confirmed he'd sold three nano-botz in exchange for drugs.

Three—I knew where the first two had turned up. One for the Clara Vista Crash that killed Raymond's own father and Frank, and one for the Baby Mine Clinic. Where was the third? Nieto already had a long string of murders to his credit. That missing nano-bot promised a still higher body count.

On the tape, Mrs. Lee's strangled little whimper became wrenching guttural sobs. It was the first time I'd ever heard her cry over her husband's death.

It was 12:30 when we pulled into the parking lot of the luxury hotel where Nieto was said to be staying. I instructed the K-9 unit and bomb squad to park way in the back, well out of sight. While they got ready, Shin and I went to talk to reception.

We took the manager up in the elevator with us.

The sniffer dog went first. Tail in the air, he checked the outside of the 22nd floor residence for explosives. The manager stood quaking well behind us.

At the same time, the guy from the bomb squad, dressed like a window washer, reconnoitered from outside on the ledge. He loosed a robot droid to get a better visual on angles outside his view.

"All clear," he said.

"All clear," the K-9 handler echoed when the dog detected nothing.

I gestured to the hotel manager. "Mr. Duarte?" the manager called as he inched forward from behind Shin and me and knocked on the door. "Management." Nobody answered, so he unlocked the door.

"Police!" As the manager threw himself flat against the corridor wall, we poured past him into the room, guns out.

We cleared the residence room by room. But no Nieto anywhere.

About two thousand square feet, the place was one of the hotel's smaller privately-owned residences. Per the manager, Nieto had sublet it from an owner who lived in London.

"There are thirty similar units on site," the manager said. "Owners like having the convenience and amenities of a hotel combined with the benefits of home."

I nodded. Opposite the front door and behind the sofa stretched a wall of floor to ceiling windows. A pale silvery floor rug shimmered faintly in the gloom. Furniture and effects were all standard luxury décor. Nothing personal.

"Think he's in the wind?" I said.

"His clothes and stuff are back here," Shin replied, staring at the neat row of suits hanging in the bedroom closet.

As Shin went through the pockets, I headed back to the living room.

Squirreled away in a sideboard, tucked behind some high-end camera equipment, sat Nieto's phablet and a couple ghost phones. With latexed fingers I fished them out from behind the phone's telephoto lens attachment. Setting the phablet on the dining room table, I turned it on.

Shin came back into the living room, shaking his head. "Nothing in the closet," he said.

Since I had Nieto's biometric faceprint, we were able to log into his phablet without much trouble. Nieto hadn't expected us, so the device hadn't been wiped clean. Nieto's recent browser history bookmarked orders he'd placed for drones. These small-scale models looked, and flew, like large dragonflies.

"He bugged people," Shin said. "Literally."

"That's how he got the bird's eye view on me up at Clara Vista," I said. Nieto had been the anonymous party who sent the news station that footage of the crash. The crash that killed Frank.

"Triggered it too." Shin held up the box for the nano-bot detonator. "Here's our proof. Nieto was sitting safe miles away, piloting the drone when he engineered the crash.

But the third bot wasn't in the hotel suite.

I cocked my head at the screen. "Look at the ego on this guy. News articles covering both the Ramirez shooting and the Clara Vista crash. He bookmarked them all."

"You got a fan, Eddie," Shin said, reading over my shoulder. "He has a big fat file on you."

As Shin bagged the phones and phablet, I stood and gazed down from the living room window of Nieto's digs to the streets below. Police Headquarters was visible from the room. So was the building that housed the new police parking lot a block away.

Still gloved, I moved quickly back to the phablet and pulled up his camera roll of photos.

"Need to wash my Porsche," I said and angled the phablet so Shin could see the pictures.

We both stared at the close ups of the entrance and exit for the police lot. The parking spot where my Porsche sat, a thin layer of dust on the trunk, was just visible. Nieto's camera roll showed other shots of my car coming and going. Ditto our detective sedan. The times were all logged in.

"Fuck me," Shin said.

"That's how he kept one step ahead of us," I said. "He kept tabs on our comings and goings."

"He's laughing at us." A look of barely muted anger had replaced Shin's typical laid-back expression. "Fuck him."

Shin called in the APB and notified eye in the sky so the police choppers would be on the lookout for Nieto as well. I copied Nieto's files onto my glove phone before forensics bagged the whole works.

I was standing to the side of the window, angled behind the plum-gray drapes out of view, looking down at the street through Nieto's camera, when a silver Mercedes ZX-20 glided down the street. The license plate read ROSE2. It was the car he'd lifted from Sandy Rose.

"He's here," I said. "Mercedes at the entrance."

The car slowed as Nieto prepared to pull into the underground parking garage.

Shin called it in to the black and white as we raced downstairs. He told the uniforms to stay back until Nieto was well inside, then to block his exit. We had just sprinted into the parking lot, when instead of turning into a space, Nieto gunned the engine. The silver Mercedes suddenly accelerated into a U-turn.

He must have seen, or sensed, the black and whites.

We raced to our sedan as he cut off another car. Bam! Nieto smashed through the wooden arm of the exit barrier.

"Hang on," I said.

Shin still had one leg stuck outside when I swerved away from the cement pillar and hit the gas. Shin grabbed the overhead grip and yanked himself fully inside the car. He was still pulling his seatbelt on when we hit 65 mph. I spotted Nieto up ahead. We were closing in on Nieto's tail two blocks from Union Station when he made an illegal left turn onto a one way street. Horns blared. Cars wove around the blur of silver we tailed. I didn't turn with him.

"You're gonna lose him, Eddie," Shin said.

I shook my head. I'd seen the little sticker on Nieto's back bumper—NorthStar, the satellite relayed real-time-help line that serviced certain high-end vehicles—including this model Mercedes. "Let him think he lost us."

I'd already called in my badge number and Nieto's license plate when I sped past the one-way street. Circling around, I saw a blur of silver as the Mercedes shot out of the one-way street into two-way traffic again. Nieto was between us and Union Station when his car stopped cold. The NorthStar people had shut down his engine.

Nieto didn't take long to figure out what had happened. He threw open the door of his Mercedes and raced for Union Station on foot—his black blazer and dark jeans a blur. I almost grazed the curb in front of the entrance as I slammed on the brakes.

"You're faster," Shin said. He started to climb over into the driver's seat as I leapt out of the car and sprinted after Nieto into the train station. It was 1:45. Lunch hour rush—and Nieto had vanished into the crowd of commuters pushing their way under the barrel-vaulted ceiling of the central hall leading to the trains.

I stood outside the Railz restaurant, scanning the crowd for a glimpse of the black suit jacket he wore.

I glanced at the light board. The eight lines stopped at more than 72 stations and covered 103.1 miles of rail plus. Those slender threads span almost the entire city. All pass through Union Station. Which would Nieto take?

That's when I caught sight of him in the crowd at the end of the hall. Nieto had spotted me too. For just a second he stood frozen, his face a mask of anger. Then he took off in a run. I sprinted after him.

Nieto ran towards the entrance to the Gold Line. The Line winds on elevated tracks from Union Station past Chinatown through brush-covered hills bordering Lincoln Heights before it hurls back down to ground level in Highland Park. The line ends in Pasadena where it intersects with the Green Line. Where the hell was Nieto headed?

He climbed over the turnstile, catching the pocket of his trousers on the tangle of metal. I heard the fabric tear as he pulled away and stepped onto the train. He pushed people out of the way, moving through the car. I vaulted over the turnstile and leapt onto the train behind him.

This car was a sardine can crammed full of commuters. I wormed my way through, following Nieto into the next car. But just as I got within ten feet of him, Nieto made it to the open doors. He leapt out of the train. I elbowed my way through the crowd. I threw myself out of the car just as the doors closed.

He had a good lead on me. Now Nieto hurried toward the Red Line—the Metro that heads northwest through Hollywood to the Valley. I sprinted, closing the distance. Nieto's face was red and shiny with perspiration he didn't bother to wipe. 75, 50, 25 feet. Nieto had his foot on the top step leading into the train when I grabbed a fistful of black jacket and jerked hard. He lurched backwards.

Nieto grabbed the pole to his left to steady himself. With his other hand, he took hold of a stunned commuter and hurled him down the steps at me. I stopped the stranger's fall with a right shoulder block. But I was blocked too. I spun back around and leapt towards the steps again, but the doors to the car had already closed.

Through the window of the train I saw Nieto's breath fog the window as he leaned close to the glass. He reached up with his glove phone hand and wrote something on the window. A word: MOOB. Then he tapped his phone. Nieto stared at me and smiled as the train pulled away from the station. I just had time to decipher the word: BOOM.

CHAPTER FIFTY-FIVE

"Lost him." My call to Shin went through as I raced back out across the station. I scanned the parking lot outside Union Station for Shin and the car. "He's on the Red Line. I think he's got the third detonator wired already." I told Shin what Nieto had written on the fogged glass of the train.

"Roger that," Shin said. "Any idea where? Or where he's heading now?"

I shook my head and alerted security on the Red Line.

Nieto could have left the country days ago, but he hadn't. That meant he had more loose ends to tie up. Sandy Rose had been one. But she was already on her way out of town. There was another loose thought. If she was still alive, Nieto would be worried about the woman whose genome started it all. He'd try to take her out too. But since I didn't know who or where she was, there was no way to warn or protect her.

"Don't sweat it," Shin said. Shin had already issued an APB and an alert at all train stations and airports. "One of the cameras will pick him up."

But from his expression I knew Shin was thinking what I was thinking. Before or after the next explosion?

"Where're you?" I said, glancing down at Shin's face on my phone. A movie trailer flashed past on the wall outside the windows where he sat. But I knew it wasn't the image of Batman chasing Dracula that moved. It was a Sidetrack ad—hundreds of LED lights hung over a quarter-mile span of familiar train tunnel.

"You're on the Gold Line?"

"The damn train took off before I could get through the crowd," Shin said with a sheepish frown. "Get the car. I'll take a black and white back to Nokia."

But the call that went out over the police radio and web news twenty seconds later made my heart sink.

On my glove phone I watched the footage.

Boom was an understatement. A tower of flame burned bright against the tarmac of the Santa Monica Airport. The explosion had taken out a Mercedes and four other cars plus a parking lot attendant.

The Mercedes' license plate was scorched, but I could still make out the letters: ROSE-1. The car itself was now a pile of burning wreckage. A funeral pyre. For Sandy and her security guards. I wasn't a fan of Sandy Rose, but it was a bad way to go.

"Guess we know where that third nano-bot detonator went," Shin said.

I gave him a grim nod. "But where's Nieto?"

Metro Security still hadn't spotted him. Back at Nokia PD, I hunkered down, scrolling through the killer's files, searching for any hint to his whereabouts.

Shin had been right. Nieto had a fat file on me. I skimmed through the usual news stories about the Sphinx case and my promotion to Homicide Special. But Nieto's file was much more detailed. It went as far back as public records would take him, and then some. He had a copy of my birth certificate at KP Medcenter in San Diego.

Ping. There it was—that familiar sensation, the slight tightening of the muscles at the pit of my stomach.

A crazy thought flickered through my mind. Nieto's research on me would have helped him anticipate our moves, but this was over and above. Could Nieto have had more than one reason for tracking me?

Sandy Rose had said the genome resistant to Alz-X came from a blood sample taken from her old company, the Global Baby fertility clinic. That inventory dated from 2010-2020. So the blood spot could never have come from Britney Devonshire. She hadn't even been born. Neither had I.

Except. My stomach did another little twist and flop as I remembered my mom's confession at my father's funeral—about her IVF. Her OB-GYN had been named Singh, and Singh was the doctor implicated in the Global Baby scandal that closed the clinic. It's a common surname, but I don't believe in coincidence. Could my mother have been a patient at Global Baby?

I did a quick search through Nieto's files for the name Lagos. There it was: Calista Lagos. Her blood spot was included. I texted Jim Mar and sent him the partial prelim.

"Who's Calista Lagos?" Shin said, looking over my shoulder.

"My mother," I said. "I think she's the source genome."

CHAPTER FIFTY-SIX

My next call was to San Diego P.D. By the time we disconnected, they were on route to pick up my mother, having assured me they would keep her safe in the downtown station. My follow up call was to Jim Mar. He'd received the blood spot from my mother and had already started on an expedited comparison with the resistant genome.

By then the fire department had calmed the blaze at the Santa Monica Airport. Forensics had found two bodies in Sandy Rose's Mercedes, a male and a female. Both were badly incinerated, but forensics would have positive identifications soon.

"We got a sighting on Nieto," Shin said a moment later. "Security cameras spotted him exiting the Red Line at North Hollywood and heading into a men's room. No sign of him exiting from there."

"He's probably disguised," I said.

"Yeah," Shin said. "Uniforms found the black jacket he was wearing in the men's room trash can. We're scanning for a facial recognition match. No matches yet."

We had a 3D biometric face print on Nieto, but fake teeth or even a hat and oversized glasses could still outsmart facial recognition software. Since he'd known enough to ditch the jacket, Nieto would probably have found a way to run interference on the software too.

"The Red Line dead ends in North Hollywood," Shin said. "That's between two airports: Van Nuys and Burbank. We're checking with the Orange Line and all the cab and ride share companies too. Plus car rentals."

The unspoken question was clear to us both. Where would Nieto go next?

"I think I know where he's headed," I said and put in a call to the Genesys CEO straight away.

Maclaren's assistant told me the CEO was "unavailable."

"Make him available. Tell him Detective Piedmont thinks he's about to get a visit from Nieto."

Shin and I raced down the elevator to the parking garage. Shin was headed for the Burbank Airport. Timbo from NOHO Homicide would cover Van Nuys. "Anybody even suspects Nieto's there," Shin said, "call for back up." Shin reached out and grabbed my arm. "Do not try to take him on your own."

I nodded as Shin took the detective sedan and I jumped in my Porsche. As I switched on the ignition, Jim Mar called me back.

"You sitting down?" Jim pulled up the two bloodspots, one the source genome and one labeled Piedmont. They floated between us on the glove phone. To my eyes they looked like a match.

"She's the source genome, isn't she?" I said, feeling my diaphragm tighten. "My mother."

"No," Jim said, shaking his head.

"She's not?" I puffed out a short breath that was almost a laugh, then inhaled in what felt like my first deep breath in days. "Then why?"

"You are," Jim said. "You're the source genome, Eddie."

CHAPTER FIFTY-SEVEN

STANDING MOTIONLESS NEXT TO MY PORSCHE, I STARED AT Jim's floating face in disbelief.

"I thought it was insane too." Jim pointed at the two bloodspots on his phone, one the source genome and one labeled Piedmont. "But it's an exact match with the uncorrupted part of the Devonshire blood spot and Lee's file. I pulled your bio-file from Nokia P.D. to confirm. You know what that means?"

"I'm a target. And now I know why." My head buzzed. No wonder Lee had said my name in his vid-log before I'd even shown up at his door. No wonder Nieto had a big fat file on me.

And if Lee knew all that, Maclaren must have known too, and lied about it, hoping to keep me in the dark.

I popped the trunk on the Porsche and pulled out my Second-Skin. Peeling off my suit jacket, I slid the silky black fabric over my shirt and fastened the Velcro strip on the bullet-proof vest. Then I headed for Genesys.

As I hurtled toward the Valley on the 101, cars on either side of me seemed to drift backwards.

The call that buzzed and pulled me out of my thoughts as I passed the Sunset exit was from Jo.

"Hey." Until I was staring at her floating image, I hadn't known just how much I wanted to hear her voice.

But Jo's face was tense and drawn, her lips the color of milk.

"What's the matter?" Jo looked like I felt.

The black Lexus in front of me slowed. I hit the gas harder and pulled around him.

"I can't see you for awhile." Jo's voice was a thin quaver. "I have to go away."

"What?" I almost snorted. "Can we talk about this later?"

Jo's eyes were bright with tears. She was fighting for control.

That pushed my pause button. I had no idea what had set her off, but Jo wasn't a drama queen. Could it be the pregnancy hormones talking? I kept my face calm, took a deep breath, and eased my foot off the accelerator.

"I'll be home as soon as I can," I said. "We can talk then."

She shook her head. Jo smiled a wan smile, her face leaning close to the phone's camera. "Whatever happens, Eddie, I love you. Remember that. I've always loved you. Try not to hate me."

She was scaring me now. "It's going to be okay," I said.

Jo just shook her head. "Why did you ever take this case?"

Voices murmured in the background. Jo was calling from an office, not from home. The painting behind her looked familiar. Where had I seen that before? I sharpened the focus and saw a pair of ceremonial swords mounted on a coffee table. Katana. No.

"Jo, where are—?"

"I'm sorry."

Before I could finish the question, she'd disconnected. But I'd recognized one of those voices in the background. It belonged to the owner of that museum quality katana: Maclaren, the CEO of Genesys.

What the fuck was Jo doing in Maclaren's office? There was only one answer I could think of, and it wasn't good. No wonder Maclaren had dodged my calls. My head buzzed and my stomach felt like I was going to heave any second.

The traffic snarled to a standstill near the Vineland exit. The bar of lights on the dash pulsed blue and arterial red as I hurtled my Porsche up on the shoulder and in and out of lanes. Fast as I could weave.

Maclaren wasn't the only one who knew my identity as the source genome. Nieto knew too, and he'd used the knowledge to pressure the Genesys CEO. Maclaren had caved to Nieto's threats, just like Fuentes-Obrador and Sandy Rose. They had to stop me, and they knew how. Jo.

"Fuck, fuck, fuck." I slammed the steering wheel with the palm of my hand and welcomed the sting.

Nieto had Maclaren in a vise. My guess was Nieto had tried to get me off the case earlier. When that didn't work, he tightened the vise on Maclaren, who found a way to get Jo to come to

Genesys. I'd gotten my mother to safety, but left Jo unprotected. And Nieto's next move would involve more than threats.

He knew I'd come for Jo.

And then he'd come for me.

Let him. I was ready.

CHAPTER FIFTY-EIGHT

IT WAS SEVEN AS I RACED INTO THE GENESYS PARKING LOT. THE gate was up. The guard was gone. Not a good omen.

The lot was nearly empty. A few cars clustered just inside the security gate, a few more near the entrance to the building. No sign of Nieto, but I tensed at the sight of a black Bentley X20 parked in the spot reserved for the CEO: Maclaren's car. Next to it stood Jo's green solar Prius. And perched up on the roof of the building—a chopper car.

Shin called as I roared to a stop and parked across the handicapped spot by the door.

"No sign of Nieto here," Shin said, circling the Burbank Airport. "You?"

"No. But the Genesys CEO is inside with Jo." I told Shin what had happened. How Nieto had Maclaren in a vise and was using Jo to lure me here. "I'm going in."

"Wait for backup," Shin said. "Units are on route." He turned the nose of the detective sedan around and headed towards Sun Valley and Genesys.

"No time," I said, checking my Laser-Glock before re-holstering. "They've got Jo. There's a helipad on the roof. With a chopper car."

"Eddie, listen to me," Shin said. "Sandy Rose didn't die in that airport explosion."

"What?"

"The body in that Mercedes wasn't hers. It was another girl from her club."

Another innocent life added to Nieto's body count. I flipped the Glock's laser option to hot. "Sandy contact you?"

Shin shook his head as he barreled down the road, lights and siren blaring. "She's in the wind. Don't expect we'll hear from her anytime soon. Forensics made the call. Over and out."

As I leapt out of my Porsche, a middle-aged man in a white coat was scurrying out of the building. When he saw me, he dropped his backpack. I stooped to retrieve it. His biometric identification card told me his name was Dr. Lozano.

"Where is everyone, Doctor?" I handed him his backpack.

"The boss sent everybody home early." Lozano nodded thanks and hurried to his car. He didn't notice his biometric I.D. had slipped into my hand.

His I.D. gained me entry to Genesys. Skipping the elevator, I raced up the three flights of stairs to Maclaren's office. No sign of Nieto. Or anyone else.

The door to Maclaren's office was wide open. But Maclaren wasn't in it. I looked past the coffee table with the katana and short sword mounted atop it near the door, to the leather couch nearby and the desk at the other end of the room. Holographic computer files floated in the air over the desk. Blood spots. And there, seated in a ghost chair and staring blankly up at the files, sat Jo. No Nieto. No Maclaren.

"Where is he?" I said, stepping into the room. "Maclaren."

Jo whirled around like she'd been struck. "Eddie. You shouldn't be here."

"I came for you." I crossed the office and knelt beside her. "Has he hurt you?"

She looked away, pained.

I took her pale face in both my hands and forced Jo to look at me. For the first time, she flinched at my touch. Standing, I took a step back. "Jo, we need to go now."

"Not yet." Jo gestured for me to take a seat in the matching ghost chair next to hers. "I suppose you had to know sometime."

As I sat, her eyes returned to the floating files above us.

"Jo, what's going on?"

"You remember when I told you I'd had a miscarriage in my teens? That there were complications?"

There wasn't time for this, but I nodded and played along. "You thought it'd made you infertile. But you're fine. You're pregnant."

Jo winced. I took her hand and started to pull her out of the chair. She tore her hand free.

"There were complications, Eddie. I lied about the miscarriage. Oh, I'd had one, but that was later, in my thirties. You know I'm older than you."

I nodded. "Let me take you home. We can talk later."

Jo shook her head. "You know I left home and came out west when I was sixteen." She fingered the tiny white scars on her forearm. Ghosts from her past.

I nodded, confused, but I let her talk.

"Had to," she continued. "My father, he was like yours. Violent. And worse. When I left, he was furious. Cut me off, so I needed to earn money. My brother put me up, but college was expensive. Coke offered to help."

"Coke?"

"Maclaren. He was a med-student and something of a science geek back then. He'd made money donating sperm. Coke told me about this clinic that would pay handsomely for donations. Egg donations."

My hands started to go numb.

"I put myself through college that way," Jo said. "They made embryos from my eggs and cloned them. They told me they'd use the embryos for research only. But one of their fertility doctors working at the clinic had a problem with alcohol. Dr. Singh implanted some of the research embryos in infertile women by mistake. The babies were born healthy, so the clinic let it slide. But another research scientist kept track of them. One of the implanted embryos cloned for research turned out to be very special." Jo turned to look at me. Her eyes were brimming with tears. She gestured to the floating files, the blood spots.

"The resistant source genome for Alz-X," I said. My voice sounded very far away and my head was buzzing. Dr. Lee was the research scientist who kept track.

Jo nodded. "You know the rest. Dr. Lee acquired the clinic's embryos and brought his research to Genesys. He developed the cure to Alz-X using the resistant genome. And then everything went to pieces."

"When did you find all this out?"

"Today. When Coke called me. You see now why we can't be together." She hung her head and crossed her arms, rocking slightly back and forth.

That's how Maclaren had pressured Jo. He'd told her we were tied by more than love. We were blood. That my birth mother wasn't my genetic mother. That Jo . . .

"No." I shook my head. "It's a scam. They're using you to get to me. Nieto has Maclaren in a vise. They lied to get me here. We have to go. Now."

"None of this was my idea," said a voice from the back of the room. Maclaren. "This was never supposed to happen." He walked towards us. With a fluid movement, he ran a hand through that salt and pepper hair and leaned against the desk. He looked from Jo to me. "But mistakes were made. And here we are. I can't sacrifice the research." Maclaren closed his eyes. His lip curled slightly. "What good would that do anybody? Millions will live because of that research. The research is what turns it all around. The only thing left is to focus on the positive and move on."

"Move on." A short burst of bitter laughter erupted from Jo.

"I know right now this is traumatic," Maclaren said, leaning towards Jo. "But I'll see you both get a fair percentage of the profits. It's the only thing to do. Let me take care of things."

"You've taken care of enough already," I growled. "Where's Nieto?"

Maclaren's shoulders dropped in a shrug. "I don't know. Why don't we have a drink and talk this through like adults?" In slow motion, he pulled a bottle of whiskey and three squat glasses out of the desk.

"We'll talk down at the station," I said. "Let's go."

"There's no need for that, detective. Let's work this out."

I stared at him. "You're like a lot of players, Maclaren. Spinning all these plates in the air. You keep spinning even when all the plates have crashed. I'll ask you again. Where's Nieto?"

"I have no idea."

With one sharp backhand, I swept the whisky glasses off the desk. They tore through the holographic blood spots and smashed into the wall.

"We all need to stay calm," Maclaren said, drawing out the syllables of each word. "Nobody needs to get hurt. His pale blue eyes were glued to my hands.

My gun was still holstered, but my hand was on it.

"Tell that to Frank, or Britney Devonshire and Dr. Lee."

Maclaren blinked. "Eddie, you have to believe me. I never wanted anyone to get hurt. Especially not you or Jossie." Maclaren blinked.

Jossie—I'd never heard anyone but Craig call Jo that.

"Shut up," I said. "Keep your hands where I can see them."

From the corner of my eye I saw Jo staring at me with a look of mingled terror and pain. I was afraid of what I might do if I met her gaze head on.

"I'm going to be sick," Jo said. She ran towards the door.

Maclaren opened his mouth to speak, but no words came out. The shrill sound of his glove phone cut the air.

Maclaren made a sudden move, reaching across his body. I saw the glint of steel leave his desk. My gun left its holster. Glock in hand, I broke his nose and hammered his gun hand down hard on the desk. Maclaren cried out.

The .9mm clanged as it skidded across the office floor. I kicked it away.

In the second it took for me to whirl back around, Nieto was standing in the doorway, a .45 pointed not at me, but at Jo's head.

CHAPTER FIFTY-NINE

NIETO HELD JO AS A SHIELD IN FRONT OF HIS BODY, HIS LEFT arm locked tight round Jo's throat, his right hand with the gun pointed at her head. Eyes glued to mine, Nieto shoved Jo back inside the door of Maclaren's office.

I stood to Maclaren's right in front of his desk as he stood behind it, cradling his hand. If I tried to shoot Nieto now, I might kill Jo. I strained for the sound of sirens.

Shadowing Nieto and Jo step for step, I searched for the clear shot as I edged closer to the door. "Let her go, Nieto. You can't get away." I was about five feet from the coffee table to the right of the door. "The chopper car won't even make it past take-off. There's already an APB out. Back-up's closing in."

"I've beaten worse odds," Nieto said, voice calm, eyes dead. "Get his gun," he snapped at Maclaren, hauling Jo another foot inside the office. "Let's get out of here."

Maclaren edged his way out from behind the desk. He slowly walked towards me, still holding his sore hand. His gun lay on the floor between Nieto and me.

Maclaren knelt. With his left hand he retrieved his Glock. But instead of rising and taking mine, he turned his head towards Nieto. "No."

Maclaren's gun was aimed at Nieto, not me. "I want to save lives," the CEO said, "not end them. I never wanted anything to do with Sandy Rose and her fertility clinic. But Dr. Lee, he dragged me in, and with her came you. No more bloodshed. It stops here."

"What a punk-ass back-stabber you are, Maclaren." If Nieto was surprised by the betrayal, he didn't show it. "You were happy as long as you didn't have to see the real work close-up. You knew what was gonna happen when you called Ms. Sloan with that bullshit about being Piedmont's egg donor. Sounds plausible. She was a teen when she made the donation. And she's had nano-work done that makes her look ten years younger now. But you knew it was a lie. So, don't pretend to yourself that you're so noble."

"See, Jo," I said. "I told you it was a lie."

Jo's eyes were bright with tears.

"Of course it was a lie." Nieto pressed the barrel of the gun to Jo's temple so tightly I could see the red impression it left on her skin. "But we needed to lure her here so you'd come after her, detective. See, you've become a problem that has to go away."

"What are you saying?!" Maclaren said. "We were going to offer them a deal. I never planned to hurt Eddie or Jossie."

"No?" Nieto cocked his head. "Then why'd you empty out the place and turn off the security cameras? You figured I'd kill them. Then you'd shoot me in the back. Leaving you in the clear to spin more lies to the cops."

I heard the distant whine of approaching sirens. Nieto heard them too.

We were three points in a line: Nieto holding Jo at the door to the CEO's office, me at the coffee table, and Maclaren kneeling between us both.

Nieto's grip had loosened. Jo must have felt the change in pressure.

She dropped her weight and broke free. Nieto's lipless smile vanished as he realized he was open. He let Jo go and lifted his gun to me.

I saw the blur of motion and fired at Nieto.

Maclaren's body jerked like a marionette on strings. Gun in hand, he'd risen from the ground just in time for my shot to punch a hole the size of a blood orange just below his rib cage. Maclaren looked down, stunned, as he crumpled and slid to the ground. He reached for the coffee table to steady himself, but grabbed only a handful of air. The katana mounted atop the glass table rattled as he fell and dropped his gun once more.

Nieto took cover right outside the office door. I was pressed flat on the wall just inside. Jo was lying flat on the ground behind the coffee table and sofa on my right. I signaled her to stay put. She nodded.

The smell of cordite and seared flesh rode sharp in the air. Yet the room had gone eerily quiet. Bubbles of blood frothed at the corners of Maclaren's mouth. As he tried to speak, the words were drowned in blood.

Then came the burst of bitter laughter from right outside the door. "Motherfucker," Nieto called out. "You shot your own father, detective."

My father . . .?

Then Nieto charged through the doorway. His first shot went wide. I pulled the trigger, but my Glock jammed.

Nieto's second shot punched my left shoulder before I could clear my gun. The impact slammed me back a foot even as my Second Skin tightened into armor. I rolled with the blow, aiming my body as I came out of the back-flip and hurled the jammed Glock at his head. It sliced open his hand as he batted it away.

The flesh on the side of my head burned. My eye stung. Blood poured down my cheek.

From the floor Maclaren whimpered. "Not Eddie. No." His gun barrel was raised towards Nieto. But his wildly shaking hands had triggered the laser. He'd hit me instead.

Nieto laughed and raised his gun barrel to my head.

In one fluid motion I unsheathed the katana on the coffee table. The sword moved in my hands with a life of its own.

He never got the chance to fire again.

As the blade connected with his temple, Nieto's face became a mask of blood. He looked down, stunned, as the top of his head fell into his hands. Nieto crumpled, face down in a pool of blood glistening around his head like a perverse halo.

The whine of sirens grew until they blared loud from just outside the building. My eyes were clouding up. Probably the blood from the laser scalp wound. I wiped them, but the fog didn't clear. The light hurt my eyes. The seared flesh on the side of my head was blistering. My ribs started to throb.

"Jo," I said, squinting. "You okay?"

"It was just a lie, Eddie. A sick lie." She wiped her mouth and flashed me a faint smile.

"Paramedics are right outside." I could hear the clatter of ambulance and police personnel scrambling in the hall.

Jo wasn't my blood relative, but Maclaren . . .

My mother's IVF confession at my father's funeral—how she'd used a sperm donor, some medical student picked from a digital menu. Jo's offhand comment that Maclaren had earned some extra cash that way back when he was in med school. It all tracked.

Maclaren lay on the floor, barely breathing.

"Nieto wasn't lying," I said out loud, "About you being my biological father, was he." It wasn't really a question.

I didn't think he'd heard me, but Maclaren opened his eyes and nodded. "Sorry," he croaked, his voice a hoarse whisper. "You deserved better."

Suddenly the counselor's words to my fifteen-year-old self echoed back over all the years—how if I didn't change course, I'd kill my father. Or he'd kill me. Of course, she'd meant Piedmont Sr., not this man in a three-thousand-dollar suit. Maclaren just wanted the golden goose with the cure to Alz X in his blood, not a son. Not me.

"When did you know?" I said. But Maclaren had closed his eyes. His head fell back. He didn't move again. "When?!" I grabbed him by the shoulders and shook him. Maclaren's body hung like a rag doll in my hands. I rose to my feet again.

"Jo?" I said. "We're safe."

I turned around. But Jo wasn't moving.

CHAPTER SIXTY

MY EYES WERE STILL HAZY, BUT AS I EDGED CLOSER, I COULD see a blood rose bloomed, staining the white of her silk shirt.

Nieto's shot. The one that went wide.

Laying Jo face up on the floor, I ripped open her shirt. I placed my hands over the wound, pressing hard to keep her from bleeding out. A wound to the gut shouldn't bleed out this fast. But Jo was pregnant. More blood vessels had grown there to feed the baby. Jo looked at me. Her face chalk white, an ocean of blood spread all around us.

I grabbed her hands, but her grip was so weak. "Eddie." Her hands loosened. And just like that she was gone.

As the paramedics rushed in and pushed me away, I sat there like a stone, helpless, staring at Jo, willing her to open her eyes and breathe again.

All my life I thought I was in control . . .

Then the adrenaline shakes started. I couldn't keep my balance. My legs gave out, and I crumpled to the floor. My head burned. The haze clouding my vision was growing thicker. Jo's face, the face I loved so much was fading. A wave of nausea flooded through me as my whole life unwound.

Then there was only darkness.

EPILOGUE

Count no man happy until he has passed
the portals of this world.
—Sophocles
Oedipus Tyrannos

Lies written in ink can never disguise facts written in blood.
—Lu Xun

I am not what happened to me. I am what I choose to become.
—Carl Jung

"Cuh," I tried to speak. My tongue was too thick. My mouth tasted of new pennies. "Where?"

"You're in the hospital, Eddie. You've been out of commission for a month." Shin's—the familiar voice was Shin's. "But you're gonna make it. You were right all along, Eddie. About everything. Nieto's death dealt a real blow to the AzteKas. We cleared a lot of cases with this one, partner." He rattled on about the Devonshire case, Dr. Lee, several gang-related murders, the bombing and Frank. All had been tied to Nieto's plan to unite his cartel's illegal drug dealing with his push into the world of legal pharmaceuticals via Maclaren's company. When I'd refused to give up the Devonshire case, I'd pulled a string and unraveled his whole operation.

"You just concentrate on getting well now." Shin babbled on, making feeble jokes the way he always did. Jo always laughs at Shin's jokes, especially the bad ones. She's kind that way.

Then I remembered. Jo. And bad jokes and clearing cases didn't matter anymore. Nothing mattered.

"We have to put him back in hypothermia to reduce inflammation and minimize brain damage," a woman's scratchy alto voice on my left said. "Induce coma stat!"

The cold hands on my right grazed my arm. The vein in my forearm began to burn. It was a relief when darkness took me again.

How many days or weeks or months had passed when I woke again? Muted voices off to the side were talking, but not to me. I heard Shin's voice, and somebody else I didn't recognize. But the place had that same awful antiseptic hospital smell.

There was something covering my eyes. I reached up and touched it. Gauze by the texture. I ripped off the bandage. Searing pain followed, but still I couldn't see.

"He's awake!" Shin shouted. Footsteps echoed out of the room. Returning footsteps were doubled with somebody else's.

I tried to blink but couldn't.

"Eddie, can you hear me?" Shin's voice was coming from the right side of my bed.

I reached out. And misjudged the distance. My hand hit his cheek. Shin's unshaven face was wet. Tears? The movement sent a sharp pain shooting behind my eyes.

"I'm Dr. Kang, detective," a new feminine voice on my left said. Her breath smelled of peppermint and garlic. "And you're lucky to be alive."

I winced. "What's wrong with my eyes?" I thrashed around, trying to get up.

"The gun's laser wiped out the optic nerve and the retina of your right eye. There was also considerable brain swelling," Dr. Kang said as two pairs of hands restrained me. Her's and Shin's I guessed. "The brain is healing, but there was too much tissue damage in your eyes. We'll try to fit you with animatronic eyes. When your condition improves."

Too weak to fight, I fell back on the pillow. The hands released their hold.

"You've been in hypothermia for seven months while your brain and your two broken ribs healed. We'll start cosmetic surgery soon." She rattled on some more, but her words didn't resonate.

"Jo," I croaked once the doctor finally left.

The sound of his shuffling feet told me Shin wasn't sure what to say.

"I know what happened," I said, wishing I didn't, wishing it hadn't. "I remember. Where is she? Her body?"

Shin cleared his throat. "Her brother Craig made the arrangements for the cremation. Jo's memorial and estate are on hold until you're better."

My throat was choked tight. I swallowed. Swallowed again and waited for the burning lump wedged deep in my esophagus to clear.

"So," I said. "Fake eyes and cosmetic surgery. As bad as that?"

I could tell from the way Shin cracked his knuckles and shifted his weight back and forth on the creaking linoleum he was weighing how much to tell me. "Look at it this way, Eddie," he said. "Nobody will be giving you grief about being the sexiest cop of the year anymore."

The next thing I knew I was laughing. Demented laughter indistinguishable from hacking sobs bent me double.

Shin was laughing too. "I'm just glad you're alive, Eddie." I heard him blow his nose.

"Shin. If I'd let the Devonshire case alone like everyone said, then maybe . . ." Jo would still be alive. I couldn't say the words. Even the thought hurt too much.

"You didn't cause this, Eddie," Shin said. "They did. Nieto and Maclaren. They wrapped their greed in a web of lies. But you stopped them. And you have the power to put an end to more than that. With Maclaren dead, Genesys is history, but your blood still has the key to ending this Alz-X plague. So, you can't die. You hear me?"

Then Shin's voice jumped half an octave. "Besides, Eddie." I heard the honk as he blew his nose again. "You got something to live for." I heard the sound of fingernails tapping something hard to Shin's right, like a large hollow plastic box.

"I told the paramedics Jo was six months pregnant. Not four." Shin's voice was muffled now. I guessed he was fussing with something inside the box. "Violated protocol to save a life," he said. "Like you would've done. Don't make me regret it."

"What?" I jerked upright in the hospital bed.

"You're a father now." I could feel Shin's breath on my face as he leaned in and set a warm bundle on my lap. Very gently, Shin placed my hands on top of the soft blanket cocoon.

"The baby survived? I don't believe it."

But my gingerly groping hands told me there was an infant inside the blanket on my lap. With great care, I wrapped my arms around the bundle and leaned in, breathing deep the new baby smell. Then the tiny creature inside the blanket began to cry. Jo's child—our child—was alive.

"Your mom moved into your place, Eddie. She's been helping out, but your baby girl needs you." And just like that, Shin's metaphorical tiger rolled over one more time.

"Shin, how the hell am I gonna take care of a baby? I can't take care of myself."

"You'll find a way. We'll help you until you do."

"No." I shook my head and held the crying bundle out to him. But Shin didn't take it.

So, I tucked the blanket more securely around the baby and pulled her in close to my chest. She stopped crying.

"See? You know what to do," Shin said.

"Sure," I said, not making an effort to keep the doubt out of my voice. "What about when she gets old enough to ask the hard questions? About Jo? What do I tell her then?"

"The truth," Shin answered. "Her mother died to protect you both. You'll figure out the rest when the time comes. She needs you. And you need her."

"She deserves better."

"You're her father," Shin said. "That's good enough. It's like kendo." I felt the air move as Shin's hand sliced through it and tapped my forearm. "The masters see the moves in full. The rest of us just practice until we get there. You got some choices to make about your life now, Eddie. And your kid's life. Do something positive."

"Like what?"

"Give your daughter a name," Shin said. "That'd make for a good start."

I could feel the sun's rays on my arm. The sun must be shining outside the window. Maybe Shin was right. My family, my blood, had always been a curse, but now I saw it was a gift too. A gift I could share with others. Starting with my kid. My daughter. Those words were gonna take some getting used to.

"Jocelyn Antigone Piedmont," I said after a long silence. "For her mother and grandmother." But I'll call her Tiggy after the tiger that rolled over.

I felt a tiny hand wrap around one of my fingers.

And with that touch a glimmer of warmth bled back into the world.

ACKNOWLEDGEMENTS

I OWE SO MANY SO MUCH. LET ME BEGIN BY THANKING MY agent Sandy Lu of Bookwyrm Literary Agency, and publisher Patrick Swenson of Fairwood Press. Both have been unfailing sources of support, guiding this debut author through the labyrinth of revision and publication. This book has been gestating for many years, and I would be remiss if I failed to mention the brilliant lecture on Sophocles delivered by my very dear friend Professor S. Georgia Nugent that originally inspired me to write it. In addition, I would never have been able to describe how Eddie performs *sabbrage* without the help of another dear friend, Georgia's husband Tom, who taught me how to behead a bottle of champagne with a saber myself. Any merit in the kendo sections is due to the generous instruction I received from the sensei of the Southern California Kendo Organization before injuries sidelined me.

But any excellence in the story itself told in these pages would not have been possible without the help and weekly doses both of support and criticism from my beloved Saturday writers group led by the intrepid Jerilyn Farmer, and the encouragement of friends and family, especially my sister Patricia. The flaws herein are entirely my own.

ABOUT THE AUTHOR

B.J. Graf is the author of *Genesys X* and four short stories, three of which also feature Detective Eddie Piedmont, including "Shikata Ga Nai" (in the Sisters in Crime 2013 Anthology *Last Exit to Murder*), "Blood Shadows" (in the Sisters in Crime 2019 Anthology *Fatally Haunted*), "Sandman" (in the Partners in Crime 2020 Anthology, *Crossing Borders*), and "Deux ex Machina" (in the Malice Domestic 2020 Anthology *Murder Most Theatrical*).

An adjunct professor of Film Studies and Classical Mythology, B. J. Graf worked for many years as V.P. of Development for Abilene Pictures. She lives and works in L.A. with her family and a menagerie of rescue animals.

NEW & RECENT TITLES FROM FAIRWOOD PRESS

The Best of James Van Pelt
by James Van Pelt
signed ltd. hardcover $40.00
ISBN: 978-1-933846-95-8

Living Forever
and Other Terrible Ideas
by Emily C. Skaftun
trade paper $17.99
ISBN: 978-1-933846-98-9

Anthems Outside Time
and Other Strange Voices
by Kenneth Schneyer
trade paper $18.99
ISBN: 978-1-933846-92-7

Unicorn Mountain
by Michael Bishop
trade paper: $18.99
ISBN: 978-1-933846-94-1

Inagehi
by Jack Cady
trade paper $17.99
ISBN: 978-1-933846-93-4

All Worlds are Real
by Susan Palwick
trade paper $17.99
ISBN: 978-1-933846-84-2

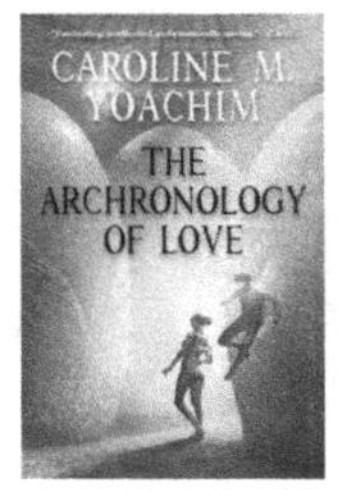

The Archronology of Love
by Caroline M. Yoachim
small paperback: $8.00
ISBN: 978-1-933846-96-5

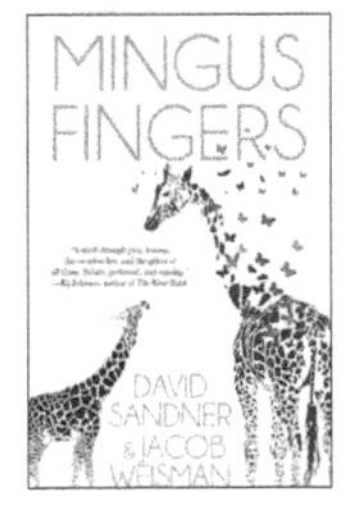

Mingus Fingers
by David Sandner & Jacob Weisman
small paperback paper: $8.00
ISBN: 978-1-933846-87-3

Find us at:
www.fairwoodpress.com